SERPENTS UNDERFOOT

DC Gilbert

FRANK!
ENJOY THE BOOK.

3/18/18

Copyright © 2017 Darren C Gilbert

ISBN: 1541240332
ISBN-13: 9781541240339

DEDICATION

This book is dedicated to all those brave men and women who, throughout the history of our great nation, fought, sacrificed and died ... to provide us with and to safeguard the freedoms we enjoy as citizens of this American Nation. Remembrance is vital because it is in the forgetting that we will lose the most precious gift we have been given ... Freedom.

ACKNOWLEDGMENTS

I would like to thank my parents, Curtiss and Ardis Gilbert, for instilling in me a love of reading at such an early age. I also need to again thank my mother for all her hard work editing this work and helping me clean up my bad writing habits ... of which there were many. Hopefully, some have, by now, been drilled out of me. I would like to thank SSG Brendan Gilbert for reading over several of the military sections. His comments were very motivational and helpful. Last, I would like to thank all the friends who supported me in this endeavor that has spanned several years.

Thank you all.

PROLOGUE

How can one man, even a dedicated servant of Allah, bring down an entire country? It would certainly take a great deal of planning and perseverance. Second, you would need an army of mujahidin ... only the most dedicated servants of Allah. It would also take a great deal of money. Rahman Atta had that. He was worth billions. Last, it would take a maniacal determination from a ruthless leader. A leader who would not accept failure from others ... or from himself.

Rahman Atta's followers soon learned that he was that leader. To those who served him well, Atta was generous. But, fail him, or worse yet, betray him ... and there was no place on earth you could hide. It was not that he was violent or given to fits of rage. Quite to the contrary, like a snake, Atta was cold, quiet and deadly. He was efficient in his decisions and in his use of resources ... including his followers.

Excellent, Atta thought to himself. Things were falling into place. A smile of grim satisfaction settled itself on Atta's cruel lips as he pressed the end call button on his cell phone. He'd planned everything to the very last detail. He was but a faithful servant of Allah and the will of Allah would be done.

He relaxed back into a soft cushion which sat on the hand-woven Persian carpet that covered most of the floor of the room. Despite the elegance of his living space, to the outside world, Atta's house was a modest one.

The house clung to the side of a mountain at an altitude of 1050 meters above sea level. It overlooked the village of Masuleh in the southern Gilan province of Iran. All the houses in the village were constructed of brick or stone with flat roofs. Those roofs often provided the streets for the level above.

Masuleh was perfect for Rahman Atta's needs. It was a small farming village with not much in the way of tourist facilities. There was an old bazaar as well as a couple of excellent cafes. There were some nice shops selling crafts, knives, and silks. Masuleh did, however, have a certain charm along with a mild summer climate. This made it a popular destination for day-trippers from Tehran. The day-trippers provided excellent cover for the frequent visitors to Atta's home. These visitors, all dedicated leaders of key radical Islamic groups, had a common purpose ... the establishment of a global Islamic Caliphate. This was Rahman Atta's dream as well, a dream to which he had dedicated much of his adult life.

Like many of his followers, Atta followed the path that began in the Paris slums. These slums were home to so many angry young Muslims. Minds numb from years of drudgery and boredom, they looked for something to give meaning to their lives. They looked for a cause.

But, unlike many of his followers, Rahman Atta was radicalized at a very early age. His uncles took great care in seeing to that. While his impoverished brothers were looking for a cause, Atta had already had one. He'd chosen to take this journey with a clear goal in mind. He needed followers. Atta needed to establish himself as a true jihadist, a leader, and a true defender of Islam. As a distant cousin to a prince of the House of Saud, Atta had more money than he could ever hope to spend. His father and honored uncle both worked hard in the service of Allah, and Allah truly rewards those who are loyal to him. Both were very wealthy ... before the hated Americans murdered them.

Jamil Amman Atta, Atta's father was one of al Qaeda's respected senior leaders. An American Predator drone blew Jamil Atta to pieces on a desolate stretch of desert highway in Afghanistan. There was little left of him, his companions or the vehicle they were traveling in. Atta's uncle, Sayyid Ismail Atta, spent almost a year as a detainee at Camp Vigilant, a detention center in Iraq. Finally released from that facility, Sayyid Atta, a British citizen, returned to the UK. He died a few years later when MI5 foiled a plot to detonate a bomb in Harrods department store in London. While fleeing to escape arrest, a London cab struck and killed his uncle as he darted across a busy street. The fact that it was an accidental death, and he was fleeing arrest, did not matter to Atta. His burning hatred of the West only grew hotter. After their deaths, Atta inherited the combined fortunes of both his father and uncle.

Rahman Atta scowled at the memory. He ran his tongue over his thin, dry lips. He despised the British and their Queen.

No woman had any business ruling over men, he thought. It defied the teachings of the Prophet Mohammed! It was written in the Hadith that when the Prophet had heard that the Persians chose the daughter of Khosrau as their Queen, he'd stated, "Never will succeed such a nation as makes a woman their ruler."

The path taken by Rahman Atta led from Paris slums to Yemen and one of many fundamentalist Islamic schools. These schools filled empty young minds with a seething hatred for the west. Especially … all things American. Atta attended the Iman University headed by Abdel Majeed al-Zindani. This also was by design. Atta knew that al-Zindani was al-Qaeda. He was Osama bin Laden's theological adviser. Al-Zindani became Atta's direct link to the inner circle.

While Atta was respected by his fellow students, it would be a mistake to say he was liked. Atta studied hard. He knew and understood the Koran and the Hadith well. He studied much harder than most of the students and because of this, he excelled. While they might not like him, his fellow students did look forward to Atta's turn to lead the theological discussions that were part of their education. His thoughts on the verses of the Koran were clear, thoughtful, and inspiring. But, not one of his fellow students thought of Atta as a friend, or as someone they even wanted to be friendly with. Perhaps, it was something in his eyes. Atta had cold, black eyes that his thin cruel smile somehow never seemed to reach. His fellow students always felt an unexplainable sense of relief when leaving his presence. It was like stepping out from a dark, cold and clammy cave into the bright warm sunshine.

Atta enjoyed his time at the school. The only sour note had been the period the American pretender was there. He had not liked the American. The man was a traitor … a treacherous dog.

What was his name? Atta remembered. *Oh yes! Walker. Steven Walker.*

Walker was an American infidel who, in Atta's opinion, only pretended to be a true believer. How Walker had managed to enter the school Atta could only guess. Atta had the misfortune of having to speak to him on one or two occasions. Atta understood the need to recruit in the west. Such dogs had their place in Allah's plans. But, they were not true believers and could not be trusted. In fact, he had heard Walker was now serving time in an American prison. Sent back to recruit new converts, the fool had even blundered at that. Atta did not know why the idiot Walker had landed in prison, but the fact it had happened proved the accuracy of his early dislike of the man.

But, the pieces were now coming into place. The time was drawing near. Allah was just and would provide … Atta would have his revenge. When his plan went into action, it would avenge both his father and his uncle as well as destroy the American Satan. This was as it should be.

Sayyid Abul Ala Maududi, an Islamic scholar, taught that Allah demanded the destruction of all other States. All people must be brought into subjugation under Islam. Islam required the entire planet … not merely a part of it. Atta was confident that his grand plan would soon help do exactly that. His will and the will of Allah were now melded into one. He, Rahman Atta, would be the instrument of Allah's vengeance.

Atta's mind returned from its ruminations to focus on the call recently concluded. It was welcome news.

Yes, Atta reflected. His followers did find the perfect candidate. Every detail, option, and contingency were covered. Every aspect of the woman's life … dissected and examined. She was a perfect choice.

Yes. This was good. Even as Allah might have the occasional need for an idiot such as the American Walker, Atta now had his own useful idiot. Allah would always provide even if, as in this case, that useful idiot was an infidel woman of the hated West.

CHAPTER 1

Dong Re Lao Mountain rose to a height of 4,879 feet over the A Shau Valley in South Vietnam. It sat less than six miles from the Laotian border. The North Vietnamese Army took control of the valley in March of 1966 when they overran the last remaining Special Forces camp in that area. Running north to south, the valley is approximately a mile wide and twenty-five miles long. Elephant grass covers most of the valley floor. Route 548, a hard-packed dirt road, splits the A Shau lengthwise. The valley is bordered on both sides by forested mountains ranging from three to six thousand feet in elevation.

The A Shau provided the NVA with a strategic and defensible stronghold. Lieutenant General Ngo Thanh, the NVA Commander, wasted no time turning the entire valley into a fortified supply depot. General Thanh commanded a garrison of between 5000 and 6000 NVA soldiers. Supplementing this force was the local Viet Cong. Under General Thanh's direction, much of the complex lay concealed in underground bunkers and tunnels. It was also ringed with a large number of anti-aircraft batteries with sophisticated inter-locking fields of fire. The valley soon became a major infiltration point into the Thua Thien Province of South Vietnam. General Thanh funneled men, weapons, and materials down the Ho Chi Minh Trail to support the communist North's effort to unify the country. It was a painful thorn in the side of the U.S. forces fighting in Vietnam and would be a very hard nut to crack!

The last time Cordell was in the A Shau Valley, his team had been deep in the shit! The six-man team, out on a long range reconnaissance patrol, almost walked into a cleverly-concealed "V" shaped ambush. Lt. Cordell, wounded in the desperate firefight that followed, also lost a good friend. Officers and enlisted were not supposed to mix, but Hicks was different. He would have made a damn good officer. Hicks was also the best point man Cordell had ever had on his team.

A Vietcong favorite, the "V" type ambush is virtually undetectable by the man on point or by flank security. The open end of the "V" is positioned toward the enemy's advance while the ambushers lay in good concealment along the legs of the "V." They lay in wait until the enemy point passes and some of the team are in the kill zone before creeping up closer to the trail. The ambushers direct enfilading fire down the enemy's line of travel. Combined with interlocking fire along both legs of the "V," this creates deadly three-way crossfire throughout the kill zone. It also provides a perfect area for the use of controlled mines and booby-traps.

Lt. Curtis Cordell awoke with a start, sweat dripping from his body. It was that same stupid dream. Smoke, heat, jungle, explosions and a young Vietnamese woman who was calmly standing there in front of him, smiling, and beckoning for something. Cordell was never sure what.

He sat up on his cot, naked except for his dog tags and skivvies. Sitting for a minute, he busied himself studying his feet on the pallet flooring of his tent. It was only six a.m., and already steaming hot. There was no escape from the heat. In the Peoples Republic of Vietnam, it was hot and wet or hot and dry, heat being the only real constant.

Curtis thought these dreams were somehow being prompted by rumors that they were going back into the A Shau. He was not looking forward to that. A lot of good men had died in that valley. He'd lost too many good soldiers there himself. The A Shau Valley was a place of death.

Cordell shook that thought off. He pulled on some shorts, grabbed a towel and his wash kit, and slipping on his Ho Chi Minh sandals, made his way to the latrine. After emptying his bladder, he checked in at the showers, one of the few true pleasures of life in the base camp. Feeling a little better in clean jungle fatigues, Curtis stopped in at the mess hall for a quick breakfast before the briefing scheduled for 08:00 hours. The scuttlebutt was flying about a possible major offensive soon. He guessed that the upcoming briefing had something to do with these rumors.

Cordell met Sergeant Walker, just finishing breakfast, at the mess hall door. While just an E-5, Jim Walker was the most experienced enlisted man on Cordell's LRRP team.

"Morning Lieutenant." Walker saluted.

Cordell returned his salute. "Morning Jim. What's for breakfast?"

"The usual …. green eggs and shit on a shingle," Walker replied grinning.

"You gonna find out the truth behind these god-damned rumors this morning?"

"Hope so," Cordell muttered. "Fill you in afterward."
"Yes, sir. See you later sir."

Cordell hoped the rumors were just that. Rumors. He still had a bad taste in his mouth from his last mission. They'd been two weeks into a six-week reconnaissance patrol along a section of the Laotian border and maneuvering along a ridge about 20 meters above a trail that had seen a lot of recent travel. It could only be the NVA or Vietcong. Cpl. Steven Hicks was on point and was about to begin to move forward again when something told him to stop. He paused, remaining very still. Hicks signaled the rest of the team to get down and take cover. He often took the point because he was famous for his uncanny ability to smell an ambush. The other team members referred to it as his "spidey sense." But, they took it with dead seriousness when they were out in the bush. Whatever was out there, Hick's "spidey sense" was tingling like hell right freaking now.

He stood stock-still, becoming part of the jungle. His eyes scanned back and forth, starting close to his position and then moving away into the jungle. His nostrils flared trying to pick out the scent of something out of place while his ears strained to hear and identify any sound that did not belong. It was too damned quiet! Then, there it was again. Not a sound ... the impression of a sound. Something that did not belong in the jungle!

Ambush, Hicks thought. *I can feel it. We're going to be in deep shit!*

From his position, the Vietcong platoon leader could see that his carefully laid ambush was a split second from being discovered. He immediately yelled at his men, ordering them to open fire. Twenty-five well-hidden

Vietcong ambushers began firing on the six-man LRRP team.

Hicks screamed "Ambush!" and dropped to the ground returning fire.

The team hit the dirt short of entering the kill zone and began returning effective fire. Even with their ambush blown, the VC still had the advantage of higher ground. Cordell's team was now locked in a desperate firefight. It was damn fortunate they stopped short of the kill zone, but they'd still been surprised, and it looked like they were outnumbered about five to one. The firefight lasted for several long minutes. Lt. Cordell caught two AK-47 rounds; one in the calf and one in the hip. Luckily, both bullets traveled cleanly through. Though hurt and bleeding, the wounds were not bad enough to take Cordell out of the fight.

Stay in the damn fight, he thought! *You can't fucking quit now!*

He dropped two VC with quick, accurate bursts from his M16 rifle. Cordell heard more firing on his left flank. He glanced in that direction and saw Big Dave Johnson, the soft-spoken son of a Texas rancher, firing away with his M16. At great risk to himself, Johnson was giving covering fire to Jim Walker and Bobby Stillwater who were being overrun by charging Vietcong fighters.

Jim Walker, a genuine White Mountain Apache warrior from Arizona, emptied one thirty-round clip into the jungle, spraying suppressive fire into the VC position along the left leg of the ambush. He'd released the empty mag and was reaching for another when he looked up to see two VC charging at him. Cordell could hear Walker howling like one of his Apache ancestors as he smashed one charging VC in the head with his rifle butt, splitting his skull wide open. Pivoting on the balls of his feet Walker turned to face the second black-clad attacker bearing down on him from behind. Cordell saw them collide and tumble to the ground, each fighting for an advantage.

Suddenly, Johnson was cut down by a burst of 7.62 from a Vietcong's AK-47 rifle. Cordell spotted the enemy shooter firing from the dense foliage higher on the ridge to his right and placed a five-round burst through the black-clad chest.

Cpl. Hicks and Mike Hightower were down as well. They'd managed to take out the Type 24 machine gun the Vietcong platoon placed in the depression at the deadly end of their "V" ambush. Hightower scored a direct hit on the machine gun with a LAW anti-tank rocket at the same time Hicks tossed a fragmentation grenade into the depression. The machine gun was silenced. The two had shifted positions to resume firing on the right leg of the ambush when a Vietcong stick grenade traced an arc out of the foliage twenty yards away and landed at their feet.

Cordell shouted a warning. "Grenade!"

Cordell could only watch as Hicks moved to grab the grenade and throw it back. He was too late. Grenade fuses are never that predictable. The grenade exploded before Hicks could get to it and the explosion took both men down.

"Damn it! Shit!" Cordell raked the dense foliage with automatic fire hoping to get the VC who'd thrown it.

And in the next instant, as fast as all the shooting started, it stopped ... the Vietcong simply faded back into the jungle.

Cordell was still for long seconds, scanning the surrounding area to make sure the VC were gone and the firefight indeed over. Keeping his eyes on the ridges he moved over to check on Dave Johnson. Pvt. Johnson was dead. Several rounds had gone through his chest killing him instantly. He'd sacrificed himself for his two teammates. Lt. Cordell collected one of Johnson's dog tags, put it in his fatigue pocket and reached down to close Johnson's eyes.

Still alert for snipers, Cordell worked his way over to where Hicks and Hightower were lying side by side, surrounded by a pile of dead Vietcong soldiers. Two more dog tags went into his pocket. Hicks was a damn good soldier as well as a friend. They were all good soldiers.

Cordell spotted Jim Walker working his way toward him carrying Bobby Stillwater over his shoulder. Bobby was alive but shot through both thighs and his left hip. Walker was gentle as he placed Stillwater on the ground. Digging into the first aid kit he found the morphine and gave Stillwater a shot and then prepared to give one to his Lieutenant.

"Save it," Cordell ordered. "Better to keep my head clear, and besides I think we'd better get the hell out of here. Just hand me a couple of field dressings."

Cordell had already packed the holes in his hip and thigh with tree moss to slow the loss of blood. They were both flesh wounds, but they still hurt like hell.

Hopefully, I won't catch some fucking kind of indigenous blood poisoning from that damn moss!

"Damn radio is shot to shit," Walker reported. "We're going to have to hoof it out of here to reach the backup landing zone ... wait for the alternate extraction tomorrow evening. It's about eleven or twelve clicks from here to there I figure."

Lt. Cordell nodded and then thought for a moment. Jim busied himself applying dressings to Bobby's gunshot wounds trying to stop the bleeding.

"Listen," Cordell said. "I won't be able to keep up with these bullet holes in me. Jim, you'd better carry Bobby and go on ahead. I will cover our six ... bring up the rear. Just hold that fucking chopper for me," he grinned.

"You bet!"

Walker adjusted his gear and checked his ammo. He hoisted Bobby to his shoulders, reached down to retrieve his M16, nodded to Cordell, and started off through the jungle toward the alternate extraction point.

Cordell hunkered down near a rock in the brush. Keeping one eye on the jungle for any VC or NVA and his rifle close at hand, he took a long swallow from his canteen. He sat, listening to the sounds of the jungle. When he was sure there was no activity in the immediate area, he headed down the trail after Walker. Every twenty to thirty yards, Curtis stopped to listen and make sure they weren't being followed.

The two bullet holes made for slow going but Cordell managed to keep moving for several hours. The sun had begun to drop from the sky when Cordell got out his compass and checked his topographical map. He figured he was halfway to the backup LZ. He was lying on his stomach in the low scrub brush at the edge of what seemed to be a wide flat clearing. It looked like a dried riverbed about twenty-five or thirty yards across. It ran as far as he could see in both directions. The clearing was covered with low brush, dotted here and there with islands of flat rocks. There were also signs of recent travel along the clearing. Maybe an NVA patrol route?

Curtis Cordell was feeling very tired. The loss of blood wasn't helping his situation any either. He had to concentrate to stay focused.

If he could make it across this clearing he'd be able to locate a secure position up on that opposite ridge. It would be concealed and have a good view of his back trail. He needed to rest a bit before moving on.

Looks okay, Cordell thought. *Here goes nothing!*

Cordell worked his way across the clearing still painfully aware of his wounds. As it turned out, he was way too slow.

He was midway across the clearing when the hair stood up on the back of his neck. He could hear in the distance the growling and clanking of machinery. Cordell dropped to the ground and froze. It was louder now.

Oh shit! An NVA tank. Damn! It must have been in a low spot or on the other side of a rise.

And of course, that meant NVA patrol.

What fucking luck!!

The North Vietnamese Army had a few Chinese-made T62 tanks operating in A Shau Valley area. Cordell fought the urge to get up and run because, while he couldn't see the NVA tank because of his low position, they would sure as hell see him if he ran. Cordell reached up to pull some scrub brush over himself for cover, flattened out onto the clearing floor and willed himself to be invisible. The clanks and roar of the Chinese tank grew closer.

Time stood still as the sounds of the approaching tank grew still louder. It sounded like the tank was right on top of him.

By God, it was!

Cordell lay very still. He could see a tank track visible to either side of him. Turning his head, he looked straight up through the brush at the steel hull of the tank itself as its engine cut off. He slowed his breathing and remained still.

Cordell woke with a start.

Shit! I guess I must have dozed off, he thought to himself. *Must be the loss of blood.*

Cordell heard the murmurings of Vietnamese voices talking off to his left. He could identify the dim light of a small concealed fire, the faint smell of wood smoke and the greasy metallic smell of the tank. It was getting dark. He heard the clinking of pots and pans, then the footsteps of someone working his way around to the rear of the tank and then relieving himself in the brush. A few minutes later he smelled the strong, pungent odor of a Vietnamese cigarette.

The smell was coming from my right side, he thought. Curtis suppressed a cough.

Next came the hissing sound of a fire being extinguished and three or four voices talking as they climbed up on the tank. Finally, silence … except for the sound of insects and an NVA soldier snoring above him.

I'll get little sleep tonight, Cordell thought. *This is insane.*

The roar of the Chinese tank's engines coming to life yanked Cordell back from his sleep into the land of the living. Startled, he started to sit up but remembered where he was and so missed cracking his head on the hull of the tank.

Just stay down and be still!

The tank started to move. Moments later the NVA tank was gone, the sound of its engine growing dimmer as it moved off down the clearing.

I'll be a son-of-a-bitch, he thought and grinned, thinking about the absurdity of the entire situation. *At least I feel a bit more rested and my wounds don't hurt as much. Guess I must have gotten some sleep after all.*

Waiting long enough to make sure that the tank was gone, Cordell got stiffly to his feet. He made it across the rest of the clearing and part way up the ridge before taking a drink from his canteen and checking his back trail. Deciding he'd already had enough of a rest, Cordell took a compass bearing and started off along the ridge toward the backup extraction point. Five or six clicks left to go. He had plenty of time and had slept some last night. Things were looking up.

The sun was now at its zenith and it was damn hot. Walker finished giving Stillwater a swallow from his canteen. They stayed hidden in the foliage, a few meters back from the secondary LZ. It was still a few hours out from the pre-arranged backup extraction time. The choppers wouldn't even be in the air yet.

Suddenly, Walker heard the call of a Great Barred Owl off to his left, maybe twenty or thirty yards away. The Great Barred Owl has a distinct call, not easily mistaken by anyone who had heard it before. As far as Walker knew, there were no Great Barred Owls indigenous to South Vietnam. Knowing that Great Barred Owls were very territorial, Walker figured he'd better return the challenge. He did. Grinning, he hunkered down to wait. In a matter of minutes, Lt. Cordell worked his way up beside him.

"Howdy Lieutenant." Walker offered him his canteen. "About damn time!"

"No thanks. I'm good. How's Bobby?"

"I'm here," Bobby spoke up in a subdued, hoarse voice. "But I confess I've felt better."

"It's been a pretty quiet night here Lieutenant," Walker whispered. "Nothing much moving out there."

"How was your night, Lieutenant?" Bobby asked in his hoarse whisper.

Cordell grinned.

"Bobby, Jim, you guys wouldn't fucking believe me if I told you."

They settled back in to wait for the choppers, each set of eyes scanning the jungle terrain around them, alert for any sign of the enemy. A few hours later they heard the welcome sound of two approaching UH-1H helicopters.

Walker threw a yellow smoke grenade to help guide the choppers into their location. While one Huey, acting as the escort gunship and taking a defensive station circled overhead, the second Huey touched down in the small clearing.

Walker carried Bobby to the chopper while Cordell limped along at his side keeping his eyes on the jungle behind them. The Huey's door gunner scanned the clearing's perimeter for any sign of the enemy, his finger ready on the trigger of the chopper's M-60 machine gun. Jumping out, the co-pilot helped Walker lift Bobby up onto the chopper's deck. Walker sprang up into the Huey and leaned down to give Cordell a hand up as well.

"Damn, we are glad to see you guys!"

"Well, we're damn glad to see you guys as well. We should be back at Evans in about thirty minutes," the co-pilot yelled over the roar of the engines. The chopper lifted off, climbing into the late afternoon sky.

Cordell settled in for the flight and thought about Steve Hicks, Dave Johnson, and Mike Hightower … all damn good soldiers. Steve Hicks was a good friend.

What a snafu!

He'd make sure their bodies were recovered and sent home. Three more letters to write.

CHAPTER 2

Mai walked barefoot, moving carefully down the village path to the river. It was a beautiful morning. Located in the Central Highlands of Vietnam, the Montagnard village was just a little to the south and east of the A Shau Valley. She approached the river to fill her water jug as the early morning sun was breaking through the fog. She moved cautiously because of the ever-present danger of NVA or VC patrols. Neither the NVA nor the VC were noted for their humane treatment of captured enemy combatants or the local civilian populace. Even close to the village, there was always the need to be alert. While the VC would often move around, their forces always operated in or near populated areas. Their base camp was usually a half-days walking distance from any populated area ... any further and their purpose for existing ... to terrorize, propagandize, harass and tax ... would be defeated.

As she knelt at the river's edge to fill her water jug a stream of sunlight engulfed her, highlighting her delicate beauty in the morning light. Mai was Vietnamese, not Montagnard. It was a direct result of Vietcong barbarism that she was now living in the relative safety of a Montagnard village.

Mai's father, Ang Dung, was the respected chief of a small Vietnamese village on the northeast edge of the Central Highlands. The hamlet was about thirty kilometers west of Da Nang. Ang Dung had a reputation as a good man ... a fair man. As village chief, he would also often act as the local constable and arbitrator of disputes. Because he was also a well-respected practitioner of Nguyen-ryu, a Vietnamese martial art, his decisions were rarely questioned.

The Montagnard are an indigenous mountain people. Most Vietnamese people considered them "moi," or savages, and because of this, there was little trust between them and the Montagnard. Ang Dung was friendly to the Montagnard folk who lived in the mountains to the west, and he treated them as he would treat anyone else. This attitude was very rare among the local Vietnamese. Ang Dung was one of the few local Vietnamese villagers welcomed and respected in the nearby Montagnard villages. One of the Montagnard village chiefs, a fierce old warrior who still aided the American Special Forces units operating in the area, asked Ang Dung to teach his son Nguyen-ryu. Ang Dung consented and soon Dish became one of his hardest working students.

Using the heavy early morning fog as cover, the well-armed VC company descended on Ang Dung's sleeping village unobserved. There had been no warning. Guards had been posted around the village. But, either they were dead ... or they had been VC.

The villagers were terrified and confused as they were dragged out of their homes and rounded up. The VC herded the villagers into a group in front of Ang Dung's longhouse.

Seventeen-year-old Mai had been up early, tending to her father's water buffalo at the edge of a field on the far side of the village. She did not see the Vietcong. Dish, also up early, was practicing a new form Ang Dung had been teaching him. Dish saw the hated VC and suspected what was coming. He spotted Mai working her way across the field, back toward the village. He felt sick to his stomach as he thought of her falling into VC hands. Fortunately, he intercepted Mai before she reached the village and silencing her protests, led her into the jungle to safety.

Ang Dung rose and went out to meet the Vietcong soldiers hoping to avoid any trouble. Behind him, several VC soldiers charged into his house. With angry shouts, they dragged his pregnant wife and three other children outside and shoved them down onto the ground in front everyone.

Realizing what was about to happen, Ang Dung fought back, lashing out with a powerful kick to the knee of the Vietcong soldier standing to the right of him. He heard a rewarding crunch as the kick struck home. With a short upward punch, he slammed the two large knuckles of his right fist into the cavity beneath the cheekbone of the VC soldier turning to face him on his left. The VC dropped and lay still. Ang Dung fought to save his family but it was hopeless. Even with his skills, there were too many Vietcong to overcome. Overpowered when a rifle butt smashed into the back of his skull, Ang Dung was wrestled to the ground and bound. His pregnant wife and three children were forced to watch as the VC cut out his tongue, slashed off his genital organs, and stuffed them inside his bleeding mouth.

The VC next went to work on his wife. She was dragged

from her crying children, thrown to the ground and repeatedly bayoneted and left to die. The VC had no mercy for Ang Dung's small children either. All three terrified and crying children were grabbed and held as sharpened bamboo lances were rammed into one ear and out the other.

Their mutilated bodies were tied to the pilings supporting their longhouse. Hand-lettered signs were hung around their necks. The signs warned the remaining villagers not to support the Saigon government or its American allies. Their savage work completed, the Vietcong force moved off into the jungle, demons returning to the hell from which they'd come.

Mercifully, Dish had kept Mai from seeing what evil had transpired. He'd heard of the atrocities committed by the Vietcong but had never actually seen it with his own eyes before now. That night, they'd hid in the jungle not too far from the village. When Mai eventually cried herself to sleep, Dish covered her with his shirt and crept back into the village to assess the situation. There were no words to describe the horror of the scene before him. The rage and sorrow he felt would stay with him forever.

Dish made his way into the longhouse where Mai's family had lived, making sure he was not seen. He'd been there many times as a guest. Mai had been Ang's oldest child. Her two brothers and sister were much younger. Perhaps this was why Ang had shown great trust in his student and shared with him a family secret. Dish had impressed Ang as an honorable, hardworking young man.

"Should anything happen to me," Ang had said, "I want my family looked after." Dish located the item he was looking for right where Ang had once shown him it was hidden. He slipped the brown leather pouch into the small bag at his waist. After again checking to see he had not been observed, he returned to where Mai still lay sleeping. He sat down leaning back against a tree. There would be no sleep for him that night.

In the morning, Dish roused Mai and led her west into the Highlands … toward his father's village. After they traveled some miles, Mai slowed her pace and then stopped walking. Dish knew what was coming. He turned around and looked at her. He waited. Finally, Mai spoke. With tears on her face and in a hoarse, quavering voice Mai asked,

"Where are we going? I want to go back to my village! Where are you taking me?"

Dish was not sure how best to tell Mai what had transpired in the village. He was pretty sure she already suspected. Finally, he decided it was best, to be honest.

"I will not lie to you, Mai. Those VC soldiers killed your family. Your father, your mother, your brothers and sister … they are all gone. My heart is filled with sorrow for you and hatred for the Vietcong for what they have done."

He paused.

"I am taking you to my father's village. You will be safe there. I do not know what else to do."

Mai stood in silence for several long minutes. Her face a battlefield of struggling emotions. There was nothing more he could say. Mai was like a little sister to him. Nothing in his life had prepared him to know how to help her handle the fear, anger, and pain she must now be feeling. He did not even know how to comfort her. He was at a loss. Finally, Mai reached for Dish's hand.

"Then we better get going," she said quietly.

When the two of them arrived at his father's village the next day, Dish told his father what had happened. The old Montagnard warrior felt a deep sadness and anger that his longtime Vietnamese friend had met such an end. Without hesitation, he reached for Mai and drew her to him in an embrace that conveyed the depth of his feeling in one heartfelt gesture. Villagers gathered around and listened to the awful story. Dish's father turned to the villagers and announced he was taking Mai into his family. She was now under his protection and a member of their village.

He turned back to his son and said quietly, placing a hand on his shoulder,

"Take care of your new sister."

And with that, he turned and walked off into the jungle.

Mai had no trouble carrying the water jug up the short path to her longhouse. Life in the Central Highlands agreed with her and over the months that passed, she became strong and healthy. Like most Montagnard homes, hers was set up off the ground on pilings. The area underneath was used to store grain and firewood. Mai also kept several little black pigs in a remarkably tidy pen under one end of the house. She had named every single one of them. Dish was not happy at all with this situation. Much to his chagrin the pigs, customarily kept as a source of food, had now become family pets. He could not kill any of the pigs without facing the wrath of a very angry Mai.

And so, Mai lived there in the Montagnard village with her adopted family, an older brother Dish and Dish's mother, Jun. Dish's father, Mund, was no longer with them. He had died in a bloody fight with the Vietcong several months after taking Mai into his family.

After the murderous slaughter of Mai's family, Mund became an avenging angel. Such savages could not be allowed to walk upon the earth. And so, he made the killing of Vietcong soldiers his life's mission. In the jungle, Mund was silent, deadly and completely without mercy.

This day he'd joined with a Special Forces team. On a patrol deep in the jungle, they picked up the trail of a group of Vietcong that had just raided a nearby Montagnard village. The marauding VC had slaughtered the village's elder and his family.

Like my friend, Ang, Mund thought. The hatred and anger were never far ... away rising quickly in his chest. The Special Forces team managed to get ahead of the Vietcong who did not know they were being tracked and so traveled in no hurry. The team set an L-shaped ambush along a section of trail on the VC's suspected line of travel. They settled down, waiting for the killers to appear. Command suspected this group of Vietcong was guilty of committing a string of atrocities on Montagnard and South Vietnamese villages. They also tortured and killed any South Vietnamese or American soldier that fell into their hands.

These Vietcong were not just especially vicious in their savagery, they were also clever and disciplined fighters. They made a determined effort to fight their way out of the ambush's kill zone and almost succeeded. Caught in the two-way crossfire of the L-shaped ambush, seven VC soldiers made a determined effort to break free. Knowing better than to charge forward into the withering fire of the M 60 machine gun on the short leg of the L and taking deadly fire from the Special Forces team members positioned above the trail on the long leg of the L, the seven VC broke off to the left in an attempt to get some jungle between themselves and the ambusher's deadly fire. They continued to circle left and headed back down the trail the way they'd come. They ran right into Mund.

When the Special Forces team found him, Mund had finally succumbed to his wounds, but not before taking the seven Vietcong with him. In a salute to his heroism and as a sign of their respect, Mund was given a full military funeral by the members of the Special Forces team. To say that this was a rare occurrence would be an understatement. Mund's American brothers-in-arms knew that besides losing an important ally, they had lost a loyal friend.

Mai, at one time, thought and maybe hoped that she and Dish would be married. After all, he was not much older and not really her brother either. But Dish now shared his father's deep hatred for the Vietcong. The hatred that filled his heart left little room for anything else. Dish would often disappear into the jungle for weeks at a time. When he was not helping American Special Forces operating in the area, he was hunting the VC on his own, seeking vengeance for Mai's family as well as for the death of his father. Dish's father was a legend among the local Montagnard villages and he felt honor bound to follow in his father's footsteps. That was his duty.

CHAPTER 3

A few hours before dawn on Wednesday, April 19th, Lt. Curtis Cordell, and his team gathered near the helicopter pads at Camp Evans. The team completed a weapons check and inspected their gear. The radio operator fired up the PRC-77 radio, authenticated, logged onto the network and completed a communications check. It was all standard concentrated routine. No one talked. Pre-operational checks completed, they sat down, settling in as comfortably as the situation allowed, to wait for word that the mission was a go. Jim Walker took out his wet stone and began sharpening his Buck General, a Bowie-style knife favored over the government-issued bayonet by many seasoned American combat veterans in Vietnam.

"Hey, Lt! Are we finally going to see some action?" asked Wilson, breaking the silence.

Pvt. Wilson was a young replacement, having just arrived in the country. He was from somewhere in Wyoming.

Young and green as hell, Cordell reflected. "Not if I can help it, Wilson," Cordell replied. "I would like to see you make it home to your momma in one piece."

"If we do," Walker added gruffly taking a pause from sharpening his knife, "you keep your god-damn eyes open and your newbie ass down! Do you hear me, Wilson?"

This terse comment from Walker drew a general chuckle from all the others. It helped take the edge off the waiting. A few minutes later the radio crackled with the message that Operation Delaware was a go. And so, with that signal, the team stood and moved toward their chopper.

The pilot of the Huey escort gunship flipped the switch, firing up his chopper's engine. His crew jumped to life.

Captain John Crandall completed the pre-flight on his HU-1H and nodded to his co-pilot, Warrant Officer, Jimmy Trent, that all was in readiness for liftoff. Crandall glanced back to see that Cordell's team was on board and in position, then reached over and flipped his own chopper's ignition switch, firing up the powerful engine.

"Let's go," Cordell yelled giving Crandall a thumb up.

Relaying orders to the pilot of the Huey gunship assigned as an escort, Crandall pulled pitch and with its rotors howling like a caged beast breaking free into the morning air, the Huey lifted off its pad with the escorting gunship following in its wake.

Lt. Curtis Cordell's team settled in for the thirty-five-minute flight. A few members of the team joked among themselves as they looked out through the Huey's open doors. It was a clear morning and the landscape below was easy to make out even though they were cruising at 2000 ft. They flew over rolling hills, clearings of tall grasses, and groves of trees some 30 to 50 ft. tall. The rest of the team sat quietly, alone in their thoughts.

Lt. Cordell spotted the charred remains of an abandoned Montagnard village. There were no signs of life.

The UH-1H, continued along on its indirect flight path, zigzagging over the jungle, small Vietnamese and Montagnard villages and farm clearings, running streams, and dry rocky stream beds.

Still no sign of recent activity, Cordell thought to himself.

Crandall changed course heading north toward the A Shau and their destination. Fourteen miles out from the designated LZ, Crandall brought the Huey down to treetop level and began flying the nap-of-the-earth, almost brushing the treetops with the chopper's skids as he made their final approach. The gunship followed, taking up a defensive station on their left flank. Birds scattered as the two Hueys' roaring engines propelled them forward at 110 miles per hour.

Once inserted into the LZ, a small clearing on Dong Re Lao Mountain, Lt. Cordell's team's orders were to establish a radio relay site on the mountain's mile-high peak dubbed Signal Hill by the staff back at HQ.

This mission should be piece of cake, Cordell thought. *Just set up the communication link, sit tight and relay any communications. Nothing to it!*

The 1st Cavalry Division (Airmobile) would launch a massive air assault into the A Shau Valley with the assigned mission of seeking out and destroying all current NVA and Vietcong capability in the valley. The radio relay site set up on Signal Hill by Cordell's team would allow for effective communications between the three combat brigades, their operational command center located at Camp Evans near the coast, and any approaching combat or support aircraft being used during the assault.

This major action designated by HQ as Operation Delaware consisted of a combined force of three brigades of the 1st Cavalry and their attached ARVN forces. With 20,000 men and 450 helicopters, the 1st Cavalry Division had more firepower and mobility than any other division-sized unit in Vietnam.

If the fucking politicians would get the hell out of the way, we could win this damn war and go home! Cordell had often wished he could say this to someone, to anyone. As an officer, he could not. Officers had to keep comments like that private. He reminded himself of that on frequent occasions.

They had been in the air about a half an hour when the ready lamp in the UH-1H turned green and seconds later the UH-1H swooped in on its initial approach. The chopper pilot made a quick pass over the small clearing designated as the LZ while the escort gunship took up a protective station, circling just overhead.

"Shit," exclaimed Cordell. "Damn it to hell!" On the first pass, the "small clearing" revealed itself to be nothing more than a bomb crater on a forty-five-degree slope ringed by fire-blackened trees. A touchdown was impossible. His team would have to rope down from an altitude of about thirty feet into the crater.

"Just once I'd like things to go without complications," Curtis muttered to himself.

The pilot broke off and began a "go around" to take up a hovering position as the team prepared to rappel down into the crater. Crandall brought the UH-1H around for its second pass, hovering over the crater at about thirty feet. The Huey's door gunner trained his M-60 on the clearing's edge, his eyes scanning for any signs of enemy movement below as the team readied for the descent. Lt. Cordell was a man who believed in leading from the front, so as the first man out, he stepped into the doorway with his team falling in behind him ready to take the rope.

As door gunner, Pfc. Jimmy Allen's eyes were in constant motion searching for any sign of enemy activity. He was careful not to look directly at anything. He'd learned well the lesson of using the corners of his eyes to pick up movement ... much quicker than direct stares. Suddenly Allen spotted a smoke trail to the left streaking up from the jungle canopy below.

"RPG!" Allen yelled, raking the area where the smoke trail had originated with a hail of 7.62 mm bullets.

The pilot glanced left, also spotting the smoke trail. He shoved hard on the cyclic stick to avoid the incoming rocket, but in the thinner atmosphere at that altitude, the UH-1H's Lycoming T53-L-13 engine suffered from less oxygen for power and the rotors found less air to bite into for lift. The pilot lost control and the Huey careened wildly, down and to the left, the tip of its rotor almost contacting the jungle canopy.

Cordell managed to keep his footing and had almost snapped the rope into his D-ring when the Huey shifted violently back to the right, the pilot fighting to regain control of the chopper. Cordell was thrown from the Huey and fell tumbling into the tree canopy now just a few feet below him. The chopper with the remaining team members careened again, this time back to the left as the pilot fought desperately to regain control.

Cordell felt like he was falling in slow motion as he tumbled his way to the ground. Fortunately, breaking tree limbs slowed his fall. His rucksack caught for a few seconds on a large tangle of vines, suspending him for a moment in mid-air. It broke loose and he crash-landed on the jungle floor.

Lt. Cordell slowly clawed his way back to a painful consciousness.

"What the fuck happened?" he asked. There was no one to answer.

Aware now that he was lying flat on his back on the jungle floor, he looked up to see daylight filtering down through the leaves of the jungle canopy above him.

Shit! Where's the damn chopper?

Instinctively he tried to roll over and locate his weapon but an intense pain shot through his body like an electric current. Mercifully, he blacked out again.

When Cordell again drifted back into consciousness the jungle surrounding him was getting dark. This time he did not move. He laid still and focused on trying to figure out what the hell had happened to him.

Okay. I was in the chopper trying to snap the rope into my D-ring and ... the door gunner was shouting and there was the sound of the M-60 firing ... and I was grabbing for the rope and ... Holy shit! I fell out of the fucking chopper.

Cordell lay still a few more minutes as that thought slowly took hold in his brain.

What the fuck do I do now? He began to mentally assess his situation. He thought about where he was ... the region they were flying into. Vietnamese civilians in the area had been under Viet Cong control for quite a while now. That meant that, for the most part, they would be unlikely to render him any assistance. Fully indoctrinated or terrorized into supporting the enemy ... they would be more likely to turn him over to the VC.

Curtis was in the mountains, so water was going to be an issue. He still had his canteen, but that was only one quart. That was simply not enough! When thinking "jungle," most folks imagine lush growth and monsoon rains. There are also long dry seasons with no rain ... where water becomes an issue even in the lowlands. They were currently in such a dry season and Curtis was not in the lowlands.

Time to see if I can move. It was a painful process but this time he managed to roll over. He discovered his M16 and his rucksack beneath him. Giving his weapon a thorough inspection, he was relieved to find that the rifle was operational. His helmet was nowhere to be found.

Just as well, the damn thing weighed about ten pounds!

Lucky for him that the soft damp soil of the jungle floor had absorbed much of the impact when he landed. It could have been a big freaking pile of Vietnamese rocks ... with a very different result.

Slowly Cordell managed to get up on his knees and then to his feet. Every inch of his body hurt like hell. He was covered with a large assortment of abrasions, lacerations, and contusions, and a good amount of his blood too. He'd have to watch for signs of a concussion ... his head really hurt and he felt a huge knot on it as well. At first glance though, it appeared that despite the considerable pain, there didn't seem to be any broken bones or internal injuries.

Cordell's primary concern at this point was simple survival. He was still disorientated and had no idea what had happened to the chopper or his team. He knew he was somewhere near the original LZ, and since there was no sign of the chopper or a crash site, it was a good bet they'd gotten away safely. And then, Cordell realized that he had no radio.

What a cluster fuck, Cordell thought!

He took stock of his present situation and concluded that it was not good. Obviously, they'd been spotted since someone had fired that rocket! The VC, or even an NVA patrol, might be on the way to investigate what they hoped to find, the site of a disabled helicopter or a crash site. Even on his best day, Cordell wouldn't be able to take on a well-armed Vietcong or NVA patrol alone. He needed to move now, pain or no pain.

"Okay Cordell," he told himself. "I know it hurts, but you've got to get your ass moving." His best option was to head downhill toward any water.

Cordell knew there were still a few Montagnard villages in the area and they would be located near a source of water. Maybe with luck, he could find some friendlies willing to help him make his way back to his unit. Cordell took a few steps in a generally downhill direction before his knees buckled and he hit the ground.

Lt. Curtis Cordell was unaware that he had an observer who was watching him from deep within the jungle foliage about forty yards away, silent, immobile and invisible.

CHAPTER 4

Dish was squatting silently in the dense foliage trying to decide what to make of the American soldier who had just fallen from the sky.

He was a Degar, or Montagnard, of the Jari tribe from the Kon Tum Province of the Central Highlands. The term "Montagnard" was a carry-over from the French colonial period in Vietnam and meant "mountain people." They generally disliked the Vietnamese who regarded the Montagnard as little more than savages. Dish might have been an exception to this, but ... he still felt great hatred for the communist North Vietnamese and their Vietcong allies.

About 40,000 of these tough Montagnard tribesmen fought side by side with U.S. Special Forces and LRRP teams in Vietnam. They had earned the respect and admiration of their American comrades-in-arms. Both the Special Forces operating in Vietnam and the Montagnard excelled in all forms of combat skills and were quite accustomed to operating under the harshest of conditions. It was not surprising that each group formed a deep respect for the other.

Dish finished his lunch, a handful of sticky rice wrapped in what was jokingly referred to as a "totally unpalatable vegetation" by his Special Forces colleagues and then worked his way down to have a closer look at the American. As he approached he saw that the soldier had lost consciousness again.

Suddenly he froze. His eyes narrowed into slits. He remained stock still, breath held, as the many-banded krait coiled itself tighter just a few feet in front of him and directly in his path. The krait was still, only its tongue darting in and out, tasting the air, searching for what had disturbed it. Dish waited, as still as a statue for long minutes. There was little Dish feared in this world, but death from the bite of the venomous krait was a painful way to go. Not a good death for a Montagnard warrior such as himself.

Eventually, the krait seemed to lose interest and with painful slowness, uncoiled itself and slithered off his path and into the jungle growth. Dish remained still for several more minutes. Kraits were known to be aggressive and sometimes to wait in ambush for unwary victims. Finally, Dish slowly worked his way the rest of the way down to the American soldier. While still breathing, it was obvious that he was in terrible shape. The American was seriously battered, scraped, and bleeding. And there was a large swelling on the back of the soldier's head, probably from being struck by a tree limb on his way down.

Dish noticed the American's rank and unit insignia and saw that the soldier was a lieutenant from the American 1st Calvary division. Dish had worked with many American Special Forces teams over the past months, but never with the 1st Cav's LRRP teams. He was impressed by the fact that, even though the American lay unconscious on the jungle floor, he'd still managed to maintain a solid grip on his rifle.

Falling from the sky was not a smart thing to do, Dish reflected. This American soldier must be very clumsy or stupid. Perhaps both. He grinned as he recalled the picture of the American tumbling down through the canopy, hanging up momentarily on the vines, and finally flopping onto the jungle floor. It was a very funny picture. It had been quite difficult not to laugh out loud.

Better not leave him here or this clumsy American would quickly become a dead American!

Dish's life of hard work in the Central Highlands, and his martial arts training with Ang Dung, had turned him into a very strong and capable young man. He scooped up the American, rucksack and all, and slung him over his right shoulder. Grabbing up the American soldier's M16 in his left hand, Dish headed into the jungle following a ghost of a trail most Americans or even the NVA would never have noticed.

Even with the extra burden Dish could travel quickly. By nightfall, he felt near enough to the village to stop for a short rest. He set the M16 down and settled the American gently on the ground, propping him up against the base of a water pine tree. Dish thought that several times on the trail the lieutenant had regained and then lost consciousness. But, there had been no struggle. Perhaps he'd noticed the crossbow hanging from Dish's hip.

Since the Montagnards were famous for their deadly use of this silent and accurate weapon, Dish figured that the American believed himself to be in friendly hands and so there'd been no struggle to get away. He unslung his crossbow and squatted down to eat a little more rice. Dish noticed that the American was conscious and watching him, so he went over and offered him a drink from the canteen he'd retrieved from the soldier's gear. The American was grateful and drank greedily. Dish helped himself to a drink too.

"You okay," he said quietly. The human voice carried a long distance in the jungle. "My village is close."

Cordell tossed and turned in the grip of a feverish dream. He was hurt, desperately trying to make his way through the jungle, searching for his team. But, everywhere he turned or tried to crawl, the jungle became an impenetrable mass of vines, thorns, and underbrush. He could not get through. The jungle floor would become hot, a steaming mass of rotting vegetation. He could not breathe, he felt like he was choking, he felt like he was being steamed alive. Then, for a brief instant, the feeling of cool relief, like a gentle jungle rain would flow over him, starting with his head and spreading throughout his feverish body. However, it was just a temporary respite, because the heat always came right back, the choking resumed, and again he could not breathe. It felt like some giant, constricting serpent was coiling itself around his chest and was slowly squeezing the life out of him.

When Cordell came to and opened his eyes he found himself looking up into the face of the most beautiful woman he had ever seen. At least he hoped she was there and he wasn't just hallucinating. She was gently washing the scrapes and cuts that covered most of his sore and aching body. He was embarrassed when he realized that he was lying naked on a woven mat in a Montagnard home. To his relief, he found that his midsection was discretely covered. When Mai noticed that the American was awake, she indicated that he should remain still until she finished cleaning his injuries. That task completed, Mai smiled at the American and gave him a reassuring pat on his arm. He was dimly aware that she'd got up and left, and an instant later Cordell was back to sleep.

Cordell awakened sometime later to find Mai returning with bowls of clear broth soup and plain rice on a tray she placed next to him. He glanced around the room and was relieved to see his M16 leaning against the wall near his mat. It looked as though it had been recently cleaned and since he could see a magazine seated in the magazine well, he assumed it was loaded.

"Please eat," Mai stated in clear English. Cordell was shocked.

"You speak English very well," he said somewhat surprised.

"Yes," Mai replied. "I learned in the mission school. I would sometimes help my father talk to the Americans when they visited our village." Being the daughter of a village chief had its advantages.

"You are not Montagnard," Cordell observed.

"No," Mai replied. "I am Vietnamese. My family was killed by the VC. I now live with the Montagnard."

Cordell nodded. "I am sorry," he replied. A look of sadness flickered briefly across her face and then she went on.

"The man who brought you here is my Montagnard brother, Dish. It is okay! You rest now. Okay?"

Cordell smiled.

"My name is Curtis Cordell. What is your name?"

"My name is Mai. You rest now. I will come back later."

It is very nice to meet you ... Mai, Cordell thought as he drifted off to sleep.

A few days later Mai went off to tend her small patch of garden and see if she could find something to add to tonight's meal. She typically did not need much for herself and Dish was rarely around for meals, but feeding the American who needed to recover his strength was putting a slight strain on her resources. She'd manage somehow.

She'd decided she liked the American soldier. He was quiet in a pleasant, thoughtful way and tried hard to stay out of her way while obviously enjoying her company. Mai was not sure that this was a good thing. He would be leaving soon and she must continue her life in the village. It would not be a good idea to become too friendly and as a young Vietnamese lady, it would not be appropriate.

Arriving at the garden Mai pulled a few weeds and repaired a hole in the wooden fence. One of the water buffalo calves had developed a fondness for her garden and she was continually chasing him away and repairing the damage he did. She found a turnip and some cabbages ready to pick and would add them to the pot. Gathering up the vegetables, she made her way back to the house where she found the American sitting on the steps enjoying the sunshine.

"What are you doing?" Mai scolded. "You should be lying down and resting."

Cordell smiled. "I just needed to move a bit. Can't get too lazy. Anyway, the sun feels pretty good right now." Mai noticed the rifle leaning on the step beside him and frowned.

"You must go inside. You should not be seen outside. Too many VC."

"Okay, okay. You might be right." Cordell, using his M16 for support, hobbled back into the house with Mai right behind him.

Cordell chuckled. "With your brother in the area, I do

not think too many VC would bother this village."

Mai admitted to herself that Cordell was probably right. The VC generally steered well clear of this village. They'd learned from experience that they didn't last long in this area with Dish and the other Montagnard men from the local villages on patrol. And too, the American Special Forces teams often passed through the area on missions to disrupt the flow of weapons and other supplies coming down from the north. Despite all of this, the horror of her painful memories had taught her the importance of always being on full alert. Lose your focus, lose your life.

Mai busied herself preparing vegetables and rice for the evening meal while Cordell found a place to sit and relax. He was feeling better but knew he still needed several more days to recover before he could even attempt to get back to his unit. His head still hurt badly where he'd gotten that prize-winning knot.

Cordell found it very pleasant just sitting there watching Mai move about concentrating on her tasks. She was so very beautiful! Her face, her hair. She moved with such grace and gentleness. He wanted to help her prepare the food but thought better of it since he still felt quite weak and was probably much safer sitting down. And, he certainly didn't want to overstep any cultural bounds.

The next morning Cordell awoke to feel much better. Mai had left a bowl of rice and vegetables sitting on a tray next to his pallet. There was also some rice tea in an old cast iron teapot sitting there along with his canteen cup. Cordell ate the vegetables and rice, discovering that he was hungry. He poured some of the tea into his canteen cup. It was still warm. Finishing his breakfast, he went over to the sink and splashed some water from a bucket onto his face.

Feeling a bit more human, Cordell worked his way out through the longhouse door and down the steps, doing so without the aid of his rifle. He made his way to a small bench and sat down to enjoy the morning sunshine. Some activity in a small clearing nearby caught his attention.

Dish had returned to the village and was engaged in martial arts practice with other men from the village. Being a soldier Cordell was always interested in such things and enjoyed watching them practice for a good while. Whatever they were doing, it looked damn practical and efficient.

Solid stuff! He was intrigued.

Dish saw him sitting on the bench and when they were done, he came over and sat down. Dish decided he liked this quiet American who didn't complain much and seemed genuinely interested in the village and its people. Dish thought Mai liked him too.

"You like?" Dish asked indicating the martial arts practice session. Despite it being morning, it was already quite warm. Cordell observed that Dish had worked up quite a sweat. However, for all the physical exertion, his breathing was very normal. "You try tomorrow. Okay?"

Cordell wasn't too sure he would be ready by then but nodded and smiled.

"Okay," he said, hoping he would survive tomorrow's practice session.

A few days later Cordell's general condition was greatly improved. He'd survived two of Dish's training sessions and was beginning to understand a little of the basics. Mai explained that Dish was showing him Nguyen-ryu, a Vietnamese martial art originally taught him by her father.

When Cordell, with Mai translating, asked her brother

about his getting back to a U.S. military base and his unit, she was surprised to realize that she was saddened to think of Cordell leaving. Dish informed him that the Vietcong and NVA were currently very active to the south, the very area they must pass through to reach the closest U.S. military outpost. His recommendation was to wait until the activity died down.

Cordell took the news translated by Mai well enough. It made sense and he found that he liked the idea of being around Mai for a few more days.

The days turned into weeks. Cordell spent the time gaining back his strength, practicing Nguyen-ryu with the village men, and helping Mai with her chores. At first, Mai resisted his help, saying that he mustn't ... that it was woman's work. Cordell countered that he could not be expected to sit around and do nothing and he needed the exercise. Finally, Mai relented and she and Cordell enjoyed their time together in the garden, fetching water, and doing other odds and ends. He'd even learned the names of all her pigs.

Today, Dish joined them for the evening meal. Through Mai, Dish explained that the NVA and their VC allies had moved off to the northwest. This meant Cordell should have no trouble getting through to an American Special Forces camp located a few days walk to the south. Unfortunately, Dish went on, he and the village men would be leading a Special Forces team north to track the NVA's movements and he would not be able to guide Cordell to the outpost. Cordell knew that he needed a guide to help him avoid any VC patrols still operating in the area. Especially since he had no radio, maps, or even a compass. All of that had been lost when he was thrown out of the chopper.

"I will show you the way," came a firm, quiet voice.

Cordell looked over at Mai and began to argue. Dish looked at Mai and nodded, and that was the end of that discussion.

CHAPTER 5

Cordell began preparations for the two-day trek south with Mai. He checked what little gear he had left from his fall from the chopper. There wasn't much.

He had his web belt, canteen, the M16 and four full 30-round magazines. He still had his old aviator's watch. Somehow it had survived.

Just like Timex, he thought, chuckling to himself. *Takes a licking and keeps on ticking.*

The Buck General bowie-style knife he'd carried now belonged to Dish, a gift in gratitude for saving his life and as payment for the Nguyen-ryu lessons. It would prove a valuable tool in the jungle and be a real status symbol among his fellow Montagnard warriors.

Cordell's rucksack was in bad shape, but with some minor repairs, it would do for a light load. Cordell's boots and camouflaged fatigue pants were in good enough shape, but his fatigue jacket had been torn to shreds by the tree limbs that had slowed his fall. One of the larger men in the village had been kind enough to provide him with a shirt. It was a dirty gray and a bit snug, but at least it was not a bright red. Montagnard men liked to wear bright colors when they were not hunting VC in the jungle.

I would have trouble blending in with the jungle foliage in a bright red or yellow shirt, Cordell mused.

He cleaned and inspected his rifle again, and then emptied and reloaded the four magazines. Mai busied herself preparing sticky rice balls wrapped in green leaves and gathering the items she would need for the trip. Cordell could feel a certain tension between them that was not there before. He was unsure what it was about and decided to chalk it up to nervousness about the journey. They would be leaving the next morning.

Rising early, Mai had already prepared their morning meal of rice and vegetables. Cordell noticed a few small chunks of meat mixed in with the vegetables but decided not to ask. Last time he'd checked, all the pigs were still present and accounted for.

They finished eating and loaded up. Cordell slung his rucksack over his shoulders and picked up his M16. Dish spoke to Mai quite seriously for some time, and Cordell saw him hand her a small brownish leather pouch. Mai checked to see if anyone had noticed before placing it into her woven back-basket for the trip. And then, she went off to say goodbye to her pigs.

Dish stepped up to Cordell, faced him squarely and in his very broken English said, "I think you good man. You take care of Mai. She good woman."

"I will," Curtis replied.

More likely she will take good care of me, Cordell thought. "She will be back safe in a few days," Cordell continued.

"She does not come back," Dish responded shaking his head. "Here no good for her."

Now, what does he mean by that? Where else would she go? Certainly not Saigon.

He decided to just stick out his hand. Dish hesitated. Shaking hands was not a Montagnard custom. Suddenly, Dish reached out and took his hand and they shook hands briskly. Then Dish turned abruptly and walked into the jungle beyond the village. Cordell and Mai watched him until he disappeared.

"Are you ready?" Cordell asked.

"I am ready," Mai replied simply. They started off traveling on a track that led them into the jungle in a southeasterly direction. In silence, Mai led the way while Cordell kept a wary eye out for anything that might spell trouble. After several hours of walking, they left the track and climbed part way up a ridge, locating a spot that offered good cover and a clear view of the surrounding terrain. They both needed a rest.

Cordell sat quietly, alert for any suspicious sounds or movements in their area. Mai also sat quietly. Finally, she commented softly, "I hope Dish takes care of my pigs and does not eat them."

Cordell thought for a moment and replied, "He knows how much you care for those pigs. I don't think he will eat them."

She smiled gratefully as she turned toward Cordell and said, "We will follow the ridge south and then east. Better to stay off the trails ... less chance of meeting VC."

Cordell nodded. "I guess we should be moving."

Mai stood and the late morning sun glistened in her jet-black hair. She was so very beautiful. Cordell felt his heart doing funny things. His breathing seemed to be misbehaving as well. During his time in the Montagnard village, he had developed a great respect for Mai. She was so strong and capable, truly amazing for her age. And, despite the tragic circumstances that brought her to the Montagnard village, she was somehow still able to find such joy and beauty in the world. She absolutely inspired him.

He chuckled to himself, *even her little pigs loved her!*

"Yes, we have a long way to go," Mai replied looking at him. Their eyes met and suddenly Cordell fully realized what Dish had already understood when he made that parting comment. Mai would not be returning to the village. They would stay together and meet whatever situations life dealt them side by side. Cordell swallowed.

Oh shit! That thought excited him. It also scared the crap out of him. He had nothing solid to base that sudden revelation on, just a few smiles, shared meals, a few shared chores, and an occasional quiet look along the trail. But he knew deep in his soul that it was true. He also knew it had the potential to cause problems for the both of them. The U.S. Army typically frowned on that kind of stuff.

Still ... it was not impossible!

Cordell picked up his rifle, motioned for Mai to lead the way and with one last look back the way they had come, followed Mai as she headed south staying just below the ridgeline.

It was going to be dark soon. Mai was guiding them along a faint path obviously not traveled for some time. The path suddenly turned up and into a small grotto containing some ancient stone ruins.

Cordell spoke softly, "Looks like an old temple."

Mai nodded. "It is a very old Buddhist temple. No one uses it now."

It certainly looked to Cordell like no one visited this temple anymore, or at least not in many years. However, just to be safe he found a secluded spot with good cover several yards off from the ruins where they would be hidden from view. Their line of travel had broken off toward the east and they were now at a lower elevation, soon they would be in the flatlands and rice paddies. They'd traveled a good distance and were making excellent time. They were about half way to their destination ... the Special Forces camp.

Mai and Cordell sat side-by-side eating their rice balls, appreciating the opportunity to rest. The jungle was still except for the occasional sounds of birds rustling in the trees and the chirping of many insects. A quiet bird call sounded. Mai tensed and looked toward the trees. The insects were no longer chirping. The jungle was silent. Cordell reached for his M16.

"It's okay," Mai whispered placing her hand on Cordell's shoulder. "Montagnard."

A few moments later the silhouette of a man appeared several yards off and slowly approached them. Mai stood. Cordell taking no chances, positioned himself slightly forward and to the right of Mai with his rifle at the ready. The man spoke to Mia in hushed tones. Cordell recognized it as the Montagnard dialect and relaxed just a bit. Mai replied and a short conversation began. The conversation ended and the silhouette turned and disappeared silently into the jungle.

Mai turned toward Cordell. He could see from the look in her eyes that something was very wrong.

"What is it?" he asked.

"My brother sent this man. His name is Tau. Tau says the NVA and VC are circling back. He said that when the VC moved to the north it was to set a trap for American soldiers who are coming. American soldiers will walk into very bad trouble. Many NVA and many VC are coming south."

"How did Tau find us?" Cordell asked.

"My brother told me of this place and to rest here tonight. That way if any trouble comes, he knows where to find us," Mai explained.

Trouble certainly did come, Cordell thought to himself. He had to try and find a way to warn the advancing American soldiers.

"Did Tau tell you where the Americans are?" Cordell asked.

"He said in the morning to head west and we will find their base camp near Chuon Ngo village. It is maybe three or four hours walking"

West, Cordell thought. That was going away from their original destination but he had no choice. He had to warn whatever American unit that was out there, probably conducting deep reconnaissance or on a combat patrol.

"We'd better get some sleep. I want to start at first light and we will have to travel fast."

Setting his rucksack down on the ground against a tree, Cordell took a quick look around. Everything looked quiet. Mai put her pack basket down and set about her own preparations for the night.

"Why don't you get some sleep," Cordell suggested. "I will keep watch and wake you in four hours so I can get some sleep."

Spreading out a ground cloth she'd pulled from her pack, Mai gave Cordell a tired but pleasant smile.

"Okay, sounds good." She retrieved a second small bundle of clothing from her pack and using it as a pillow, made herself comfortable on one side of the ground cloth, indicating Cordell should use the other side. It was far safer than sleeping directly on the ground.

Cordell hesitated for a moment and then shifted his rucksack to the ground cloth and sat down using the rucksack as a backrest. He could tell from Mai's breathing that she was already asleep. He sat there quietly listening to the sounds of the jungle. It was too dark to see much more than a few yards.

It was still dark when Mai gently shook Curtis awake. He awoke with a start, reaching instinctively for his rifle.

"Everything is okay," Mai whispered. "We must go." Mai quickly packed up her bundles and the ground cloth, and after a shared cold breakfast of sticky rice and water from Curtis' canteen, Curtis slung on his rucksack and picked up his M16.

"Okay Mai," Curtis spoke quietly. "Let's go. You lead and I will bring up the rear." Mai nodded. They started off without another word. The gray light of dawn was just enough to allow them to make their way back down to the main track. Curtis trusted Mai to lead the way, keeping his eyes out for any signs of danger. It would not do to run into a VC patrol now. They were headed in a generally southward direction, but after a few miles, Mai veered off to the right, following a narrow, less used trail that Curtis had failed to notice. They continued west along this trail for quite some time before cautiously stepping out onto a dirt road that continued along in the same westerly direction. They had been traveling for almost four hours.

"Chuon Ngo village is close. Maybe one mile." Mai smiled. "We should be okay unless they think you are VC."

Curtis grinned at that. His current uniform was not exactly regulation.

"Let's hope they talk first and shoot second." Staying to the right side of the road and close to concealment if needed, they started down the road to the village.

The 1st and 2nd platoons of the U.S. Marine's First Force Reconnaissance Company, tasked with supporting the United States Special Forces A-Team, A-104, were conducting a deep reconnaissance probe to collect intelligence on any enemy activity near the mountain approaches to the south. This area was part of the U.S. Marines' assigned area of operations along the Laotian border. Under the command of Captain Kevin Sparks, the two platoons, with a contingent of South Vietnamese soldiers, were ordered into the area after reports came in that a large force of NVA and their VC support were moving to the north. It was their job to find out what the hell the NVA were up to.

"Captain Sparks, you have company," a voice called from outside his tent. His unit was conducting its operations from a small base camp set up near Chuon Ngo village. There was not much to look at ... just a few tents, a field kitchen, a latrine and a chopper landing pad.

"Looks like an MIA from 1st Cav."

"Thanks, sergeant! Show him up." A few minutes later, Staff Sergeant Tindell arrived at Captain Sparks' tent with Lt. Cordell and Mai in tow.

Cordell followed by Mai, stepped into the tent. Cordell saluted. Captain Sparks returned the salute and greeted Cordell.

"Welcome Lieutenant. What can the U.S. Marines do for you on this fine afternoon?"

Cordell replied with a smile, "Lieutenant Cordell at your service, Sir. Actually, I am here to assist the U.S. Marines."

Omitting only that he had "fallen" out of the chopper, Cordell quickly relayed the story of his becoming injured and separated from his unit, his recovery while in the Montagnard village, his current efforts to rejoin his unit with Mai as his guide, and the change of plans because of the information Tau had provided just last night.

Cordell grinned. "However, I didn't know it was the U.S. Marines over here … or, I wouldn't have bothered to hike all this way! I am sure you guys can handle whatever Comrade Ho sends your way."

Captain Sparks laughed. "All the same, we appreciate the heads up!"

Cordell's face turned serious, "But seriously sir, I know the source of this intelligence. The man is her brother," indicating Mai standing there quietly. "He is a good friend and absolutely hates the VC. You guys are probably going to get hit hard in the next few days. Better be ready."

Sparks got up, nodded appreciatively to Mai and walked over to the tent flap. "Sergeant," he yelled.

"Yes Sir," came the reply.

"Get on the horn. Notify 1st Cav we have an MIA that belongs to them, one Lieutenant Cordell, and that he and his South Vietnamese guide have warned us of a probable major NVA assault on our position in the very near future."

"Yes, Sir!"

"Then get HQ on the horn and tell them we have good intelligence that the NVA and their VC comrades will be launching a major assault on our position in the next 12 to 72 hours. We want immediate resupply of ammo, food, water and medical supplies. First thing in the morning, no later. Also, any reinforcements they can send our way would be damn well appreciated. And, tell them to wake up the artillery boys and to have close air support standing by."

"Yes, Sir!"

"One more thing! Have somebody double check our pre-arranged firing coordinates with the artillery guys again. Make sure they cover any probable lines of attack the NVA might use. I'll be up back up to the command post in a few minutes."

"Yes, Sir." Sergeant Tindell took off toward the command post.

Sparks turned back to Cordell. "We can find a place for you and your South Vietnamese ally for tonight. Not much room in these tents, especially for a lady, but we will make do," he said smiling at Mai. "You two can catch a hop out on one of the resupply choppers tomorrow morning. If they give you any shit about taking your guide, have them talk to me. I figure the Marines owe her one."

"Yes, Sir." Cordell saluted.

"Why don't you stop by the field kitchen and see if they can't scare up a meal for the two of you. I'm going up to the command post and I'll send Sergeant Tindell over to get you settled as soon as I can."

Cordell and Mai left Captain Sparks and walked over to the field kitchen. Cordell was looking forward to some American food even if it was Marine Corp chow. Rice and vegetables were great … but he needed a break.

CHAPTER 6

Two days later with Mai at his side, Cordell reported to his commanding officer at Camp Evans. They'd had no trouble getting out on one of the resupply choppers and soon landed at Phu Bai, one of the several operational bases for the Marines of First Force Reconnaissance. Cordell found a marine corporal who was delivering a jeep to a Colonel with the 4th Marine Regiment stationed at Camp Evans willing to give them a ride.

Arriving at Camp Evans, they were met at the gate by the battalion's command sergeant major, Sergeant Major Rausch, who'd gotten word of Cordell's resurrection from the dead and imminent arrival. Rausch raised an eyebrow when he saw Mai in the jeep with Cordell. But, once Cordell explained the role she had played in his rescue and safe return, he took her under his wing. Within minutes a nurse from the 326th Medical Battalion arrived and led Mai off to find a place for her to stay and a much-welcomed bath. Cordell's platoon was notified he was back and still in one piece.

"I'll be a son of a bitch! You're one lucky bastard. I was

sure you were dead!" Walker exclaimed, a huge grin on his wide Apache face. Thrusting a cold beer into Cordell's hand he went on, "And here you show up with a beautiful Vietnamese girl on your arm! I don't fucking believe it!"

Pvt. Wilson was there as well ... happy and relieved to see him, and looking a bit less like a newbie.

"Yep, Wilson ain't got himself killed yet!" Walker said as Wilson came up to greet Cordell. Wilson didn't know whether to salute or extend his hand and tried awkwardly to do both at the same time.

Cordell laughed slapping him on the back and said, "Glad to see you are still with us, Wilson."

There were several new faces in the platoon including a new second lieutenant who looked like he was trying to decide whether to introduce himself or make a beeline for the latrine and was stuck somewhere between the two. Walker jumped into the potentially embarrassing situation and saved him.

"This is Lieutenant Peters. He's alright. Our team's been assigned to break him in right. Not sure what will happen now. Probably send you stateside for some R&R, Sir."

Cordell nodded shaking Peters' hand and kept the pleasantries short so Peters could continue his way to the latrine. There was a lot to get used to for any newbie, regardless of rank.

It turned out that Crandall, their chopper pilot, had successfully regained control of the Huey and then inserted the team at an alternate LZ a few kilometers from the original site. No enemy rockets this time. Walker assumed command, the communications relay site was set up and Operation Delaware was declared a military success.

"We radioed in the location where you got thrown from the chopper," Walker explained. "They sent out a rescue team ASAP but you were nowhere to be found. It was like you just disappeared."

Cordell laughed. "I was carried off by a friendly ghost." He then explained to Walker the circumstances that caused him to arrive back at post with a beautiful Vietnamese girl on his arm.

Walker laughed shaking his head, "I'll be damned! Only you could pull that off, Sir."

Cordell had time to enjoy a hot shower, some new fatigues, and a couple of cold beers before Sergeant Major Rausch returned to get the full story from him. Rausch confirmed that they had received word from Captain Sparks and the U.S. Marines through division HQ that Cordell was alive and on the way back with a Vietnamese guide. They'd not been prepared for Mai.

Cordell laughed. "I wouldn't be here now if not for Mai and her brother."

The Sergeant Major went on to say that he'd just spoken with the battalion commander, and thanks to Cordell's warning, the Marines were reinforced and more than ready when the NVA attack came the very evening of the day Cordell and Mai left on the resupply chopper. The NVA figured they would catch the marines off guard, but they were the ones in for a shock. It was a short, bloody fight with the Marines suffering light casualties. The NVA and VC paid a very heavy price.

"The fucking marines will probably put you in for a god-damned medal just for saving their sorry asses!" Rausch chuckled.

Sergeant Major Rausch stood up, "Relax. Get some sleep. Lieutenant Colonel Ellerson wants to see you and your Vietnamese lady friend at 0700. I'll pick you up in my jeep at 0645." Rausch turned and left the tent. Cordell lay back on his bunk very happy to be back but he was also worried about what tomorrow morning would bring as far as Mai was concerned.

At precisely 0645 Sergeant Major Rausch pulled up in his jeep. Mai was seated in the jeep's back seat wearing a pale blue-gray Ao Dai, the traditional Vietnamese dress. Her jet-black hair, freshly washed and shining in the sun, fell gently against the left side of her face. Once again Cordell was dumbstruck by her delicate beauty. Mai noticed his reaction and smiled. It made her happy that her looks pleased him.

"For Christ's sake lieutenant, get in the jeep!" the Sergeant Major growled. "Ain't you ever seen a pretty girl before?"

Cordell recovered and climbed into the jeep's front passenger seat. Rausch shifted gears and pointed the jeep in the direction of battalion headquarters. They pulled up alongside the Quonset hut that served as battalion HQ, and Rausch killed the jeep's engine.

"Colonel Ellerson is waiting for you in his office," he announced.

Cordell climbed out of the jeep and helped Mai extricate herself from the jeep's cramped back seat. A short freshly raked gravel walk led to the Quonset hut's front door. Cordell opened it for Mai and followed her in. The buck sergeant serving as "NCO of the Day" sat at the front desk. He got up when he saw Mai enter with Cordell following close behind.

"Welcome back Lieutenant Cordell." The sergeant saluted. "Good to see you again. Good morning Miss." He waved them on. "The Colonel is expecting you."

"Thank you, Sergeant. Glad to be back," Cordell replied returning the salute. They walked down the narrow hallway to the Battalion Commander's office.

Mai was deeply concerned about how this meeting might affect her. She'd entered a new world and couldn't help wondering how she'd manage if she had to return to her old one, or even if she could. Cordell sensed that she was very worried and, well damn, so was he. He reached out and took her hand, giving it a reassuring squeeze. Mai squeezed back. It was the first real familiar interaction between them and it sent an electric jolt through his system.

Colonel Ellerson looked up from his desk. "I'll be damned! Come on in Lieutenant!"

Cordell stepped into the Colonel's office with Mai right behind him. Cordell saluted.

"Lieutenant Cordell reporting, Sir!"

"At ease Lieutenant. Welcome back. And this is the young woman responsible for getting you back to us in one piece." Ellerson smiled at Mai. "We are in your debt, young lady. The lieutenant here is one of our finest officers. I could ill afford to lose him."

The Colonel indicated they should sit.

"Proceed with your report, Lieutenant."

Cordell left nothing out as he related the events beginning with his team's assigned mission to establish the communications relay station on Signal Hill, the VC rocket's near miss of their chopper and his being thrown out and falling to the jungle floor. He told of his rescue, his recovery time in the Montagnard village, the plans to return to his unit and the delays, first by large-scale enemy activity in the region he'd need to pass through, and then by his decision to warn the Marines of an imminent NVA attack. When Cordell finished his report, Colonel Ellerson nodded.

"That tracks very closely with what I have heard, Lieutenant." Ellerson leaned back in his chair.

"I do know that the Marines kicked major ass when the NVA attack came thanks to your warning. That Captain Sparks spoke very highly of you and wants to put you in for a medal. I'm not sure how that will fly."

"I didn't do it for a medal, Sir," Cordell replied.

"I know that, Lieutenant. You may get it anyway if the Department of Defense approves. I am putting you in for a Silver Star."

Cordell started to object, "That's not necessary, Sir."

"Forget it. It's a done deal. There's more. You have new orders. First, you have been promoted to Captain effective the first of last month. Second, the army is sending you stateside for a tour. You've earned a rest. You will be commanding a training company for the Infantry School at Ft. Benning, Georgia."

Cordell frowned. "I'd rather stay here, Sir," he stated simply.

"I know that, Captain. This is not a step-down. Your experiences here will serve to greatly improve the training our new recruits receive, and the command experience will stand you in good stead on your next tour here if that happens." The Colonel smiled. "I am sure you will have no trouble getting back here if you want to."

Mai sat quietly, but her hands gave her away. They were white-knuckled with the stress of the moment as the conversation went on between the Colonel and Cordell. Mai had a strong sense of destiny and duty and it seemed so right at the time to leave her village and travel south with Cordell, but she'd done so at great risk. While she suspected he loved her, she was also afraid that he had not yet recognized these feelings for what they were. There was no future for her if she returned to the Montagnard village. While she knew she was attractive and certainly accepted by the villagers, the Montagnard men were of no interest to her. Most were much older; too many of the younger Montagnard men had died fighting the VC. Young single women in Saigon had little hope of finding suitable husbands now. For them, it was a question of finding a way to survive day by day. Any plans for a future had to be put on hold.

Mai had very little experience with Americans before now and she had been somewhat frightened of Cordell at first because he was both an American and a soldier. In her past experience, all soldiers were very tough and hard, many were cruel. But, it didn't take her long to see that, at his core, Cordell was kind and a gentleman. And, he was never cruel. He was certainly a soldier and could be hard as nails when the situation required it. But, he could also make her laugh and she hadn't been able to do that in a long time. It only took a few weeks for her to realize she had fallen in love with this American. He was not simply a way out. Mai wanted to share her life with him even if that meant traveling to a strange land.

"And now, what are we going to do with you, Miss?" Colonel Ellerson smiled kindly at her.

"I will do whatever the Captain tells me to do." What else could she say at this point?

Cordell spoke up. "Sir, Can I speak to you privately for a few minutes?"

"Sure," Colonel Ellerson replied. He punched the button on his intercom. "Sergeant Brooks!"

"Yes Sir," came the response.

"Come here, get this young lady and see if you can find her a cup of tea, or maybe coffee. We will be a few more minutes."

"On the way Sir," Sergeant Brooks replied.

Colonel Ellerson rose and showed Mai to the door. "Don't worry young lady. Sergeant Brooks will take good care of you. The Captain and I will have a few words and he will be right back with you." Mai followed Sergeant Brooks to the outer office.

"Permission to speak freely, Sir?" Cordell asked after the Colonel had sat back down behind his desk.

"Go ahead, Captain."

"Sir, I am sitting here today because of this woman. She nursed me back to health and guided me here. I owe her a great deal. Hell! The U.S. Marines owe her a great deal. But there's more. While she was living in a Montagnard village she is, as you can see, Vietnamese … and the daughter of a village chief. Her entire family was butchered by the VC. She has nothing and nowhere to go. And, she is also brave, intelligent, just amazing in so many ways. I've never met a woman quite like her and if she is willing I want to take her stateside with me as my wife."

Cordell found himself a bit surprised by what he had just said … but there it was. He did love her, and he wanted this woman to be his wife.

Colonel Ellerson leaned back in his chair. "You know the army's policy on that sort of thing, Captain?" he asked.

"Yes Sir, I do. However, I am not some newbie private who just got laid for the first time in the village and now wants to marry a business girl. Hell! I've never even kissed her and I don't think Mai has ever even had a boyfriend!"

Colonel Ellerson frowned. "I am not sure this would be such a good idea for your career."

"Colonel, I know several married officers. You yourself are married, Sir. And I think Mai already understands pretty well the concept of being a military spouse and what that might entail." Cordell paused and then went on. "You've told me that I am a damn good officer and I do plan to make the military my career. Furthermore, I believe Mai would be an asset, not a detriment to my career ... and I think the U.S. Marines would agree."

Colonel Ellerson chuckled at that. "Rein in your horses, Captain. If you are bound and determined to get married, I am not going to stand in your way. And if this girl, Mai, is half the woman the U.S. Marines seem to think she is ... I am damned sure not going to get in her way." Colonel Ellerson paused and then grinned. "You still have to ask her and she might be smart enough to run like hell."

Cordell stood and with a grin on his face saluted. "Thank you, Sir!"

Colonel Ellerson returned the salute. "Don't thank me, Captain. Thank the U.S. Marines."

Cordell turned to leave.

"Captain."

"Yes, Sir?"

"See the supply sergeant, Staff Sergeant Cooper, about this. And ... I don't know a damn thing about it. Can't have Staff Sergeant Cooper knowing I am privy to his little side businesses."

"Yes, Sir!" Cordell headed down the hall to find Mai.

Cordell walked back down the hall and found her in a small side office sitting on a folding metal chair, holding a now empty cup of tea and looking out the window. It was obvious to Cordell that she was worried, but she still managed a little smile when she saw him approaching.

"Mai, can we take a walk?"

Mai nodded and stood.

"Have a nice day Ma'am. You too, Sir," the sergeant called after them as they left the building.

Once outside they turned left at the end of the gravel path heading off nowhere in particular. After walking for a bit, they came across a group of picnic tables near the mess tent and sat down.

"I am not sure where to begin," Cordell said. Mai waited quietly. Cordell took a deep breath and began again. "Mai, these last several weeks have been wonderful for me. I've enjoyed being with you so much." He continued, "I think you feel what I am feeling. I think your brother Dish saw it too and told me, but at that time I did not understand what he meant."

"What did my brother say?" Mai asked in a quiet voice.

"He said that you would not go back to the village. It was not for you. He also said you were a good woman and that he thought I was a good man, and he asked me to take good care of you." Curtis paused. "At first, I thought he just meant on the trip here. But, while we were on the trail together I began to understand what your brother saw and what he meant."

Mai considered Cordell's face for a few seconds before she replied. "What do you think he meant?" she asked.

Cordell took another deep breath and continued. "He meant for us to be together. I love you, Mai. And not just because of what you did for me. I think you are an amazing woman." Mai looked away. Cordell stopped for a brief minute ... almost afraid to continue.

"I have orders to return stateside, to America. I would like very much for you to come with me as my wife. I know it will not be easy but I believe the two of us together can make it work."

Mai turned back to face Cordell and he could see tears running down her cheeks.

"I want to be your wife and I will go with you to America."

Cordell reached over and drew Mai into his embrace. His heart felt like it had just been set free from a steel trap and was now soaring high overhead. He held her close for several minutes and then whispered into her ear.

"I really do love you, Mai."

Mai drew back a bit and smiled at Cordell. "I know that, Captain Cordell. I love you too."

"Then do me a couple of favors, Mai, if you will?"

"What do you want me to do?"

"First, I want you to stop calling me Captain Cordell! Please call me Curtis. Second, I want a kiss."

"Okay, Curtis"

Their lips met in a kiss that took Cordell's breath away. He could not remember another time when he had felt such pure joy and raw emotion.

Finally, Mai pulled away. "Was that O.K, Curtis?" she asked.

"I'd say a bit more than okay." They were both laughing when he pulled her to him again and said, "If you don't mind, why don't we just try that again."

CHAPTER 7

Captain Cordell would assume command of Bravo Company, 1/19 Infantry Battalion, 198th Infantry Brigade located at Sand Hill, one of the four main cantonment areas at Fort Benning, Georgia. He and Mai had lots of ground to travel before they got there though. Cordell knew that the transition from single army lieutenant and young Vietnamese guide to a married military family would be something of a roller coaster ride.

Staff Sergeant Cooper was a bit shocked to be approached by a newly-promoted captain who needed to push his marriage to a local Vietnamese girl through the military red tape. It was usually enlisted men who sought his help in such situations. The U.S military frowned on such marriages and made it difficult to get them approved and finalized. However, once the initial shock wore off and the specifics of the situation were clarified, Staff Sergeant Cooper was happy to help. Strings got pulled and paperwork, blood tests, and physicals were done in record time. The Staff Sergeant was even able to procure a simple wedding band for the ceremony and having gotten caught up in the excitement of it all, forgot himself and presented it to the couple as a wedding gift. It was sized just a bit big, but some string wound around a section of the band took care of the problem for the time being.

Two weeks later an army chaplain pronounced Cordell and Mai "husband and wife." Since Dish was nowhere to be found, Sergeant Major Rausch insisted on giving the bride away. Jim Walker served as Cordell's best man and one of the nurses served as Maid of Honor. Captain Matthew Sparks showed up to represent the U.S. Marine Corp and Lieutenant Colonel Ellerson was there as well, sitting quietly at the back of the large general-purpose tent that functioned as a sometime movie theater, recreation hall, meeting room, mail distribution center, and now ... a wedding chapel.

A small reception was held in the mess tent. In addition to those attending the ceremony, there were other members of Cordell's old team and several of the nurses who had befriended Mai. The cook, Staff Sergeant Pearson, provided a light buffet of assorted finger foods, thoughtfully including some Vietnamese dishes for Mai. He'd even managed to create a very passable wedding cake and as the old saying goes, "a good time was had by all."

Exactly one hour later Private Wilson pulled up in a jeep. Wilson had clear orders to get Captain and Mrs. Curtis Cordell to Saigon in time to catch their Military Airlift Command-chartered TWA flight to the United States. Curtis settled Mai in the jeep's front seat despite her objections and climbed into the back with the two duffel bags containing most of their worldly belongings. The remainder of Captain Cordell's gear would catch up with them later at Fort Benning.

After two or three rounds of well-wishing to the newlyweds, Curtis prodded Pvt. Wilson in the shoulder.

"Wilson, let's get going. After all this, we sure don't want to miss our flight." Wilson pressed the starter switch, shifted the jeep into gear and away they went. The ride to Saigon was uneventful if a bit long, but Wilson did his duty and got them there in time for their flight. Curtis and Mai boarded the Boeing 707 at 11:30 PM. Of course, Mai had never flown before and was nervous and excited all at the same time. Nineteen hours later the 707 landed at Travis Air Force Base and the tired but happy couple caught a cab into San Francisco.

Mai found herself in a completely new world. Everything dazzled her, the lights and sounds of the city, the landscape, the architecture, just everything. While she had gotten somewhat used to the American military look from her experiences with Cordell and the base they'd just left behind, she was now deep in the world of American civilians. Everything and everyone fascinated her. Curtis found himself caught up in her excitement and soon the two were having the time of their lives laughing and enjoying each other's company in a way they had not had the opportunity to before. Mai reached for Curtis' hand and clasped it in both of hers, holding it to her chest. Never had he seen such a look of pure, complete happiness on anyone's face, and there it was on hers … it filled his heart with an indescribable joy. He put his other arm around her and they spent the rest of the ride quietly enjoying just being close.

Cordell checked them into their room. He'd dipped into his savings and booked three nights at the Ritz-Carlton. He felt a bit odd when the Bell Hop grabbed his duffel bags and led them to the elevator. But, after all, weren't they at the Ritz-Carlton? They were shown their room and Curtis tipped the Bell Hop as he left. It was 8:15 PM California time but for their bodies, it was 10:00 AM the next morning. Surprisingly neither of them felt all that sleepy but they most definitely were very hungry. After unpacking what little they had and splashing some water on their faces, they ventured out to explore the food options that were available. Settling on a small but friendly looking diner, Mai experienced her first American hamburger complete with French fries and a strawberry milkshake. Seeing that the diner offered breakfast twenty-four hours a day, Curtis ordered two eggs, toast, and coffee. Mai enjoyed the hamburger and fries but did not care for the milkshake.

"Too sweet," she commented.

Their most immediate need now taken care of, Curtis' mind turned to other things. Mai did not have a lot of belongings in his duffel bags. Stuffed in the bottom was a little bag containing some clothes, a hairbrush, and toiletries, and her mysterious leather pouch that Curtis had seen only twice and Mai never commented on.

Curtis decided that Mai needed some additional clothing and other necessities right away, so after they finished eating they left the diner to find a department store. They located a J.C. Penny store where, with the help of a wonderfully understanding saleswoman named Rebecca, Mai picked out a couple of summer dresses, a few casual outfits, dress shoes to match the summer dresses, and a pair of Reebok sneakers. Curtis stood by, thoroughly enjoying the shopping process. She looked so beautiful as she spun around modeling the dresses and Curtis found himself amazed by what she did for those jeans! Mai was totally amazed at the wide, almost endless selection items in the store. She had never seen anything like it. She browsed through the selection of ladies' underwear in total wonderment while Curtis blushed a bit, thinking to himself how wonderful she would look in those as well. Lastly, they selected a small suitcase for Mai's new belongings. Purchases in arm they returned to the hotel.

Once they were back in their room, Mai unpacked and went over all the purchases, removing any labels, once again examining everything for defects or wrong sizes. Mai seemed happy and at ease. She seemed quite content checking out her new clothing and accessories. Curtis couldn't help but remember how beautiful she had looked when he first saw her in that traditional Vietnamese Ao Dai.

It suddenly occurred to Curtis that, since their marriage, this was their first time to be alone together as husband and wife. They were on their honeymoon. Curtis smiled at Mai as he got up from the chair where he had been sitting, nervously thumbing through one of the "local attractions" brochures provided by the hotel.

"I think I will take a quick shower. Probably feel pretty good after the flight and shopping."

"Okay, Curtis," Mai replied. "Sounds good to me too. I will shower after you."

A little while later Curtis emerged from the bathroom wearing just a clean pair of underwear.

"That shower certainly did feel good. It's all yours now." Curtis found the remote and turned on the television. He sat on the foot of the bed and began looking for something to watch while Mai took a shower.

Mai glanced up as she finished examining her new suitcase and watched Curtis as he moved to sit on the foot of the bed. She felt her pulse quicken. She had seen Curtis unclothed before but that was different. He'd been injured and she was caring for him. Now he was healthy and strong, and he was her husband. He was, she decided, a very handsome man. Mai quickly finished putting up her things. She smiled, leaned over to kiss Curtis softly on the cheek and went into the bathroom. Curtis, not finding much worth watching on the television, lay back on the bed and closed his eyes ... half listening to some sitcom. He had no interest in listening to the news. It would all be about the war in Vietnam and he had enough of that for the time being. It felt great to simply lie there and relax for a few minutes.

"Curtis?"

Curtis opened his eyes and turned to see Mai. He felt his blood racing through his veins and wondered if Mai could hear his heart as it pounded away in his chest. Mai had finished showering and was walking toward him, her long jet-black falling to frame her delicate face. She had a towel wrapped around her midsection and the effect was simply stunning. Her golden skin, freshly scrubbed, was still glowing from the hot shower. Mai's muscles were strong and toned. Her long, slender neck drew his eyes to shoulders that were somehow strong and delicately feminine at the same time. Mai's firm breasts sloped gently, her nipples covered by the towel that wrapped around like a sarong, down to her narrow waist and gently flared hips. Her legs were long, their muscles taut and supple, her ankles were delicate, her feet small. Curtis had never seen a more beautiful sight. Mai, seeing his reaction, gave Curtis a happy, slightly nervous smile.

Curtis got up from the bed and walked over to where Mai was standing. He felt a surge of raw emotion welling up within him, a strange mixture of happiness, love, admiration, fear and strong desire. He tentatively reached out with his hand as if to stroke Mai's cheek and then suddenly pulled her into his embrace. His strong lips sought hers and Mai returned his kiss with equal passion. After long seconds, she pulled away.

"Do I please you, Curtis?" Mai asked shyly.

Curtis could barely breathe. He felt his stomach tighten. He answered, his voice almost a whisper.

"Mai, I am the luckiest man alive." Mai smiled happily. Curtis felt the heat of her hand as she gently pressed it against his well-muscled chest. The touch of her fingertips caused an electric sensation that made his thighs began to tremble.

He scooped her up in his arms.

"Oh!" An involuntary cry escaped from her lips as he laid her on the bed and moved over her. As Mai lifted her arms to encircle his neck the towel covering her midsection fell open revealing her small firm breasts, her dark nipples already long and hard. She pulled him down to her and her mouth opened under his, their tongues probing. Curtis felt the warm length of her body pressing against his, the heat building between them.

His lips gently traced a path down her long neck and along her collarbone. Mai shivered and moaned as his mouth moved slowly to her breasts. Curtis felt her hands move tentatively toward his briefs and shifted enough to help her slide them down and then kicked them off. Her touch sent exquisite sensations of pleasure coursing through his body.

Mai closed her eyes and another soft moan escaped her lips as Curtis gently kissed his way down her belly and moved between her spread thighs. His lips found the soft flesh of her inner thighs and worked their way upward. Curtis pressed his mouth against her and Mai's legs convulsed upward, her ankles locking themselves against his spine. Mai's entire body hummed as she cried out, soaring to greater heights of pleasure. Another moaned escaped Mai's lips and Curtis felt her shudder against him, feeling the tension flow from her body.

She reached for him, pulling him up, her lips kissing him wildly as she drew him towards her. He felt her heat as she guided him. A brief hesitation, a short cry of pain and Mai thrust her belly toward him. Curtis groaned with pleasure at the sensation. Mai wrapped her arms around him, her hard nipples brushed his chest. They moved together, two souls intertwined, inseparable, becoming as one. Her mouth found his neck, teeth gently biting as his hands roamed over her body, caressing her, enjoying the feel of her silky-smooth skin. Their movements slowly became more urgent. Mai found herself again teetering on the edge, and sensing Curtis' approaching release, hugged him tightly to her as she rode the waves of intense pleasure rolling through her body. Finally, they collapsed together in a tangle of arms and legs, neither of them wanting to break the connection. Mai placed her hand against Curtis' cheek and smiled up at him. Her eyes were shining. Curtis smiled.

"I think I have just died and gone to heaven," he whispered in her ear.

Mai giggling nodded. "Me too. That was very wonderful! Can we go again?"

Curtis laughed. "Okay, okay. Just give me a minute!" Then his face took on a more serious look. "I really love you very much, Mai."

Mai smiled. 'I love you too, Curtis. Also, very much."

Curtis and Mai spent three wonderfully lighthearted days exploring the San Francisco Bay area. It was just what they both needed. They immersed themselves in the hustle and bustle of this beautiful city, especially enjoying China

Town and the shops on Union Square. Later that same evening in the North Beach area, Mai had still another unforgettable experience, eating her first wood-fired pizza.

I can't believe how happy and content I feel right now just being here with Mai, Curtis thought to himself. It was amazing to him how much pleasure he got simply by watching Mai smile while she enjoyed the pizza. *I want this feeling to continue forever.*

The nights were spent exploring the physical side of their feelings for each other. Raised in traditional Vietnamese and Montagnard cultures, Mai certainly was aware of the role of sex in the lives of men and women, but simply as an act that usually led to children, an important duty to be performed for the survival of her people. The concept of pleasure for the woman as well as the man was foreign to her. But, she'd discovered that she loved how Curtis made her feel and she was eager to learn. And Curtis, while certainly no Casanova, having had some short-lived romances prior to his going to Vietnam, realized that they had been nothing compared to his feelings for Mai when they made love.

Curtis lay on his side close to Mai as they held each other, enjoying the afterglow of their lovemaking. He pressed he nose into her hair inhaling its sweet fragrance. Mai snuggled still closer feeling safe and loved in the quiet strength of his embrace.

"You are the best thing that's ever happened to me," he whispered into her ear. Mai rolled over to face him and reached up to stroke his cheek. She looked deep into his eyes, into his very soul and recognized the depth of the love that was there, his total sincerity and the wonderment at his own feelings. She closed her eyes … smiling.

"Toi yeu ban mai mai," Mai whispered back. "I love you forever."

The next morning while Mai packed for their flight to Knoxville, Tennessee, Curtis took time to make a quick trip to the San Francisco VA Medical Center. Knoxville was Curtis' hometown and they were going to stop to visit for a few days before continuing on to Ft. Benning, Georgia where Captain Curtis Cordell would assume his new command.

Curtis found Bobby Stillwater rehabbing under the watchful eye of a young physical therapist named Becky. Bobby lost his left leg when two rounds from an AK-47 struck it during a VC ambush, one round shattering his hip and the other striking the femur. Despite the efforts of Jim Walker who carried him out and the medics who worked on him and got him to the base hospital, too much time had passed to save Bobby's leg.

"Hey Bobby," Curtis called out as he headed across the room where Bobby was working on a parallel-bars type contraption. "How're you doing?"

"I'm alright, Lieutenant," Bobby replied nodding his head toward his therapist. "Got this cute nurse keeping me in line. It's good to see you, sir. I'm glad you stopped by."

"It's captain now," Curtis laughed. "Sending me to Ft Benning to train new recruits. Glad to see you're doing okay. Tough … about the leg."

"Well shit! I'll be alright," Bobby replied. "They can't send me back now." Bobby laughed. "Once I am done here, my Dad has a temporary job for me at his car dealership. Then I will take stock and see what happens." Bobby paused. "My girlfriend is sticking with me. I told her she didn't have to but she is. She must really love me I guess."

Curtis grinned. "Even without that left leg, you're a

better man than a lot of those assholes out there these days. I couldn't believe some of those idiots at the airport! I'm on leave and was in civvies so nobody bothered me. Some of the guys traveling in uniform caught hell. I saw one girl even spit on one of them. Couldn't believe what I was seeing."

"No accounting for assholes," Bobby acknowledged and then laughed. "So, what else is new?"

"Well, I just got married."

"To who?" Bobby asked. "You haven't been stateside long enough."

"To a Vietnamese princess," Curtis replied smiling. He then gave Bobby a condensed version of his story starting with falling out of the chopper and ending with marrying Mai."

Bobby sat there dumbfounded for a few minutes. Then he grinned. "She must be something special if she put a rope around you, Captain!" He laughed. "I would like to meet her sometime."

"That'd be great," Curtis replied. "Get yourself out of here and resituated and then come down to Benning for a visit. You'll like her and it would be great. Spend a few days and we'll burn some steaks and drink a few beers."

Bobby nodded. "Sounds great!"

"Well, I better shove off. Flying out to Knoxville to see the folks for a few days before heading down to Benning. Our flight leaves this afternoon." Curtis shook Bobby's hand firmly. "I mean it, man. Come for a visit when you can. You'll like Mai and we will have a great time."

"Yes, sir!" Bobby grinned as he saluted. "Now get out of here, sir. I have to get back to my rehab!" Curtis returned the salute, turned and left.

Later that afternoon, Curtis and Mai boarded their flight to Knoxville, Tennessee to visit his parents. From time to time he'd told Mai stories about growing up in Knoxville and his family activities and "adventures." They certainly sounded like fine people but she still worried about their reaction to her.

"They are going to absolutely love you!" he promised. "Especially since you probably saved my life. And besides … you are absolutely wonderful!"

Curtis had written to his parents before leaving Vietnam. In his letter, he explained the circumstances leading up to his sudden marriage and he was pretty sure his parents would understand. Unfortunately, as luck would have it, they'd beaten his letter to Knoxville.

Jacob and Marjorie Cordell were a bit surprised, to say the least. They knew that Curtis had been listed for a while as Missing in Action and were promptly notified when he'd made it back to his unit. The U.S. Army had been less forthcoming with any real details. But when they heard the full story of their son's impromptu insertion under fire, his subsequent rescue by Mai's adopted brother Dish, and then his full recovery under Mai's care, they were delighted and warmly welcomed her into the family. Mai was a little shy at first, but in no time at all everyone was having a wonderful time just being in each other's company.

Marjorie and Mai went into the kitchen to prepare dinner. This was Mai's first exposure to a typical East Tennessee meal and she enjoyed helping with the preparation. Dinner consisted of Marjorie's famous meatloaf, mashed potatoes and gravy, fried okra, buttered corn, and sweet tea. They were even treated to some homemade sourdough bread. Marjorie had also recently baked a pecan pie, a favorite of Curtis', but that would have to wait since everyone was still very full of that wonderful meal! While Marjorie and Mai cleaned up the kitchen, Curtis and Jacob retired to the living room to talk. By the time the pecan pie was served, the entire Cordell family was a very relaxed and happy one.

"Mai seems like a very wonderful girl. Beautiful too," Curtis' Dad commented. "Your mother and I both love her and we are very grateful for her role in getting you home safe." Jacob paused. "You know, it could be kind of hard on her … new life, new country, new language and all that."

Curtis nodded. "I know that Dad, but she is tough and smart. She had my back in Vietnam and I'll have hers here. We'll be fine."

"Will you have to go back to Vietnam?"

"Possibly. Probably. I have a little more than two years left in my commitment to the army. So, it is likely. You know I was planning on making the military my career but now I think when my time is through, I'll get out. This war is different. Things are changing. I know we are doing the right thing over there, but people here seem so different." He told his father about what some of the returning soldiers had been subjected to at the airport.

"There is no call for that," his father replied. "They're just doing their job … what their country sent them to do. It's those damned hippies …! I think they're a bunch of communist sympathizers."

"Maybe," Curtis answered, then changed the subject. "How about a beer Dad? Got any? I'll go grab a couple."

"Sure, Son. Sounds good. Should be some PBRs or Buds in the refrigerator in the basement."

Curtis got up and left the room in search of the beer. After a few minutes, he was back in the living room with two cold PBRs. They quietly talked about the weather, the local economy, and local politics. It was so pleasant just catching up.

Curtis' Dad was a retired Naval officer based on the USS Boxer during the Korean War from which he'd flown F4U Corsairs. After the war, he went to work for Boeing at a plant in Oak Ridge, Tennessee where he met Marjorie, a floor manager at the local Millers Department Store. They dated for several months before Jacob worked up the nerve to propose. They married and about a year later Curtis, their only son was born.

Marjorie and Mai, carrying glasses of wine, joined the men in the living room and the rest of the evening was spent in pleasant conversation. Mai felt like she was home.

On July 1, Captain Curtis Cordell took command of Bravo Company, 1/19 Infantry Battalion located at Sand Hill on Ft Benning, near Columbus, Georgia. Curtis and Mai were assigned a nice two-bedroom house in the East Main Village on the post. Marjorie had made the trip down in Curtis' old Camaro. She'd be able to help Mai get settled and they'd have a car. And, when Mai caught a glimpse of Curtis' old Camaro … she was instantly interested in learning to drive.

While Curtis busied himself with the important work of assuming his new command, Marjorie and Mai set up housekeeping. Between the two of them there were very few possessions, so much was needed to make their housing a home. Curtis had never been the sort of guy who threw money around and of course, there hadn't been much to spend money on deep in the jungles of Vietnam, so Mai and Marjorie had some "working capital."

Marjorie's assistance would prove invaluable. She'd been married to a fighter pilot after all and knew how to prioritize what was needed. They found good quality used furniture including a bed, chests of drawers, a dining room table and chairs, a couch, and a recliner for Jacob when he visited. The Camaro's trunk had been packed with dishes, pots and pans and other household items. The back seat contained clothing that might still fit Curtis, his collection of books, and an old Remington bolt-action .22 ... his first rifle.

Marjorie also found time to take her new daughter-in-law shopping. She introduced Mai to the wide world of options available to her ... the many restaurants, grocery stores, pharmacies, and department stores. The easy availability and convenience of anything and everything in America amazed Mai.

Marjorie stayed for about two weeks, the time it took to have all the basics of housekeeping in place. The finishing touches would be in Mai's hands, and she'd do just fine.

"I have to get back and make sure your Dad is eating right," she joked with a smile. They drove Marjorie to the airport on a beautiful Saturday morning. They stopped at the gate. Marjorie gave Mai a big hug and a kiss on the cheek. She smiled and whispered into Mai's ear, "My son is in wonderful hands. I couldn't be happier for both of you." Mai took Marjorie's hands in hers and pressed them to her heart, saying softly and with such sincerity, "Thank you for everything." There were tears in Marjorie' eyes when she turned to her son. "Curtis, you have a real jewel of a woman for a wife. Take good care of her."

"I know that, Mom. I certainly will." He hugged his mother and then Marjorie was off through the gate with a smile and a wave.

The two of them enjoyed learning about married life together. Curtis took Mai out on the post's remote roads and taught her to drive. The 65 Camaro had a 383 Stroker engine with a manual four-speed transmission. Once Mai got the hang of the clutch and four-speed there was no holding her back. She loved driving that car. She was hard at work studying to get her driver's license. Curtis enjoyed the interesting combinations of Vietnamese food with experiments in American cooking and he also enjoyed, much to Mai's feigned chagrin, helping her with the dishes.

One Sunday afternoon a few weeks later, Mai watched Curtis through the kitchen window as he moved about trying to remember the Nguyen-ryu forms he had learned from Dish while recovering in the Montagnard village. He was having trouble. She went out.

"Curtis, would you like some help?" Mai asked.

"That would be great if you can," Curtis replied.

"I am my father's daughter," Mai replied with a smile. Mai demonstrated the series of movements Curtis was having trouble with, and her mastery of the technique was obvious.

"Can you show me how they work," Curtis inquired wondering if she could make them work on him.

Mai laughed. "Of course, I can."

Giving her husband a mischievous smile, she beckoned him to advance on her. Curtis did and immediately found himself flat on his back. He felt like he had just struck his funny bone, but the funny bone extended through his entire body.

"Wow," was about all he could muster for a few seconds.

Mai sat down next to him. "Before my father was killed by the VC, I worked on Nguyen-ryu every day since I was maybe eight years old," she explained. "My brother Dish is very good." Mai smiled. "But I am better."

Curtis sat up and looked at Mai. His wife never ceased to amaze him.

"If you like, Curtis, I can teach you."

Curtis shook his head and laughed.

"I like," he said and reached over to hug Mai with his, at least for the moment, one good arm. Mai leaned in and gave Curtis a kiss on his cheek.

"When you can move, come into the kitchen. I have something to show you," she teased.

"Just be a minute, love," Curtis replied with a grin.

A few minutes later Curtis joined Mai at the kitchen table. She had placed a shoe box on the table.

"What's up, baby," Curtis asked as he sat down. Mai looked serious.

Mai began, "I have several things to tell you, Curtis. First, I want to say to you that you are a wonderful man and a good husband to me, and I love you very much. I could not be any happier. But I want to contribute to our family. Since I was a young girl in Vietnam, I dreamed of being a doctor. It was not possible until now, here in America with you. I have talked to people on the post and I have a plan to get my American high school degree here at the base. Then I will work on becoming a doctor … or maybe a nurse if that is not possible."

Curtis whistled a long slow whistle. "Mai, I will support you in whatever you want to do. But that will be a long hard pull and it will cost money." He thought for a few seconds. "We could probably get loans or something if needed."

Mai opened the shoe box on the table and took out a brown leather pouch. It was the one Curtis had seen Dish give to Mai before they left the Montagnard village in Vietnam.

"This was my father's. My brother retrieved it from the

village after my family was murdered by the VC. Dish kept it for me and gave it to me when we left the village to go to your army post. I asked him to take some but he would not. He said I would need it in America. You are my husband. It is now yours. It will help." Mai handed the pouch to Curtis. He looked at Mai a few seconds before opening it to see what it contained. What he saw in there made him blink in surprise. Curtis reached in and pulled out several gold coins. He spread them out on the table. There were more in the pouch. When he was done he'd removed twenty-five such coins from that old leather pouch.

"What are these?" he asked quietly. The coins had four Chinese characters surrounding a radiant sun on one side and a dragon on the reverse side.

"They are gold coins from the time of Thieu Tri. He was the third emperor of the Vietnamese Nguyen Dynasty. He died in 1847," Mai explained. "My great-grandfather was a retainer at the court of Thieu Tri. This is all that is left from that time. It would have gone to my oldest brother if the VC had not killed my family."

"I wonder what they are worth?" Curtis spoke quietly.

"Your mother helped me to have them valued. One day when you were at work we drove to Atlanta to visit a man your father knew. To the right buyer, they are worth about $10,000 each."

Curtis whistled again. He was looking at $250,000. Quietly he put them back into the leather pouch and tied it closed. He looked at Mai.

"Honey," he began, "these are yours. I am honored that you want me to have them, but they are yours. They are your inheritance from your father. How they will be used is not my decision, but if you want to use some of them to go to school, then that's what you should do. I think your father would like that. But, we should find a safer place to keep them than in a shoe box, probably a safe deposit box." He handed the pouch back to Mai who placed it back in the shoe box.

"You will help me with that, Curtis?"

"Of course, I will." Curtis paused, then laughed. "Mom never said a word to me."

Mai smiled. "I asked her not to. I wanted to tell you when it was the right time for us."

Curtis leaned back in his chair. "Well, is there anything else we need to discuss right now." He smiled. "I thought we might go into Columbus tonight for pizza and a movie if you like."

"I'd love that," Mai replied. "But, there is one more thing I need to tell you, Curtis."

"What's that?" he asked.

"I'm pregnant."

Curtis took a second to process that information.

"You're pregnant?"

Mai nodded. "We are going to have a baby."

Curtis got up from his chair grinning and took Mai into his arms, hugging her close.

"Have I told you today that I love you?" he asked quietly.

Mai smiled. "Yes, I think it was just about three hours ago."

CHAPTER 8

JD was born on March 1, 1969, at the Martin Army Community Hospital on Ft. Benning. A 7.8-pound bouncing baby boy with a head full of jet black hair. Mai announced that his name would be Jacob Dish Cordell.

"Jacob for your grandfather and Dish for my brother."

There was a little sadness in her voice. Since leaving Vietnam, they'd had no word of Dish and no way of knowing what had become of him.

Curtis nodded. "Okay then. It's a done deal and it's a good name. I guess we can call him JD for short."

Several of Curtis' company training officers and NCOs stopped by the nursery to congratulate their captain and his wife on the new addition. His First Sergeant, Nathan Dorch, even dropped by with a box of cigars.

"Just in case you forgot to bring some to hand out, Sir." Curtis had indeed forgotten that minor detail, but from that point on everyone who stopped by got a cigar if the supply held out.

JD grew to be a handsome, athletic young man. Once

he entered the seventh grade, he began participating in wrestling and basketball. He had quite a knack for wrestling. Being strong for his size as well as quick and agile, he soon began winning most of his matches, even against much bigger opponents. And, while shorter than most of the other members of the basketball teams he played with, he was a very good ball handler. By his second season, JD was starting most games at the guard position and had developed a deadly accurate jump shot. Mai became quite a serious basketball fan and soon knew the rules of the game better than the referees. She often let the referees know that in no uncertain terms.

Even before he started high school as a freshman, JD was well liked. He had already earned the reputation among his friends as being a friendly, laid back kind of guy, but one that you really did not want to mess with. Not that he was mean or a troublemaker. Far from it. JD was a nice kid. It was just that, as one of his better friends noted in their junior year, "JD just did not have a lot of patience with assholes."

You also did not want to mess with his little sister, Annie.

While Curtis and Mai came from extremely different worlds, they both were raised in an environment where hard work, responsibility, loyalty, and honor were valued ideals. Both knew they wanted those same values instilled in their children. Values like earning what you get through hard work and an appreciation of those who came before, making it possible for their family to have the life they have today. Curtis and Mai both wanted their children to grow up to love the country that had provided them with so much opportunity. They made a conscious decision to participate in activities designed to bring success and fulfillment to both their marriage and their children's lives.

Curtis was a cradle Episcopalian and wanted to share this important part of his life with his wife and children. Mai very soon came to love the traditions, the beauty, and mystery of the Episcopalian Church.

It was through the church that JD would make his first very good friend, William Peterson. They would soon become inseparable. When they reached the age of eleven years, they joined the Boy Scouts together. Troop 88 was a great scout troop with dedicated leaders who understood that the real purpose of scouting was to teach young boys how to become good men. Troop 88 was an active troop, always camping, pioneering, knot tying, learning survival skills, and about edible or medicinal herbs. There were countless outdoor adventures made even better because of Curtis' enthusiastic participation. All the troop members thought it was very cool to have a genuine army veteran around on their many adventures.

JD didn't mind Sunday school too much either. Their Senior Youth Sunday school teacher was Joe Trenton. Joe, a retired police detective, was an interesting man with a great sense of humor and a twinkle in his eye. Joe had started out with the Knox County Sheriff's Office, had transferred to the Knoxville City Police Department and worked his way up to detective. He had seen it all but somehow had still managed to keep a sense of balance in his life. Both William and JD enjoyed his Sunday school class. While his classes always began with the prescribed lesson, Joe always found a way to use his past experiences with the police force to make the lesson relevant to the modern world, at an age-appropriate level, of course. For today's class, the topic was the Garden of Eden.

When they got to the part about Eve and the serpent, one of the girls, a pretty redhead William had a big crush on, commented on how much she hated snakes.

"They're so slimy," she said with a shudder.

"They aren't," argued William. "They are actually quite dry." William had a pet garden snake he kept in a large class aquarium in his room. While JD did not especially like snakes, he had no dislike for them either. He certainly had no need to keep one as a pet!

"Snakes are God's creatures too," Joe Trenton had laughed. "I guess maybe just like people, there are good and bad snakes in the world." Joe paused and then went on. "We all have seen black snakes in our yards at one time or another. They eat a lot of pests including poisonous snakes." Joe chuckled. "Snakes do get somewhat of a bad rap in the Bible, don't they?"

Lucas Taylor, a tall thin quiet boy spoke up, "But in the Garden of Eden, that wasn't a real snake. That was really the Devil disguising himself as a snake!'."

Joe chuckled. "Lucas, you raise a good point."

"JD, what about you?" Joe Trenton asked. "Anything to add to our discussion?"

JD thought for a Moment and shrugging his shoulders said. "I have nothing against snakes but I want to know where they are when they're around. As long as they leave me alone I will leave them alone."

"Now that's a pretty good philosophy I'd say," Joe Trenton observed.

Back when he was in sixth grade JD had asked his father about karate lessons. His father, Curtis Cordell, had tried to teach both his son and daughter the Vietnamese martial art of Nguyen-ryu. It required a lot of stance training and seemingly endless drills of basic techniques. While very practical and effective it included little in the way of jumping, spinning, somersaulting, or board breaking. Not cool! Annie quickly lost interest. Even JD eventually lost interest.

Several years later, JD and his good friend, William Peterson, returned from checking out the new Premier Martial Arts Center that had just opened near West Town Mall. Grandmaster Barry Sykes really impressed the two boys with his amazing abilities, leaping high into the air to smash a board held by one of the assistant instructors. Grandmaster Sykes went on to demonstrate some awesome self-defense techniques. JD was excited. He was dying to learn the things he'd just seen. Understanding how his son felt and pleased that he was interested in martial arts again, even if it wasn't Nguyen-ryu, it was agreed that they would find him a good martial arts school.

To say that fifteen-year-old JD Cordell was disappointed would be an understatement. The place he stood now, a few days later, was not impressive. They'd entered through a door with a little sign on it that read Isshin-ryu Karate-Do and were now standing in the main room of an old dance studio someone converted into a karate dojo. It was sparsely furnished ... a few leather padded punching posts along one wall, some weapons hanging on a rack in a corner, and a small section of mirrored wall at the front. The dojo had a hardwood floor polished to a gleaming shine by many years of bare feet. Pictures of revered Okinawan instructors hung on the wall over a small table-like shrine. JD's father was talking to the instructor, an Okinawan gentleman in his late fifties or early-sixties, dressed in a simple white gi with a faded black belt tied around his waist.

He doesn't even have a master's sash, JD thought to himself.

After a few minutes, Curtis called his son over.

"JD, this is Tokumura Sensei. Sensei, this is my son, JD."

"Good day young man." Tokumura Sensei bowed politely.

Shocked, JD returned the bow and managed to get out a polite, "Hello, Sir."

Cordell, bowing to Tokumura Sensei excused himself and his son as he pulled him to the side. He spoke quietly to his son for a few minutes and JD seemed uncomfortable with the conversation.

"Sensei, with your permission I am going to leave you two to get acquainted." JD's father smiled. "When should I return?"

"Give us a couple of hours," replied Tokumura Sensei nodding to JD's father. Curtis left the dojo.

Tokumura stood quietly for a few minutes. He seemed to be trying to decide about the young man standing in front of him.

"Well JD, your father says you have had some martial arts training with him."

JD shrugged. "He showed me a little I guess but I wanted to learn real karate."

Tokumura smiled.

"Real karate you say? What is real karate?" Tokumura inquired with an inscrutable look on his face.

"I went by Premier Martial Arts at the mall a few days ago," JD replied. "That Grandmaster Barry Sykes is pretty awesome. He is a real Grandmaster! I saw him do some amazing stuff. He taught me a couple of moves."

"Really?" Tokumura replied with a slight twinkle in his eye. "I would very much like to see them. Do you think you can demonstrate some of them for me?"

"I don't understand it!" None of the techniques were working for him. They seemed to have no effect on Tokumura Sensei at all. Every kick or punch he tried to throw was instantly and effortlessly shut down. When he tried some of the joint locks, Tokumura Sensei just stood there and smiled at him.

JD blurted out, "Well these techniques worked when I used them on the instructor over at Premier Martial Arts!" He felt embarrassed and angry.

"Even the poorest technique can work with a cooperative attacker," Tokumura said, keenly aware of the young man's sensitivity. "Unfortunately, most real-world situations do not involve cooperative attackers. True karate is simply a matter of properly understanding body mechanics, applying the correct technique, and having the proper focus. The attacker never really enters the equation. He simply experiences the results of his foolishness."

JD looked at Tokumura Sensei. "I am not sure what you mean."

Tokumura replied, "Would you like me to demonstrate?"

"Sure," JD replied a bit hesitantly not sure what to expect.

Tokumura signaled that JD should come at him. JD attacked and the Sensei's techniques shut him down quickly and completely. Tokumura seemed to use no strength or force, and at times barely moved at all. But his techniques always hurt. JD had to admit that much of it was very like what his father had tried to teach him.

They took a break. JD felt like he had just finished a summer double session work out for football except that he hurt more. Tokumura Sensei, on the other hand, showed no evidence of their just finished activities.

JD stood there, looking down at the floor. He did not quite understand everything that just happened. He did know that he was completely amazed by what he'd experienced. Grandmaster Barry Sykes' flash and theatrics were completely gone from JD's mind. They'd been obliterated by something that, until that minute, JD would not have thought possible.

Tokumura Sensei asked, "What do you think now?"

"I have never seen anything like that," JD replied.

"Sensei," JD added as an afterthought.

Tokumura smiled. "Would you like to learn this art?" Tokumura asked.

"Yes Sensei, I would like that very much!"

Tokumura stood up and motioned JD to stand. "Then we shall make an agreement you and I," Tokumura smiled. "I promise to teach you karate. You promise to do what I say. What do you say to that, JD?"

JD did not hesitate. He bowed to Tokumura Sensei, "Yes, Sensei!"

Satisfied, Tokumura returned the bow and went on.

"JD, to build real skill in any physical endeavor you have to start with a firm foundation. We must start at the beginning. First, you need to learn to walk. Are you ready to do that?"

Again, there was no hesitation in JD's reply. "Yes, Sensei!"

When Curtis Cordell returned to the dojo two hours later he was astounded to see JD practicing crescent steps as he moved up and down the entire length of the dojo floor. These gliding steps were already showing fluidity and power.

Tokumura saw Curtis and nodded.

"Good job, JD. That's enough practice for today."

JD stopped and walked to where Tokumura Sensei and

his Dad were waiting. He was dripping sweat but had a very satisfied look on his face.

"Good first day?" Cordell asked his son. JD grinned and nodded

Turning to Tokumura he said, "Thank you Sensei. Can I come back and practice tomorrow?"

Tokumura nodded.

"The dojo will be open."

When JD and William reached the rank of Life Scout, their respective parents sent them to the Philmont Scout Reservation in New Mexico. It was the adventure of a lifetime for boys their age, a two-week trek into the Rocky Mountains of New Mexico. They saw herds of elk, they panned for gold, they drank ice cold root beer in a lumberjack bar after sawing logs and climbing poles! But, ... and it was a big one ... they hadn't seen a single grizzly bear. Of course, it would have been exciting to see a grizzly ... but maybe that was not such a bad thing.

It was William and JD's turn to prepare the bear bag. Everyone in their group gathered any belongings with a smell; soap, toothpaste, food items ... anything with a scent that a grizzly bear might consider food. All these potential food items went into a waterproof heavy-duty nylon bag which was tightly tied shut. While JD picked up the bag, William hoisted a heavy coil of strong rope over his shoulder. Under the watchful eyes of one of the adult leaders, they headed into the woods. About fifty yards from the camp, the boys chose two stout-looking trees. William uncoiled the rope and JD secured the heavy-duty nylon bag to its center with nylon cord.

"Okay," JD stated as he checked his knots.

"I've got two good rocks," William replied. The boys

each took a rock and secured it to an end of the rope. Each boy took his rock with its trailing rope and taking aim at an appropriate limb, threw it up and over the limb, the rocks carrying the rope up behind them. Collecting the rope ends and removing the rocks, the boys pulled on the ropes hoisting the bag about fifteen feet into the air and then, securing the ropes to their respective tree trunks, stepped back to admire their handy work.

"Looks good,' William commented.

"That'll work," JD agreed.

"Yep! Good job boys," the Scout Leader stated.

William grinned. "Like to see a danged old grizzly bear get our stuff now.!"

"Fat chance," JD laughed.

A few days later, JD had to try riding one of the donkeys they used for one section of their backpacking adventure, despite, of course, being warned not to.

"These are pack animals. They do not like being ridden. They will throw you off or knock you off using a tree. They will kick you and they will bite. I repeat, do not try to ride these donkeys!" the donkey wrangler warned before they started out on this section of the trek.

William was the one who placed a splint on JD's broken arm and went for help. Fortunately, the trek was ending the next day, so JD didn't miss too much. Of course, Curtis and Mai flew out to check on their son. William got praise and thanks, while JD got a stern admonishment to be more careful in the future.

A year later, both boys earned their Eagle Scout awards and later completed the God and Country Award program as well.

Back at home also meant back at the dojo for JD. The

weeks quickly turned into months and the months became years. He had learned so much. He'd spent countless hours working the basic techniques of Isshin-ryu Karate. He studied the kata, a physical repertoire of the techniques of Isshin-ryu in their simplest form. And, he explored their bunkai, the many possible applications of the techniques from the kata. JD also became intimately familiar with the makiwara … the punching post of Isshin-ryu Karate. And, while it was difficult to decipher, he studied the Kenpo Gokui, the eight maxims essential for a thorough understanding of the philosophy upon which the art of karate is based.

JD practiced three days each week after school. Mai would usually pick him up after training, then home for supper and homework. JD found time for other activities such as scouting and the occasional date. But his primary passion was his martial arts. William Peterson took an interest in karate and they trained together for a while. However, he was not as dedicated as JD and when a cute redhead in chemistry class caught his eye, he suddenly lost interest.

Annie had no interest in Nguyen-ryu or Isshin-ryu whatsoever. Her interests and talents lay in music and she had grown to become quite a violin player while in middle school. She also loved movies. She and her friends Tasha and Gina were standing outside the Downtown West Theater waiting for JD. Mai had dropped the three girls off for an early showing of The Breakfast Club. JD, because their mother was working that evening at UT Medical Center, had agreed to pick them up. A group of four older teenage boys, who seemed to be aimlessly wandering around the parking lot, spotted the three girls and approached.

"Hey sweet thing," one of them called at Gina.

"What're you chicks doing? Wanna have some fun." The tone of voice was anything but friendly.

"No thanks," Annie answered for the three of them. "We're not your type." Annie always did have a little bit of a smart mouth.

"You're not? What type are you?" One of the boy's snickered at that.

"Smart," Annie replied.

"What the fuck do you mean by that, bitch," one of the boys snarled.

"She means she is too smart for you," came a male voice from behind the four teenage thugs. It was JD.

"And just who the fuck are you?"

"The smart one's older brother."

"You better get the fuck out of here before we kick your ass."

JD just looked at him. "Well, you are welcome to try. But it would not be your smartest move of the night." The four teens looked at each other. The smart-ass girl's older brother did not look very scared. In fact, he didn't even look nervous. He was just standing there waiting and ready. Finally, one of the boys said, "Fuck him. They're too young anyway. Let's get the fuck out of here."

Three of them turned to go. The fourth stood looking at JD. "Who the fuck do you think you are?" He seemed to be working up the courage for a fight.

JD smiled. "Just someone here to pick these three girls up and take them home before they get into real trouble, and maybe keep you from making a stupid mistake if it's necessary."

The fourth teen shook his head, seeming to make up his mind. "Whoever the fuck you are, you got balls!" He turned toward his three friends. "Let's get out of here." JD watched them walk off toward the shopping center and

Kingston Pike.

"Alright ladies, let's go," JD said after the four had gone. Tasha and Gina were speechless, not knowing what to say. Both had mixed looks of fear, relief, and admiration on their faces. Only Annie seemed totally untouched by the whole situation.

"Let's go," she repeated brightly and started toward the Ford Explorer. Once in the car the girls were back to their jabbering happy teenage selves, comparing the relative merits of Emilio Estevez and Judd Nelson, and whether Molly Ringwald should choose one or the other of the two young men as a boyfriend. JD drove, listening with an amused disinterest to the conversation.

JD completed his senior year of high school. Curtis and Mai decided to throw a graduation party for their son and invite some friends. After much discussion and some compromise, they settled on a celebration dinner at The Chop House. By 7:00 pm, JD was back at the dojo practicing kata.

JD's eighteenth birthday was just around the corner and he'd been training for almost four years. He ran through the eight empty hand kata practicing them slowly to work on balance and form. The second time through he worked them for speed and power, and finally performed them all focusing on proper breathing. He performed each kata in turn … Seisan, Seiuchin, Naihanchi, Wansu, Chinto, Kusanku, Sunsu, and finally, Sanchin. JD finished his last exhalations in Sanchin, bowed out, and went over to the makiwara to finish his workout.

Tokumura Sensei, working technique with a few black belts in the center of the dojo floor, called to him.

"JD, please come over here," JD approached the group,

stopping a few feet away to bow.

"Yes, Sensei?"

Tokumura selected four black belts at random from the group and directed them to form a rough circle around JD. "Now we shall see how well you have come to understand the Kenpo Gokui and the kata of our system." Tokumura backed away and signaled the test to begin.

JD began to control his breathing. The attacks that would come while not intended to injure, would certainly hurt if they landed. JD relaxed, his arms hung loosely at his sides, his weight rested gently on the balls of both feet. He softened his gaze and waited.

The first attack came from his left side. JD pivoted on the ball of his left foot. His left arm rose smoothly up through his center-line deflecting the powerfully thrown left-hand straight punch to the outside as he smoothly transitioned into a Naihanchi stance close to his attacker's left side. Instantly his left leg slid straight back to form a hook stance, allowing him to pivot sharply on the balls of both feet and drive his left elbow into his attacker's kidney area with enough force to cause pain and drop him but not actually cause injury. JD settled back into a ready stance and quietly waited as the remaining black belts continued to circle him ... perhaps a bit more respectfully now.

The second and third attacks came almost simultaneously from the rear and from the right. JD angled away to the left by pivoting again on the ball of his left foot effectively controlling the distance between himself and both attackers. Completing the pivot, he landed in an angled Seisan stance with both attackers now within his field of vision. The rear attacker was almost on him. JD shifted his right leg, dropping into a Seiuchin stance while his left forearm deflected the attacker's reaching arm upward. JD drove the two knuckles of his right fist down into the center of the attacker's left thigh dropping him to the floor. The third black belt made his way around his fallen comrade and launched a powerful front kick toward JD's groin. JD angled back and right, again dropping into Seiuchin stance while deflecting the kick with his inner left forearm. The deflection took the attacker's balance and JD immediately seized the advantage. Shifting forward into a Seisan stance, he struck the black belt solidly in the chest with the heel of his palm, setting the black belt down on his butt … a stunned look on his face. JD settled back into a ready stance and waited for the fourth attacker.

The fourth black belt approached slowly assuming an aggressive stance while gazing fiercely at JD hoping to intimidate him. JD stood relaxed and ready, his breathing slow and steady. The black belt abruptly shifted into another stance but still drew no reaction but calm confidence from JD. Seconds passed, stretching into minutes. Suddenly the black belt straightened up and respectfully bowed to JD. Surprised, but trying to not let it show on his face, JD returned the bow. The black belt backed away, then turned and walked over to Tokumura Sensei. The other black belts, one with a slight limp, approached JD and they all exchanged bows. Leaving JD alone in the center of the floor, the three joined their comrade.

"Very good," Tokumura stated as he approached and handed the coveted black belt to JD. "You have trained hard and learned much. Understand, JD. This is just the beginning of your journey. This black belt signifies that you are now ready to begin learning the deeper teachings found in Okinawan Karate-do."

Shocked, JD bowed to his Sensei. "Yes, Sensei. Thank you, Sensei," he managed to get out.

Tokumura returned JD's bow and headed off toward

his office.

JD left the dojo and spotted his mother down the street in the Ford Explorer. She was waiting to give him a ride home after training.

"Hi, Mom." JD climbed into the passenger seat. Mai could tell her son was excited."

"What's up, Jake?" Only his mother called him Jake. JD's full name was Jacob Dish Cordell. He'd been named after his grandfather and his mother's Montagnard brother. JD knew the story of his father and Dish, and his mother's life in Vietnam. He was not ashamed of his middle name but it certainly raised a lot of questions whenever it came up, so he simply went by JD to avoid a lot of questions.

"Sensei gave me my black belt today."

Mai was proud of her son's accomplishments in martial arts. Curtis taught JD some Nguyen-ryu and even his mother threw in a lesson or two. JD was not too keen on that at first, but since meeting Tokumura Sensei and knowing the respect his Sensei had for his father's abilities, his view changed. JD was shocked when his father had told him that his mother was a much better martial artist than he was. Eventually, the shock wore off and JD blended a lot of the Nguyen-ryu into his Isshin-ryu. There were a lot of similarities. After all, body mechanics were body mechanics; regardless of system or style.

'I don't believe your Sensei gave it to you, Jake. I'd say you earned it." Mai smiled at her son. They rode along in silence for a few minutes. JD was obviously deep in thought.

"Mom, can we talk about something."

"Sure."

"Well, I know you and Dad have been talking about

which college I will be attending and all that." He had been accepted at all three institutions he had applied to ... The University of Tennessee, Carnegie-Mellon, and Georgia Tech.

"Yes," Mai replied waiting.

"Well, I don't want to go to college ... at least not yet. I have been thinking about this for some time now. I really want to enlist in the Navy. There will be plenty of time for college while I am in the Navy or after I get out."

Mai was not surprised. In fact, she had been waiting for this.

"I think, JD, that you need to talk to your Dad about this. But whatever you finally decide to do, I know you will do it well."

JD smiled. "Thanks, Mom."

"No problem. I was wondering how long it would take you to bring it up," Mai smiled. "You are your father's son." Mai paused smiling and then reached over and put her hand on his forearm. "But there is a lot of me in you as well."

"What are you going to do in the Navy," Mai asked.

JD did not hesitate. "I want to be a Navy SEAL."

CHAPTER 9

Dawn broke over the northwest Afghan frontier, the border region between Afghanistan and Pakistan. It is rugged terrain comprised of tall jagged mountains, cliffs, deep crevasses and broken shale. It was cold, the air crisp and clear. JD could see his breath. He adjusted the sling of the .300 WIN MAG on his right shoulder.

The head shed had received information placing Abdullah Al-Wahsari in their area of operations. Al-Wahsari was a high-value target ... a courier between the Taliban and many other radical Islamic groups. Intelligence placed him in a small village controlled by the Taliban to the north. Captured alive, Al-Wahsari could provide very valuable information for the war on terror. Golf Platoon, SEAL Team 5 would chopper to the landing zone twelve kilometers north of the village. The team would hump the rough terrain to a position on the ridge overlooking the village. Establishing Al-Wahsari's presence in the village, they would move in and grab him. Once the package was secured, they would proceed to the extraction point ten kilometers south. Simple!

It was still dark when the Blackhawk lifted into the air. The team was pumped. SEAL's are warriors, consummate professionals at taking out the bad guys. They live to do their job. It is the time between missions that is hard on them. The chopper flight would take approximately thirty minutes. A few team members filled the time loudly making bets on whether Al-Wahsari was even there or not. A few sat alone in their thoughts. The noise of the Blackhawk's twin General Electric T700 engines made conversation difficult.

JD leaned back against his rucksack. He'd been a member of a SEAL team almost for twenty years now. He thought back on the early months of brutal SEAL training, the many subsequent missions, the comradery, and friends he'd made. It had all been worth it. The training that started all this had been even tougher than JD had expected.

Like his mother, JD's father was not surprised when JD approached him about his decision to join the Navy. They were in the backyard digging a hole for his mother's newest acquisition, a Japanese purple plum tree.

His Dad had chuckled and said, "At least the food is better in the Navy." They went on digging for a few more minutes before his Dad took a break and got serious.

"Son, there has been a Cordell in darn near every war our Country has been in. Thomas Cordell marched with General Braddock and George Washington on Ft. Duquesne in the French and Indian War. Jacob Cordell fought in the Revolutionary War at the Battle of Oriskany. Another Cordell spent the winter at Valley Forge with George Washington and was still alive when the British surrendered at Yorktown. You have a great-grandfather who fought in the Spanish-American War. Both of my grandfathers fought in WW II. My Dad's father fought his way across Europe and my mother's father went island hopping in the Pacific." Curtis paused to wipe some sweat from his forehead.

"My Dad flew Corsairs in Korea and I fought in Vietnam. I guess I got out because I got sick of politicians deciding whether we could win a war or not. But, this country will still need good soldiers in the future. So, you see, JD, you are just carrying on the family tradition."

JD grinned. "That's quite a speech, Dad!"

Curtis laughed. 'Yep ... it was. Anyway, if that is what you want to do then that is what you should do."

"It is what I want to do, Dad."

"Then it's settled." Curtis slapped JD on the back and then gave him a warm hug. "Remember to keep your butt down and your socks dry, Son."

JD snapped back to the present when a voice crackled over their SEAL comm units.

"Five minutes out."

SEAL Team 5 prepared to un-ass the chopper when it touched down. JD heard Chief Whitley bark, "Somebody fucking wake up Axel." JD grinned. Axel could sleep through anything.

This border region remained a real hot spot despite the stories in the media. JD's team knew the Taliban and Al Qaeda moved weapons and supplies through these passes. It was common knowledge that Pakistan did nothing about it. To JD, this did not seem like the actions of an ally in the war on terror. It was also the considered opinion among the teams that President Hardeman's administration had its head so far up its own ass ... it could not tell a radical Islamic terrorist from a blond Swedish bikini model!

JD and his team moved out to cover the twelve kilometers to their first objective ... the ridge above the village. Sweeney took the point, the team falling in behind him. Each man kept several meters between himself and the next man. They traveled silently, eyes scanning the terrain for movement, ears listening for any sound that was out of place. It was starting to warm up. JD could feel a sweat beginning.

Three hours later, the team approached the head of the narrow valley, they split up and moved to two observation points. Situated above the village, they began the process of verifying Al-Wahsari was there. JD settled into a position with Chief Whitley, Sweeney, and Jackson at the high end of the valley. He unpacked his Nikon DCS 425 M, a black and white DSLR. It was damn near indestructible and was completely waterproof without any casing. The inner workings, designed by Eastman Kodak, sent images to the rear via satellite uplink. Nikon and Eastman Kodak both publicly denied the camera's existence, but it was an essential tool for surveillance under extreme conditions.

JD used the powerful telephoto lens to zoom in on the village. He began snapping photos of any inhabitants he spotted, taking care to get good facial shots whenever possible. Maddux, Axel, and Jonesy were on the ridge to the East side of the valley. They were also busy trying to identify the target.

The comm unit in JD's ear crackled.

"Target verified." It was Sweeney. He had gotten a good shot of a man walking with a group of four others toward one of the larger village structures. It was Al-Wahsari.

"Ready to make the world a safer place?" Maddux

quipped.

JD snorted in disgust. At a press conference, the Secretary of State had announced that al Qaeda was now "in full retreat."

Guess somebody forgot to tell the terrorists, JD thought to himself. The team settled into concealed positions and waited for dark. Jackson took first watch. Some of the team members napped. JD was too wound up to sleep. His brain kept returning to the chain of events that brought him to this remote mountaintop in Afghanistan.

The graduation ceremony for JD's SEAL class was quite impressive and stirring. JD's family had flown out to San Diego to attend. Even Annie was impressed. After the day's graduation celebrations were over, Curtis drove back to the hotel with Mai and Annie. They had an early morning flight to Knoxville to catch and the day's festivities, while enjoyable, were quite tiring. Annie was the center of attention for several young men during the celebration. She was bubbling over with excitement during the drive to the hotel. Curtis and Mai both hoped she would calm down enough to get some sleep.

Jimmy Stiles, JD, and two of the other new graduates caught a cab downtown. They were going to the Stumble Inn, a local beer joint for a little celebration SEAL style. While not looking for trouble, they were brand-new Navy SEALs. This meant that backing down from a fight was not going to be in their nature. After a few beers, the recounting of memorable moments in their training got a little loud. Their boisterous attitude was rubbing a few local boys the wrong way. It did not help that the ladies present began showing more interest in the young SEALs than in them.

One of these locals, Wayne Morrison, had been sucking down Budweiser like Kool-Aid. Morrison was an instigator. He liked starting trouble, so he could watch the fights that usually ensued. Wayne reached over and poked his buddy, Junior Willis, in the ribs.

"Hey Junior, you going to let those Navy boys steal our women folk?" he asked. Junior Willis was a mountain of a man. He stood about 6 ft. 7 inches tall and weighed in at a little under 300 lb., very little of which was fat. Junior was usually easy going, but tonight he'd consumed enough beer to override the good sense he so often prided himself on having.

"No fucking way," he replied. Junior paused the game of snooker he was playing with another local named Gordy Wallace. "Be back in a minute, Gordy."

Junior headed for the table where the four young men were enjoying themselves. They were laughing about how Jimmy fell asleep while they were waiting for the medic to check them out. Several of the local young ladies were now sitting at their table as well and seemed to be really enjoying the "war" story. JD was just finishing describing how they spent last Christmas morning sitting chest deep in the icy Pacific. They'd been singing Silent Night for their instructor's enjoyment. Just short of freezing to death, the instructors ordered them out of the water and lined them up on the grinder. A medic was present to check them for hypothermia, or shock, or whatever. Stiles, waiting his turn to see the medic, had simply collapsed, landing flat on his face. To the amusement of some, he started snoring. The medic, who was almost to him anyway, immediately checked him out and was able to rouse him. Unfortunately, his snoring had not gone unnoticed by the instructors. Jimmy was okay, but his little nap had cost their boat crew several hundred pushups. The young ladies, enjoying the tale, were laughing. They enjoyed the good-humored company of these four young men. The SEALs, who'd enjoyed little in the way of female company for some time, were enjoying the attention.

Junior approached the table where the group was laughing and having a great time. Because of his Asian looks and slighter build, JD probably stood out as the easier target. Junior homed in on him.

"Hey, shithead! What the fuck do you assholes think you're doing here? You Navy boys piss me off, coming in here and trying to steal our women."

JD smiled. "Hey man. Relax. We're having a good time talking and drinking a few beers. Your lady friends will still be here when we're gone." Jimmy and the other three SEALs pushed their chairs back a bit and turned to get a better look. This was promising to be interesting.

"Fuck that shit," Junior growled. "I'm going to kick your scrawny little chink ass on general principle!"

JD stood up, keeping the smile on his face.

"Don't hurt him, JD" one of the SEALs offered with a grin.

Another SEAL, a genuine cowboy from the great state of Montana, sized Junior up with an appraising eye. The cowboy whose name was Kyle, let out a low whistle.

"Careful, JD, this guy is pretty damn big!"

JD moved away from the table, hands open, palm outward and in front to show he wanted no trouble.

"Listen, dude, take it easy. My scrawny little chink ass is going to drink a couple of more beers and then it is going back to the base. If you get in the way of that you will be in for a world of hurt. How about I buy you a beer and we call it even?"

Junior Willis seemed to weigh this idea in his head for a few seconds. His response came in the form of a lunging step forward as he swung his huge right fist at JD's head. JD slipped the punch. His right foot kicked out, the toe caught Junior midway up his inner right thigh near the femoral artery. The kick did not stop there but continued through, JD's heel smashing into the same spot on the other thigh. JD used enough force to make his point but do no real damage. Junior let out a surprised grunt. He teetered there for a long second, his two legs splayed out at awkward angles, off balance and unable to move. JD reached up and placing his palm against Junior's sternum, set him back down on the floor.

Junior's snooker partner, Gordy, had moved closer to get a better view of the fight. He still held the pool cue in his hands. He wanted to see Junior rip this little Navy puke's head off. Seeing his big friend taken down so easily shocked and angered him. Gordy let out a yell as he swung his pool stick over and down at JD's head. JD, seeing this coming, stepped inside the swing. Both hands met the pool stick inside its arc, trapping Gordy's hands on the cue in vise-like grips. JD circled the cue around and down, giving it a sharp powerful twist. Gordy felt his wrists turned back against themselves. Stepping back with his left foot, JD gave a focused tug that left him in sole possession of the pool stick. Reversing the tug, JD gave the pool cue's former owner a solid poke in the chest with the butt end of the stick. The poke rocked Gordy back on his heels. JD then shifted his grip on the pool stick and presented it to its former owner.

"Would you like to try again?"

Gordy stood there a moment, a look of sheer disbelief on his face.

"Hell no," came the reply as the stunned man took another step back raising his hands to show he quit. The bar was silent. JD set the pool stick down on a table and walked over to where Junior was still sitting on the floor. Junior was shaking his head in amazement. Reaching down, JD held out his hand.

"Buy you a beer now?" JD asked smiling. Junior Willis looked up at JD for a few minutes, a look of incomprehension on his face. Suddenly, he grinned.

"Why the fuck not!" He took JD's offered hand and was helped up off the floor. "That was some pretty slick shit you just pulled."

JD laughed. "Yep. Pretty slick chink shit."

"Where did you learn that stuff?" Junior asked.

"My mother taught me!" JD replied slapping Junior on the back as they headed toward the bar.

When darkness fell, the team prepared to descend on the village from two directions. The night was dark and cool. Clouds covered the moon while a few stars showed through isolated pockets of the clear night sky. The night air felt refreshing to JD and his night vision equipment handled the darkness well. JD could see fine, although the device did bathe everything in an eerie greenish hue. The team would sweep in from the North and East and grab Al-Wahsari. Then, move off South toward their extraction point. JD would provide overwatch for the operation and then circle to the West. He'd rejoin the team South of the village.

JD moved with caution below the ridgeline so not to silhouette himself against the night sky. Each footstep could dislodge a stream of small rocks or cause the shale to slide and betray his presence. His team had tangled with these Afghan tribesmen on several occasions now. They were not pushovers. Though they might lack the expertise of the SEALs, they'd been fighting in these hills for many years.

Using his L-3 night vision goggles, JD scanned the village below looking for any signs of activity. He carefully worked his way toward an outcropping of rock some distance below his previous position. It was a good position to shoot from, high enough to provide a good view and field of fire on the village. JD's assignment was to provide cover for the team during the mission and to cover the team's asses if things went to shit. He would shoot any Taliban fighters who came running if the team was compromised. JD continued working his way toward his chosen position.

Reaching the rock outcropping, JD settled into his position and unslung his M91A2 .300 WIN MAG. The .300 WIN MAG was his weapon of choice for this kind of work. There were certainly rifles that shot farther, but this versatile rifle could reach out 1000 plus yards and it had a flat trajectory past 100 yards. The rifle was fitted with an AN/PVS-26 long-range night sight so it was perfect for this kind of shooting. JD eased into a prone shooting position and pressed the switch to power up the sight. Using the sight, he scanned the village. All was still quiet.

Maddux, Axel, and Jonesy worked their way down the valley slope and made their way toward the structure Al-Wahsari had entered earlier. The three approached the building from the left side. Chief Whitley, Sweeney and Jackson approached from the north. All six men arrived at the structure at the same time. Chief Whitley and Jackson would remain positioned outside and help JD provide cover. There was only one door in the front, a window on the right side, and a couple of windows high on the rear of the structure. The windows were dark, and nothing stirred within. JD had the building and his fellow team members in view with his night sight and was alert for any sign of trouble. Satisfied that all was quiet, four SEALS positioned themselves at the door. It was an old wooden door consisting of planks and old rusty hinges. It would not take much to kick it down. The team was ready. Sweeney prepared to kick in the door. Almost as an afterthought, Axel reached over and tried the door latch, finding it unlocked. Either it was a trap or Al-Wahsari felt very safe deep in his own territory. Hoping it was the latter, Axel opened the door and the four SEALS entered.

Four Taliban fighters lay sleeping on mats on the floor with their AK-47's at their sides. One of them was Al-Wahsari. Five Taliban had entered the building. They noticed the fifth mat with nobody sleeping on it.

Where is the fifth man, Jonesy wondered? Just then, another Taliban fighter stepped into the room from an inner doorway. Shocked to see four U.S. Navy SEALS standing in the room, he let out an angry shout and charged Maddux. Maddux dropped him with two rounds from his silenced MP4. Unfortunately, the noise was still enough to wake the other four sleeping Taliban. Startled, they reached for their weapons, shouting in surprised anger. Jones, Axel, and Sweeney each took a fighter down with quick bursts of their weapons. The fourth Taliban fighter got one shot off before Maddux dropped him. Luckily, that shot flew wild and buried itself in one of the structure's wooden roof beams. The sound of the shot from the AK-47 brought two more Taliban fighters running toward the building. JD dropped them both, firing two shots from his .300 WIN MAG. Nothing fancy, he simply aimed center mass. They dropped and lay still. As quickly as it started … it was over. The night was quiet once more.

Maddux squatted down and checked the one identified

as Al-Wahsari.

"Damn," he muttered. They aren't going to like this. Al-Wahsari was dead.

"The package is dead," Maddux spoke into the SEAL comms link.

Whitley's voice came through the earpieces, "Get a quick search for anything worth grabbing and let's get the hell out of here. You got three minutes. JD ... keep your eyes open."

"Got it covered," came the response. JD, his shooting eye glued to the eyepiece of his night vision scope, swept the village for any other signs of activity.

The team executed a quick, professional search of the building and recovered several spiral bound notebooks, two IBM laptops, and a pre-paid cell phone. Captured intelligence secured, they moved out to the south, disappearing into the night. As they neared the top of the ridge, JD rejoined them. The team turned left keeping just below the ridgeline and headed south toward their extraction point, ten kilometers away. The chopper would soon be on the way.

"Damn. Too bad the package had to go and get himself killed," Axel commented through the SEAL comms link. "Hope there's some good shit on the stuff we grabbed."

"Hope so," Whitley replied. He did not like it when a mission did not go as planned. Sometimes shit happens that way.

"Well, at least there are six or seven less terrorist assholes in the world," Sweeny muttered. "That alone is worth something!"

"On the bright side, Chief," Axel joked, "we should be home for breakfast."

"Shit!" Jackson piped in. "All you ever think about is food."

Jonesy and JD chuckled at that observation. It helped relieve the tension. Axel was always hungry and they enjoyed reminding him of that every chance they got.

"Cut the chatter!" Chief Whitley ordered. "We are not out of here yet!"

The comms link went silent.

The V-22A Osprey set down on the deck of the Nimitz-class carrier, USS George Washington. The team had met the Blackhawk and its escorting Apache gunship in the desert as planned. Within minutes they were onboard and flying to Bagram Airbase. Once on the ground, SEAL Team 5 was shuttled immediately to the waiting V-22A. There had been a change of orders. Their new destination was a carrier somewhere in the Gulf of Aden. They would turn the collected intelligence over to a CIA contact who was already on the carrier. JD and his team would get a few hours rest before being briefed for a high-priority direct-action mission. Once that mission was completed, they would return to Bagram for a few days downtime.

Just another day in the life of a U.S. Navy frogman, JD reflected. Axel was really bummed over missing breakfast.

Filing off the Osprey, they headed toward the carrier's ready room for their debriefing. Axel took off on a quick detour through the galley to see if he could grab a snack. He was hungry. A voice yelled out.

"Hey JD! You damn swabby! How the hell are you?"

JD turned. *Who the hell was that?*

Then he spotted the man doing the yelling.

"Son-of-a-bitch! Will? Is that you?" William Peterson was JD's best friend in high school. They had shared a lot of the pains and successes of growing up together. "What the hell are you doing out here? I thought you went to school to be a damned accountant?"

William grinned. "I did and I am. I'm just a damned accountant who works for the CIA." JD gave Will a big bear hug and slapped him on the back.

"It's good to see you, man! What do you know ...? A bean-counting spy! What the hell are you doing way out here?"

"I got promoted. I now work for the CIA's military affairs department. Somebody has to keep you guys out of trouble," Peterson laughed! "I flew out to take Al-Wahsari off your hands. But, I understand from what I heard that part didn't go so well."

"No," JD replied. "The son-of-a-bitch had to go and get himself killed. We did manage to grab some notebooks, a couple of laptops and a cell phone. The mission wasn't a total loss."

"Shouldn't be with all that," William replied. "I'll get that stuff back to Langley and see what we can extract from it. Hey man, I have to hit the head. See you in the debriefing in a few minutes." William took off toward an open door in the carrier's island superstructure.

Sweeny came up to JD. "You know that guy?"

"Yeah! We went to high school together. We were best friends. How weird is that meeting him again way out here?"

"Yeah!" Sweeny replied. "Crazy man! We better get going." Heading to the ready room, they met Axel coming down the gangway with a huge turkey sandwich grasped in one hand.

"Axel, you're going to eat yourself to death," Sweeny joked making a half-hearted grab for the sandwich.

"Not today, Sweets!" Axel laughed as they turned into the ready room.

After the debriefing and the captured intelligence was

inventoried and secured, the team headed to the galley for some chow.

"Come on, Axel," Jonesy kidded. "Let's see if they have more turkey left … or did you eat it all."

"Fuck you, Jonesy!"

William was already in the galley. JD and William caught up on the last several years. JD learned that William married a beautiful. red-headed pediatrician and now had two little twin girls, Becky and Janet.

JD laughed. "You always had a thing for red-heads!"

William learned that JD stayed busy doing his SEAL thing. While he had enjoyed a couple of short-lived romances, for the moment, there was no one special lady in his life.

Maddux came in and sat down at the table.

"You guys hear the news. Some fucking genius college kid got in trouble with the FBI over some virus scam he created. Guess it was pretty big time and he was going to do some time in the pen ... so he got religion."

"What?"

"Yep! Seems he converted to Islam, then somehow ended up in Iran. The FBI knows where he is and still want him … but as long as he stays in Iran, they can't touch him. No extradition! It is all over the news!"

"Shit! He'll end up getting his head lopped off on some Al Jazeera video," Jonesy commented. "He would have been better off spending a few years in the federal pen."

"I'd like to set my cross-hairs on a few of those assholes cutting off heads on TV. That's a sick new twist these assholes have taken," JD growled. "Now that would make the world a safer place!"

"Amen, brother," Maddux responded.

JD turned to William. "When are you headed out?"

"Got a chopper to catch in about an hour. Ought to be

getting my shit together. Hey man! Next time you get stateside stop in for a visit. We're living in D.C. My wife would love to meet you. Grill a few burgers, maybe some steaks, and have a few beers."

JD laughed. "Sounds great man. I sure will." They stood and shook hands.

"It was great to see you again, JD!"

"Same here, Will. Take care. I will definitely look you up when I get some time stateside."

William turned and headed off to pack his gear for the upcoming chopper flight.

Chief Whitley came out of the Head Shed. He spotted Axel returning from the patch of sand the team used for their workout area. The "gym" consisted of a roman chair, a few weight lifting benches, and a chin-up bar. There was also a picnic table that served well for team briefings and general shit shooting. Axel was making his way toward his B-hut.

"Hey Axel," Whitley yelled.

"Yes, Chief," came the reply.

"Tell JD I want to see him at the head shed. ASAP!"

"Sure thing, Chief, I'll let him know."

Axel entered the B-hut and made his way down the hallway toward JD's cube. A B-hut usually houses eight single individuals. Made of plywood, they were typically divided into eight separate one-man rooms with a common walkway down the center. A typical B-hut usually has two entrances, one at each end. There were fluorescent lights and small ductless air conditioning units above each door. Each room has a window with a latch to aid in climate control and one electrical outlet. B-huts provided no protection from enemy fire, but they did offer a certain amount of privacy. That was a rare luxury for deployed SEAL teams.

Axel pounded on JD's door.

"Yeah?" came the response from behind the plywood door.

"Chief wants you up at the head shed," Axel replied.

"What for?" JD inquired.

"How the fuck should I know?" Axel pounded on the door one more time for good measure. "The Chief said ASAP, JD," he added before returning down the hallway toward his own room.

"Headed that way," JD returned.

JD entered the head shed and spotted Chief Whitley sitting at a desk over in the corner. He was pouring over a topographical map of the border region.

"You wanted me, Chief?"

"Yep ... have a seat," Chief Whitley replied. "Got some orders for you."

"Orders? For what?" asked JD as he took an empty folding metal chair near the desk. He spun the chair around and took a seat, resting his arms on the chair back.

"I'm sending you to Ft. Bragg. You should be there about six months."

"Ft. Bragg? What's at Ft. Bragg? My team is here."

Chief Whitley shrugged. "Seems the U.S. Navy has decided Team 5 is going to get a K-9 member."

"A what?" JD asked.

"That's a dog, in case you did not know," Whitley responded.

"What the hell are we going to do with a dog?" JD asked.

"How the fuck should I know?" Chief Whitley replied. "I guess that's for you to find out. I suppose the dog can sniff out Tallies, explosives, IED's, whatever."

"Why me, Chief?"

Whitley laughed. "Hell, JD, I need to send someone who has at least some chance of being smarter than the damn dog. Can't send any of those other shitheads!" Chief Whitley paused a minute before going on, "This should be a good thing and I want you to handle it. It's not some kind of shit detail. Enjoy the six months stateside. See your folks. Meet your dog and enjoy the training. Be fucking ready to put your new partner to good use when you get back!"

What else could JD say? "Okay, Chief. When do I leave?"

"Got you on a C-5 Galaxy leaving for Germany day after tomorrow at 14:00 hours. You'll go from there to Ft. Bragg compliments of our Air Force friends."

"Okay. I'll get my gear together," JD replied.

Chief Whitley grinned, "Don't forget to pack your toothbrush. Who knows, you might even meet up with a few ladies while back stateside. I hear they kind of like guys with cute puppies!"

CHAPTER 10

Pakistan, officially, is an ally of the United States in the War on Terror. Whether this is true or not, could be the topic of some serious debate. Pakistan is a nuclear power. This fact, by itself, seems too many to be a good reason to position Pakistan as an ally. Western allies needed the means to keep an eye on Pakistan's nuclear arsenal.

Health issues forced the U.S. Ambassador to Pakistan, Warren Goldsby, to retire early. He'd served at his post in Pakistan for the last two U.S. Presidents. Goldsby, a well-respected diplomat, understood the finer points of Pakistani politics. He suffered under no illusions and wore no ideological blinders. He was a realist and saw things as they were. Goldsby was very successful at keeping the more radical players in Pakistani in check. Only a deadly enemy like pancreatic cancer could force Warren Goldsby from his post. Goldsby was now in the fight of his life and, unfortunately, it was not looking very good.

President Hardeman tapped Margaret Stannsbury as the interim Ambassador to Pakistan. She would serve out the rest of Goldsby's term. Since this was an election year, there was no guarantee beyond that. But for Margaret, it was the experience of a lifetime.

A smart, ambitious young woman, Margaret graduated from Harvard Law School. After graduation, she completed an internship with the State Department. When her internship ended, she landed a job as an assistant district attorney for the city of New York. She earned a reputation for being tough but fair and became quite respected in the courtroom.

However, her time in Washington had given her new ideas for a career path. Margaret looked for and landed a position at the State Department. She rose rapidly through the ranks, starting as a low-level staff member for the Secretary of State. She then got postings at U.S Embassies in both Germany and the United Kingdom. Margaret served as a senior adviser at the U.S. Embassy in Afghanistan. Finally, she was appointed as the charge d'affaires for the U.S Embassy in Seoul, South Korea. Margaret Stannsbury was a rising star. Now she was a U.S. Ambassador representing the President of the United States.

Margaret had some big shoes to fill in following someone like Warren Goldsby. She was someone who needed to lead by example. But, Margaret also was smart enough to listen to those with more experience. That approach had always worked well for her in the past. She saw no reason to change.

At 09:15 hours, the convoy pulled out of the U.S. Embassy compound and turned left on Khayaban-e-Suhrwardy. Lieutenant Jimmy McCray rode in the lead Humvee. McCray commanded the detail protecting Ambassador Stannsbury. There were three other marines in his lead Humvee. The second vehicle, the typical U.S. government Chevy Suburban, carried the U.S. Ambassador and her entourage. A third vehicle, also a Humvee, carried four more U.S. Marines.

Stannsbury mentally reviewed the files on the Pakistani government officials she was meeting. While riding, she directed questions to her staff members who had more time in Pakistan. She listened to their responses. Margaret wanted to make a good impression. She wanted to know as much about the officials she was about to meet as she could.

It was a ten-minute drive to the Pakistani Ministry of Foreign Affairs. The Ambassador's meeting started at 10:00 hours. They had given themselves extra time. The traffic in Islamabad was unpredictable at best. In the lead Humvee, McCray kept his eyes moving. He watched both the street and other vehicles traveling it. Pakistan was an ally and things were quiet now. However, Pakistan's intelligence service, ISI, still ignored al Qaeda activities along the border between Pakistan and Afghanistan. While not aiding them, they did little to prevent the flow of supplies that crossed the border. Of course, both Pakistani and U.S. State Department officials would deny this.

Still, Lieutenant McCray thought, *you could not be too careful. You never know who you can trust in this country.*

"Keep your eyes peeled," McCray admonished his team. He'd seen action in both Afghanistan and Iraq and knew how fast a situation could change. "Seems quiet enough, but it can all go to shit pretty fast!"

'Yes Sir," came the quick responses through his comm unit's earpiece.

McCray's eyes caught a movement of the canvas top covering a utility truck parked across the traffic circle. The convoy had entered the circle to turn right onto

Constitution Avenue. An instant later he saw the flash from a rocket-propelled grenade and yelled.

"RPG!" The rocket-propelled grenade struck the lead Humvee but somehow, failed to detonate. Gunfire erupted immediately, coming from several directions. Struck in the head, McCray's driver lost control of the vehicle. It swerved, crashed into a lamppost, and came to a stop. The two other convoy vehicles braked hard, swerving to avoid a collision. The convoy came to an abrupt halt. Two marines were out of the second Humvee and beginning to return fire. LCpl Davis, in the second Humvee, was on the radio calling for help. A second rocket-propelled grenade struck his vehicle. Davis and the fourth marine manning the turret .50 Cal died in the explosion.

The marines in the first Humvee were now out of their vehicle and returning fire. The attackers were firing from vehicles and alleyways on both sides of the street. Lt. McCray, firing controlled bursts from his M-16 rifle took down four of the attackers. Two of the marines in his Humvee were now dead, killed by enemy fire. On the other side of his Humvee, he heard PFC Taylor still returning fire. A bullet struck McCray's helmet and grazed his forehead. The blood was running down into his eyes, making it hard to see. A second bullet struck his right calf. His years of training took over. His next burst killed another attacker. More firing to his right! He heard PFC Taylor grunt and go down, his rifle clattering on the pavement. No more sound came from the other side of the Humvee ... silence.

McCray shifted his gaze to the suburban a few yards away. The driver was dead, slumped over the steering wheel. The engine compartment and tires looked shot to shit. But, the passenger area seemed untouched. Then it hit him. This was not just an ambush ... this was a kidnapping attempt!

The Ambassador ….! He tried to rise.

Two more bullets struck McCray; one slammed into his hip, another into his upper back. He was still alive but it was getting harder to breathe. His breath came in loud, labored rasps. McCray slumped back against the front tire of the Humvee. He dropped his rifle, feeling himself drifting into unconsciousness. All went dark. There was no more shooting from the second Humvee.

What's that? More gunshots? McCray drifted back into consciousness and squinted his eyes trying to see. The attackers were all over the suburban. McCray watched as they dragged the Ambassador's team from the vehicle one at a time and executed them.

Where was the Ambassador? Then, he saw them drag her from the suburban and shove her into the back seat of an old sedan that appeared out of nowhere. In a few short seconds, the Ambassador and the sedan were gone.

How did they know? They must have someone in the fucking Embassy! Damn it, he thought! McCray coughed again, a deep cough … and blood. There was a slow rattling exhale and McCray was gone. The entire ambush and kidnapping, start to finish, had taken about eight minutes.

Josephine Warren-Brookstone was born on August 7, 1962, in Chicago, Illinois. Her family roots in that city ran wide and deep. Her grandfather Simon Markham was a steelworker during the Great Depression. When the Japanese bombed Pearl Harbor on December 7, 1941, Simon volunteered in the U.S. Army. He fought his way across Europe with General Patton's 3rd Army.

While Josephine's grandfather fought in Europe, her grandmother, Gertie, worked at a munitions plant near

Chicago. The war ended for Simon in May of 1945. Adolf Hitler committed suicide in his Berlin bunker and Germany surrendered. Several weeks later, Gertie met Simon with a big hug when he stepped off the train in Chicago with his duffel bag in tow. Simon was able to return to his steel working job and life seemed to take a turn for the better. They both used the GI Bill to further their education. Later, they upgraded their standard of living by buying a home through the Federal Housing Program.

Josephine's mother, Jean Markham, grew up in Chicago. Her father, Henry Warren, was born in Detroit, Michigan. Henry never knew his parents. Killed in Detroit during the mob-related violence, Henry had to grow up as best he could. He was in and out of the foster care system but managed to somehow get through public schools in Detroit. He was a bright enough young man with a winning personality and a real way with words. He could convince anyone of about anything. Henry also worked very hard. He was eventually able to leave Detroit to attend the University of Illinois in Chicago. During his second year there he met, Jean Markham. They fell in love and married on February 20, 1962. Josephine arrived six months later.

Young minds are very impressionable, and Josephine was no exception. A charismatic high school English teacher introduced Josephine to literature promoting causes like wealth redistribution and social justice, which quickly consumed her. Josephine was soon under his spell. She thought she loved him, believing him to be brilliant. And so, by her junior year, she was sleeping with him. When she caught him in bed with a male classmate of hers, she saw him for what he really was. But by then, she was too well indoctrinated. That painful discovery did nothing to undo what she had come to believe over those three years. When Josephine entered Wellesley College, she was committed to her cause.

It was 11:30 PM. Josephine sat in a dark office at her campaign headquarters in Chicago. Her mood ranged somewhere between depressed and angry. Her campaign team, led by her campaign manager, Carl Sundstrand, had done a terrific job. The crowds always responded enthusiastically to her well-crafted talking points. Her speeches rang with phrases like "joining together to build a brighter future." Her team had tested many similar phrases on focus groups and they'd assembled quite a good number. They just rolled off Josephine's tongue. She'd inherited the gift of gab from her Dad. Back at Wellesley College, her friends often kidded her that she could sell horse shit to pig farmers.

Josephine should be feeling ecstatic. She was watching Secretary of State Andrew Perry's campaign go up in flames. And, he was the only opponent with any real chance of beating her in the Primary. Perry's tenure as Secretary of State, riddled with scandal, was coming back and kicking his ass for her. Josephine only had to sit back and watch him self-destruct.

The implosion started when the news stories broke about his extravagant state dinners. They were at taxpayer expense of course. That was not so unusual on its own. His problem was that officials from certain terrorist-sponsoring states were often in attendance. It may have simply been bad judgment on his part, but it was still enough to raise eyebrows in certain circles. In an interview, Perry defended their presence, arguing it was necessary to secure the interests of the United States.

However, less than three months later, another story

broke. This one put Secretary of State Perry in the spotlight for brokering a secret weapons deal with Iran. The U.S. would sell 25 F-16 fighters to Iran for their help defeating the Taliban in Afghanistan and Iraq. The U.S. would also release $1.7 Billion in Iranian assets frozen during the Hostage Crisis in the late 1970s. Iran's Arabic neighbors were outraged at the unilateral attempt to secure Iran's aid. The Israeli Prime Minister was absolutely livid. The releasing of frozen assets was one thing. But, no one in the region wanted to see a better-armed Iran. Iran was a thorn in everyone's side. The story especially angered our military leaders at the Pentagon. Improvised explosive devices manufactured in Iran had killed or maimed many American servicemen. Iran trained many of the insurgents fighting against the American forces operating in Afghanistan. The Pentagon also expressed some serious concern that there was no guarantee Iran would ever live up to their end of the deal. And indeed, there was ample evidence to support this concern. This second scandal really hurt Perry's campaign.

The last nail in Perry's coffin was the brutal beheading of Margaret Stannsbury. Margaret was the new U.S. Ambassador to Pakistan. The Pakistani terrorist group, Lashkar-e-Taiba, took credit for the Ambassador's death. The group shared common goals with al Qaeda. That goal was the establishment of an Islamic State, a Caliphate, in South Asia and beyond. The terrorists videotaped the entire grisly execution.

The civilized world watched in horror, seeing the poor woman, kneeling in an orange jumpsuit. Black-garbed masked terrorists formed a circle around her. It had taken the executioner three chops with a machete to separate her head from her body. Even in the black garb the executioner wore, all could see that he was a fairly young boy.

Reports told how eight Marines had fought valiantly to the last man to protect the Ambassador. The attackers ambushing her convoy were just too many and the Marines were far out-gunned. A second disturbing video aired later that same day on Al Jazeera. It told the whole story in living color. Soon that video was all over social media. The terrorists, armed with AK-47's and rocket-propelled grenades, had launched a major assault. It was a very well-planned and executed military-style ambush. Al Qaeda immediately congratulated Lashkar-e-Taiba for striking such a blow against the hated Americans.

Someone on the embassy staff had leaked the Ambassador's schedule to the terrorists. There was no other explanation. The vetting process for Pakistani employees working at the Embassy was sloppy at best. Departmental cuts to the security budget to fund appeasement programs had seen to that. This effectively ended Secretary of State Andrew Perry's campaign.

Josephine was, of course, ecstatic. In her bid to become the first woman President of the United States, the stars seemed to be in perfect alignment. She was in the right the place at the right time to achieve her dream. And then, today of all days, her campaign treasurer called to tell her that her campaign war chest was empty. Her campaign was broke. Josephine knew that money had become an issue, but thought she could make it last a few more weeks.

What a time for this crap to happen. It was so unfair! Perry was out of the race. All she needed were a few more good speeches and a positive TV spot or two. A decent jump in the polls and more donations would come. Her Party's nomination was hers, but she needed to now take on the opposition party.

Damn it, she thought!

Her campaign team had spent like crazy to get out in the front right away. This strategy had succeeded. Though it wasn't official, she'd essentially won the primary. Now she would need to mount a massive smear campaign against the other party's candidate. That is if she were to have a chance at winning.

It looked like her opponent would be a well-liked black Senator with an impressive political history. Benjamin Steele served in the U.S. Army Rangers. He'd participated in the U.S. invasion of Grenada in 1983. Steele also deployed during the invasion of Panama to capture General Manuel Noriega. Noriega was a politician, a General and a long-time informant for the CIA who went rogue and became a military dictator and a thug. The U.S. had no choice but to go in and clean up the mess they created.

After leaving the military, Steel returned home to New Mexico where he became the state representative for his district. Steele served two terms before managing to get himself elected to the U.S. Senate. He served with distinction on the Senate Intelligence Committee. Steele also co-sponsored several bills that passed through Congress. Steele was young … in his mid-fifties with the reputation of being a good man of solid character and integrity. Many on his staff referred to Benjamin as "Stainless Steele," but never in his presence.

Brookstone had a very different political history. She was a little-known senator from Massachusetts with a totally unremarkable record of accomplishments. She'd served on just enough Senate committees to earn some name recognition. But, she carefully avoided taking any stance that might later hurt her political aspirations.

Josephine did have a real knack for appearing as an activist on the right side of popular issues, especially those favored by the typical low information voter. Luckily for her, these same voters never seemed to notice how often her actions didn't match her rhetoric. Her blue-collar background helped make her appealing to potential voters from Middle America. And finally, she could always play the "sexist" card if she needed to.

It was being reported by some news media outlets that she was an admirer of Saul Alinsky. In fact, she was a student of his methods and tactics. Fortunately for her, many Americans did not know or care who Saul Alinsky was. Following the tactics in Alinsky's book, Rules for Radicals had taken her this far. It was his tactics that would take her the rest of the way. Her team was already out there, digging up whatever dirt they could find on Steele. Everyone had dirt.

Smooth sailing, she thought to herself. *Maybe! But right now, I need to find more money.*

CHAPTER 11

Zev Weiss had lived in Masuleh for almost seven years. In Masuleh, he went by the name Salim Abbas and owned a small cafe with a reputation for serving great kabob, fine tea, coffee, and delicious pastries.

Zev's mother, Yana, was a Syrian Jew who came to Israel along with several thousand other Jews during an ex-filtration operation. The Israeli government ran several such operations during the early 1970s.

Yana soon met and married a successful Jewish businessman named Abraham Weiss. Abraham owned a custom tailor shop in Tel Aviv which provided clients top quality suits, dress shirts, and ties. Many of Tel Aviv's successful entrepreneurs, government officials, celebrities and visiting dignitaries frequented his shop.

Two years after their marriage, Yana gave birth to beautiful twins ... Zev the elder by six minutes and Ola, his younger sister. The day after Zev and Ola's fourteenth birthday, both Yana and Ola were killed on a bus in downtown Tel Aviv. A Palestinian suicide bomber had detonated his explosive-packed vest on the bus. The loss of his mother and sister devastated Zev. He also lost his father. Abraham Weiss never recovered from the loss of his wife and daughter. Instead, he retreated into his business and never emerged again. Zev never forgave the Palestinians.

After serving his mandatory two years in the Israeli Defense Force, Zev was approached by the Mossad for recruitment. He'd been an exceptional soldier. He was intelligent and quick-witted, a crack shot, and very skilled at unarmed-combat. These skills had not gone unnoticed.

After several years as a highly successful agent, Zev's superiors approached him about a deep cover mission in the mountains of Iran. They wanted to set Zev up as Salim Abbas, a cafe owner in Masuleh. Rachel Weinstein, another Mossad agent would pose as his daughter, Nadir. There was a lot of chatter coming out of Iran lately. Something big was brewing. And, the Mossad wanted to know what it was. Zev jumped at the opportunity.

Rahman Atta caught Zev's watchful eye several months later when he came into the cafe for kabob and tea. Atta was soon joined at his table by a man named Al-Wahsari. Al-Wahsari was well-known to the Mossad. He was a mid-level courier between several radical Islamic groups including the Taliban. The Mossad allowed Al-Wahsari to go about his business so that they could use him to catch bigger fish. Zev would keep a close eye on Atta with the help of Rachel, who in her guise as Abbas' daughter, Nadir, served food to the tables in the cafe.

Over the next few months, Al-Wahsari regularly met with Atta and another man Zev soon identified as Hakim. It was clear to Zev that Hakim was no errand boy. He had the look of a desert warrior ... one used to commanding respect. It was only when Hakim met with Atta that Zev saw any kind of acquiescence in his attitude. That observation nagged at Zev. Atta was a new variable in the equation. Zev's suspected something very big was brewing here in the mountains of Iran. He needed to know more about Rahman Atta. Zev sent an encrypted message to his handler, requesting more resources. A few months later that resource arrived, allowing Zev to place an asset close to Atta.

That asset was a former Israeli officer, Major Alek Cohen. Cohen was wounded in combat during the Six Day War. The wounds were bad enough that he was forced into an early retirement from the Israeli Defense Force. He now spent most of his time tending to his beautiful gardens at his home. He had no family and very few visitors.

One dark and cloudy afternoon, a middle-aged woman did pay the retired officer a visit. Since it was a dreary day, Cohen was sitting at his kitchen table, reading the paper and sipping coffee. The gardens could go one day without his care.

The woman's visit turned out not to be a social call. As a recruiter for the Mossad, she was looking for another deep-cover agent to place in Masuleh. They needed someone to assist with surveillance of a suspected radical Islamic leader. Major Cohen, fluent in several Afghan dialects, could pass as a native. The recruiter stressed that this was a matter of national self-defense. If something big was being planned, Israel could well be the target.

A few months later, a shabby looking beggar wandered into Masuleh. He was looking for work as a gardener. Hadi, a crippled Afghan freedom fighter, tortured by the Soviet army during their invasion of Afghanistan, was a sorry sight.

Rahman Atta strolled along through the busy Masuleh

bazaar at the heart of the small town. It had changed very little in almost one thousand years. The fog long since burned off, the bright sun was shining, and the sky was a beautiful azure blue. It was warm but pleasant. It seemed to Atta as if all two thousand inhabitants of Masuleh had picked this precise moment to descend on the bazaar. It was a beehive of activity.

The shops were busy selling a variety of handicrafts. Atta walked past a shop with a wonderful smelling assortment of freshly-baked pastries. There were blacksmiths selling an assortment of knives. Several shops sold assorted weaves and colors of silk scarves.

Atta turned left into an alley and took the flight of ancient stone stairs up to the next level. There he again turned left, making his way toward his favorite cafe for lunch and a meeting. This cafe offered great kabob. And, it also provided a pleasant view of the lower town levels and the valley stretching out below.

"T'faddal." The restaurant's owner greeted Atta as he entered the cafe.

"Assalamu Alaikum," Atta replied. He ordered his kabob and strong black coffee to drink. Despite government attempts to close coffee shops, coffee remained very popular. Atta had to admit he was glad the "morality police" were not too successful in this effort.

The kabob came and Atta enjoyed it, washing it down with sips of the strong black coffee. Finished, he wiped his lips with a cloth napkin. He belched politely. And, now for some tea and gheliyoon, the traditional water pipe used for smoking tobacco.

Atta's mind wandered back to his time spent in France as it often did when he enjoyed good coffee. He hated the foolish French infidels. However, Atta did miss the coffee shops and patisseries.

Atta despised the French socialist government. They strutted around proclaiming their tolerance for all. They pretended to be an enlightened socialist democracy. Atta chuckled. It was not a pleasant chuckle. France could proclaim to the western world that they had no Muslim problem but Atta knew the truth. The French kept their Muslim population hidden away in Paris slums, out of sight and out of the news. Atta smiled to himself. France would atone for its sins. It was the will of Allah. The Islamic revolution would become inseparable from the French government system. It would happen under their very noses. The people of France would live with the Islamic revolution even if they did not like it. The majority of Paris' residents, Atta knew, were already Muslim. Soon, Allah willing, most of the French system would function under Sharia law.

He recalled the writings of a fellow Mujahidin, Marwan Muhammed. Muhammed had written, "Who has the right to say that France in thirty or forty years will not be a Muslim country? Who has the right to deprive us of it?"

French law forbids the collection of statistics on the race or religion of its citizens. But, Atta knew there were about 6.5 million Muslims currently living in France. They would not rest until Islam dominated France. He dreamed of the day when Islam dominated not only France but also England, Germany, Russia and the United States. The whole world ....

"Assalamu Alaikum Wa Rahmatullah." Rahman Atta returned from his thoughts.

"Assalamu Alaikum Wa Rahmatullah Wa Barakatuh," he replied. "Please, sit. How are you my good friend Hakim?" Atta gestured to the empty seat at his table, "Some kabab or coffee?"

"Thank you but no. Some of their excellent tea would

be nice," replied Hakim taking the offered seat. Atta signaled for Nadir and ordered tea for his visitor as well as more coffee for himself. Hakim went on. "It is a beautiful day here in Masuleh. You are truly blessed to live in such a lovely place."

The beverages came and Atta poured for his guest. The waiter disappeared leaving them alone on the patio to talk.

"How are things in Tehran?" Atta asked. "How is our American doing? Our plans are progressing as expected?"

Hakim smiled. "The software works as promised. And, we have tested many times."

The American, Michael Stanley, was a brilliant programmer and hacker. He'd received his BA in Computer Science from Harvard University. Stanley was the stereotypical computer geek. He had never dated very much. He was not particularly comfortable around women. Or, maybe it was simply that women had never seemed to pay much attention to him.

He was, however, an entrepreneur. To make a little money on the side, Stanley created and released a new Ransomware, or Lucky1024 as he called it. It was an annoying little virus that locked its victims out of their own computers until they paid up. Unfortunately, his little enterprise had aroused the interest of the FBI. Stanley was not too keen on spending time in a federal prison. He didn't figure he'd make it too far without becoming some lifer's bitch. Stanley needed a way out of the country fast.

Always intrigued by Islam, he'd made some friends in the Muslim community. Stanley had approached one such friend. He had the needed money. A few days later, Stanley converted to Islam and with fake papers made his way to Canada as Ali Jal Hammad. From Canada, Stanley flew to Turkey. His destination was Iran.

"Of course," Hakim continued, "the real test will have

to be when we actually put it to use. But, all signs are that it will work as expected."

Atta took a sip of the strong, black coffee before he went on, savoring its strong, rich flavor. "Please explain to me again how this software works."

Hakim went on. "It is quite clever but also very simple. The American has explained this to me. We use the American Internet to make many legitimate-looking financial campaign contributions. American politicians are now using their Internet to raise campaign funds. It can be for any American political candidate we choose. Any large sum you send will appear as many small sums paid by individuals."

Hakim paused, both men remaining quiet as Nadir brought more tea to their table. The young woman poured Hakim's tea and made her way back toward the cafe's kitchen.

Once the woman was gone, Hakim continued. "The American has used his computer skills to gain access to the candidate's political party voter rolls. Through our Chechen brothers, we have a list of valid stolen credit card numbers. The American created a file that continuously updates with new stolen credit card numbers. The file holds the stolen credit card and other information needed to complete these contributions."

Hakim took another sip of his delicious sweet hot tea. "We run the program, it connects names from the voter rolls with credit card numbers and the political donation happens. It is quite amazing, yes?"

Atta nodded. "Allah has provided."

Absentmindedly stroking his short beard, Hakim continued, "The contributions will surely pass all but the most diligent inspection. The American tells me that the program leaves little evidence and the American FBI will have a difficult time discovering what we have done. And if by chance they ever do, it will be too late to stop us. The second phase of our plan will already be well underway."

Atta chuckled. "Then we should have nothing to fear. It will matter little if they discover what we have done after the election. It will only serve to deepen the distrust between the American government and the American people. And, once the American election is finished, phase two of our plan begins."

Hakim smiled at that. It was not a pleasant smile. "Our second phase has progressed as well. The North Korean government has agreed to our offer and the training at our facility in Somalia continues. Our new recruits will finish their training on schedule."

"And the American border with Mexico remains wide open," Hakim commented. "The American infidels will soon pay for their arrogant stupidity. As you have so often said, Allah will provide." With that, Hakim finished his tea and stood.

"And now if you will excuse me, I must return to Tehran to make our final arrangements. It is a long ride on the bus. Thank you for the tea and the pleasant afternoon."

Atta's black eyes hardened. "One more thing, Hakim. When we are ready to transfer the money to the campaign account, give the American hacker to our brothers in Syria," Atta paused, sipping some tea. "On second thought, it would be better to wait until after the initial deposit, but still … there is no need to pay him. He is nothing more than a treacherous infidel, an American dog, and a thief; not a true follower of Allah. Our new brothers are very ambitious. They can use him to film another beheading or better, a burning. The world will see him die an infidel dog's death. Allah is just after all."

Rising to take his leave, Hakim commented, "It will be

as you so ordered. I have the men to handle such an important task. Allah Akbar."

"As Salaam Alaikum," replied Atta. Hakim made his way off the patio and down to the next street level in time to catch his bus back to Tehran.

A few days later, Rahman Atta again stepped into the cafe. He was immediately greeted by the restaurant's owner. "T'faddal."

"Assalamu Alaikum," Atta replied. "How are you on this beautiful day, Salim?" Atta seemed to be in a friendly mood.

That did not happen too often, Zev reflected.

"How are you Rahman, my friend? Indeed. It is a beautiful day. Allah is gracious. What can I get you today?"

"Some tea. Thank you." Atta let his eyes drift around the cafe. It was a pleasant sort of place, the big ceiling fans slowly turning overhead. In the cool mountain air of Masuleh, it was enough to keep the cafe comfortable except on the hottest of days. Atta's black eyes came to rest on a man sitting at a corner table sipping on a cup of tea. He had never seen this man in Masuleh before.

Nadir approached with the tea Atta had ordered, set it down, and disappeared back into the kitchen area. A few minutes later Salim reappeared and set a plate of fresh dates on the table.

"Compliments of the house, my friend. Enjoy the beautiful day and the dates."

"Thank you, Salim. But, may I ask … who is the man sitting at the corner table? I have not seen him here before."

"That is Hadi, a beggar. He has not been here long. I hear he is a most excellent gardener, Rahman. He is looking for work."

Rahman took a sip of the tea and reached for a date. Salim went off to wipe clean a nearby table and then returned to where Atta was sitting. He continued in a quiet tone.

"I hear he fought with Osama bin Laden in the jihad against the infidel Russian invaders. His health is not good. I am also told he spent many months as a prisoner of the Russians and suffered horrible torture. I've seen he has a bad leg, and he is also deaf. He comes in here sometimes and I give him tea. Allah commands us to be charitable, does he not. And, he bothers no one."

"It is a sad story, Salim," Atta replied. "And, for a true defender of Islam to live thus. You are kind to give him tea."

Emboldened, Salim went on. "Rahman, could you perhaps give him some employment? I hope I am not being to forward. But, I do know your home has beautiful gardens. He might be of help to you in keeping them up."

Atta's eyes narrowed. Zev went on in an attempt to lighten the mood.

"It would be nice if the poor man could one day pay for the tea I give him."

Atta chuckled at that. Zev noticed that the laugh had no real warmth ... it never reached his eyes.

Atta is a cold-blooded creature, Zev shivered thinking to himself.

"It is possible. Send the man to my house tomorrow afternoon. Say at two o'clock. I will speak to him and see if he is as good a gardener as you have heard. It would not do to have a true warrior for Allah, a hero of the war in Afghanistan, living so ... if we can put him to honest work."

"Thank you, Rahman! You are a wise and generous

man. A true servant of Allah. And, I am sure he will work out well."

"We will have to see, my friend." Atta finished his tea and popped the last date into his mouth. Rising, he placed a few coins on the table, turned and left the cafe.

CHAPTER 12

Rahman Atta was an avid reader of newspapers. He prided himself on being very knowledgeable about world events. He did not watch television. Atta was a man who accumulated knowledge and then applied that knowledge to further Allah's will. To defeat your enemy, you must know your enemy well. To that end, he'd studied this infidel woman, her beliefs, her life, and her ambitions.

Atta knew she was a follower of Saul Alinsky ... who'd taught his followers not to flaunt their radicalism, but to hide it. He had them cut their hair, put on suits, and become part of the system. Alinsky taught his followers to work toward bringing down the system from within. This woman understood Alinsky's principles well. All this met with Atta's purpose. Indeed, this candidate was a great choice. Atta would use the same methods Alinsky taught. First, put the woman in power and then use her to destroy his hated enemy.

Atta's thoughts turned to the pitiful man he and Abbas had discussed in the cafe yesterday. The Russians, those Godless communists, were no friend to Islam either. It was unspeakable what the Russian soldiers had done to the people of Afghanistan. Praise Allah, the jihadists had driven the Russians out. Their turn would soon come. Allah was patient. The Russians were simply another face of the same evil decadence.

His plan was simple. Because of his research, Atta knew all about this infidel woman. He knew her politics and followed her campaign. More to the point, he knew her desperate financial situation. Atta would ensure she had the funding needed to win the presidential election. He would buy the infidel woman's election and she would become President of the United States. She would control the most powerful nation on the planet and Rahman Atta would control her. Then, praise Allah, he would begin the process of destroying America from within. The time had come and Atta was ready.

He left the cushion he had been reclining on and selected a cell phone. Atta walked out into the small walled garden in front of his house. He had time for the call. The gardener would not be arriving for another hour. It was such a beautiful day. While the sun was warm, the higher elevation kept the humidity to a pleasant level. Atta sat on the bench along the garden wall. He pressed the speed dial button for a number one of his regular visitors had recently provided. The phone was ringing at the other end.

Josephine sat in the back seat of her limo. Sundstrand sat across from her. They were returning from a fund-raising dinner in nearby Alexandria, Virginia. It was late and she was tired. There was very little conversation. It had been a long day for little return. The event had raised almost $250,000 but it was nowhere near enough. They could burn through that in a week, even a few days. There were months of campaigning ahead and it would be a tough battle. She would need a lot more money.

Josephine's mind went to next week's fundraiser in Miami, Florida. If they were smart, they should be able to both raise money and chip away at Cuban voter support for their opponent. Steele's support among Cuban-Americans was strong. They liked his position on the Castro regime. Steele strongly criticized the Castro government's treatment of dissidents and the Cuban people in general.

Josephine's cell phone chirped.

Who would be calling at this hour, she wondered? She did not recognize the number. "Hello?"

"Is this Josephine Brookstone?" a voice inquired. It was a pleasant voice with a slight accent.

European, Josephine thought.

"This is she," Josephine replied. "Who is this?"

"Ms. Brookstone, I am a friend I hope. I have taken a great personal interest in your campaign."

"Okay," Josephine replied, thinking she needed to cut this phone call short. She had more important things to think about. "That is so nice. If you would like to talk to a member of my staff I can arrange...," Josephine began.

"Ms. Brookstone, that is not necessary. You need to talk to me. I understand your campaign is having financial difficulty. I would like to help."

"That's great!" Josephine responded. "Donations are always welcome. Would you like to visit our campaign website and donate with your credit card?"

"Ms. Brookstone," the voice continued. "I want you to win the election and I am prepared to provide you with a sizable sum of money to see that you do win."

She frowned. Was this idiot for real or was this someone's idea of a practical joke? She didn't need this shit right now!

"How nice," Josephine quipped. "And how much of a donation would you like to make?"

"Ms. Brookstone, I can have $50 million in your campaign fund by the end of the week." The voice paused. "There is a contingency fund of up to $100 million more if needed."

"Bullshit!" Josephine Warren-Brookstone exclaimed. "Did Fielding or Sexton put you up to this? I don't need this shit right now!"

"Ms. Brookstone," the voice continued. "The offer is quite real. The money is real. It is there for you with no strings attached."

"Sounds like 100% horse shit to me whoever you are," Josephine laughed this time. "$50 million with no strings attached." Sundstrand perked up, suddenly interested in the conversation.

"I assure you it is real. So is the $100 million contingency fund." The voice chuckled. "I guess I could ask you for a few minor political favors if it would help ease your mind."

"It's not legal or even possible, even if the money was real," Josephine observed aloud.

"Ms. Brookstone, allow me to explain. By tomorrow evening, I will donate $1 million to your election campaign. The money will arrive in varying amounts from many sources. They will withstand scrutiny by your election commission or law enforcement agencies. Once the money is in your campaign account, your treasurer can verify what I have said. Once satisfied, call this number." The voice recited a 10-digit phone number with a Washington, D.C. area code. "We can arrange for any future donation at that time."

Josephine laughed. "Mister, I don't know who the hell

you are, but if there is $1 million in my campaign war chest by tomorrow night, you have a deal!"

"Excellent, Ms. Brookstone. It's been so nice to do business with you."

Josephine heard the click of the call ending from the other end.

"What a nut case," she muttered to Sundstrand as she settled back into the limo's comfortable seat. Josephine felt a real need to get back to her condo, have a drink and try to get some sleep.

Atta hung up smiling. You can always count on Western greed. He stood, walked across the garden and entered a small room that served as his kitchen. He took a date from a bowl on the table and popped it into his mouth.

Delicious, he thought.

Walking to the counter, he picked up another cell phone. There was quite a selection of cell phones of various makes and models. All were pre-paid phones ... a security precaution. Atta punched a speed dial number.

"Yes?" a voice inquired.

"Begin the first transfers, Hakim. I want the money in place by 3:00 PM Eastern Time in America."

"It will be done."

"Excellent!"

Atta helped himself to another date, then he continued.

"How are things with our North Korean friends? They have received their payment and all is in order?"

"Payment has been made and arrangements for the cargo to be picked up are completed. We have acquired an Iranian freighter, the Hamad, with a Captain who is a loyal follower of Islam. He is anxious to help." Hakim replied. "Also, our Syrian friend says the North Koreans were very enthusiastic. Their government appreciates the money we are paying them." Hakim chuckled, then continued. "I am sure that their petulant leader will use the money to buy new toys for his own amusement."

"That is all good to hear my friend. Allah always provides. Please let me know if anything arises which needs my personal attention."

Atta ended the call. Time for tea, he thought to himself. Atta made his way out through the door, across the garden and out into the street. His mind was already at the cafe a few blocks away. They did serve such wonderful tea. He thought of the lovely young lady who waited on tables there. She wore the traditional modest dress of a good Muslim, but a man could still tell she was quite attractive.

Atta had never married, having devoted his life to furthering the will of Allah. But, perhaps when he had achieved his goal? It would be most suitable to take a wife at that time. Atta had never wanted children. But, a family would help to secure his position as leader of the new Caliphate. After all, that was his goal. It would become necessary to have a son to continue the lineage. Even all-powerful Allah could not provide Atta with immortality.

Yes, Atta thought to himself. He would discuss a marriage to Nadir with Salim once the time became appropriate. She was pleasing to the eye and a woman did have her uses in a man's life. She would bear him many strong sons.

An elated Michael Stanley left the work area. Under Hakim's watchful eye, he had successfully completed the first "production" run of his program. The $1 million had transferred smoothly to the campaign fund account of Josephine Warren-Brookstone. His program worked well.

It was perhaps, some of his best work. The hard part had been hacking into the party's voter database. He'd piggy-backed on their web server connection that provided access to their regional campaign offices. The rest was straightforward, especially with his programming and hacking capabilities.

The building serving as their project headquarters sat in downtown Tehran. Stanley made his way up the stairs to the third floor and turned down the hall toward the room he had been given for his own sleeping quarters. Hakim had provided everything he'd needed. It was all enterprise-grade equipment. Powerful Dell blade servers ran his programs and housed the data. He had a powerful laptop to work on in his sleeping quarters as well. All in all, it had not been a bad job. He was well-treated and they provided for his needs.

Hakim had congratulated him. "You have done well, Mr. Stanley. Everything has performed as you have promised. I am very pleased. You will receive the reward you have earned."

"Thank you, Hakim," he'd replied. "I am happy you're pleased with my work." Stanley was under no illusions. These were dangerous men and he tried very hard to stay on their good side. He knew he needed to keep them happy. It did not bode well to have them unhappy with you ... for any reason!

Now that his program had proven itself, his big payday was finally here. In a few days' time, there would be $2.5 million deposited into an account he'd set up in the Cayman Islands. He just needed to lay low a few days and figure out how to get back into Turkey. From there he could work his way to another country and start a new life.

$2.5 million should go a long way in Costa Rica, he thought.

As Stanley approached the door to his room, strong

arms seized him from behind. Before he could even cry out in alarm, everything went black. He felt his legs folding beneath him.

Stanley was terrified. He came to lying on the steel bed of a covered truck ... bound and gagged. Someone had tied his arms behind his back. He could do nothing to stop himself from bouncing around in the back of the truck as it traveled to wherever they were taking him. Stanley did not know how long he had been unconscious or in the back of the truck. In a panic, he struggled, trying to free himself from his bonds. There was no play at all in those knots. The circulation to both his hands and feet was cut off ... they were now completely numb. He began to cry, but the gag prevented any sounds from making it much beyond the canvas top that covered the truck. The rough ride took most of the night and the next day and included several fuel stops. Finally, the truck came to a more permanent sounding stop.

Stanley had no way of knowing he was in al-Bab, the stronghold of an al Qaeda splinter group in Syria. Al-Bab was a twenty-hour drive from Tehran. He heard two men exit the cab of the truck. Voices speaking in an Arabic tongue chattered outside the canvas that was blocking his view.

Oh God, he thought. *Where am I?* Stanley did not notice the fact that, despite his recent conversion to Islam, he had not called on Allah for help. It was very hot under the canvas that enclosed the back of the truck and he was covered in sweat. However, not all of it was from the heat.

The back of the canvas was pulled open. Bright sunlight invaded the darkness that had filled the back of the truck. Two men climbed up into the bed of the truck. Roughly grabbing Stanley by his feet, they dragged him out of the truck bed. He landed hard on the packed sandy ground. He again tried to work free of his bonds but to no avail. They were very secure. His eyes began to search his surroundings. He saw thirty or forty men gathered around him in a large circle. Stanley felt his lower body turn to water. Most wore what he recognized as the typical garb of al Qaeda fighters. All carried weapons. His eyes came to rest on a tripod with a video camera mounted on its top and he looked in the direction the camera seemed to be pointing.

Michael Stanley screamed into the gag that was still tied across his mouth. There in the center of the circle was a fire-blackened metal cage. Stanley screamed again. He was oblivious to the fact that his bladder had released its contents. Again, his eyes searched the crowd, every face held a look of intense hatred or cold indifference.

One man approached the video camera on the tripod and pressed a button on its side. He swiveled the video camera around. The lens now pointed at Stanley, who began to make whimpering noises into his gag. Two more al Qaeda fighters approached. Grabbing the terrified man, they dragged him over to the cage ... the video camera recording their every move.

From the crowd came loud trills and shouts of "Allahu Akbar." Michael Stanley was oblivious to any of this. He had lost all control of his senses. They were now near the cage. One of the men dragging Stanley released his grip and reached up to fling the cage door open. Reaching down, he ripped the gag from Stanley's mouth. This seemed to bring Stanley back around to some state of awareness. His terrified screams were now easily heard by all the radical Islamic killers in the circle and only added to their murderous frenzy. Stanley was shoved into the cage, the door clanged shut and was secured with an old padlock. The shouts and trills of the crowd became louder. A man approached with a gas can and doused the cage and its screaming occupant with its contents. The strong smell of kerosene assailed Stanley's nostrils and he could taste it in his mouth. He vomited.

There was a rapid burst of gunfire as an AK-47 fired into the air. The shouts and trills stopped. It was suddenly very quiet. Another man, the group's leader by his bearing, approached the cage carrying a blazing flare in one hand. He stopped near the cage and turned to face the video camera. The man stood, holding the flare and pointing at the cage containing the terrified, screaming man. The leader's features were hidden by the black and white checked shemagh wrapped around his head. He spoke in English with a strong British accent, his voice betraying his Middle Eastern ties.

"Look upon this American criminal! This traitorous dog! This is the fate that awaits all criminal infidels and enemies of the Islamic State." He raised the flare above his head and shouted, "Allahu Akbar!" Turning he threw the flare into the cage. Michael Stanley did not die a good death. The camera did not stop filming until the screams came to a complete stop.

Josephine woke to feel refreshed. So nice not setting the alarm for a change. The sun peeked through the heavy drapes of her bedroom windows.

And, a good morning to you too! She got up, slipped on a robe and went downstairs to get some coffee. After a second cup, she called the office to tell her team that she was going to work from home. She returned some calls and emails and initiated a few more calls and emails of her own. She hated the never-ending cycle of trying to raise campaign funds.

Well, it went with the turf.

Josephine had a quick lunch of tuna salad and grapes. She then turned to the review of a speech written for the town hall meeting scheduled in two days in Cleveland, OH. It was a little after 3:00 PM when her cell phone rang.

"Joey, its Sundstrand. You are not going to believe it!" Sundstrand was clearly excited.

"What's up?" Josephine asked.

"We got $1 million in campaign contributions today!" Sundstrand exclaimed. Josephine almost dropped her phone.

"I'll be right in!" Josephine headed toward the shower.

The drive to campaign headquarters took thirty-five minutes. Josephine burst into Sundstrand's office.

"Show me!" she exclaimed.

Sundstrand turned his computer's display so she could see. "Look."

Josephine looked at the account statement showing a long list of donations. The statement listed personal donations all within the legal amounts. The balance was just over $1 million more than it had been the day before.

Josephine was dumbstruck and had to sit down.

"It all looks good to me," Sundstrand. "Nothing fishy looking here. It just looks like a healthy day of your supporters making donations!"

Josephine smiled. "It's like a miracle. Money from heaven."

Sundstrand snorted. "I don't believe in God, but if I did … I'd say he wants you to win."

"Somebody sure does," She recalled the late-night phone call she'd received just last night in the limo.

She stood there a few minutes, thinking.

"Are you alright?" Sundstrand asked.

"What … ummm, yes, I'm fine," Josephine replied. "I'll

be in my office. Double check all this and make sure it really looks good. We can't afford any legal problems down the road."

"Damn straight," Sundstrand replied as Josephine left his office.

CHAPTER 13

JD arrived at Ft. Bragg three days after boarding the C-5 Galaxy. Two days later he met his new partner, a Belgian Malinois named Ajax. The Belgian Malinois is named after the country of Belgium, and the city of Malines where the breed developed. The origin of the breed goes back to the mid to late 1800's. The Malinois was first registered as a breed in the United States in 1911. The Malinois breed is noted for its intelligence, trainability, and willingness to work hard as herders and trackers. They are very similar in abilities and disposition to the German Shepherd. The one advantage of the Malinois is they are smaller, averaging sixty-five pounds. This is about ten to fifteen pounds lighter than the average German Shepherd. This is a big advantage when jumping into hostile territory with your dog strapped to your chest.

Ajax had already undergone a great deal of training before meeting his new handler. Ajax's early training had been with Petty Officer Jim Broggan. JD met Petty Officer Broggan and Ajax that afternoon at the kennel.

After basic introductions, during which JD had given

Ajax a tentative scratch behind the ears, Broggan led them to a smaller training room with a few seats. JD watched in amazement as, without a command, Ajax fell in and trotted along at Broggan's left side. All three took a seat. JD and Broggan in chairs, Ajax on the floor right between them. Petty Officer Broggan began to fill JD in on his new partner.

"You're getting a great dog! Ajax is going to be one of the best"

"How so?" JD asked.

"First, you need to understand we don't take young dogs or puppies. Ajax was a two-year-old dog when we got him and was already a certified Schutzhund. This means he's qualified to be a German police dog."

"I see," JD replied. "Did he come from Germany?"

"He came from what used to be East Germany," Broggan went on. "Many breeders in the U.S. over breed or breed for show thanks to the AKC. Breeders behind the wall missed out on all that, and because of it ... they have much healthier dogs." Broggan gave Ajax a pat on the head, then pointed at the floor. Ajax lay down on the floor between them and waited.

"Anyway, you are getting one hell of a dog. His prey drive is over the top! That's a good thing! Ajax needs to be able to charge right in there and do his job ... no hesitation, no concern for his own safety! He's got that and then some! The biggest problem we're going to have is to train you to control and direct that drive."

"Okay, so Ajax has one big pair of balls!" JD laughed. "Sounds easy enough. I catch on pretty quickly!"

Broggan laughed. "Shouldn't be too bad. That is if you are half as smart as your dog is!"

"Let's hope so," JD grinned.

"The other key point to understand is that Ajax also has

a great nose," Broggan continued. "Ajax has a very strong hunt drive. If Ajax signals it's there ... it's there!"

JD grinned. "The nose that knows!"

"Exactly," Broggan responded. "Come on, let's take Ajax out for a run on the obstacle course. Let you see what he can do!"

"Sounds good!"

To say JD was impressed would be one hell of an understatement! Ajax attacked that obstacle course like any of the best-trained Navy SEALs would have. The obstacle course was like the many courses JD had run over the years. The only noticeable difference was that some of the obstacles were sixty-five-pound dog size. It was not easy.

They finished that first day with JD working some basic commands with Ajax using a sixteen-foot training leash. The leash was not for Ajax, Broggan explained. It was more for familiarization for JD. By the end of their full day of training, Ajax seemed to have decided JD was okay for a human being. They were getting along well. JD was picking up the training but reflected it was a good thing Ajax had a lot of patience.

The day ended with Ajax back in his kennel and eating the dinner JD was now responsible for preparing. The kennel, JD noted, was very clean and orderly. Even the K9s-in-training lived in pristine barrack conditions. JD followed Broggan back to the parking area near the kennels. Broggan was giving JD some last key points for the training that lay ahead.

"What you must understand JD, is that dogs are nonverbal animals. They respond to the sounds of our words, but they react more to the intonation, in other words, the pitch and volume of the commands. That makes all the difference in the world."

JD nodded.

"Another key is positive reinforcement. We want a dog that does his job because he loves to ... he loves the reward he gets for doing a good job. He respects his master. A dog like that won't quit, he won't let you down! He would die first."

JD understood that concept well. It was the same for the human species of SEALs.

"What we do not want is a dog that is only doing his job because he doesn't want to have his ass kicked! A dog like that is ruined. That dog fears human beings and it fears pain. You can't rely on a dog like that in a dangerous situation. A dog you need to trust to stop bad guys in a war zone can't be afraid of anybody."

When JD got back to his quarters, he gave his folks a call. His father answered the phone.

"Hey Dad, how are you? I wanted to let you know I am at Ft. Bragg for at least the next six months."

'That's great, JD. What are you doing at Bragg?"

JD explained about his new K9 partner, Ajax. Curtis thought that was terrific.

"We had some dogs in Nam ... German Shepherds. I never worked with any ... but from what I heard they were great. Saved a lot of lives."

They talked for several more minutes before JD hung the phone up. His Mom was at the store. She would be disappointed she'd missed his call, but he would call again. He'd have to get home for a visit or two while at Bragg. JD missed his mother's fried rice. He went over to the refrigerator and grabbed a cold Heineken. Popping the top off, he took a long swallow. Heineken was always best very cold.

Okay. Time to finish off the beer and then grab a hot shower. Tomorrow was going to be another busy day.

The training progressed. JD learned more than he ever thought it was possible to know about the psychology and anatomy of dogs. Ajax, JD learned, was a large breed dog and his skull was mesaticephalic in shape. This meant that his bite strength varied from 617 to 550 pounds of force at the molars. At the canines in the front of the jaw, the bite strength was 170 to 150 pounds

"Even a pet dog playing tug-of-war will start out grabbing with the front teeth. But, they will chomp forward, shifting the toy to their rear teeth," Broggan explained. "That means if Ajax is taking somebody down, he will work to use his back teeth. Those canines will draw blood well-enough. But, to drag an attacker to the ground, Ajax will need the bone-crunching power of those molars. We want him to do exactly that … which, since it is instinctive anyway, is pretty simple."

Several days later, JD learned commands to have Ajax take down an aggressor. Luckily, the "aggressor" was dressed in a protective bite suit. JD was again very impressed.

The first thing that caught his attention was that Ajax rarely left the ground. JD had seen videos and movies with dogs launching themselves at bad guys from twenty feet away. Ajax stayed low, seizing the aggressor in those powerful jaws and dragging him to the ground.

"Son of a bitch," JD exclaimed. "Even in a bite suit … that had to hurt." JD developed a still deeper respect for the abilities of his partner. During a break, he asked Petty

Officer Broggan why Ajax never jumped at his target.

"Several reasons," Broggan replied. "Any athlete or serious martial artist knows you can't change directions once you leave your feet. That's just physics. The dog jumps at you, you move over a few feet, the dog misses. That is not a good thing."

"I guess not," JD agreed, thinking about his own martial arts training.

"You watch football?"

"Some," JD admitted. "I like Rugby better."

"Well, you know how cool those flying tackles look in the NFL. But, when they miss, bad things happen. Often the other team scores. We don't want the other team to score."

JD nodded. "I get that."

Broggan continued. "So, from a rugby point of view, a good rugby player has both feet planted when he tackles. He wraps the ball carrier up and takes him down. That kind of tackling is fundamentally and tactically more sound. And, it could inflict much more serious punishment. Fortunately, in Rugby … they have rules."

That evening JD cleaned up and called home before grabbing a quick supper at the local McDonalds. You were not able to get a Big Mac in Afghanistan. JD talked to his mother this time. It was great to hear her voice.

"When are you going to be able to come home for a visit?" his mother asked.

"Not sure, Mom. This training has been intense. We have several weeks tactical training coming up. I should be able to get a weekend after that. I will call you as soon as I know for sure."

"Can we meet Ajax when you come?"

"I'll see. He's a great dog! You and Dad will love him. He's smarter than I am."

Mai laughed. "I kind of doubt that, son … maybe as smart as you are! I bet you two make a great team."

"Well, time will tell," JD replied laughing. "Mom, I had better say good night and get to bed. Early morning tomorrow. I'll call again in a few days. I do need to get up there. I bet Ajax would love some of your fried rice."

Mai laughed again. "Hopefully, he will leave a little for you … that is if you are lucky! Good night, Jake. Talk to you soon."

'Good night, Mom." JD hung up the phone.

Curtis Cordell came into the kitchen, just back from his trip to the mailbox. He found Mai was busy making egg rolls for a get together with friends later that evening. Mai was a wonderful cook. Curtis enjoyed the many dishes she'd added to her repertoire over the years, an interesting blend of Vietnamese, Chinese, French and American cuisines. The egg rolls smelled delicious. Curtis especially loved her egg rolls.

"Looks like a package for JD in the mail," Curtis observed. "Came to him in care of me." Curtis set the mail on the kitchen table and slid up behind Mai to give her an affectionate squeeze.

"Careful," Mai laughed. "Hot stuff."

"You got that right," Curtis whispered into her ear. After all these years, he was still so in love with his beautiful wife. They had such a wonderful life together.

Mai laughed again and turning in his embrace, give her husband a playful kiss.

"Guess you should call and let him know. This will give him an excuse to come home for a visit. That would be wonderful! I want to meet Ajax too!"

"Absolutely," Curtis replied. "I'll give him a call this

evening. I'm sure he'll be busy this time of day, but they should be about done with the tactical training he was talking about a few weeks ago."

Curtis tried JD later that evening. JD answered the phone.

"How's the training going, son," he had asked once the obligatory greetings were dispensed with.

JD chuckled. "Ajax is scary smart. He knows his stuff. I am not sure how much of a part I will play in all this."

Curtis laughed. "Don't worry, son, I am pretty sure Ajax will need you for something. Hell, someone has to feed him and point him in the right direction." JD laughed at that.

"Sheesh, Dad, you should see the great equipment Ajax has. It's impressive stuff. You should see this K9 Storm Intruder Body Armor he gets to wear. Pretty high-tech. My gear isn't nearly that cool!"

"Yeah! Probably come a long way from what we had in Nam," Curtis replied.

"No doubt about that," JD responded. "We did our first tandem jump last week. No big deal for Ajax. We've sure been through it all together. Machine gun fire, explosions, mountains, desert, mud, jungle, swimming, helicopters! He seems to love it ... just takes it all in stride."

"That's great, son. Sounds like you have one hell of a dog there." Curtis paused. "Hey JD, I almost forgot. We have a package here for you. No idea who it is from. The return address is someone in Idaho. Military buddy perhaps?"

"Maybe," JD replied.

"I could send it on, but your mother was hoping you would come home for a few days. Maybe pick it up while you are in."

"I can probably take next weekend off. I think Ajax and

I have earned a little rest and relaxation. Let me check with the Chief. I will get back to you tomorrow, Dad."

"Okay, JD. Sounds good. Want to talk to your Mom a minute? She is standing right here," Curtis grinned. "Well, truthfully, she is jumping up and down."

JD laughed. "Sure thing, Dad."

Mai feigned anger as she gently and jokingly kicked Curtis in the shin. He laughed, handed her the phone and pretending injury, limped off down the hall. In the den, Curtis turned on the TV to see what the news had to say.

CHAPTER 14

Arik Daniel grew up in Borough Park, a neighborhood of southwest Brooklyn. Borough Park is home to one of the largest populations of Orthodox Jews in the world … outside of Israel, that is. The Daniel family was well to do. Arik's father was a podiatrist who ran a very successful clinic associated with the Maimonides Medical Center. His mother ran the business side of the practice.

Arik was the youngest of six brothers and sisters. For his part, he did well-enough in Borough Park's public-school system. Many Orthodox and Hasidic families sent their children to small private schools called yeshivot. The unintended consequence was Arik's classes were very small. The Principal knew each student by name and the halls were orderly and quiet. It was an excellent atmosphere for learning. By the time Arik reached the fifth grade, his reading level was already two grades higher than most public-school kids in other systems.

Fascinated by the history of Israel, Arik decided he wanted to spend a summer living and working on a kibbutz. He'd become fascinated by the idea after learning of the Kibbutz Program Center and their Israeli Experience trips. Supportive of Arik's interest in Jewish history, as a high school graduation present his parents decided to send him to Israel.

Arik found a spot in the Kibbutz of Sde Boker in the center of the Negev Desert of southern Israel. He would stay there for a period of three months. Arik chose this kibbutz because of its historical significance. This kibbutz was the home of David Ben Gurion, the first Prime Minister of Israel.

Life sometimes takes some strange twists. Arik never made it to Sde Boker. He flew into Tel Aviv where he planned to spend a few days getting acquainted with Israel. Arik was walking on the busy sidewalk when a young Palestinian woman detonated a suicide bomb vest at a busy pizza parlor. The concussion threw Arik to the ground …stunned, but otherwise uninjured.

Arik did not leave Israel. Through his family, he already had dual citizenship. He joined the Israeli Defense Force, where because of his aptitude, he was trained as an intelligence analyst.

"Son of a bitch," Arik muttered. "I do not like the looks of this.

Years later, Arik Daniel now worked for Seawatch, a privately-owned maritime intelligence service. Seawatch, founded by a group of former Israeli naval officers, kept an eye out for suspicious behavior by maritime vessels belonging to Israel's enemies. While still a new security company, Seawatch had already established a good track record. The agency was gaining the respect of friendly intelligence agencies around the world.

Seawatch helped western intelligence agencies track and

seize shipments of illegal arms in the Gulf of Aden and off the coast of North Korea. One such shipment had a value of over $250 million. It was also thanks to Seawatch that a U.S. guided-missile destroyer, the U.S.S. Belmont, seized over 700 kilos of heroin. The heroin, destined for the United States, was concealed in a large shipment of oil drilling equipment in the cargo hold of a Libyan freighter intercepted in the Arabian Sea.

Daniel sat at his desk and read through the file he had open on his computer screen. The activities of one Iranian cargo vessel were really bugging him. Any single segment of the vessel's activities viewed on its own could seem legitimate. That was a big part of the problem. Too few saw the complete picture. A NATO vessel might see an Iranian vessel off the coast of Yemen, then later a U.S. destroyer might spot it plying the waters of the Gulf of Aden. But, they could not always put that together with the other pieces of the puzzle that made up the complete picture of that vessel's activities. That is where Seawatch came in.

The 30,000-ton Iranian cargo ship, Hamad, left the North Korean port of Nampo and disappeared into the open sea. After more than ten days at sea, the vessel reappeared at the Iranian port of Bandar Abbas. There the Hamad's Captain, Achmed Suhani, reported his ship fully loaded. This caught Daniel's eye because there was no record of the Hamad ever entering the port of Bandar Abbas. Then, later that very same day, the Hamad set sail for Yemen.

The Hamad arrived off the Yemeni port of Hodeida, dropped anchor and sat outside the port for twenty-nine days. Finally, the Hamad entered the port of Hodeida, refueled and took on supplies. One week later, the Hamad again left port and this time sailed north without disclosing her next port of call.

Arik Daniel wondered exactly where the Hamad had set sail for. He had a nagging feeling that he needed to find out. Arik wanted more information on the Hamad's movements.

He reached down and opened a drawer in his desk, pulling out a small but rather thick booklet. After grabbing a pen and a notepad, Arik opened his code book. Several seconds later he had his "code in" number calculated. He reached over for his phone and dialed a number.

A phone rang in a small office in a rundown building on the outskirts of the Jinhae-gu District on Masan Bay. The Jinhae-gu District housed a large naval base and served as the main base for the Republic of Korea Navy.

"Hello? Seawatch" The voice was professional and direct.

"Hello, this is Arik Daniels. I'm with Seawatch here at Haifa. I need waybill information on a ship we are tracking."

"Code in please."

"Sure, I have it right here," Daniel replied. The number was a sixteen-digit security code used to identify Seawatch personnel before the exchange of any information.

Arik Daniel read the code from the slip of paper he had written it on. He would destroy the slip of paper as soon as he'd finished. Simple technology, but very effective.

"Right, let me check." There was a pause of a few minutes. "Yes, good. What do you need?"

"I need to establish the destination of the Iranian cargo ship, Hamad." It left Hodeida sailing north, but with no declared destination. Previously, it had been to Nampo in North Korea, then to Bandar Abbas. The Hamad reported being fully laden at Bandar Abbas but took on no cargo. I believe it left North Korea with cargo they are trying very hard to hide." Arik paused. "It is nothing I can put a definite finger on, but I have a gut feeling from its activities that they are up to no good. I need to know where the Hamad is going. I need to know whatever you can find on this vessel."

"Okay. Got it. I will check this out and call it in if I find anything."

'That's great. Thanks." Daniel hung up the phone. He stood up and stretched a bit, then walked down the hall to the office suite's small kitchen. Pouring a cup of coffee, he leaned against the counter and took a sip.

CHAPTER 15

Julie Spencer showed her ID badge to the security guard at the gate.

"Hi Julie," the guard greeted her with a smile.

Julie knew he liked her. "Hi, Rob." She gave him a friendly return smile and drove on through the gate.

Julie was an attractive woman of twenty-seven. She wore her blond hair cut short and had a perky disposition that matched the smile on her face. Julie was intelligent and friendly, well-liked by the members of her team.

She'd earned a Bachelor of Science degree in Computer Programing from North Carolina State University. After graduation, she landed an internship with the CIA. Julie started work on her Masters of Science in Cyber Security from Western Governors University while still an intern with the CIA, and was now a full-time employee.

Finding a great parking spot for her 1998 Honda Accord, she grabbed her shoulder bag and made her way toward the tech lab deep in the complex. Julie worked as a data retrieval expert for the agency.

On the way to the tech lab, Julie stopped by the

complex coffee shop for a large black coffee. She really liked the flavor of a good cup of coffee. Sipping her coffee, she made her way through the maze of long corridors. Finally, Julie made one last left turn and stopped at a door. Punching in her access code, she went in to begin her day. Things were beginning to settle into a routine. It had been a while since Julie had anything interesting at her workstation.

Hopefully, something exciting would pop up soon, she thought to herself. Julie checked the progress of the tests she was running on some new equipment. As technology advanced, the tools needed to crack that technology also needed to advance. It was a never-ending game of catch-up.

Little did Julie know, she was going to get her wish.

"Oh shit!" It was late and Peterson was tired. He'd set his mug of coffee down on his desk a little too hard. Coffee splattered onto pages of the report that lay scattered across his desktop.

What the hell? Peterson stared at the report he'd been reading. The report stamped Top Secret, laid out some disturbing information.

Peterson had worked his way up through several positions at the CIA. He'd graduated with a Bachelor's Degree in Finance from the University of Texas, McCombs School of Business. Then taking the next year off, Peterson traveled throughout Europe, making extended stops in Berlin, Paris, Rome, and Vienna. Peterson found he enjoyed immersing himself in different cultures. He worked hard at learning their languages. Exploring their cuisines was great fun as well.

It turned out that Peterson had a knack for languages,

and soon become fluent in both German and French. Completing his European tour, Peterson returned to the University of Texas where he earned his Master's in Professional Accounting. The time he'd spent abroad, however, made the prospect of working as an accountant a little less appealing. On impulse, Peterson applied for employment with the CIA. Surprised when he got an interview, he was ecstatic when the CIA offered him an entry-level position as an Economic Analyst. He did not hesitate, accepting the position. Soon after, he married his girlfriend, Ginny, a pretty redhead he met about a year earlier. Ten months later, twin girls arrived.

Peterson had a good mind for this kind of analytical work. He enjoyed his job and worked hard at it. A promotion soon came and Peterson was transferred to the Office of Military Affairs, a CIA section providing intelligence and operational support to the United States armed forces. That transfer had put him on an aircraft carrier a week ago.

It'd was great seeing JD again, William thought. *What a surprise bumping into him in the middle of the Arabian Sea! I always figured JD would end up a U.S. Navy SEAL or something like that. He really loved all that karate training ... all that duty and honor stuff.*

Peterson brought his mind back into focus. It was wandering and he needed to concentrate.

Must be because I'm tired, he thought. With an effort, he refocused his thoughts on the task at hand.

The CIA had immensely powerful resources to gather and process intelligence. It was the processing of that intelligence that was the hard part. Peterson knew that there was no substitute for using your God-given brain. It was much more import how you put the puzzle pieces together ... rather than just looking at the pieces themselves. Often there were millions of puzzle pieces … all bits and pieces of intelligence. The real question was how did they connect? Peterson seemed to have a real knack for connecting those dots. Part of his success, Peterson knew, was an intuition-like gift he seemed to possess. But, that gift was also a danger. Relying on intuition alone could get you into real trouble. There had to be enough real intelligence to keep your intuition under control.

The report he now read detailed the contents of the notebooks grabbed by SEAL Team 5 during their mission to snatch al-Wahsari in the mountains of Afghanistan. Unfortunately, Al-Wahsari died during the ensuing firefight, but the SEAL team did retrieve a couple of laptops, a cell phone, and several notebooks. The laptop's hard drives were encrypted and were now in a clean room where a CIA tech team was working to crack the encryption. The cell phone's SIM card did reveal records of several calls and coded text messages. Several calls to the cell phone had originated in the Gilan Province of Iran. That piqued William's interest. There was also a text message that clearly referred to Michael Stanley and arranging the delivery of Stanley to al-Bab in Syria for execution.

Poor slob, Peterson thought. Stanley had converted to Islam and fled the U.S. to escape federal prison time for computer fraud charges stemming from a Ransomware virus he'd created. He'd then somehow made his way to Iran. The poor schmuck had later managed to get himself burned alive by terrorists in Syria. The whole execution was videotaped by the terrorists and the video aired by Al-Jazeera.

What a God-awful way to go, Peterson thought! The poor guy did not deserve to die like that … even if he was a real slime-ball!

Peterson took another sip of his coffee.

These terrorists are getting bold … and sloppy. Peterson believed it was the direct result of President Hardeman's incompetent foreign policy. The problem was that this administration lacked anything resembling testicles. There could be an unintended benefit to the CIA though … especially if the terrorists remained sloppy and continued to make mistakes.

He turned back to one of the pages he had skimmed over a few minutes ago.

But this? This is plain crazy!

The reported stated that one of the spiral-bound notebooks contained a scribbled 10-digit number in one of the margins on the last page. It stood out because it seemed so out of place with the rest of the notebook's written Arabic text. To the analyst's eye, it looked like a very important number jotted down in a hurry … so somebody would not forget it. The technician had run a check on the number and received the surprise of her life. The number was an exact match for the personal cell phone number of Josephine Warren-Brookstone. And, Brookstone was one of the leading contenders in this year's presidential election.

The Media had, for all practical purposes, already anointed her as the first woman President in U.S. history. Peterson hated to admit it, but according to most polls, this was likely going to be the case. While her campaign had run a flood of brilliant, well-crafted campaign ads distancing her from the current administration's incompetence, Peterson found it interesting that she retained the same political agenda. Her campaign ads argued that President Hardeman actually had the right policies, but that his administration had simply been careless and sloppy in implementing them. The bills passed by the President's allies in Congress had the right intent but were simply poorly written.

Peterson had to admit that he agreed with the Brookstone campaign ad's assertions that President Hardeman's administration had been careless and sloppy. There seemed to be a lot of that going around.

I would have added arrogant and incompetent as well, he thought. It seemed obvious to Peterson that legislation should be read and understood before being signed into law ... not after the fact. He had a very hard time comprehending why that was so hard for so many to understand.

It was funny how many of his colleagues agreed in principle, but still, voted the way they did.

It makes no sense! No sense whatsoever!

Josephine Warren-Brookstone's campaign platform stated that if elected, she would continue the policies put forth by the former administration, but that she would put policies in place the right way. Peterson had to admit it was a brilliant well-run advertising blitz and it was reaching a lot of people.

So, the question is, Peterson thought, *why is Josephine Warren-Brookstone's personal cell phone number in the margin of a terrorist's notebook found on the other side of the world?*

It shouldn't be. A coincidence? Could the number be something else ... some kind of account number or passcode? Peterson's guts were telling him that this was not the case. That it was Brookstone's cell phone ... that damned intuition thing again. He reached for his phone. Peterson decided he needed some guidance on how best to proceed, especially with such a politically explosive bit of intelligence. If this was indeed Josephine Warren-Brookstone's cell phone number, this was going to get very ugly. Peterson reached for his intercom.

"Buzz the Deputy Director for me, Wanda. I need to come up and talk to him. Thanks!"

"No fucking way," was Mike's initial response as Peterson explained the situation.

"That's what I thought," Peterson replied. "But the number is definitely a match. We are checking on phone calls coming into that number from the Middle East to see what, if anything, pops up." Stanton got up from his desk and moved over to his window. He stood there a minute, gazing out over the parking lot. His right hand reached up, scratching the back of his head.

"Could the number be something else?"

"I guess the number could be an account number, or a password or security key, or one of many other ten-digit possibilities. Hell! I don't know!" Peterson paused. "But, if it is her cell phone number, and my instincts say it is, there will be some serious implications for national security, to say the least."

Mike nodded his head. He had to agree. He walked back and sat in his chair, silently thinking for a few more seconds. Finally, Stanton reached a conclusion.

"We will need to proceed with a great deal of caution. The CIA will have to have something more than a damned suspect ten-digit number before we try to connect Josephine Warren-Brookstone to radical Islamic terrorism."

"I couldn't agree more," Peterson replied. "Let's not jump in with both feet until we have an idea how deep this goes … or if it even goes at all."

Stanton got up from his chair and paced back and forth behind his desk.

"We can't afford to have this blow up in our faces and, you're right, it may turn out to be nothing at all. There's no fucking way we can say anything about this and then have that number turn out to be some terrorist's fucking Swiss bank account number." Stanton paused. "Have the files sent up to my office, Peterson. I want to see that number in context with any other available intelligence. We'd better keep a lid on the whole thing until I've had a chance to see what we have. I may want to kick this upstairs after looking at it."

"Yes, Sir." Peterson got up to leave.

"Go ahead and make some quiet inquiries. See if any other connections might exist between Brookstone and charitable Islamic organizations, known Islamic leaders, the Muslim Brotherhood, Mosques, or terrorist front organizations like CAIR … anything like that."

William nodded as he opened the door to leave Stanton's office.

"But for God's sake, keep it quiet. Keep a very low profile, right?"

"Will do," Peterson affirmed as he left Mike Stanton's office, shutting the door behind him. He was feeling no better about any of this.

After Peterson had gone, Stanton remained thoughtful for several minutes.

What the hell … as the old saying goes … nothing ventured nothing gained! Stanton pulled his cell phone from the inside pocket of his sports coat. Opportunities like this didn't come around every day and if Mike Stanton was nothing else, he was an opportunist. Selecting a name from his contact list he pressed the call button. The call was answered on the third ring.

"Hey, Richard! How are you? It's Mike Stanton."

"Mike! What a surprise, What's up?"

"Well," Stanton began, "you folks may have a bit of a problem campaign-wise. I think we need to talk. When and where can we meet?" Mike paused, waiting for the reply.

"Jeez Mike, we are all pretty busy right now. Sometime next week?"

"No, I am afraid that simply won't work. It needs to be sooner! Tonight would be best if possible. It is important, but to your campaign team … not to me."

"I see," Richard replied. "Let me look at my schedule." There was a pause. "I can meet you tonight at Le Diplomate … say at 7:30. It will have to be short … we're flying out to Dallas for a campaign rally tomorrow morning."

"Okay, that sounds good. I'll meet you there at 7:30 sharp." Stanton ended the call. He got up and walked over to his office window and looked out over the complex. There was not much to see from his window at Langley, especially since it was raining so hard.

Stanton viewed himself as a D.C. power-broker, an inside-the-beltway big shot! Over the years he'd managed to build up some pretty good connections. And, a lot of people owed him favors.

Now, Lady Luck had dropped a big fat opportunity right into his lap … and he was going to make the most of it. Stanton knew that he now had in his possession some serious dirt, dirt that either side in this presidential race would want to know about. Either way, it went, someone was going to owe him a big favor. And, if worse came to worse, he could push it right back to Peterson and let him run with it.

Ain't politics great?

Mike was smiling as he left his office and made his way

down the hall to the men's room. On the way back to his office, he detoured by the cafeteria for a cup of coffee. Stanton spotted Julie Spencer sitting at a table eating some yogurt. Julie was an attractive young woman who worked as a data recovery technician. Mike had tried on several occasions to get into her pants but had met with no success.

Nothing ventured, nothing gained, Stanton thought to himself. He made his way over toward her table. Julie saw him coming and steeled herself. She found him repulsive.

"Hey there Julie! How's my favorite little techie doing today? On break?"

Julie looked up and somehow managed to force a smile. "Yes, but I have to get back to the lab now. My break time's up." Julie absolutely did not want him sitting down at her table. "Got to get back to those laptops you know."

"Sure thing," Mike replied. "Keep me in the loop with whatever you find, Okay?" Julie nodded, and to her relief, Mike turned to walk off. Then he stopped and turned back to her.

"Hey, Julie! By the way, I am having dinner at Le Diplomate tonight at 7:30. Do you want to join me? A little dinner …. a few drinks?"

The thought of that nearly made her lose her yogurt. "Geez Mike, sorry. I already have plans for dinner with my sister tonight. She is having a tough time of it right now."

"Alright then. It's your loss," Stanton smiled. "Just kidding, Julie. The family is important after all. Another time perhaps. See you later."

"Later, Mike."

Mike headed back to his office whistling some off-key tune with no recognizable melody.

Julie finished up her yogurt and left for her work area. *What a sleazeball,* she thought still thinking about

Stanton. The way he talked to women made her skin crawl. Her mind turned to William Peterson. It was too bad Peterson was already married. He seemed like such a nice guy. Julie sighed.

Why are all the good ones already taken?

She punched her access code into the keypad. The door unlocked. Julie entered the clean room and returned to her task of extracting whatever secrets were hidden on the laptops recently recovered in Afghanistan.

At 7:15, Mike Stanton walked into the small Washington eatery called Le Diplomate. The maître d' seated him at a private table toward the back. A favorite place of his, the quiet restaurant offered a prime view of Lafayette Park and the White House. He ordered a scotch on the rocks and perused the menu while waiting for Sexton. Stanton decided on the grilled Rockfish with rainbow Swiss chard, little-neck clams, and achiote broth. He was ready to order when Richard Sexton, a key member of Josephine Warren-Brookstone's campaign team slid into the seat across from him.

"Richard."

"Mike," Sexton returned.

"I was about to order. Will you join me?" Stanton asked.

"Sorry no! I am in a bit of a rush. Can we get down to business?"

"Well sure … if we must," Stanton replied. He didn't like to be rushed. Mike had wanted to prolong this moment.

"Then I will get right to the point. One of my operatives came across your boss's personal cell phone number in a notebook. That particular notebook was picked up by a U.S. Navy SEAL team during a raid on a village in the northern mountains of Afghanistan."

"What kind of bullshit is this?" Sexton asked. Stanton ignored the question and went on.

"This notebook was recovered during an attempt to capture a known terrorist … a courier for several radical Islamic groups. The terrorist's name was Al-Wahsari. I am sure his capture would have yielded a lot of good intelligence. Unfortunately for us, the terrorist died during the mission. It seems he was not too keen on being captured." Stanton paused and took a sin from his scotch. "The SEAL team killed six other terrorists as well. The mission was not a total loss because the team came out of the Taliban safe house with a couple of laptops, several notebooks, and a cell phone." Mike paused for effect and took another sip of his scotch. Sexton slumped back into his seat, a look of disbelief on his face.

"Now, the question we have on the table before us is this. What the fuck is your boss's cell phone number doing in that notebook. And, a second question comes to mind, who the fuck has been calling her from Afghanistan?"

Sexton's whole demeanor had changed. He looked like he'd been told that he had a terminal disease with only months to live. Sexton felt that way at that moment. Brookstone's campaign was surging into the lead and November was not far off. She was the squeaky-clean working-class candidate, the candidate who would listen to the people and do what was best for them … not the special interest groups. If word leaked out that she was under investigation for connections to radical Islamic terrorist groups? Sexton didn't even want to think about it. Steele's people would extract every bit of blood they could from a scandal such as that. They'd have a field day.

Sexton recovered himself enough to ask, "So why are you telling me all this?"

Stanton smiled, "I like being on the side that wins, and I also like it when the winner owes me favors." There it was … no pretense. It was right out in the open.

Sexton sat back in his chair.

What the fuck has Josephine gone and done? He'd now recovered his composure and was all business.

"This is bad enough as it is. But, if your operative makes any further connections, and mind you, I am not saying that he will, the threat presented will have to be squashed. Can we trust him to play ball? There is too much at stake here." Sexton shifted in his chair before going on. "What about the SEAL team that recovered the intelligence?"

"They have no idea what was on the stuff they grabbed. As soon as they landed on the carrier, my operative took possession of everything they'd recovered." Stanton took another sip of scotch. "Sounds like maybe it was a good thing the package got himself and the others killed."

Sexton nodded, leaning forward to speak. He was an old-time Chicago-style politician and knew how to get things done.

"Our candidate is going to win, Mike. Take care of this mess. Clean this up for us. See that it gets swept under the carpet and you will be set. Maybe even CIA Director. Who the fuck knows?"

Stanton swirled the remaining swallow of scotch in the glass before downing it. "I'd like that. I'd like that a lot."

Sexton got up to leave just as the waiter brought Stanton's dinner order to the table.

"Have a nice night, Richard," Stanton called as Sexton walked quickly toward the exit. Sexton did not look back.

CHAPTER 16

It was a hot mid-August Masuleh afternoon. On this day, Rahman Atta's pleasant little house was playing host to a meeting between the who's who of the radical Islamic world. Rahman Atta had requested this meeting with all the major players in the world of radical Islamic terrorism. While they were often at odds with each other, they all had one thing in common … a deep hatred for the western world and the United States of America. Atta was setting the stage. Today, he would unveil his plan for dealing a decisive blow to their hated common enemy, the United States.

He'd insured their attendance with the promise of a large financial contribution to each attendee's war chest. As directed, each attendee arrived in secret with their arrivals spread out over several days. Some arrived by bus, others by private automobile. One arrived posing as a merchant with a camel caravan loaded with trade goods.

They spent time relaxing and enjoying the sights and shops of Masuleh. Taking care to blend in with the day trippers from Tehran, they looked to most like anyone else not from Masuleh … people simply seeking a place in the mountains, a place to get away from the oppressive desert heat. Atta was certain there was little chance of them being observed by western agents here in the mountains of Iran, but one never knew.

Atta could not have been more correct in his assumption. Where he went wrong in his thinking, however, was that Salim Abbas was not a westerner. He was a Jew by the name of Zev Weiss, and an agent for the Mossad.

Several of Atta's guests wandered into Salim's cafe to enjoy some tea and the café's famous baked delicacies. Weiss had recognized three of them. It was clear something big was afoot in Masuleh. No doubt they were here to meet with Rahman Atta. Weiss wondered how many more might be in attendance.

This is unbelievable, he thought to himself. *All these top-level radical Islamic terrorist leaders meeting in one place! There is no way this could be a good thing.*

Abbas motioned for his daughter, Nadir, to take over for a few moments. He made his way upstairs where their living quarters were. He needed to get a message to Tel Aviv right away.

Later that day, the guests were all assembled in what served as Atta's sitting room. Present were Malachi Abdul Razi, the First Deputy of the Taliban's Council of Ministers. Then there was Khalid Ali Mohammed, a senior member of Hezb e Islami Gulbuddin. Hezb e Islami Gulbuddin originally formed as a political party during the Russian invasion of Afghanistan but was now listed as a terrorist organization by Canada, the European Union, the United Kingdom and the United States. Another guest was

Abdul Jamal Mohammed, a Syrian known to have had a long relationship with Osama bin Laden and who, it was rumored, had important connections in the North Korean State Security Department. There was Ismail Ahmoud, a senior officer in the military wing of Hamas who now sat, reclining on a cushion in one corner waiting for the proceedings to begin. In another corner of the room sat Abu Bakhr al-Suwani, a former colonel in the Iraqi army and now the commander of his own militant group. Al-Suwani was one of the cruelest military leaders currently operating in both Iraq and Syria. Atta's loyal lieutenant, Hakim, was also present. Hakim had been with Osama bin Laden battling the Soviet invaders during their invasion of Afghanistan. Several years later he'd gone to work for Rahman Atta. Hakim had many connections in the Taliban as well as with terrorist insurgents in Iran and Afghanistan. He'd proven very useful to Atta and thus, had been well rewarded.

Rahman Atta entered the sitting room and greeted his guests.

"As-Salaam Alaikum." Atta had provided a nice assortment of refreshments for his guests. They had a choice of tea or ice-cold water with sliced cucumbers. There was also a nice assortment of pastries and other delicacies from his favorite café.

His guests responded, "Wa akaikumus salaam."

Atta made his way to a vacant cushion and sat. He gazed around the room … letting the anticipation build. Atta enjoyed a sip of tea. A few moments later, Atta raised his right hand and the room became quiet.

"My brothers, I have asked you here today so I can share with you the fruit of my many years of labor in the service of Allah. I know each of you to be a dedicated servant of Allah and a true warrior of Islam. You are all soldiers in our jihad to rid the earth of the vileness and corruption of the decadent west. We share a common goal ... to destroy its foul leader, the United States of America."

Heads nodded around the room and murmurs of "Allahu Akbar" rose from several in attendance. Atta went on.

"As some of you know, I was blessed by Allah, as well as by my father and honored uncle, with considerable resources. I have used these resources to put into operation a plan that has been several years in the making. This plan will destroy the American Satan once and for all. If you would all be so kind, I would like to share with you the details of my plan."

Atta paused for another sip of tea before continuing. He was enjoying his moment.

"The plan comes in two parts. You all know that our friends in Syria recently executed, with Allah's cleansing fire, an American infidel dog. That American criminal worked for me for some months. While the American was a treacherous dog, he was also a brilliant computer programmer ... a computer hacker.

Before I turned him over to our brothers in Syria, he created a software program, a computer virus. This virus allows for the backdoor transfer of large sums of money into the campaign fund of a candidate in this American presidential election. This virus makes these transfers appear as many smaller legitimate financial contributions. I have chosen a candidate who will serve the needs of my plan and I will aid her in winning the election. She has received approximately $50 million from me and is now well in the lead. I have made an extra $100 million available to her as needed. Greed and a thirst for power will turn their President into a puppet for our use."

Rahman Atta paused, sipping his tea. His now captive audience waited for him to continue.

"Once she is in power, I will use her to continue the policies that are tearing our hated enemy apart from within … the same polices implemented by her predecessor. The stupid Americans do not see that these policies divide and weaken them. Her policies will continue to pit Black against White, Hispanic against Black, White against Hispanic. She will pit the wealthy against the poor and the American people against their own government. Her policies will continue to disarm the American people, weaken their military, and exhaust their financial resources. Our puppet President will cause the Great Satan to sink deeper into ruin."

There were murmurs of approval and appreciation from the meeting's attendees.

"But my brothers, that is but the first part of my plan. Ten American citizens, recruits who are true Islamic warriors, are training at a camp I have been funding in Somalia. Hakim has been in touch with our brothers from Somalia and the training progresses as scheduled. After completing their training, these ten warriors will travel back to the United States. They will enter through South America and across the American border with Mexico." Atta paused for another sip of tea. Hakim saw that Atta had the undivided attention of his guests.

"Before crossing into America, each of our ten brothers will receive a device … a small nuclear device … known as a suitcase bomb. The American border with Mexico is as porous as the desert sands. They will have little trouble getting through. If the Americans manage to catch a few, those that remain will be enough to do the job. Each of our ten brothers will, with the aid of other Islamic brothers already present in America, make their way to their assigned targets. Once all ten have reached their assigned cities, they will detonate their devices at the specified hour. The cities I have chosen include New York, Boston, and Atlanta on the American east coast and San Francisco, Los Angeles, Seattle, and Portland on the American west coast. Chicago, Illinois and Charlotte, North Carolina will also be targeted."

A voice raised a question. "Why are our brothers making their way to America through Mexico? Have we not excellent passport makers? They could fly to America. Crossing the border may be an unnecessary risk."

"A most excellent question, my friend," Atta replied. "They will cross over from Mexico because the American CIA, or perhaps their FBI, may be watching for these returning warriors. Therefore, they will walk across the American border disguised as common immigrants. It also will be much easier to get the devices to Mexico and carry them across the border into American. The American border presents no obstacle. My candidate will ensure that this same open-border policy continues.

As I stated earlier, once in America, our brothers will meet other true followers of Islam who will assist them in reaching their assigned targets. While the weak-minded American infidels war with themselves, we will inflict a deadly attack on their nation. We will destroy ten of their key cities. The resulting devastation will be very great in the eyes of Allah."

More respectful murmurs of approval sounded from around the room. Hakim arose, excusing himself … and left the room.

Atta waved his hand for silence before continuing. "This phase of the attack comes only with the help of my good friend, Abdul Jamal Mohammed, who is here with us today. My friend, through his connections with the North Korean Department of State Security, has provided the nuclear devices we will use to bring down our hated enemy."

The murmurs of approval for the planned attack Atta was describing was now very enthusiastic. Abdul Jamal Mohammed was congratulated for his role in obtaining the nuclear devices. Atta called for quiet once more.

"While the foolish Americans squabble like women, we will unleash Allah's vengeance upon them … a vengeance of such magnitude has not been seen since before the Prophet Mohammed walked among us. This plan will kill many hundreds of thousands of infidels. We will bring down their financial infrastructure. The American people will riot among themselves and against their government! Total collapse will follow. As a result, the only true obstacle to our new Islamic Caliphate with control of the entire globe will be destroyed."

Rahman Atta smiled as he leaned back into his cushion and enjoyed another sip of tea. The tea was almost as enjoyable as the applause of his guests.

And, I will be in a position to become the next Caliph, Atta thought to himself. Allah's will would be done.

Hadi was kneeling outside the window of that same sitting room. To the casual viewer, he was busily weeding a section of Rahman Atta's flower garden. Hadi was shocked by what he was hearing through the small earpiece in his left ear. The tiny microphone he'd managed to plant with some cut flowers in the sitting room worked very well. And, what he was hearing through that microphone was sheer madness! Murdering hundreds of thousands of human beings in the name of a barbaric seventh-century religion. It was hard to believe such evil existed. Hadi hoped Zev was getting all this as well. He'd hidden a small but powerful signal repeater within the garden. It boosted the microphone's signal and relayed it to a receiver in Salim Abbas's apartment above the restaurant. Hadi was so shocked by what he was hearing, he failed to hear Hakim approaching him from behind.

Hakim had stepped out to check the grounds. While making his way back to the house, he'd noticed Hadi kneeling to weed the flower beds below the sitting room window. That old gardener was always puttering around. Even Hakim had to admit that Hadi kept the gardens in immaculate condition. Then Hakim paused. Something was very wrong here. He frowned, thinking. Suddenly he knew what was bothering him. It looked to Hakim like the old man was not gardening, but listening. Listening? To what? How?

A strong hand covered Hadi's mouth. Hadi's head was jerked violently back as a knee pressed into his lower back. He began to flail with his arms, trying to break free but the effort was futile. There was a quick flash of metal and a razor-sharp knife slashed across his throat, severing his carotid arteries and his wind-pipe. Hadi's body went rigid, then sagged as he drowned in his own blood. Hakim released Hadi's lifeless body to fall to the ground among the flowers. Performing a quick search, Hakim grimaced as he discovered the earpiece in Hadi's left ear.

There must be a matching microphone in the sitting room, perhaps in other rooms as well. It was a good thing he had come across Hadi when he did. At least the traitor had died before he could report whatever he'd heard from within the sitting room.

Hakim left Hadi's lifeless body where it lay, returning to the sitting room. He would have the body properly disposed of later.

Hakim was unaware of the signal repeater hid in a flower-filled urn a few feet to his left.

The formal meeting was ending when Hakim returned. Atta's guests were enjoying the last of the tea and the few remaining pastries. Murmuring voices were discussing the sheer brilliance of the plan that had just been laid out for them. Atta listened quietly, smiling as comments like "Rahman Atta is a true servant of Islam" and "Allah has chosen his true servant well" floated about the room.

Hakim said nothing, concentrating as his gaze swept the entire room. His eyes came to rest on a vase of flowers sitting on a low table in the center of the room. The many cushions Atta and his guests had been reclining on during the meeting surrounded the table. Hakim went over to the vase and peered at it as if to admire the blooms and their fragrance. He selected a flower and held it to his nose for a second. Hakim took it with him as he left the room. Once in the kitchen, he placed the flower in the microwave and pressed the one-minute button. Something popped in the microwave and there was a slight odor of hot metal in the air.

Hakim returned to the sitting room. Helping himself to some of the excellent tea and selecting a delicate-looking pastry from a serving tray, he joined the festivities. He circulated among the guests, offering a smile and an occasional comment about Atta being chosen by Allah to lead the future Caliphate. His whispered comments often drew a surprised look, but not one guest seemed to totally reject the idea.

A few hours later the party was over. Atta's guests had left to prepare for their return journeys. They would not meet as a group again. Like their arrival, their return trips would be undertaken in a variety of ways. Even terrorists understood the need for operational security. For instance, Abu Bakhr al-Suwani would leave Masuleh disguised as a lowly trader … leading a camel bearing a load of firewood. He would change disguises and modes of travel several times as he made his way back to Syria.

Hakim shared his discovery of Hadi's betrayal with Atta. Atta's eyes flashed in anger upon hearing the news.

"And you certain the dog spoke to no one of our plans?" Atta demanded.

"Before tonight, I cannot say. But I slit the dog's throat before he could tell anyone of anything he might have overheard tonight," Hakim replied.

Atta thought about that for a few moments before he spoke again.

"Before tonight is of no consequence. Our plans were not discussed in detail before tonight. I see no reason to change our plans now. Allah's will be done."

Hakim nodded, "As you say, they can know nothing of what you discussed tonight."

Atta sighed. "It is a shame that Hadi turned out to be such a traitorous dog. He was a wonderful gardener."

"Too bad," Hakim agreed. "And now, if you will permit me, I will retire for the night."

"Just a moment, Hakim." Atta was thinking. "Was not this gardener, Hadi, recommended to us by our friend from the cafe, Salim Abbas?"

Hakim thought for a moment. "Yes, he was. But it may be nothing more than a coincidence. Hadi was new to Masuleh. Abbas has lived here for many years."

"You may be right," Atta spoke, his eyes cold and dark.

"Yet, I never would have suspected Hadi of being a traitor and a spy. Let us dig a little deeper to be sure. Allah would be most displeased if his servants were less than diligent in their work."

Hakim nodded. "It will be done."

"Then I will say good night, Hakim." Atta turned and went through the door into the room that was his sleeping quarters. It was an eventful day and he was feeling rather tired. He needed a good night's sleep.

CHAPTER 17

Julie let out an involuntary gasp of surprise. What she discovered on the laptop's encrypted hard drive was simply astounding.

The hard drive was encrypted using the AES-256 algorithm which, realistically speaking, is unbreakable. Its weakness is the encryption key ... a 77-digit number. So, the question really becomes one of where the laptop's owner hid the encryption key.

It is virtually impossible for most people to memorize a 77-digit number. So, often the key is encrypted with a simple password and then stored next to the data on the hard drive. Unless the password is very long, say fifty characters, it is far simpler to crack the password than the encryption key. Most civilians, including many terrorists, believe an eight-character password is long enough. Some might even go fifteen or sixteen characters to play it safe.

However, Julie was very good at her job. She'd cracked the password using a rainbow table, a precomputed table for reversing cryptographic hash functions such as password hashes, in less than 15 minutes. Once she had access to the data, Julie used a translator program to translate the Arabic into English.

Julie had sifted through files containing propaganda for jihadi organizations and several motivational videos by Osama bin Laden. There were also manuals on how to make bombs, a terrorist's guide to torture techniques, instructions for stealing cars, and on using disguises. It was all typical stuff. Then, she began checking the laptop's hidden files.

"Oh shit!" Julie exclaimed as she came across a hidden file named Brookstone. Julie had seen the cell phone number found in the notebook. She began browsing through the file documents and spotted a reference to Michael Stanley. That was the name of the American hacker who'd been burned alive in Syria a few weeks ago! As Julie read more, it became clear that Stanley was working on software for someone named Rahman Atta. Then, a few pages later, there was a notation that all was ready for the transfer to "the American woman's" account.

Was the woman mentioned Brookstone? Julie wondered. Seemed likely.

Still browsing Julie came across another folder named North Korea which contained information about some kind of a purchase. There was no description of what was being purchased. Only a reference to 10 packages ready to be delivered. Another file contained a list of 10 American citizens, some of whom were of Middle Eastern descent and some of whom were not. This file mentioned a new training camp in Somalia. Julie felt a chill. She was not sure why. Terrorists often opened training camps. They transferred money often enough … despite U.S. efforts to freeze their assets whenever possible.

"Shit," Julie exclaimed again. Her mind had just made the connection between the ten U.S. Citizens and the ten North Korean packages.

Julie began shaking. She did not know what the ten packages were, but if terrorists were talking with a rogue nuclear state, it could not be good. She needed to tell Peterson what she'd found. He could take it to that slimeball boss of his. Julie copied all the pertinent data to a secure jump drive. Then on impulse, she made a second copy. Securing her workstation, she left the clean room and hurried down the hall. Taking the elevator up two floors, she made her way to Peterson's office.

Peterson stared at the files on his computer screen. He was shocked by what he was looking at. Julie Spencer had presented him with the data she had extracted from the laptop and it was worrying, to say the least. He could not believe what his eyes were seeing. There was more evidence of a connection between Josephine Warren-Brookstone and someone in Afghanistan or Iran. It was obvious to Peterson that she was the "American woman" mentioned in the file and the transfer of money to the "woman's account" did not bode well.

There was also this software program created by the American fugitive, Michael Stanley. Stanley, a recent convert to Islam, had somehow ended up in the hands of a new Islamic group based in Syria ... and had been burned alive by them.

This information might possibly explain his death at the hands of these terrorists in Syria. Stanley was probably executed in lieu of payment for services rendered.

What kind of software program did he write for these terrorists? Could it have to do with the money transfers mentioned? That would fit the narrative.

There was also information on a new training camp in Somalia. That, coupled with the ominous mention of these ten possible suicide bombers who, if the file was correct, were all U.S. Citizens was alarming enough. But then add to that the information about a probable weapons purchase from North Korea and Peterson did not like the sound of that at all.

Several years ago, the Mossad had blown up a nuclear plant North Korea was building in Syria. A rogue nuclear state selling anything to Islamic terrorists was not something Peterson was happy to hear about.

And all this seemed connected to one individual based in Iran named Rahman Atta. It was so crazy. Yet, there had been a good bit of chatter lately connecting the Taliban with the North Korean Department of State Security. William shook his head.

Holy shit! What in the fucking blue blazes was this Atta character up to!

Julie had also done something very odd ... she had gone one step further, warning him to be careful.

"I have a funny feeling about this," Julie said when she'd handed him the thumb drive, her voice almost a whispered.

"This thumb drive contains a copy of everything I have uncovered from the laptops, the cell phone SIM card, and the stuff from the notebooks. Please keep it safe. I don't mind telling you this scares the hell out of me." Julie paused. She knew she could be treading on thin ice with where her mind was going.

"Terrorists funding the Brookstone's campaign as part of some crazy attack on the U.S.? It's hardly conceivable! This will be bad ... very bad! Her campaign will not want word of this connection to get out. And, with these terrorists involved, if it's true, people could get killed." Julie paused again, biting her lip.

"And, coordinating that with some possible weapons buy from North Korea? I'm thinking dirty bombs or something. It's like a crazy movie plot!"

William nodded in agreement. "It's almost beyond belief!"

Julie's next words caught William Peterson completely off guard.

"There is more. I don't trust Mike Stanton. It's not just a feeling, there's more than that."

William looked up at Julie in amazement. "What the hell do you mean?"

"He asked me to dinner at Le Diplomate the other night. And, he told me to keep him posted on what we found on these laptops"

"So? Of course, he wants to be in the loop on this. It's his job!" Peterson ignored the part about the dinner invitation. He knew Mike Stanton considered himself to be something of a lady's man.

"I know that," Julie replied. "But that restaurant? Le Diplomate is a favorite meeting place for Josephine Warren-Brookstone's people and other members of her Party here in D.C. It is hardly a place I would expect Stanton to go. Except," she paused. "Stanton thinks he is some kind of player. He's a snake in the grass and I don't trust him."

William frowned. "I don't know …."

Julie went on, "I have another copy, a backup, of the thumb drive locked away in my office."

Peterson took a minute to absorb all this. "Okay. I am going to talk to Stanton. I will be careful," he added seeing the look on Julie's face. "Give me your personal cell phone number. I will call you now so you will have my number. If I need to get in touch with you, I want to be able to do so."

William Peterson was even more perplexed after leaving Stanton's office. Peterson was not sure exactly why ... but he had not told Stanton everything.

Was it Julie's warning? Or was it that he agreed that Stanton was acting a bit odd.

Peterson had reported that there was a real possibility that someone, probably a Rahman Atta, in Iran was planning a major terrorist attack on U.S. targets. And, that the plan involved ten packages, possibly dirty bombs, purchased from North Korea. He also told Stanton there was evidence that Rahman Atta, was also training ten recruits, all U.S. citizens, at a new training camp in Somalia.

Stanton already knew about Brookstone's cell phone number in the notebook. Peterson did not mention the additional evidence of a connection between Josephine Warren-Brookstone and this Rahman Atta. Peterson simply told Stanton that he might have additional information, but needed a bit more time to verify things before he could share them.

Stanton seemed angry about that at first. He seemed less concerned about the possible terrorist attack with North Korean connections than with the possible connection between Brookstone and Islamic terrorism. Stanton tried digging for more ... but Peterson held firm.

"I didn't even want to mention it ... until I know there is some grain of truth behind these possible connections. If they don't pan out it would be bad for both of us if anything leaked."

Finally, Stanton reluctantly agreed. Peterson could tell he dearly wanted to know what it was.

"I should know shortly ... a couple of days at most"

Peterson had reassured Stanton. "I will let you know as soon as I am sure."

At least, Peterson knew, the CIA wheels would begin turning in response to the threat of the attack. A new terrorist training camp in Somalia would not be too hard to verify or even take out if needed. They would need to dig into the North Korean connection and try to discover exactly what the 10 packages were.

And, Peterson needed a little time to dig deeper into this Brookstone - Atta campaign connection.

Mike Stanton paced back and forth behind his desk. His face was flushed. He was angry and frustrated; a bad combination. He'd already notified his superiors of the probable attack on the United States with North Korean involvement. That part was covered. He'd just returned from Connor's office.

Director Connors had sat behind his desk as Stanton briefed him on the intelligence gathered from the notebook and electronics the SEAL team had recovered in Afghanistan.

"Is this threat credible?" Connors asked.

"Definitely," Stanton replied. "We can connect way too many dots for it not to be."

"No chance it's all a smoke screen?" Connor's asked, still not wanting to accept that.

"I don't think so," Stanton went on. "All available intelligence points to this being a viable threat by a radical Islamic terrorist group. The leader seems to be based in Iran and we are pretty sure we've identified him as a man named Rahman Atta. We do have the recent execution in Syria of Michael Stanley, that computer hacker who recently converted to Islam and fled the country. And, it is also very probable that the attack will involve ten "packages" originating in North Korea. That jives with the 10 U.S. citizens who are reportedly at a camp in Somalia. We have no real intelligence about what the packages are. Peterson thinks maybe dirty bombs. I tend to agree … given North Korea's history as a rogue nuclear state. There has also been a good deal of chatter connecting certain radical Islamic leaders with the North Koreans."

"Shit," mutter Director Connors.

"What we don't know is how the fuck they are planning to smuggle the ten Americans back into the U.S. They do have passports, but I doubt that they will try to fly them in on commercial airlines."

"I'd guess they are planning to smuggle the suicide bombers and these packages across our southern border with Mexico," Connors observed. "Canada is less likely. Canadian customs would be much tougher. Our border with Mexico is pretty much wide open."

But, Connors knew they could handle this. Plots like these were always being discovered and shut down. That is what the NSA, CIA, and FBI were there for. Though he had to admit, nothing on this scale this had previously been discovered. This had the potential to make the damage from 9/11 pale in comparison … dirty bombs set off in ten U.S. cities! That would be catastrophic.

Director Connors reached for his phone.

"We need to alert all agencies including the border patrol. I'll get a satellite tasked to take some eye-in-the-sky pictures of Somalia. Let's see if we can identify this new camp. We should be able to spot it without too much trouble."

"Are you going to notify the President?" Stanton asked.

"Guess I'd better," Connors muttered. "Shit! He's not going to like this one bit."

Stanton managed an appropriate response. What had him worried was that he suspected Peterson was holding out on him. Peterson knew something about the Brookstone presidential campaign and was hesitant to tell him. This could simply mean he was not sure enough to say anything. But, it could also mean Peterson did not trust him. The former was not a big deal. The latter meant that Stanton could have a problem.

"Okay." Mike got to his feet. "I'll head down to the tech guys and see if anything else has surfaced from the electronics grabbed in Afghanistan that might help us." He headed toward the office door.

"Let me know right away if there is anything else, Mike."

"Will do!"

On the way to the tech labs, Mike entered the Men's room. After ensuring he was alone, he reached for the cell in his sports coat pocket and punched a speed dial number. He lifted the phone to his ear and waited.

Richard Sexton was sitting down at his desk with a fresh cup of coffee when his cell phone rang. Josephine sat across from him. She had come into Richard's office to discuss a campaign issue.

Richard saw the caller ID and indicated to Josephine that he should answer the call. Josephine nodded and sat back in her chair to wait.

"Hello Mike," Richard answered, the disdain evident on his face. "What's up?"

"We have a problem," Stanton replied. "My operative, William Peterson, has some new evidence tying your boss to terrorists in Iran and Afghanistan. I don't know what that evidence is and he won't tell me … which means he feels he needs to dig deeper and verify what he has first. If he is doing that, he must think it is real." There was a pause. "He is pretty good at his job, Richard."

"Shit," Richard muttered. Josephine sat up, suddenly interested in the conversation. "Mike, my boss is here. I am putting you on speaker phone. She knows we have talked." Richard set his smartphone to the speaker and laid it down on the desk.

"Mike, this is Josephine. Please tell me exactly what the problem is." Mike Stanton did exactly that, starting with the SEAL operation several weeks earlier. Stanton explained the recovery of the laptops, notebooks and cell phone from the village in northern Afghanistan. He described the discovery of her cell phone number in a notebook and the resulting preliminary investigation. Stanton made it clear he could not have stopped the process. But, that he did order Peterson to keep any investigation efforts discreet. This meant that currently, it was only Peterson and the data recovery technician, Julie Spencer, who had access or had seen the information. Josephine listened, asking a question here and there to clear up a detail. When Stanton had finished, Josephine looked at Richard. He nodded.

"Mike, thanks for bringing this to us. I appreciate it and we take good care of our friends. I'll handle this problem. You relax and keep yourself clear of whatever happens. You know what your subordinate reported to you and that is it. Understand?"

"I understand completely," Mike replied. "And, I will do whatever I can to help."

"Just stay clear. We will be in touch." Josephine ended the call. She sat thinking for a few minutes as Richard sipped his coffee, waiting.

"Richard, we will have our benefactor take care of this.

This is his mess and he will have to clean to up. There are only a few weeks before the election and we can't get involved. To borrow an often-used cliché, we will need plausible deniability. And besides, our benefactor will not want to have the entire weight of the U.S. executive branch brought to bear on him once we do win the election."

Richard nodded. Josephine had taken Richard into her confidence after Mike Stanton had approached him and Richard had then confronted her. Richard knew someone in the Middle East was bankrolling her campaign. He did not know who and did not want to know. He wanted "plausible deniability" for his own protection as well.

"Okay then. I will go back to my office and give him a call," Josephine stated. Rising from her chair, she left Richard's office.

Richard sat back in his chair and took another swallow of coffee. He shook his head.

I hope she knows what the hell she is doing, he thought.

Josephine felt a cold chill run down her spine. She had finished her call to the man she had taken to calling her benefactor. It had struck her recently that he had a Middle Eastern accent. Now, with what Mike Stanton had said on the phone, there was little doubt. The man had listened, asking only a few pertinent questions. When she had finished explaining the situation, he spoke with little emotion.

"It was good that you called, Ms. Brookstone. You will contact this Mr. Stanton and find out more about this operative and where he lives, and this Julie Spencer. I have contacts in your country who will handle this. They will also take care of Mr. Stanton. We simply cannot trust him to keep silent once we eliminate the other threats. He poses too much of a danger to our plans. And, we certainly cannot have him blackmailing our President."

Josephine suddenly felt an icy chill. This man was talking about murdering Stanton and his operatives like he was talking about the weather.

What the hell have I gotten myself into? she wondered to herself. But, it was way too late to back out now and she knew it. Her benefactor had been true to his word and her campaign war chest was already a little over $50 million in his debt.

She heard herself say, "Okay, if that is what needs to happen. I will get you the information you requested."

"Good," the voice replied. "When you have it call this number," giving her a 10-digit number.

She wrote it down, noticing it had a Washington, D.C. area code.

"Give the person who answers the information and then do nothing else. Concentrate on winning your American presidential election."

"Yes ... yes. I will do that," Josephine replied. The line went dead. She had noticed the reference to "our President." It had struck a strange chord in her mind, but she dismissed it. Once she was the President, she would handle this Middle Easterner, whoever he was.

Atta put that cell phone down and picked up another one. He hit a speed dial number. It rang a few times before being answered.

"Yes." It was Hakim.

"We have a couple of problems which need correcting in Washington, D.C."

"What has happened?" Hakim asked.

"When Al-Wahsari was murdered in Afghanistan, the American's got hold of some information connecting us to the woman, Brookstone. They cannot have much, but we need to stop it from going any further."

"I see," Hakim replied. "Surely, Al-Wahsari would have known better than to keep detailed information where it could be found, so I too suspect they cannot have much."

"Let us hope so. We have come too far to stop now. But, there is a senior member of the American CIA who is trying to make political gains with the information his operative brought to him. He has approached the woman, Brookstone, with it. The infidel dog has told his operative to await further instructions from him before proceeding, so we have a short window in which to act."

"And what is the American dog's name?" Hakim asked.

"His name is Michael Stanton. The Brookstone woman will get his operatives' names and addresses. There is a man, a CIA operative who works for this Stanton, and a woman, a technician, who has seen the information as well. I told Brookstone to call one of the cell phone numbers our brother in Washington, D.C. uses for such things. She will give him the information on Stanton, his operative, and the woman. You should have him put his most loyal warrior on this. It must be soon."

"It will be so," Hakim responded. "It is the will of Allah." Hakim was confident. He had the perfect assassin for this job and she was already in Washington, D.C. She had never failed. These three problems would soon be eliminated.

CHAPTER 18

When Zev Weiss entered the cafe, it was near dark. Salim Abbas had been out for a stroll enjoying Masuleh's cool evening air.

"Nadir, my child, are you down here?" Weiss made his way to the back of the cafe where the stairs went up to their second floor living quarters.

She must be sleeping, he thought to himself. He started up. Rachel used the room to the left at the top of the stairs. Weiss turned right down the short hallway toward his room. He paused. It was too quiet. Weiss noticed the small closet to his right in which their radio set was hidden. The door was not quite closed. He froze. It was always closed. The radio was kept hidden in a reed basket and covered with linens. When in use, a thin wire antenna that ran up the back wall and along the edge of the roof was connected to a terminal on the back of the radio. The wire was well concealed and so was very hard to see.

Weiss reached for the closet door handle. A sharp pain exploded at the base of his skull. Weiss dropped to the floor like a sack of rice, out cold. Hakim worked quickly, binding Weiss' hands behind his back. He then went to work on the unconscious man's ankles. Rachel, who Hakim knew as Nadir, was already trussed up and lying on the floor in her room.

Zev Weiss slowly recovered his wits. It took him a minute to take in his surroundings. He was sitting in a wooden chair in what seemed to be a small dirt-floor hut. He could see out the open door. Zev realized he was probably in a goat herder's hut, somewhere in the peaks above Masuleh.

He tried to move and discovered his arms were bound to the chair back. His ankles and knees were bound to the chair's legs. He literally could not move. A sound made him look to his left. It was Rachel Weinstein. She lay on the floor, arms and legs bound, a gag stuffed in her mouth. Zev could see a large bruise purpling the left side of her face. Her eyes were open and she looked terrified.

Suddenly the small door frame was filled as a man stepped into the hut. It was Hakim. He walked over to a small table that stood in the corner of the hut and when he returned to stand in front of Zev, he was holding a knife with a wicked-looking long, curved blade. Zev felt his insides turn to water. Hakim spoke. His tone of voice was almost cordial ... conversational.

"My good friend Salim Abbas. Who are you? Before you speak, you should know that Hadi is dead. I slit the treacherous dog's throat myself. I found him listening in on our meeting with an electronic bugging device. An interesting tool for a gardener, is it not?"

Zev remained silent, working hard to gather his courage for what he knew was going to come. Hakim continued, his voice still pleasant.

"You recommended Hadi to our mutual friend, Rahman, did you not?"

Weiss responded to this. "I'd heard he was a good gardener. All who knew Hadi said it was so. Rahman was looking for a gardener. I know nothing of any bugging devices!"

"That is not quite true, my friend. Rahman was not looking for a gardener. He hired Hadi as a gardener only on the suggestion from you. It is such a shame, Salim ... if that is your true name. Hadi was an exceptional gardener."

Hakim stepped closer and pressed the point of the knife against Zev's chest. It was very sharp.

"I did find your radio, Salim. It is an interesting radio for a café owner to have. So well hidden. It makes me wonder why?"

Weiss remained silent. He knew they were both dead already. He was determined to give Hakim no more information than he already had.

"You will talk to me, Salim. I wish to know who you know in the United States. We have plans there after all, and I can leave nothing to chance."

Zev fought to keep the fear from registering in his voice. While he was terrified, he was also a soldier. He knew the risks when he took this assignment.

"Do what you must. I will say nothing."

Hakim smiled. "I would expect nothing less." Hakim walked over to where Rachel was lying on the floor of the hut. He slid the knife into his belt. Reaching down, he grabbed Rachel by the ankles, dragging her over in front of Zev. He removed her gag.

"You can scream all you want to here in these mountains. Nobody will hear you, and if they do, they will say nothing." Hakim paused as he withdrew the knife from his belt. He smiled, almost pleasantly.

"But you will hear the screams, Salim. I will ask you again who you are? And, why you are in Masuleh? Each time you fail to answer to my satisfaction, I will cut off a piece of this woman."

Rachel could not stifle the gasp that left her lips. She too was a soldier. Rachel had seen much in the way of violence and pure evil as an agent for Mossad. She would not let this terrorist beat her.

Rachel spat in Hakim's direction. She turned toward Zev, "Tell this terrorist dog nothing. Let him do his worst. It will be over soon enough."

"The woman is incorrect in that it will be over soon. Tell me what I want to know and I promise you both a quick and merciful death. Allah is merciful after all." Hakim paused. "So, Salim Abbas, who are you?"

Weiss steeled himself, "I will tell you nothing."

Salim shrugged. He reached over and grabbed Rachel Weinstein by the hair. The knife slashed down fast. Rachel screamed. Her right ear lay on the floor at Zev's feet.

"I will kill you … you son-of-a-bitch!"

"Who are you, Salim Abbas?"

"Fuck you!"

The knife flashed again. Another scream and Rachel's left ear lay beside her right one.

"I will start with her fingers next."

Zev gathered himself. "You will pay for your sins. Our people will hunt you down and kill you."

"Do you work for the Mossad? The CIA?" Weiss stared hard at the floor of the hut, a look of grim determination on his sweating face.

Hakim shrugged. It was going to be a long night. He would get the information he wanted. He had the time.

CHAPTER 19

The cargo ship, Hamad, now flying under a Liberian flag to disguise itself, steamed toward the Venezuelan seaport of Punta Fijo. The sun had recently disappeared beyond the horizon. The night was quiet and the sea calm. A full bright moon gave the water a silvery glow. It was all quite beautiful.

Achmed Suhani plotted a careful course designed to avoid major shipping lanes. It was tricky. He did not want to draw attention to his vessel but understood the need to appear normal to any observers.

With the help Allah, they would succeed, he thought to himself. Suhani did not know what the North Koreans had hidden in his cargo hold. He did not want to know. Whatever it was, it lay concealed under a full load of 80-lb. bags of concrete mix. He did know, however, that he did not want his ship boarded by either the U. S. Navy or the U.S. Coast Guard. His secret cargo was important to defeating the western devils and Suhani assumed it was explosive devices. He knew better than to ask any questions. And, after all, he was being well paid. Allah was

209

most generous to his loyal servants.

Suhani was tired. He turned to his Chief Mate and grunted. "I am going to get some sleep. Maintain this course and speed. Wake me in six hours."

"Yes, Captain," the Chief Mate replied. "Do you wish me to have anything sent to your cabin?"

"Thank you but no. That is not necessary. I am tired and just need a few hours of sleep." The captain left the bridge and made his way to his cabin.

It had been a smooth voyage so far. If it was the will of Allah, it would continue to be so.

Arik Daniel was back at his desk pouring over charts showing the major shipping routes from the North Korean port of Nampo. He was checking shipping routes from the Yemeni port of Hodeida as well as the port of Bandar Abbas in Iran and jumped in his seat when the phone rang, picking up the phone on the first ring.

"Daniel."

They repeated the same code-in procedure used on the earlier call. It was correct, the authentication completed.

"What did you find out?"

"According to our assets in the field, the Hamad left the port of Nampo with 20,000 tons of bagged concrete mix bound for Venezuela. It was to stop at the port of Bandar Abbas and take on 5,000 tons of oil pipeline materials, also bound for Venezuela. According to the manifest, the pipeline materials are headed to Punta Fijo."

Daniel frowned. "But we know they never entered the port at Bandar Abbas. So, whatever is on that ship had to have been loaded in North Korea. And, with all the effort put into appearing legit, I would suspect something besides concrete is in that cargo hold."

"It looks like that must be the case. I would also suspect that whatever it is, it lies buried under all those bags of concrete mix. North Korea has always been a thorny proposition at best. If they've sold something to an Islamic terrorist group, it is not good. Especially as it seems the destination is somewhere in the Americas."

"Right!" Daniel decided. "I am going to notify the Mossad. And, since it is heading toward the Caribbean and Venezuela, I will notify the CIA as well. Might all prove to be nothing ... but my gut does not think so."

"I would agree. Anyway, better safe than sorry." The phone went dead.

Director Connors sat at his desk pouring over the report he had requested just the day before. The report, put together by a team of analysts, outlined all the material surrounding the terrorist plot uncovered by SEAL Team 5. It was scary stuff to be sure. But, the CIA, together with the FBI and NSA, handled these kinds of terrorist plots on a routine basis. Most of the time ... when they were successful ... the foiled plots remained out of the news and the public remained blissfully unaware. That was simply the world in which we currently lived. Americans could usually sleep at night because of these agencies. They were very good at their jobs.

These agencies existed to protect the American people. As far as Connors was concerned, these two agencies needed to remain above the pettiness of politics. He worked very hard to ensure the CIA remained apolitical ... concerned only with the safety of the American people. If political partisanship or corruption raised its ugly head, Connors squashed it immediately. He owed no favors and was respected by both parties as a fair-minded professional.

But, this terrorist plot really got under Connors' skin. Its scope was massive, and it must have been a long time in planning. The idea of cooperation between Iran, al Qaeda, the Taliban and North Korea was very scary. The fact that the CIA had only recently gotten wind of this plot was evidence of patience and tight operational security. That was troubling in and of itself. But Connors could not shake the gut feeling that they were still missing something. Something felt odd about all this. There simply had to be more ... to justify such a complex plot. The question was ... what were they missing!

The intercom on Connors' desk buzzed to life. It was his administrative assistant.

"We've received a call from an Arik Daniel at Seawatch." Connors was very familiar with the private intelligence agency and had dealings with them on several previous occasions.

"Yes?"

"I think you should talk to Mr. Daniel yourself," his assistant continued. "He is being very insistent ... says it is an urgent matter involving Islamic terrorists and a connection to North Korea."

"Alright, put him through." Connors reached for his phone.

"Son of a bitch," Connors exclaimed. The phone conversation with Arik Daniel had not been overly long ... however, it had been interesting. Daniel had laid out his facts and then, went on to include his "hunches." It had all fit the evidence as well as the narrative. To Connors, it all made sense.

The CIA had been on high alert since Stanton had

briefed him on the intelligence gathered by SEAL Team 5 on their raid in Afghanistan. All American intelligence agencies were busy searching for anything to help connect the many dots. The 10 American jihadists, a training camp in Somalia, the 10 packages and their probable connection with North Korea. And, now the Hamad, and its unusual activities as reported by Seawatch ... all pieces of the puzzle. The intelligence game was like trying to put together a thousand-piece jigsaw puzzle that had ten thousand pieces ... knowing that not all the pieces would fit and trying to determine which ones mattered and which ones were not important.

Connors, if he'd been a betting man, would have bet that those ten packages Stanton had referred to were on the Hamad, and were now approaching the Caribbean Ocean. They were destined for Punta Fijo, Venezuela on route to the Mexican border. Connors hit the button on his intercom.

"Linda, get me the President and Rear Admiral Spence at Naval Special Warfare Command on the phone. I want to talk to them ten minutes ago. And, I want William Peterson and Mike Stanton in my office ASAP!" He paused. "And Linda, better get me the Coast Guard Commander as well."

"Yes sir, right away sir" Linda replied. The intercom went dead. Her boss's tone had been serious. She wasted no time.

Connors sat back in his chair. He knew his hunch was right. Armchair intelligence experts and the media always had the benefit of 20/20 hindsight. The intelligence officer in the field did not.

The intercom on Director Connors' desk crackled to life. Linda's voice spoke.

"I've got President Hardeman and Admiral Spence on

the phone. Still working on Stanton and Peterson."

"Thanks, Linda. Let me know about Stanton and Peterson."

CHAPTER 20

Fatima Hadhari lived alone in a small one-bedroom apartment on Old Briggs Chaney Rd. Her apartment was a short walk from the Islamic Society of the Washington Area. She was not a member. But, living in this area allowed her to blend in well with other members of the Muslim community in Washington, D.C.

The apartment was sparsely but comfortably furnished. A table and two chairs stood in the kitchen. A small radio and a laptop sat on the kitchen counter. A small couch and a comfortable old wingback chair shared the living area with a well-used vanity. Her bedroom contained a full-size bed with a comfortable mattress, a bedside table with a lamp and an alarm clock. There was also a chest of drawers in the corner.

The most lavishly furnished area of her apartment was her clothes closet. Being able to alter and disguise her appearance was an essential part of her profession. Fatima owned a wide selection of clothing. She would have no problem dressing for any occasion.

Fatima spent most of her free time working out. She

alternated between a kickboxing gym down the street and a local 24/7 fitness center two blocks west. She did not have to work very often and therefore, had a great deal of free time. As a result, she was in excellent shape. When she did work, the compensation was very good and living a simple life, the money she earned went a long way.

At 6:45 AM, Fatima's alarm clock went off, the loud buzzer rousing her from a deep sleep. She always slept well. Last night had been no exception. Pushing back the bed covers, she swung her legs off the bed, sitting for a minute on the edge of the bed. After a quick stretch, she stood and headed for the bathroom to empty her bladder.

Proceeding to the kitchen, Fatima put a kettle of water on the stove for tea. She was still naked. Fatima had learned since coming to the United States, that this was a very comfortable way to sleep. Of course, her employer would not have approved of her lack of modesty. But this did not bother her at all. Fatima was not a particularly devout Muslim. She would never wear a burka ... or submit to the will of some disgusting fat pig of a man, Muslim or otherwise!

Fatima walked over to the laptop sitting on the kitchen counter. Logging into her MySpace account, she checked to see if she had any new messages. Fatima created her MySpace account under the pseudonym Aisha Kuwadi. She smiled to see that she had a message from her dear old uncle in Kuwait. The message meant that she had another job to do. She did enjoy her work.

Fatima was Syrian. She had come to the United States four years earlier at the age of twenty-two. Hakim had embedded her in a group of Syrian refugees who were fleeing the Syrian government's oppressive regime. Fatima, was in fact, was fleeing nothing.

Hakim recruited her at the age of seventeen. Fatima's parents were killed during a violent crackdown on protesters by the Syrian government. Her parents were part of a group of protesters calling for several political reforms and the reinstatement of civil rights. They also called for an end to martial law, which had been imposed during a proclaimed state of emergency back in 1963. The protesters were dealt with harshly, the government using armed military force. Fatima's parents were shot by Syrian soldiers during the erupting violence.

Fatima found herself orphaned and surviving on the streets of Damascus as best she could … part-time beggar … part-time thief. She'd tried to steal Hakim's money purse while he was distracted by a scuffle that occurred one afternoon in the open-air market. Hakim often frequented the market to buy his favorite tea. Fatima was good … but not that good!

Hakim, who was no stranger to surviving on the streets himself, caught her by the arm as she tried to make good her escape. He was about to turn her over to the authorities, which might well have ended Fatima's life. But, Hakim saw something in Fatima's eyes that caused him to pause. He saw something in her that he was looking for. She was young and tough and filled with hatred. And, she was intelligent. Once bathed, it turned out Fatima was also quite pretty.

While Hakim was a devout Muslim, he was also pragmatic. He certainly believed that women should remain in their proper place … according to the teachings of the Prophet and the Hadith. But, he understood that an attractive young woman could also be a valuable tool in certain situations. Especially when those situations occurred in the hated West. So, Hakim took Fatima under his tutelage. He sent Fatima to various training camps in Yemen, Somalia, Saudi Arabia, and Iran where it was discovered she had a real knack for killing. Fatima's preferred weapons were knives and she became very good with them. She also excelled with poisons and mastered several secretive methods for their delivery. Even Hakim was sometimes amazed at how her hatred allowed her to kill as easily as she did. She killed without feeling or remorse! Not just westerners, which he could well understand. But, she killed Muslims as well. Men, women, she simply did not care. She killed whomever he told her to kill. She would prove to be very useful.

Opening MySpace, Fatima read the message from her dear uncle in Kuwait. She knew that her "Dear Uncle" from Kuwait was Hakim. It was a short message, but it told her everything she needed to know for the present moment.

I have learned that three family members in your area are now in very poor health. I hope you will be able to find the time to help with caring for them. I am sending money to help ease your financial burden and aid in their care. May Allah's will be done.

Fatima smiled. She replied to her uncle's message.

Dearest Uncle, Of course, I will do everything I can to help. I will check in on them tomorrow evening. The money is appreciated and will be put to good use. Your loving niece, Aisha

Time to go to work. Fatima knew that tomorrow there

would be an envelope in her locker at the kickboxing gym. It would have the required information on the three sick family members. It would also contain $60,000 in cash. Fatima was no mindless suicide bomber to be wasted in an explosion on a street corner or in a coffee shop. She was a highly-skilled assassin.

Fatima never saw who left the communications and she never would. The envelopes were only delivered at night when the gym was typically empty. She made it a point to be nowhere near the gym during those hours. She prided herself a great deal on her professionalism and tradecraft. Hakim paid her $20,000 for each ill family member she took care of. It was more than enough to support her simple lifestyle. She was a soldier after all and did not need much. Her greatest reward was being able to kill more of her hated enemies.

A few days later, Mike Stanton walked into Le Diplomate. He headed straight to the bar. He needed a drink. While Stanton certainly had no compunction about doing whatever he needed to further his own career, this current situation was taking an ugly turn.

"How are you, Mr. Stanton?" It was Senga, a cute bartender who often flirted with Mike in a friendly way. "Can I get you a drink?"

"Please! Bourbon on the rocks. Make it a double, Senga. Thanks."

Stanton slid into a stool at the bar and surveyed the scene. It was early but the bar was still quite busy. He glanced up at the large flat panel TV mounted above the bar to his left. It was set to CNN. Some talking head was blabbering endlessly on about how great Josephine Warren-Brookstone was doing in the polls, stating that she was surely a shoe-in to win the election. The talking head went on with his pontification.

"Her opposing candidate, Benjamin Steele, is doing well enough with his base, but his position on immigration reform is unpopular with many Hispanic voters."

Stanton knew that Senator Steele liked to regularly point out that terrorists could easily blend in with illegal immigrants ... and use America's porous southern border to cross into the United States. Unfortunately, this argument seemed to fall on deaf ears. Brookstone's campaign team's answer was simply to run almost continuous ads describing Benjamin Steele as a racist. Stanton thought that was humorous since Steele was black.

Oh well, he thought. *One's man racist ...*

Of course, many in the media felt it their duty to repeat the racist mantra ad nauseum. It was just the sort of thing that some voters just loved to hear ... whether it was ridiculous or not, didn't seem to matter. Of course, the media also continued the non-stop apologies for whatever it was that the U.S. supposedly did to cause the radical Muslim world to hate us enough to want to murder innocent women and children.

What a bunch of crap, Stanton thought to himself. He knew that the radical Islamic mind simply did not think that way. What American policies caused the attack on September 11? Was it the policy of helping Osama bin Laden by providing him money, training, and weapons to fight the invading Russian army in Afghanistan? Stanton understood that, for the terrorists, it really was a religious war.

So many "experts" never bothered to read the fucking Koran, he reflected. They bought into that "Islam is a religion of Peace" crap and simply ignored all the evidence to the contrary. But that was not Stanton's problem, at least not

His problem was how to get through this current situation … and come out in a more powerful position on the other side.

Stanton again glanced around the bar. He noticed a very attractive young woman seated at a booth across the room. She looked to be in her late twenties and Middle-Eastern or Italian. She also seemed to be alone. The woman looked up, meeting his glance. There was a suggestion of a smile.

Jeez, Stanton thought to himself. *Now that's a damn good looking young woman! An hour or so in the sack with her would put a smile on my face.*

The woman checked her phone as a waiter brought her a glass of red wine. Well, nothing ventured nothing gained. Stanton signal the waiter who had served the young lady.

"Yes Sir, Mr. Stanton" the waiter inquired.

"I would like to buy the lady you served a second glass of whatever she ordered."

"Yes, sir. It is a very nice Merlot, Sir. Very nice."

Stanton knew that meant expensive. She had money and good taste. That was better yet!

"That's fine. Please bring her another glass in a few minutes."

"Yes, Sir." The waiter walked off.

A little while later Stanton saw the waiter arrive at the woman's booth with a second glass of wine. Surprised, she glanced in Stanton's direction as the waiter spoke to her, indicating the origination of the second glass. The woman looked directly at Stanton and smiled, tipping her glass in thanks.

Stanton smiled back.

In like Flynn, he thought to himself.

for the present.

His problem was how to get through this current situation … and come out in a more powerful position on the other side.

Stanton again glanced around the bar. He noticed a very attractive young woman seated at a booth across the room. She looked to be in her late twenties and Middle-Eastern or Italian. She also seemed to be alone. The woman looked up, meeting his glance. There was a suggestion of a smile.

Jeez, Stanton thought to himself. *Now that's a damn good looking young woman! An hour or so in the sack with her would put a smile on my face.*

The woman checked her phone as a waiter brought her a glass of red wine. Well, nothing ventured nothing gained. Stanton signal the waiter who had served the young lady.

"Yes Sir, Mr. Stanton" the waiter inquired.

"I would like to buy the lady you served a second glass of whatever she ordered."

"Yes, sir. It is a very nice Merlot, Sir. Very nice."

Stanton knew that meant expensive. She had money and good taste. That was better yet!

"That's fine. Please bring her another glass in a few minutes."

"Yes, Sir." The waiter walked off.

A little while later Stanton saw the waiter arrive at the woman's booth with a second glass of wine. Surprised, she glanced in Stanton's direction as the waiter spoke to her, indicating the origination of the second glass. The woman looked directly at Stanton and smiled, tipping her glass in thanks.

Stanton smiled back.

In like Flynn, he thought to himself.

A few hours later, Stanton followed the woman down a hallway on the third flow of an upscale Washington condo. He was enjoying the view. She was clearly in great shape. Together, they had walked to her condo complex only a few blocks away. These condos were often leased by politicians, lobbyists, or congressional staff members. The stunning woman, who had introduced herself as Fatima, suggested they come here ... rather than to a hotel or his place. It was closer, and she did not care much for hotels.

"You never know who was last in that bed," she had said with a distasteful grimace. Stanton was fine with her place. He wouldn't be stuck with the bill for any fancy hotel room.

Fatima unlocked the door to her condo and headed straight to the bedroom. Stanton followed her. On a side table stood a bottle of excellent Kentucky bourbon. Fatima excused herself, returning a few minutes later with a bucket of ice from the kitchen. She poured a bourbon on the rocks and handed it to Stanton who had made himself comfortable sitting on the edge of the king-sized bed.

"I don't want you to think badly of me. I don't do this kind of thing very often," Fatima smiled, her eyes dancing as she spoke.

"That's okay," Stanton responded. "I understand. I don't either. I have never met a woman quite like you."

"I just don't want you to get the wrong idea," Fatima smiled. "But, I like you and somehow, something seems to feel right about this."

"I feel it too baby." Stanton grinned. He took a swallow of the bourbon and reached for Fatima who laughing, danced away.

"Sorry. Let me just use the bathroom while you get undressed. I'll be right back."

Stanton nodded, smiling in anticipation. "Okay honey

… hurry back!"

Stanton began to remove his clothing. He heard the toilet flush and the sound of running water. He was standing there in his boxers when Fatima appeared in the bathroom door. She was wearing only black lace bikini panties. Fatima paused long enough in the doorway for Stanton to take in the exquisite view. He was now very excited. Fatima was one of the most beautiful women he'd been with.

The Gods must be smiling on me tonight, Stanton thought. His eyes were transfixed … dark hair, flawless skin, proud firm breasts with their dark nipples, a narrow waist and long legs. Clearly, Fatima exercised and took pride in how she looked. Her body was well-toned and finely muscled. She moved toward him like a big, graceful cat, reaching up with her left arm to encircle his neck. Stanton could smell her perfume, a mysterious, exotic Far East scent. She was intoxicating. Her lips brushed his cheek. Stanton inhaled, taking in the delicious scent of her dark hair. He had never been so aroused. His right hand reached up to cup her breast, thumb searching for her nipple. His thumb never made it.

Fatima's left hand covered his mouth with a tight grip.

"You will never have such as this, you foul infidel dog!" Fatima whispered through clenched teeth. Her right hand came from behind her back and thrust a dagger upward into his groin.

Searing pain raced up through Stanton's body and exploded into his brain. The dagger was withdrawn and thrust upward again. Stanton's body convulsed. Once again, the dagger was withdrawn. Fatima spun Stanton around, running the razor-sharp edge of the dagger across his throat. Blood gushed from the gash. Fatima released her hold and Stanton slid to the floor. His blood began to pool on the carpet around him. He gasped spasmodically once ... twice ... and then lay still.

Fatima tossed the dagger down onto Stanton's chest and peeled the latex glove from her right hand. In no hurry, she showered and then cleaned the tub. Dressing, she wiped down anything in the room she might have touched. With a final glance to be sure all was in order, Fatima gathered up her belongings and left. Several blocks away she tossed the latex glove into a street-side storm drain and disappeared into the quiet night.

CHAPTER 21

Peterson sat at the desk in his office at home. He was trying to find another explanation for the evidence Julie had extracted from the captured laptop's hard drives. He could not. To make matters worse, Julie had handed him the evidence along with a warning not to trust his immediate supervisor. Julie had based her warning on some kind of women's intuition. While his brain wanted him to disregard it, his gut would not let him.

The two girls were upstairs asleep. His wife was sipping tea while she read more of the newest Sheila Jackson novel in the next room. It was some Viking warrior romance novel with a picture of some hunky blond weightlifter on the cover. Peterson decided the guy was way too pretty to be a real Viking.

The ring of his cell phone interrupted his musings. The voice on the other end of the call was female. It sounded hesitant, scared, mysterious, and sexy as hell ... all at the same time.

"Is this William Peterson," the voice inquired.

"This is he," William responded. "and who am I

speaking with?"

"My name is Eva," the voice responded. "I was asked to contact you by an old friend of yours, Zev Weiss."

"Zev Weiss," Peterson heard himself repeat quietly. Now there was a name he had not heard in quite some time.

Eva continued, "You know him, I am correct? I have the right person?"

William felt himself being sucked in by her voice. The voice went on to explain that she was given his number by his old friend's daughter. Zev's daughter had contacted her because she lived in the Washington, D.C. area. The voice was mesmerizing ... hypnotic... it went on.

"I must admit I do not know Mr. Weiss very well at all. His daughter said that her father was in some serious trouble and really needed help." Peterson was intrigued. He had crossed paths with Zev Weiss on two occasions while traveling to and from Israel.

The first time had been in Tel Aviv. They had both been present at a joint security briefing attended by representatives of the CIA, Mossad, and MI6. After the meeting ended, they'd struck up an interesting conversation on great blues guitarists. Zev and William, as it turned out, were both big fans of Eric Clapton. They had continued the discussion over dinner and several cold beers.

Sometime later, they'd had a second chance meeting on a U.S Naval destroyer in the Indian Ocean. Peterson had been in Indonesia on CIA business and was hitching a ride, courtesy of the U.S Navy, to the United Arab Emirates. Peterson hated flying and loved traveling by sea. He sometimes reflected that he could have been very happy in the Navy. Fortunately, he often found the opportunity for such little excursions provided by his job. Zev Weiss, it turned out, was on the destroyer to make a rendezvous with a U.S. Submarine. The U.S. Navy was helping its ally, Israel, insert Weiss into Iran for a covert deep cover mission. Peterson doubted the Hardeman administration would have sanctioned such help. That had been many years ago. Peterson had since lost track of Zev.

'How do you know Zev Weiss?" Peterson asked.

"He is my uncle," the soft voice had replied. "His daughter is my cousin. But I have not seen them in many years."

There was a pause in the conversation. Eva seemed to be searching for something to say. Peterson waited.

"Look," she went on. "I know how crazy this sounds. Can you meet me in a public place at 7:00 tomorrow evening? I have some information to give you, a letter sent to me by my cousin. She says it is very important and will help Uncle Zev. I have no idea at all what this is all about. All I know is that it has something to do with a man named Mike Stanton.

William Peterson froze. "About Mike Stanton," he repeated.

"Yes," Eva went. "I don't know who he is but my cousin says you may know him. "

Indeed, I do know him, thought Peterson. "How did you get all this information?"

"My cousin sent me a package. It contained a note to me and an envelope I am to give to you." Eva paused. "I think the note was to give me enough information to convince you of the urgency of my uncle's troubles."

Peterson didn't reply. He was still trying to wrap his mind around this new twist. These last few days had started an interesting chain of events.

"I work in a coffee shop near the Mall. Can you meet me on the front steps of the Lincoln Memorial tomorrow at 7:00 p.m.?"

"I can do that," Peterson replied after a moment.

"Good. How will I know you?"

Peterson thought for a moment. "I will be wearing jeans and a gray sports coat," Peterson replied. "And my sunglasses." He suppressed the urge to add, "And a red carnation in my right lapel."

"Okay good. But please come alone. I am not sure what this is all about but it scares me."

"I will be alone," William heard himself reply. Fatima ended the call.

Tomorrow, number two, she thought!

It was getting late. William Peterson leaned back in his chair after ending the phone call. So much was happening so fast … it was hard to wrap his brain around it all. Clearly, the plot uncovered by JD and SEAL Team 5 was not only viable, it was real. Despite its almost fantastic scope, it was happening. Whoever hatched this plan was a maniacal genius and must have almost unlimited resources.

And now, Mike Stanton's name is dropped in a phone call with a Middle Eastern woman claiming to be the niece of a Mossad agent he had not seen in many years. And, this Mossad agent needed his help? It smelled to high heaven! Peterson was pretty sure it was a trap of some kind.

The part of this terrorist plot that concerned him most was the possibility that some Iranian terrorist mastermind was bankrolling a presidential candidate's campaign.

Talk about a Manchurian Candidate!

Despite the intricacies of this particular terrorist plot, American intelligence agencies were darn good at dealing with terrorist threats. The public had no idea how often plots such as these were discovered and foiled. Peterson knew that all agencies had been alerted to this probable terrorist attack. They were already bringing their considerable resources to bear on this. He had heard that the new training camp in Somalia had been identified. That camp would not be active much longer. A SEAL team, DELTA Force, or British SAS ... somebody would be tasked with taking it out soon enough. They would also intercept the 10 packages, whatever they were, as well. Peterson was not too concerned about that.

But, he had kept the intelligence on Josephine Warren-Brookstone from Stanton based on a gut feeling. As far as he knew, the only other person who knew about that was Julie Spencer. And, that was what worried him the most. Peterson was very sure that Brookstone and her campaign team, not to mention the mastermind behind all this, would want to keep things quiet. They would work hard to clean up any loose ends or possible breaches of their operational security. And now, there was this phone call! This thought caused an icy chill to run down his spine.

"Trap or not, I have to see where this phone call leads," he said to himself. He'd already decided he would keep the meeting tomorrow at the Lincoln Memorial with Zev's "niece" and see what this woman was up to. It was a public place and he would go armed.

Should be safe enough at the mall, he thought.

Once that was done, he would put all this intelligence and his thoughts together and take it to someone. At this point, he was not sure who to trust. Suddenly, Peterson knew what he had to do.

He reached for his cell phone and sent a text message to Julie. They had exchanged personal mobile phone numbers when she had brought the jump drive to him and warned him of her suspicions. It was a simple message that read,

You were right. You have been working too hard on this case. You should take a few days off. Remember to secure anything you were working on. Try to breathe some clean air for a bit. Don't forget, JD may call.

It was simple enough and might even pass as a harmless suggestion to take a few days off. The reference to JD would mean nothing to her now. But it might soon enough. Especially if things went the way he now thought they were heading.

Next, he got the jump drive Julie had given him from his office wall safe. He went to his desk and pulled a U.S.P.S. flat-rate mail pouch from a drawer. He did not need the drive, knowing what was on it. And, there was still a copy in Julie's safe as well as the records at the office. He needed to get it away and to someone he trusted. He addressed the mailer to JD Cordell, C/O Curtis Cordell in Knoxville, Tennessee. Peterson used a fictitious return address from somewhere in Idaho. Then taking a sheet of paper from his desk he wrote the message,

Important! Watch your step. Please be careful. Contact: Julie 2022181821. Use my name. William.

Taking the jump drive and folding the note around it, he slipped them into the mailer and sealed the pouch.

Sorry to bring you into this, JD, he thought, *but I don't know who else to trust.* And, JD was already involved whether he knew it yet or not. William got up and went over to a small walnut table against the wall on which he kept a bottle of good single malt scotch and a few glasses. He poured himself a drink. William did not feel too much like sleeping at the moment.

"Morning baby." William kissed his wife as she handed him a mug of hot black coffee. He took the coffee and sat down at the kitchen table where he poured cheerios into a bowl. He reached for the milk.

"Ginny, please come and sit down for a minute. I need to talk about something with you." Ginny finished loading the girl's breakfast dishes into the dishwasher and grabbed her coffee. She sat down at the small breakfast table across from her husband. Ginny was a striking redhead. JD had often teased Peterson about his predilection for redheads back in school. Peterson smiled at that thought. He was a lucky man.

"What's up, Will?" Ginny asked. She was the only one who ever called him Will.

"I have a favor to ask," he began, "I need you and the girls to go stay with my family in Knoxville for a few weeks. Mom and Dad will enjoy the visit with the girls. I have some work-related things to deal with here and I will not be very good company I am afraid."

"That sounds serious, Will, can you tell me what is going on?"

Peterson hesitated. It was CIA business and there was not much he could tell Ginny without violating protocols.

"I can't tell you much, Ginny, and you know why. I can tell you that I am worried and that I want you and the girls to be safe. I am involved with something big and it involves people who do not like to be crossed. It may even involve folks from the agency. I am going to be very busy trying to stop it and cover my ass at the same time. I need to know you and the girls are safe and out of harm's way ... so I won't have to worry."

Ginny took a sip of her coffee and looked at her

husband. William was a good man, and a good husband and father. He was not one to go off half-cocked.

"Okay, Will. We will do that. I will talk to the school and get some work they can do so the girls won't fall too far behind. When should we leave?"

"Pick them up at lunch," Will suggested. He got up from his chair and walked around the table to hug his wife. "Thanks, baby, I love you."

"I love you too, Will. Please be careful. Okay?"

"I will. I promise. Right now, I must go. Got a couple of things I need to do this morning. But first ..." He reached out for Ginny's hand and gave it a squeeze. Then giving his wife a kiss, he left the kitchen. When he returned from his office, he had two disposable cell phones in his hands. He handed one to Ginny.

"I will call you when I can. These are disposable cell phones in case my phone is tapped. They will be nearly impossible to track if we only use them to call each other and limit any conversation to family stuff. No shop talk."

Ginny forced a smile on her face. "That's pretty cloak and dagger, Will."

He almost laughed. "I know, baby. But, you married a spook!" He paused. "It's just a precaution, honey. Better safe than sorry. That's all."

With that, he got up and kissing her again, left. Ginny watched him go. She shivered, not quite sure why. It was plenty warm in the house. William liked it a bit on the warm side. She got up and went over to the kitchen counter to retrieve her cell phone. She dialed the number for the girl's school.

Peterson headed downtown in his Ford Mustang GT. Ginny and the girls would take the Explorer to Knoxville. Before going to bed that night, William had taken the time to unload his Glock, check the action and reload the magazines. He racked it, chambering a round and then ejected the magazine. Adding one more round to the magazine, he replaced it. Peterson slipped the Glock back into its holster. He carried his weapon because it was part of his job. He shot well enough at the agency range but he'd never drawn his gun as part of any mission. He was an intelligence analyst ... covert ops were not his typical fair. For some reason, he'd felt the need to make sure his firearm was in good working condition before meeting the woman at the Lincoln Memorial. William knew it was important to listen to those gut feelings.

Father Joe stood at the Sanctuary door of the Church wishing his congregation well as they left. He had delivered an especially thought-provoking sermon. Mai enjoyed it very much. Father Joe was an interesting priest. He'd started out working at a local Chevy dealership after high school and worked his way up to sales manager. Suddenly at the age of 42, he decided to become an Episcopalian priest. His sermons were usually very good ... with a common sense, real-world sort of approach to the point he was making.

Father Joe gave Mai a quick hug and shook Curtis' hand as the two of them passed through the big red doors. They made their way across the parking lot and toward the car. They always drove Curtis' old '65 Camaro SS to Church. Mai loved to drive that old car. The 383 Stroker with its four-speed manual transmission was a genuine thrill to drive. Curtis loved to tinker with it. It was his baby ... his retirement project. While the car was almost fifty years old, he kept that Camaro in showroom condition. It still ran like a scalded dog. Curtis sometimes teased Mai that the only reason she married him was for the car.

"Don't be silly, Curtis," she always teased back. "I married you before I knew about the car. The car is the reason I stay married to you." As they approached the Camaro, they heard a familiar voice.

"Curtis! Mai!" It was Bill and Nancy Peterson, William's parents. They were accompanied by a red-headed lady and two young girls. Both Bill and Nancy were grinning proudly, each holding the hand of one of their twin granddaughters.

"Bill! Nancy! How are you? Nice to see you. And who are these adorable young ladies?" Curtis responded. Mai went to Nancy and gave her a big hug. Then she gave Bill a friendly peck on the cheek.

'So nice to see you," Mai added. "And these beautiful girls are your granddaughters?"

"Yes, they are," Nancy exclaimed. "Curtis, Mai, you remember Ginny, William's wonderful wife?"

"Of course," Curtis and Mai both replied. Mai gave Ginny a big hug.

"And these two lovely young ladies are Becky and Janet," Bill added. Both girls giggled at that. Mai gave each girl a warm, welcoming hug. Curtis gave them each a high five. Both girls thought that was very cool.

"Ginny and the girls are visiting for a few weeks while William is working on a particularly important matter. It is so nice to have them here"

"I am sure it is," Curtis offered.

"We heard JD is at Ft. Bragg for a while," Nancy commented. "Will you get to see him while he is there?"

"You bet," Curtis responded. "He should be coming in next weekend."

"And, how is Annie?" Bill asked.

"Annie is off at school," Curtis replied. "She's driving all the boys crazy at Clemson." Mai punched Curtis in the arm.

"She is also studying very hard," Mai added.

"Of course, she is," Curtis agreed rubbing his arm. "She is doing very well. She is a finance major. Like William."

"That's great," Nancy smiled. The three ladies started chatting and fussing over the two twins. Bill nodded at Curtis and stepped off a bit. Curtis followed.

"So, William is working on something import at the agency?" Curtis inquired.

"So, it seems," Bill replied. "Frankly, I am a bit concerned."

"How so?"

"Well, for one thing, Ginny is scared. She can't tell me much. But, she said William was worried as well. Whatever it is, it is big and may involve agency personnel. They are using disposable cell phones to stay in touch. I think William is worried about their safety. Which means he is worried about his own safety as well."

"Shit!" Curtis took a few minutes to absorb everything he had heard.

"Yeah," Bill agreed.

"Listen, Bill, if there is anything I can do to help, let me know. I still have a few connections in certain circles."

"I appreciate that, Curtis. Not sure what anyone can do at this point. Hopefully, it will all work out."

"I am sure it will," Curtis replied. "William is smart and careful ... and he is damn good at his job."

William Peterson stood on the steps of the Lincoln Memorial. It was a pleasant evening with rush hour traffic beginning to subside. Tourists dotted the Mall, strolling between the various memorials. A Japanese family passed up the stairs to Peterson's left. They smiled and nodded as they headed into the memorial. Peterson waved, returning the greeting.

Peterson had dressed to be recognizable to the woman he was meeting. He was wearing jeans, a light blue button-down shirt, and a gray sports jacket. Gun-metal gray Oakley sunglasses kept the evening sun's glare out of his eyes. His eyes moved, scanning the tourists. He was trying to spot the young woman who had called him. He felt the reassuring weight of his 9 mm Glock 17 on his right hip. It held eighteen rounds of 9 mm ammunition, seventeen rounds in the magazine ... one round in the chamber.

Fatima Hadhari approached the Lincoln Memorial from the rear side to avoid crossing the Mall. She did not want Peterson to see her approach. It was part of the mind game she liked to play with her targets. She had asked Peterson to meet her on the front steps of the Lincoln Memorial. And, she wanted to be sure neither of them was followed.

Fatima wore a light blue summer skirt with a gray sleeveless blouse. She was wearing gray flats and a thin jacket. Fatima never wore makeup because she needed none. She wore very little jewelry, but today had a single ring on the ring finger of her right hand. It was a simple but attractive ring. A gold band whose plain setting encircled a large green stone ... a finely cut emerald.

Male pedestrians watched as she strolled by. They could not help but look. She was a lovely, desirable young woman. Her long, dark hair flowed over her shoulders stopping short of her full breasts. Her outfit accentuated her curves and the narrowness of her waist. Its light colors contrasted well with her tan well-shaped legs and flawless complexion. A knowing, flirting smile graced her striking face. Men always noticed Fatima when she was around. Her smile was electric. But, very few got close enough to her to see that her flirting smile never made it to her dark, almost black, eyes.

"Are you alone?"

Fatima's voice was quiet and soft. It startled Peterson. He'd been caught off guard. He turned and his eyes focused on Fatima a few short steps away. He had not sensed her approach at all. A funny feeling, a warning, wormed its way into the pit of his stomach. But for some odd reason, he silenced it. She was even more beautiful than she had sounded on the phone. Peterson was a happily married man, but he still appreciated a beautiful woman when he saw one.

Peterson looked at the woman for several seconds before responding, "You must be Eva." It was simply an observation.

Fatima nodded, giving Peterson a shy, almost fearful smile. She then looked around to see if anyone was watching them. Peterson felt his guard drop just a little.

"I came alone. You have an envelope for me?" he asked, trying to keep his voice calm and reassuring.

"I do. It is in my purse," Fatima replied. Fatima looked around and spotted a vacant bench not too far from them.

"Can we go over there and sit a minute? My knees are a little wobbly." That smile again. "I am afraid I am just not used to this type of thing. It is all a bit hard on my nerves." Peterson looked over at the bench, a slight frown formed on his face, but he could see nothing that aroused his suspicions.

"Okay," Peterson replied. "We can sit a few minutes. But, I have to get back to the office." He paused. "I am sorry you got caught up in this. I haven't spoken to your uncle in several years. I did not even know he had a daughter. What is her name?"

"Rachel," Fatima replied. "We were not very close as children and I have not seen her in many years. I think she contacted me only because I live in Washington, D.C.

When they reached the bench and sat down, Fatima smiled again, "You must work for the CIA or something like that." A warning bell went off in Peterson's head.

"What makes you think that?" Peterson asked.

"Because my uncle is in another country and is in trouble ... and is requesting help from you. I think you are maybe with the CIA or the State Department."

Peterson accepted that and the feeling of alarm quieted.

Peterson's government issued secure cell phone gave a quick chirp. He retrieved it purely by habit.

"Eva, please excuse me just a second." He turned away from the woman and unlocking the screen looked down at the message. He read the message twice, making sure he had read it correctly the first time. It said,

Report in. Condition: Red AMRIVER

"Oh shit," Peterson muttered under his breath. This was not good. Peterson knew that AMRIVER was Mike Stanton. He was either down, missing, or dead. It could not be a coincidence. He needed to go right now.

Peterson started to turn toward the woman to make his excuses when he felt a sharp prick in his neck followed by a burning sensation. He saw the ring as Fatima pulled her hand back from his neck, her beautiful face now masked in hatred. Peterson tried to stand, his hand instinctively going to the Glock at his right hip. But, his arms and legs suddenly felt very heavy. He sat heavily back on the park bench. Peterson felt his chest beginning to tighten and it was suddenly getting very hard to breathe. His last thought was of his wife and children.

Fatima leaned over as if to kiss Peterson on the cheek and shifted him into a more natural position. She got up and waived as if saying goodbye to a friend and walked off in no apparent hurry, continuing along the walkway that ran parallel to the Mall. She began to hum a tune that was now at the top of the pop hits chart. Easily blending in with the pedestrian traffic, she disappeared.

CHAPTER 22

"Mai, come here! Quick!" Curtis exclaimed, suddenly sitting upright in his recliner.

"What is it, Curtis?" Mai entered the room, alarmed by the sound of his voice.

"Look at this," Curtis pointed at the television. The local news network was airing a follow-up to a story that had aired earlier that morning. A man had been found dead on a park bench on the Mall near the Lincoln Memorial. They'd only been able to identify the man as an employee of the U.S. Government. The news anchor was now saying that, while there were no obvious signs of foul play, authorities were treating the death as a potential homicide. The reporter went on to explain that authorities were suspicious because just hours earlier, another government employee, who had worked in the same office, was found stabbed to death in a vacant upscale condominium. That man had already been identified as Michael Stanton, an Assistant Director for the Central Intelligence Agency. The reporter continued, "Since this second victim's next of kin have now been notified, his identity could be released to the public." Curtis and Mai were horrified when they heard the name. It was William Peterson.

Mai dropped the glass of water she was holding in her hand. She turned to Curtis, concern and horror written across her face.

"Oh, my dear God," she exclaimed. "I've got to call Nancy." Mai tore off toward the kitchen.

Curtis stood still. He was remembering Bill's worried comments. Feelings of concern, sadness, and anger swirled through his mind. Curtis, by his nature, was a man of action. But right now, ... there was nothing he could do.

I can call JD, Curtis thought. He will want to know. Curtis headed to the phone in the den.

Ajax waited quietly beside him in the hallway of the barracks while JD listened in stunned silence to his Dad on the phone. After the call, JD felt a cold anger creep into him. His Dad had been unable to tell him very much. JD had never met Ginny or William's two little girls. He could not even imagine what they would be feeling right now. Without thinking, he reached down and scratched Ajax's ears. Ajax licked his fingertips in response. He seemed to sense something was wrong.

What the hell do I do now? he wondered

JD thought about it for a minute and then left the barracks. He headed straight for the training brigade commander's office. He needed to take some leave time. There would be a funeral ... and other things he should be there for. Ajax followed at his left side. No command required.

William Peterson's funeral took place on a sunny

Saturday afternoon. Bill had asked JD if he would mind saying a few words at the funeral. JD was moved by the request, but he was unsure of what to say. He had never met William's beautiful wife, Ginny. And, he was totally unprepared to meet William's now fatherless twin girls, Becky and Janet. It broke his heart to see the pain on those two little faces.

William's parents took the time to introduce JD to both Becky and Janet. Bill shook JD's hand and they chatted a few minutes about happier times. Bill and Nancy had always been like second parents to JD. The two boys had been inseparable as friends for many years. They had survived school, scouting, church, girls, and many an adventure together. William had even trained with JD's karate Sensei for a little while before deciding karate wasn't for him.

Annie came home from Clemson for the funeral. She was about finished with school and was on track to graduate next June. It had been some time since JD had seen his little sister. Annie had blossomed into a beautiful young woman. It was unfortunate he had to see her again under such sad circumstances.

Father Joe led a beautiful mass. It was very well attended. The Petersons were a well-liked family and had a long history with the church. When it was time, JD stood and went to the pulpit. He scanned the faces in the Sanctuary for a few moments. He recognized many people in the congregation, including his old Sunday teacher, Joe Trenton. Sensei Tokumura sat in a pew next to his parents and his sister, Annie. There were teachers from school and parents of other boys he had known through scouts.

Nothing JD tried to prepare seemed right. Countless drafts ended up crumpled and in the trash. Finally, he'd given up and decided to wing it.

"We are here today because of a sad and tragic event. That event is the death of my best friend, William Peterson. I have known William Peterson most of my life." JD paused.

"Things do change. Often adult life separates us from those we knew as children. It dawned on me while I was trying to come up with something to say here today that, for the biggest part of my life, William Peterson was, in fact, much like a brother to me. William was my best friend. We played together. Sometimes we fought each other. We got in trouble together. And, often we suffered the consequences together. We joined the Boy Scouts together and we even earned our Eagle Scout awards together. As we got older, we often double-dated with our girlfriends.

Our parents were also friends. When we graduated from high school, our families had dinner together. Then William went to college and I joined the U.S. Navy. Our lives went in separate directions. I did not see William for many years. Then, out of the blue, our paths crossed again just a few weeks ago. I ran into William again on an aircraft carrier in the middle of the Arabian Sea. During that chance meeting, I learned that William was now employed by the government. That he was happily married and was the proud father of two beautiful little girls. It was wonderful to see my friend again." JD paused and took a breath.

"As I look around the Sanctuary today, I see eyes filled with tears, faces filled with sadness. And, it is indeed a sad day. But, I decided to take this time to celebrate my friend's life. I want to share some of my best memories of the adventures William and I shared as we grew up together, because … that is the William I knew and the William I will always remember."

About twenty minutes later, JD was finished. The

Sanctuary was very quiet. JD left the pulpit and made his way back to his seat in the pew. As he got close, Nancy Peterson stood and stepped into the aisle. She gave JD a hug and whispered in his ear,

"Thank you for that, JD. That was beautiful. Thank you."

JD nodded and hugged her back. He was out of words. He turned and slid into the pew, sitting next to his mother. Mai reached out and gave her son a hug. There were tears streaming down both of their cheeks.

After the graveside service and burial, a few people lingered and talked. JD made his rounds, talking to many people he had not seen in several years. He spent several minutes with Tokumura Sensei and promised to stop by the dojo to train while he was in town. JD also spent a few minutes talking to Joe Trenton.

Weddings and funerals, he thought.

By the time JD made it back to his parents' house, it was getting late. Annie had already left for her drive back to Clemson. She'd said her goodbyes at the end of the service. Annie had some midterm exams she needed to study for and it was a pretty good drive. She did not want to leave too late and then have to make the drive in the dark.

It was also time to feed Ajax who'd been left pretty much to his own devices for most of the day. He'd made himself very comfortable, sprawling out on the brand-new dog bed Mai had picked out for him at a local pet store. It was much more comfortable than the crate he usually slept in at Fort Bragg.

After Ajax finished his dinner, the two of them went for a brisk walk around the neighborhood. They both needed some exercise. In the morning, JD planned on he and Ajax having a good run. Five miles should do the trick.

After returning from the walk, JD and his Dad retired to the den, both drinking a beer. Mai was making herself busy in the kitchen. JD hoped she was making fried rice. The thought cheered him up a little. Ajax looked very comfortable once again sprawled out on the dog bed.

"Your Mom's going to spoil that dog rotten!" Curtis chuckled. Suddenly he jumped to his feet. "I almost forgot something." He retrieved the USPS shipping envelope from a small table in the corner of the room and handed it to JD.

"This is the package I called you about. It is from someone named Ray Culp. There's a return address in Idaho."

"I am quite sure I don't know anyone in Idaho," JD replied. "And, didn't Ray Culp pitch for the Boston Red Sox? I'm not sure Idaho even has a baseball team."

JD ripped open the end of the envelope and slid the contents out into his hand. The envelope contained a small slip of paper and a USB thumb drive.

That was odd, JD thought. He turned the thumb drive over in his hand examining it. It was fairly new technology. Not too many people were using thumb drives yet, never mind mailing them to other people. JD unfolded the slip of paper and turned it to read the short hand-written lines.

Important! Watch your step. Please be careful. Contact: Julie 2022181821. Use my name. William.

JD could not believe his eyes.
Son of a bitch … what the hell is this?
"Dad?"
"Yes, JD. What is it?"

"Does your computer have a USB port? I need to look at this."

"Sure thing, son. I've never had a chance to use it before though. Let's go to my office."

Curtis led the way to the desk in his office and pressed the power button on his Hewlett Packard desktop computer. Once it had finished booting up, JD located the USB port on the front panel and inserted the thumb drive. Going through the process, the drive opened and a window popped up asking for a password.

Damn it, JD thought for a minute.

The cryptic phrase *Use my name, William* immediately now made sense. JD entered "William" and the jump drive opened to display a series of files.

JD did not have to read much of the information contained in the files before he let out an exclamation of disbelief. He was stunned. Then slowly, that quiet, steady anger began to set in. He read on. Understanding immediately that this was the intelligence his team grabbed in Afghanistan some weeks ago, he read the files along with Julie's analysis. It was all there, … the connections between Iran and North Korea, the ten American jihadists training in Somalia and ten "packages" shipping from North Korea. There was information about Michael Stanley, the poor slob who managed to get himself burned alive by what appeared to be a new, more violent stain of al Qaeda based in Syria.

Finally, his eyes fell on the comments about the presidential candidate, Josephine Warren-Brookstone, and her cell phone number.

"I do not fucking believe it," JD muttered to himself. Curtis was shocked more by the tone of JD's voice than the language.

"What is it, JD?" he asked.

"Dad, have a seat and read this. This stuff I just read is insane. I need a minute to wrap my head around it. I'll take Ajax upstairs and settle him in his crate. Be back in a few minutes. It's going to take some thought to figure out what to do with this." JD stood.

"Come Ajax, let's go." Ajax got lazily to his feet and followed JD upstairs. Curtis took his seat at the desk and began to read the files on his computer screen.

JD returned a few minutes later. Curtis looked up from the computer screen.

"Son of a bitch," he muttered.

"Exactly," JD replied. "So, what are we going to do?"

JD's Dad sat quietly for a moment. He leaned back in his chair and let out a long, tired sigh.

"It's clear to me that William was killed because of what is in these files. Bill could not tell me what it was about, but he did tell me he sent his family here to keep them safe. William was into something big, and it scared him."

JD nodded. "I agree. And, he obviously did not know who to trust."

Curtis looked at his son, "Yes he did, JD. Obviously, he trusted you."

"Looks that way," JD admitted. "So, we have a group of ten terrorists training in Somalia and ten Packages coming from North Korea. That must be dirty bombs or something like that. We can assume the targets are in the U.S. Ten dirty bombs cannot be flown in and they'd be difficult to smuggle through our customs. I am betting they will cross over from Mexico along with the terrorists. The border is wide open. Much less chance of being caught."

Curtis frowned, "I can't see anything wrong with that logic. I'm not sure how that Stanley guy figures into this, but that and Brookstone's cell phone number being involved tell me there is much more to this … this looks pretty bad."

JD nodded. Just then Mai came into the den,

"I'm going to bed. Do you boy's need any …" She stopped mid-sentence seeing the looks on their faces. "What's wrong?"

Curtis looked at his wife. "It's not good, honey. I'll come up in a minute and fill you in. Just let JD and me finish up our discussion. I'll just be a few more minutes."

Mai hesitated before saying, "Okay. But don't take too long. I can see you are both worried. I won't be able to sleep until I know what is going on."

"I know, honey," Curtis replied. "I will just be a few minutes … promise."

"Alright, Curtis. But, please hurry." Mai gave both men a kiss on the cheek and started up the stairs. Once Mai was gone, Curtis glanced over at JD.

"So, what do we do now."

JD did not answer right away. His mind was churning. Finally, he spoke.

"I think I need to find this Julie and talk to her. She may have more information, especially about things that have happened since William mailed me this information. A lot that we couldn't know about may have happened in the last several weeks."

"Makes sense," Curtis replied. "Can we make a copy of this information? On another thumb drive? I don't want it on my computer. But, having another copy might be smart." JD nodded.

"I think so. I know we can buy one at a computer store easily enough. We can copy the files over to it."

"Good," Curtis continued. "I do have an idea. My former commander in Vietnam, Colonel Ellerson, is a

General on staff over at the Pentagon now. He's probably about ready to retire. I know I can trust him. I think I will give him a call and see if I, or we, can meet him." Curtis paused. "If we get this information into the right hands, it should be okay and something will be done. But, if we get it to the wrong people, we will all be in serious trouble. I have your Mom and Annie to think about … but we must do something. There is no way either of us can sit by and just let this happen."

"I agree," JD acknowledged. "There is no way I am letting these terrorist criminals get away with this … no way at all. We'll do everything we can to keep people safe."

"Alright then, good night JD. Better get some sleep. I have a feeling it's going to get a bit exciting around here. And, now I have to go explain all this to your mother."

"If I know Mom, she will agree with us one hundred percent."

"Yep! You certainly do know your Mom, son."

CHAPTER 23

Julie hadn't been to Langley in almost a week … or to her condo either. She was scared.

She worked out three days each week at World Fitness on Connecticut Avenue. On the day Peterson was killed, she'd finished her cardio-kickboxing class at 7:30 PM.

After Julie finished her workout, she stopped at the juice bar for a strawberry flavored revitalizing smoothie. Leaving the gym, she turned left down Connecticut Ave. As she passed through the door, she noticed three Middle Eastern men across the street appearing to be engaged in conversation.

As she approached the first intersection and began to cross the street, she noticed the same three men were now on her side of the street, walking behind her.

Are they following me? she wondered. *No way! That's silly. I am just being paranoid.*

One more block to go before the Safety Park lot. As she turned into the lot, she glanced behind her and there they were again. Seeing she had spotted them, they stopped and pretended to be looking a merchandise in a storefront window. Julie had no doubt now. They were following her.

Don't panic! Get in your car and get out of here, she told herself. Moving quickly to her car, Julie got in and locked the door. Starting the car, she quickly backed out of her slot, exited the parking lot and sped off.

Julie had spent a long sleepless night in her condo. She'd sat up all night in a chair in her living room … thinking.

How had they found her at the gym? Did they know where she lived? It seemed likely since they knew where she worked out. Surely finding her home would be easier. Or had they followed her from work to the gym. That was possible. They might not know where she lives. But, they might ….

Julie went to the kitchen and got a drink of water. She didn't own a gun. Living alone like she did, she'd often thought about getting one. Washington, DC's laws made owning a gun way too difficult and eventually, she had decided against it.

I could sure use one now, she thought.

Julie had to settle for one of her kitchen knives which she kept by her side on the table. She did not turn on the TV. She wanted to be able to hear any noises near her condo. At 6:00 AM, she showered and went to work. Julie had to talk to Peterson. He would know what to do. Arriving at Langley, she stopped at the coffee shop and sat down at a table. It was early, but Langley never closed.

Sipping her coffee and waiting for Peterson to show up for work, Julie thought back over the last 12 hours. Those men yesterday … it had to be connected to the plot they'd uncovered. It was the only thing that made sense.

Julie checked the time on her phone. She figured he'd be in his office by 8:00 or so. That was another hour … she would check then.

Or, I could give him a call, she thought. Julie decided against that. Instead, she went to the lab to see what she could do to take her mind off things.

Maybe I'm just being paranoid or silly, she reflected. *I mean really!*

Julie left the lab a few minutes after 8:00 AM and went to Peterson's office. He was not in yet. A little later ... about 9:00 AM, she heard the news about Stanton from a co-worker. Peterson had still not made it in at lunch. Then, at 3:45 PM, Julie had heard the news that Peterson was dead as well.

For Julie, the deaths of Mike Stanton and William Peterson simply proved her worst fears. When Stanton had been reported dead, Julie was shaken up. But, who knew what kind of crap Stanton had gotten himself into. Julie did not like or trust Stanton. And, knowing Stanton, he'd probably made enemies. He could have even been killed by the vengeful husband of some woman he'd had an affair with. But, when Peterson was found dead as well ... Julie could add. She did not go home to her condo after work.

Julie left her workstation with her cell phone and the jump drive. Stopping at a Walgreen for a toothbrush and a few other necessities, she drove straight out of the city. Julie was smart. The fact that Peterson was dead told Juliet somebody was doing damage control. She didn't know if they had her name, but she was taking no chances.

Julie eventually found herself in Chesterton, Maryland where she checked into the Driftwood Motel. It was an old motel, a small family-owned place ... nothing fancy but it was clean, and she could pay cash.

Julie kept the small television in the room turned to the news, listening for any follow up on what was going on.

But, outside of reports that the investigation into these deaths was still ongoing, there was little. She kept her cell phone charged. It would ring occasionally. Julie had talked to a few people she knew … family and close friends, telling them she was just taking an impromptu vacation. Other than that, she would not answer the phone. Callers could leave a message.

The hot water felt wonderful. It helped her muscles relax and eased the tension she felt. Other than walking to the diner across the road to eat, Julie hadn't left her room. She knew she couldn't go on like this forever. She really needed to go to her condo. There were things she needed to do if she was going to lay low for any length of time. She needed more clothes for one thing. She needed to arrange for her bills, pick up her mail, and grab her laptop.

I can be in and out in less than 20 minutes … tops, she thought. Julie turned off the water in the shower. Reaching for a towel, she stepped out of the tub and began to dry off. Her cell phone rang. She didn't recognize the number and let it ring. On the sixth ring, her phone kicked over to voicemail.

"Hello … umm … Julie. You don't know me. I am a friend of William Peterson's. My name is JD …"

Remember JD. The thought crashed into her brain. William had mentioned JD in the text message he had sent to warn her.

Julie picked up the phone and pressed accept button, but she said nothing.

"Hello … hello … Julie. Are you there?" There was a pause. Then the voice continued.

"Julie, I know some crazy things have just happened. I know you are scared. My name is JD. These people killed my friend, William. I have seen the intelligence. William

253

mailed me a package containing a jump drive." Another pause.

"Julie. I am here to help. I want to help. You can trust me." Julie was not sure what to do. Finally, she spoke.

"How can you help? These are bad people. If you've seen the files, you know about Brookstone's campaign and its connection to all this. These are powerful people."

"I know that, Julie. I have resources and connections as well. I can help. But, we need to meet and talk. I want to make sure you are safe. Where can I meet you?"

"I want to go to my condo. I need to get some things. You can meet me there." There was a pause as JD considered this. He did not like that idea at all.

"That is not a good idea. If these people are looking for you, they'll be watching your condo."

"I know that, but there are things there I need. I won't have to go back again and I can be quick."

"Okay, Julie. Give me the address. I will meet you there." Julie gave him the address and he wrote it down. "Please wait until I get there to go in ... okay? We go in together. Ten minutes and we are out of there. Then we find someplace safe to talk things out. That sound okay?"

"That sounds okay," Julie replied. "I will meet you there at 4:00 PM tomorrow afternoon."

"4:00 PM," JD repeated. The call ended.

JD had an eight-hour drive to get to Washington, D.C. He threw a few things in his duffle bag and loaded Ajax into the back of his jeep with his K9 traveling gear. That included Ajax's crate, leash, assorted chew toys, food and water bowls, a jug of water, and several days' worth of dog chow. He pulled out of the driveway and headed East on I-40. Once he and Ajax were well on their way, JD called his Dad.

Curtis told JD that he had purchased another USB jump drive at a nearby Office Depot. He and JD's mother were now headed home.

"Once there, I will copy the files over to it."

"Sounds good," JD replied. JD filled his Dad in on the conversation he'd had with Julie, that he would meet her tomorrow afternoon at her condo in Washington. Curtis listened. He only had one comment to make.

"I think you are right about her going to her condo, but you are also right in that there isn't much you can do about it except be there. Be careful, JD."

"I will. I'm taking Ajax for backup."

"Good," Curtis replied. "I also got in touch with General Ellerson. I didn't tell him too much over the phone but he understands that you and I have stumbled onto something big ... and something that affects national security. I get the impression that the feds are already aware of the planned terrorist attack and are working on that. He wouldn't say anything of course, but what little information I gave him on that ... it sounded like he had heard it before. I don't think they know about Brookstone's presidential campaign connection to all of this though. I mentioned the possibility of presidential campaign interference and from his reaction ... I would say that was news to him. Your Mom and I are flying down to Washington tomorrow and I'm meeting with him.

"Mom is going with you?"

"She refused to be left behind." Curtis laughed. "Said she needs to come along to keep me out of trouble. Your Mom plans to do some sightseeing while I meet with Ellerson. Hell, she'll probably keep us both out of trouble."

JD laughed at that. "Probably so ... see you soon."

"I'll let you know where we'll be staying once we make reservations. Talk to you tomorrow, JD." Curtis ended the call.

CHAPTER 24

JD turned right onto N Street NW. He was looking for the 700 block and Julie's condo. Her unit was M205. It looked like a nice community. JD spotted a beautifully laid out pool area as he drove through the grounds. He quickly discovered the M block of condos, spotting Julie's condo a few seconds later. JD glanced at his watch. It was almost 4:00 PM.

Julie had arrived at her condo a bit earlier. Parking her car a few spaces down from her assigned spot as a precaution, she sat for a minute checking the area. She didn't see anything out of place.

But, she reflected, *I'm not sure what to look for either.* Still, it all seemed quiet ... normal.

Julie created a mental checklist of the things she needed to grab and where they were located. She decided that to wait for JD was silly. She could get what she needed gathered up and then be ready to leave when he arrived. Julie took a last quick look around and still saw that nothing seemed out of place. She opened her car door and got out. Walking quickly to the entryway to her condo, she let herself in. Julie had not noticed the black Honda Accord that was parked a few spaces down. Three Middle Eastern men sat in the Honda. They'd been staking out the condo for most of the day. Allah rewarded those with true patience, and besides, the woman who'd hired them paid very well. They saw the infidel woman described to them enter the condo.

The three men got out of the car. This was to be done quietly so they were armed only with knives. The lone woman would prove little trouble. They made their way purposefully toward Julie's condo. Reaching the entrance, they paused as one man tried the door. It was locked. Two of the men shifted to block any view from the street. The third man kicked the door in. All three rushed into the condo ... each intent on being the one to have the honor of killing this infidel woman.

JD had just let Ajax out of the back of the jeep to relieve himself on a nearby fire hydrant when he spotted a woman who had to be Julie walking toward unit M205. She unlocked the door and went inside.

Damn! JD thought.

Ajax finished the business at hand and JD started toward the condo with Ajax trotting along at his left side. His pulse quickened when three men made their way to the same doorway. He saw one of them try the door. There was an audible crash when the condo's apartment door was kicked in.

Shit!

Ajax heard it too. The dog sensed the immediate change in his handler's attitude and was instantly in working mode. JD knew Ajax could get there much quicker. Reaching down, he unsnapped the lead from Ajax's collar.

"Stellen!"

Ajax took off like a bolt of lightning for the open door

with JD right behind him.

Julie was in the bathroom gathering some toiletries when she heard the door being kicked in. Glancing out through the open bathroom door, she saw the three men rush into her condo's foyer. Julie quietly shut the bathroom door and locked it. They had not seen her. But, it was a small condo and wouldn't take them long to find her.

Oh my God! What am I going to do now?

The men fanned out into the condo. One of the men started toward the closed bathroom door when there was a sound at the open entryway. Ajax hurtled through the door with a low growl. Seizing the closest man's forearm in a bone-crushing bite, Ajax dragged him to the floor. The man punched at the dog, screaming in pain, but Ajax held on ... not releasing his grip. The other two Syrians moved closer to try and help their comrade and never saw JD burst through the condo's entrance.

JD closed the distance to the closest assailant quickly. Hearing him coming, the killer, who was crouched to try and get at the dog, turned his head to see who or what was coming. The angle was perfect. JD struck downward hard, the two large knuckles of his right fist slammed into the corner of the man's jaw. There was a sickening crunch as the man's jaw splintered. He collapsed to the floor, unconscious. JD spun, moving toward the last man. The would-be assassin was crouched ...waiting. His right hand held a knife, its long, lethal blade pointing toward JD, the sharp side up. The man, his eyes filled with unnatural hatred and rage, circled to JD's left looking for an opening. Suddenly he lunged, thrusting the knife at JD's midsection. JD's open left hand deflected the thrust inward and down. Both hands closed on the attacker's wrist. JD pivoted sharply to his left and his powerful hands twisted the wrist back on itself. The Syrian bellowed in rage and pain as his wrist snapped. He was propelled to the floor at JD's feet. JD's right knee lifted, his heel slamming down in a crossing stomp kick that impacted the left side of the assassin's face. There was another sickening crunch and the attacker lay still.

"Afblijven," JD commanded. Ajax released his hold on the third assassin's forearm and backed up a step, still intently focused on the screaming man. "Zit!" Ajax sat. He did not take his eyes off the man on the floor in front of him.

'Julie … are you okay? It's JD. Everything is alright. You can come out now." The bathroom door opened a crack. Julie cautiously peered out. She stepped out and into the living area and surveyed the scene. It was hard to believe. Two Middle Eastern-looking men were sprawled on the floor in awkward positions and were not moving. A third man laid on the floor clutching his right arm staring in terror at a large dog who simply sat there, watching him, daring him to move.

"Julie, meet Ajax … my, ah, partner." Julie just nodded.

"Are those two men dead?" she asked.

"No. Just out cold. A few broken bones but they will live. I need something to tie them up with. Do you have any rope or duct tape … anything like that?"

"I do have duct tape." The shock of what had happened was wearing off. Julie rummaged around in the kitchen and returned with a roll of duct tape.

"Why don't you collect your stuff while I deal with these three … so we can get out of here."

"Yes … yes! Good idea," Julie replied. She moved off toward the bedroom. JD used the tape to secure the three assailants around the ankles, knees, elbows, and wrists. He was not overly gentle with the conscious man's broken arm as he pulled it around behind the man's back to tape his wrists together. JD had little sympathy for three men who would have enjoyed murdering an innocent woman. By the time JD had the three men securely bound and gagged with the duct tape, Julie was back with two overnight bags.

"Is that everything you need?" JD asked.

"That's it," Julie replied.

"Let's get out of here then. We'll take my Jeep just in case they know your car … and besides, it has all of Ajax's stuff in it." JD grinned.

Julie smiled for the first time. "Okay."

"Ajax, Kom Hier … Volg" Ajax fell in at JD's left side and they went out the door … JD, Ajax, then Julie. Moving quickly to his Jeep, JD opened the back hatch and Ajax jumped right in, settling into his crate. JD secured the crate door and shut the back hatch. Julie stowed her overnight bags in the back seat and got in the front passenger seat. JD slid into the driver's seat and started the engine. A few minutes later they were headed toward Chesterton, Maryland at Julie's direction. For several minutes, they rode along in silence. Then Julie spoke.

"You saved my life. Thank you."

"That was more Ajax than me," JD grinned. "I just took care of clean-up."

"He's a smart dog. What kind of dog is he?"

"He's a Belgian Malinois." JD laughed. "I hope someday to be as smart as he is."

Julie stayed quiet for a few more miles.

"Who are you, JD? Where did you come from and why are you here? Why did William tell me to remember you? I don't even know you."

"It a long story," JD replied. "But, I guess we have the time.

"William and I grew up together. We were best friends all through school … up until he went to college and I joined the Navy. I hadn't seen William in several years. Then I ran into him on an aircraft carrier in the Arabian Sea somewhere off the coast of Oman. Total surprise! But, great to see him. I learned he was working for the CIA, had married, and was the proud father two little girls." JD frowned at that. He thought of those two little girls now being fatherless. It tore at his heart."

Julie nodded. "I knew William brought the laptops, a phone and some notebooks a SEAL team had grabbed during a raid in Afghanistan back to Langley. I work in the tech lab." Julie paused. "I'm the one who cracked the encryption and got the files from the laptops."

"That explains why William's note told me to contact you. He mailed me a thumb drive that had copies of the files on it."

"Scary stuff," Julie replied.

"No shit!"

"So, where did you get your dog?" Julie asked. "He's amazing."

"Ajax is a Trident dog," JD replied.

"A what?"

"Ajax is a trained U.S. Navy SEAL … of the four-legged variety," JD explained. Julie put two and two together.

"So, you are a Navy SEAL as well then. You must have been on the team that grabbed the laptops!"

"Rumor has it," JD replied. His cell phone started to ring. It was his Dad. They talked for several minutes while Julie looked out the window at the passing scenery. JD told his Dad about the three men he'd left bound and gagged at the condo. Curtis said he'd let General Ellerson know about them as well. Ellerson could notify the proper authorities to have them picked up. There was no hurry. The three of them were securely bound and not going anywhere. JD figured they were all on terrorist watch-lists or had criminal records of some kind.

"That was my Dad. Military as well ... well former ... a Vietnam vet. He has seen the information as well. My Dad has a former commanding officer who is now a General working at the Pentagon. We weren't sure who to trust, so my Dad is going to meet him tomorrow. They've talked once on the phone. Dad said that he got the impression that the national security folks are aware of the planned terrorist attack ... what they do not know about is the connection to Brookstone and her presidential campaign."

"That makes sense," Julie added. "Stanton would have told them about the terrorist plot. But knowing him, he would have kept the connection to Brookstone to himself, to use as political leverage. He was a real slimeball." Julie thought for a minute and went on. "I know William was told by Stanton to see if he could find any additional evidence of this connection between someone in Afghanistan or Iran and the Brookstone campaign. But Stanton told him to keep it discrete ... meaning not to tell anyone."

JD nodded. "Makes sense ... if he was horse-trading with the Brookstone campaign folks. But, to the terrorists, both Stanton and William, and apparently you as well would be loose ends to be eliminated. They would want to protect their investment."

Julie shuddered. "I suppose so. It certainly looks that way." She turned to look at JD, "That's right ... I forgot. They have reported on the news that there is a person of interest, an attractive Middle Eastern woman, who was seen on security video footage, both at the place Stanton was killed and at the Mall by the Lincoln Memorial ... where William was found."

"Some of these pieces are beginning to fall into place," JD observed. A few minutes later, they turned into the parking lot of the Driftwood Motel. Julie was in room 12, the last room on the end.

"I will see if I can get a room next to yours," JD said as he parked the Jeep. Julie waited in the Jeep while JD checked on a room. He was back in a few minutes.

"Well, no vacancies. They're booked up. We may need to go someplace else." Julie looked over at him.

"It's late. You and Ajax can stay in my room. There are two beds. That is if you don't mind ...," she hesitated, "I would feel a lot safer after what happened today. We can move somewhere else tomorrow."

"Okay. If you are sure. Ajax and I will try not to take up too much room ... or be any trouble."

'I am sure," Julie replied.

Once settled into the room, JD fed Ajax and put him back into his crate so he and Julie could walk to the diner across the street and get a little late supper. JD was starved. He hadn't eaten all day.

"Ajax doesn't mind being in the crate?" Julie asked.

"No. He's used to it. It's like his den. I'll let him out when we get back." JD grinned. "Just want to keep the dog hair off the beds."

Both Julie and JD ordered bacon, egg and cheese sandwiches with fried potatoes. JD had coffee while Julie settled for water with a slice of lemon. The conversation was minimal while they ate. Julie, it turned out, was quite hungry too. JD was finished eating and sipping on a refill of his coffee when Julie looked up from her plate.

"Are you married, JD?"

"No," JD replied. "Kind of hard on a woman ... being married to a SEAL is rough."

Julie nodded. "I can see where that might be the case. It would take a special kind of woman to handle that I think."

"What about you, Julie? Are you married?"

Julie laughed. "No, still waiting for the right guy to come along. Way too many jerks out there."

They finished their meal. Julie insisted on paying.

"It's the least I can do to repay you for saving my life."

They crossed back to the motel. Ajax stirred but gave no indication he wanted out of the crate ... just shifted his position, let out a long, satisfied exhale and went back to sleep.

Julie turned on the television and found a channel showing a Clint Eastwood western movie, The Outlaw Josey Wales. There was not much choice and after all the day's excitement, Julie really couldn't take watching the news.

During a commercial break, JD got up from the bed Julie had so kindly offered for his use and announced he was going to take Ajax out for his last walk of the evening.

"We'll be out about twenty minutes. Why don't you take a shower? I bet it'd feel good after all we've been through today. I can take one after you're done and Ajax is settled down for the night."

"I think I will. That does sound good."

"Don't worry. We won't be very far."

Julie smiled. "Okay."

Ajax stirred himself when JD opened the crate door. He stretched, went over to sniff Julie's hand and giving it a quick lick, turned and followed JD out the door. When JD

returned with Ajax a little over twenty minutes later, Julie
was showered and in her bed propped up on one elbow
and watching the continuing saga of Jose Wales. With Ajax
settled back in his crate, JD grabbed some gym shorts and
a clean t-shirt.

"Did you leave any hot water?"

"Nope," Julie replied smiling. "Felt so good I used it
all up. Guess you'll have to settle for a cold shower."

JD laughed. "Hell, that's no problem. I'm used to cold
water." With that, JD ducked into the bathroom.

The hot water really felt good. JD scrubbed off and
turning the water off, reached for a towel. When he was
dry, he put on the gym shorts and slipped the t-shirt over
his head. It was then he realized he had forgotten
toothpaste.

Damn, he thought. He wondered if Julie would notice if
he used a little of her toothpaste and decided to risk it.
When he was finished, he stepped out of the bathroom just
in time to see Josey Wales charge out of the sun to take on
a whole company of Comancheros. JD walked over to the
light switches on the wall and turned off the main lamp,
leaving only the lights on their bedside tables on.

"Is that okay?" he asked. "That's a lot easier on the eyes
right now."

"Sure," Julie replied. "That's fine. That overhead lamp
was a little bright." Julie could not help but notice how fit
JD was ... especially in the gym shorts and t-shirt. He was,
she decided, a very good-looking man. And, he seemed to
be a good man as well. Julie felt something stirring deep
inside her. Maybe it was simply the excitement of the day,
the fact that she'd almost died today. She was not sure. But,
for whatever reason, she felt very much drawn to JD.

He stretched out on the second bed and glanced over
at Julie. She was lying there watching him.

"Feels pretty good to lie down," JD commented. "This was one heck of a day."

"Yes," Julie replied. "It does feel good. The hot shower helped a lot. I was pretty tense after all that … ummm … you know, at my condo."

"I understand. It got really exciting there for a few minutes."

Julie laughed. "I guess it did at that. So, what language were you using when you were talking to your dog. It sounded German or something."

"Close. It is Dutch. Lessens the chances strangers could give Ajax commands he would obey. I'm not sure he would obey just anyone, but it's a precaution we take."

Julie laughed again. "Damn! That's one smart dog. Takes out assassins and even speaks Dutch." JD laughed at that. She liked his laugh.

"I guess tomorrow we'll meet up with my parents … after Dad meets with General Ellerson. Try to figure out what to do next."

Julie nodded. "Okay. That sounds like a plan." She sat up suddenly.

"Well darn, I forgot to brush my teeth. Be back in a minute." Julie threw back the covers and slid out of bed. JD couldn't help but notice Julie was wearing a New England Patriots T-shirt that did little to hide her well toned body and a pair of blue bikini panties. She was very cute! JD caught himself staring and quickly averted his eyes.

Darn! Too late. Julie had caught the look on his face. A few seconds later, JD heard the sink running and then the sound of Julie brushing her teeth.

"I borrowed some of your toothpaste. I forgot to pack some. I hope you don't mind." There was no reply. A minute later Julie came back into the room. Stopping to look down at JD, she smiled.

"That's getting fairly personal, isn't it ...? I mean borrowing my toothpaste?"

"Why, I guess it is at that. I didn't think you'd mind." He looked up at Julie who was still standing there, looking down at him.

"I don't mind, JD ... can I call you JD?"

"Certainly ... if I can I call you Julie."

"That would be nice," Julie replied. "And since we are now being so ... umm ... intimate, there is something else I want to tell you."

"What's that?"

She hesitated. "I'd really like to get in your bed tonight ... that is ... if you don't mind."

JD decided he didn't mind at all. He pulled the covers back and moved over to give Julie room as she slid in beside him.

Julie snuggled up to JD, pressing her face into his neck. She said nothing. The heat coming from her body was intense. JD reached over with his left arm and pulled her in closer, Julie's hand gently curled around his bicep, a touch so electrically tender it caused an involuntary sigh of pleasure to slip through his lips. They lay together like that for a few minutes. Then Julie moved ... turning to look up at him. Her eyes were so blue ... electric.

Beautiful, JD thought. He leaned forward and his lips sought hers. Her mouth opened under his. He was amazed by the passion in her kiss. He could feel her pressing her body against his, molding to him.

God, she tastes good! He felt his own passion begin to rise. She felt so hot to his lips as they traveled from her mouth, across her cheek and caressed her neck.

JD's hands pulled at the Patriots t-shirt, lifting it over Julie's head. She raised her arms to make it easier ... his fingertips caressed her spine. He could feel her shiver, she moaned as his lips sought her nipple. It was already hard. Suddenly Julie pushed him away. She pulled urgently at his shirt, helping him pull it up and off. There was an urgency in her that simply would not be denied. She turned and tugged at his shorts, pulling them down his legs. JD kicked them off. His hands moved to Julie's slender waist, pulling at her panties, working them down and over her feet. He felt her mouth close around him. The feeling was incredible. He was afraid to move, enjoying the warm, wet exquisite sensations. In a few seconds, he was totally aroused. He needed to be inside her ...

Julie slid him from her mouth and pushed him back down onto the bed. She climbed on top, straddling him and reaching down with her hand, urgently guided him into her. Her eyes were closed. Julie rocked slowly back and forth. JD's hands reached up to cup her perfectly firm breasts. He began teasing her hard nipples. Julie moaned and the intensity of her rocking increased. JD's hands moved over her body. Her skin felt so amazing to his touch. He couldn't get enough.

Julie could feel JD's hands, his touch, the gentle friction adding to her pleasure. She was breathing harder now. Her eyes opened and met his gaze. JD was amazed by the intense look of concentration on her face. He reached up and pulled her face down to his, kissing her hard. Julie's mouth opened in response. As his tongue began exploring, she let out a low moan and her pace quickened again. JD could feel the pressure building, the heat, the indescribable sensation ... suddenly Julie gasped. She pitched forward, collapsing onto him. That was all he needed. JD exploded into her. He wrapped his arms around her, holding her tight as the spasms of pleasure racked through both of their bodies. Slowly, they relaxed, coming to their senses and enjoying the warm feelings of closeness.

"Oh God!" It was all JD could manage. Julie laid there in his arms, her breathing slowly returning to normal.

"That was awesome," she whispered into his ear. "God, I needed that."

"That was better than awesome." He reached over gently stroking her breasts with his fingertips. He kissed her cheek. His fingers traced down her abdomen and across her thighs. Her skin felt so good … cooler now … and silky smooth.

"Let's clean up a bit and do that again … maybe a bit more slowly this time," he added. "I would like to take some time to get to know you better … and enjoy you."

Julie smiled happily. "That sounds just lovely."

CHAPTER 25

When Curtis spoke to General Ellerson on the phone, they arranged to meet at a great little German restaurant Curtis had been introduced to a few years earlier. Called Cafe Mozart, the little restaurant was located on H Street in downtown Washington.

Four years earlier, Curtis volunteered to help with a disabled Vietnam War veteran's tour of the Vietnam War Memorial. While on tour, Curtis stopped in to see an old war buddy, Congressman Stillwater, now representing the great state of Wyoming. Bobby Stillwater had served with Curtis in the Vietnam War, losing a leg in a VC ambush. Stillwater, Sergeant Walker who'd carried Stillwater out, and Curtis had been the only survivors. It had been a bad firefight lasting several minutes. Some good men had died including Steven Hicks, a close friend of Curtis' back in those days.

Bobby recommended they eat lunch at the Cafe Mozart. The Sauerbraten was terrific and the atmosphere was authentic ... right on down to the Bavarian lady playing traditional German music on an accordion. If you liked that sort of thing, it was the best!

Curtis got there a few minutes early. It was necessary to pass through a deli to reach the restaurant at the back of the building. Stepping through the door was like stepping into a little German restaurant in Wiesbaden, Germany. It brought back some great memories. General Ellerson showed up right on time.

"Captain Cordell ... long time no see ... how the hell are you?"

"I'm fine, General. How are you?"

The waiter came and took their order. They both ordered Schnitzel sandwiches with French fries and a salad. Ellerson ordered coffee and Curtis decided on unsweetened ice tea.

"And how is Mai?"

"She's fine, General. Out shopping right now. We're planning to see a few sights while in Washington. Mai has never been to the Capitol."

"Nice time of year for that ... not too hot," Ellerson replied. The General's face turned serious.

"Okay, Cordell. Tell me what's on your mind." Curtis reached into his pocket and pulled something from it. He slid the thumb drive across the table to Ellerson.

"It's all on here. You can read it for yourself. I don't know whether the information on it would hold up legally ... chain of custody and all that. And, I am certainly not cleared to have this at all. It would be top secret at least." Curtis paused, taking a drink of his ice tea.

"My son, JD, has seen it. Being a SEAL, that might be okay. I'm not sure about that. But Peterson mailed it to him. He knew what he had and he knew the trouble he was in. That's why he sent his family to Knoxville and the files to JD. Peterson, as you know, is dead. He was a good friend of my son's. They grew up together." Ellerson nodded, knowing what that would mean to him. "JD has taken this somewhat personally, but he's is also a professional. Right now, he's with Julie, the CIA tech who pulled these files off the laptops my son's SEAL team grabbed in Afghanistan. Three men, terrorists I assume, tried to kill Julie at her condo yesterday. JD and his K9 interrupted their plans. He left them tied up in her kitchen. I thought you could get the right folks to police them up. They aren't going anywhere."

Ellerson nodded.

"I can do that. We'll want to talk to them."

"I thought perhaps someone would," Curtis replied. He took another sip of his iced tea.

Curtis frowned, shaking his head, "You can't make this shit up!" They paused as the waitress brought their food to the table. When she headed back toward the kitchen, Curtis continued.

"I think you know about the terrorist plot, including the 10 American citizens who are now jihadists-in-training at some camp in Somalia. You probably know about the packages coming from North Korea. I am pretty sure the combined intelligence agencies are all over that."

Ellerson looked at Curtis but said nothing. There was nothing he could say without violating all kinds of national security protocols.

Curtis went on. "Do you know about the connection to Brookstone's presidential campaign?"

Ellerson looked up from his schnitzel sandwich, "What the hell did you just say?"

When Ellerson got back to his office, he went straight to his receptionist who was making coffee.

"Marie, I need to talk to the President, the Secretary of

Defense, the Director of the CIA and the Director of the FBI, and I need to talk to them ASAP!"

"Yes, Sir! Right away, Sir." From the look on her boss's face and the tone of his voice, she knew it couldn't good. Marie ran to her desk and grabbed the phone.

General Ellerson sat down at his desk. It would take Marie several minutes to locate all four of the people he needed to talk to and get them on the phone together. Using that time, he called the Washington, D.C. Chief of Police. They'd gotten to know one another, and while not exactly friends, he figured he could count on Dave's professionalism.

"Washington, D.C. Police, David Harris speaking."

"Dave, It's General Ellerson. How are you doing these days?"

"General, I'm fine. To what do I owe this call?"

"Dave, we have a situation. I need your help. I am trying to get in touch with the FBI Director, but it may take a while. I have three incapacitated terrorists I need rounded up and held until we can figure out what the hell is going on here."

"Son-of-bitch! Okay. I understand. Where are they?"

"They're at the condo of Julie Spencer over on N Street." Ellerson gave him the address. "Julie works for the CIA. They tried to kill her. A Navy SEAL, who is on leave, managed to interrupt their plans. Julie is currently with him and they are both safe, but he left them bound with duct-tape in her condo. We need them picked up and held for questioning. I understand they might need medical attention. It was a pretty desperate fight and the SEAL had a K9 dog with him at the time."

"Okay. Understood. I'll get a couple of units right over there. We'll patch them up if needed and put them on ice until we hear from you or the FBI. Just let me know if you need anything else. "

"Thanks, Dave. I appreciate it. I'll be in touch soon."

"No problem, General. We have a real dislike for terrorists."

General Ellerson hung up the phone. He sat back in his chair and waited for the conference call Marie was setting up to come through.

What a day!

Director Connors was not in a good mood. He had two dead agents; one … an assistant director and the other … one of his top military analysts. He'd liked Peterson. And, Peterson had been a family man. Stanton was an asshole but he seemed to do his job well enough. The loss of these two men was a real problem. On top of that, he had a major terrorist plot unfolding before his eyes. It was like something out of a damned James Bond spy-thriller.

Connors had been on the call with Ellerson, President Hardeman, the Secretary of State, and the Director of the FBI. Not long after that, General Ellerson paid him a visit at his office and spent over two hours. He'd provided printouts of the files Curtis Cordell had passed along to him on a thumb drive.

At first, Connors had not been able to believe what his eyes were reading. However, it had connected a great many dots. The strange collection of events of the last few days were beginning to make some sense. Especially when Connors added Ellerson's information to what he'd found out during the recent call from Arik Daniel at Seawatch.

Daniel had filled Connors in on the activities of the Hamad and his suspicions surrounding what may be hidden in that cargo hold. An Iranian freighter loading secret cargo from North Korea … Connors had not liked the sound of that at all. The good news was that it was all coming together.

The next meeting with President Hardeman and Rear Admiral Spence had been productive. The President had authorized the deployment of a SEAL team to board and search the Hamad. He hadn't liked having to do it … not a bit.

While no President wants to send the military into harm's way, President Hardeman seemed reluctant to stand up to anyone. Hardeman feared it would somehow make him look bad to his base. In the end, however, he was smart enough to know that he could not afford to have a successful large-scale terrorist attack occur on U.S. soil. He was also on board for an air strike against the training camp in Somalia. Both Connors and Spence were against that action unless there was no other alternative.

"The problem with the air strike is that any possible intelligence the camp contains is lost. If we send a team in, we can still take out the camp and, if we are lucky, bring back some good intelligence. That could be a real bonus."

The President shook his head. "I don't know. Sounds risky to me. American troops on the ground. What if some of our soldiers get killed … or it's seen as just another example of American aggression."

"Maybe then … a joint action with an ally or two. Make it a cooperative effort by allies in the battle against terrorism," Connors suggested.

Admiral Spence suggested that he contact his counterpart with the British SAS. They'd been active in that area and already had teams close enough to take out the training camp.

"Perhaps a joint U.S. SEAL/SAS mission in Somalia?" Spence suggested. "We might get the French involved as well, but this needs to happen in the next few days so we can't complicate things too much either. The risk to the U.S. is too damn high." Connors liked the idea. The President finally agreed on the condition it remained, at least publicly, a 'British" operation. The mission was officially a go.

Connors knew that Bravo and Echo Platoons from SEAL Team 3 were already operationally underway aboard the destroyer, USS Redmond. Their task was to intercept the Hamad and find out what was in that cargo hold. A U.S. Coast Guard cutter had been tasked to assist as needed. And even better, Admiral Spence had called a few hours earlier to let him know the SAS was very enthusiastic and already planning the operation.

The SAS would work in close cooperation with Delta platoon from SEAL Team 4. Delta platoon was on board the aircraft carrier USS Ronald Reagan currently cruising somewhere off the southern coast of Africa. They would be flown to Djibouti the next day where they would connect with the SAS team for the pre-operational briefing and the usual weapons and equipment checks. Then they'd board British military-owned V-22 Ospreys and be inserted near the terrorist training camp. Hopefully, those damn suicide bomber trainees would still present at that location! That would sure make things operationally cleaner.

But, what bothered Connors much more than all this was the new information General Ellerson had just dropped in his lap. Ellerson was a top-notch military mind. He had one heck of a reputation stemming from his command with the 1st Cav during the Vietnam War. If Ellerson had delivered it personally, there had to be something to it. According to Ellerson's information, some fucking Iranian terrorist mastermind named Rahman Atta was behind this entire fantastic plot which included a plan to buy the American presidency.

Fucking incredible! Absolutely insane!

On the surface, it did seem crazy. But, Connors had to admit … it really was the best way to ensure the current policies stayed in effect. For instance, the policy of maintaining an unprotected border with Mexico … very helpful if you wanted to smuggle a few bad weapons across the border into the U.S. It would make sense for Atta to "buy" the candidate most likely to keep the border wide open.

The files Ellerson turned over contained evidence tying the presidential candidate, Josephine Warren-Brookstone to this same Rahman Atta. They'd found that some terrorist in Afghanistan possessed Brookstone's damned cell phone number. It was scrawled on a page in a spiral bound notebook of all things.

God-damn-it! I don't fucking believe it, Connors thought to himself. Since his call to the NSA this morning, they had identified several phone calls originating in Masuleh, Iran that had been made to her phone. Connors also felt that the death of Michael Stanley, computer hacker and Ransomware developer, at the hands of terrorists in Syria was making more sense now.

Connors' people had identified Rahman Atta as a wealthy man, currently believed to be residing in the mountains of northern Iran. He was possibly a distant cousin of the Saudi royal family. If Rahman Atta was financing Brookstone's campaign …! Connors was not looking forward to his upcoming meeting with the Attorney General and the Director of the FBI.

CHAPTER 26

The lawyer, Assad Al-Joud, called Fatima on her way to the gym. He was a Saudi Arabian known in certain circles to be sympathetic to those jihadists who managed to get themselves in trouble with the authorities.

Fatima was furious. The incompetent fools could not even kill one infidel woman. One infidel and his dog had taken them down as if they were children. And, to make matters worse, they were now in federal custody. They wouldn't talk. Fatima was certain of that. They knew what would happen to their families if they did. Better to spend the rest of their lives in an American prison than have their families wiped out. And, if the Saudi lawyer could secure their release … well … for the time being, they were safe from her anger. She could attend to them later if needed.

Fatima had a good sweat going. She was working combinations on the heavy bag, repeated combinations of punches and kicks hoping to rid herself of some of her frustration. It wasn't working. After she'd finished her kickboxing on the heavy bag, Fatima made her way over to the treadmill.

Al-Joud, a true believer and loyal to the cause, had eventually gotten in to see the three men being held for breaking, entering and assault. He'd been the one to bring her word of the American interloper and his dog. Both the man and the dog obviously had some training … probably military or law enforcement. Her assassins had been put down fast and hard. Fatima scowled at that. It didn't sound like police, more likely U.S. Special Operations. She would find out who this American infidel was, and he'd pay dearly.

I will kill him! I will kill his dog and the woman. I will kill him and his entire family, Fatima swore to herself. The rage was surging through her … like fire coursing through her veins. *If the man came to help the woman, he must be connected to her somehow. I will find out how and I will find out who he is.*

Fatima took another sip from her water bottle. She still had 20 minutes more to run on the treadmill before beginning her work with the free weights. The running did nothing to lessen her rage. After her workout, she would go visit Yana. She was angry … stressed and tense. She needed to relax so she could think better … to plan.

Fatima was smiling now. She didn't smile very often. Only Yana made her smile. Fatima, if she was capable of anything resembling love, loved Yana. She could even make Fatima laugh occasionally. This was one reason Fatima enjoyed being with her. The second reason was Yana's body. Yana was slender without being too thin. She was perhaps a shade taller than Fatima. Yana had long jet-black hair. Fatima loved how it smelled. She could get lost in Yana's hair. It was only in her arms that Fatima could forget the constant rage that seethed within her … at least for a little while.

Like Fatima, Yana was also Syrian. Her skin was a beautiful golden brown. Yana worked out regularly and was in great shape. They had met at the gym where Fatima worked out three times a week. Their relationship started with the occasional glance, a tentative smile, a few friendly comments. Fatima didn't consider herself a lesbian. It was not that she particularly loved women, she just hated men for the brutality she'd experienced at their hands during her childhood. She did find that she could tolerate Hakim, but he was more like her mentor ... maybe an uncle. But, for the most part, anything resembling a relationship with a man, had for her, never been anything at all pleasant or desirable.

Then she met Yana. They had lunch one afternoon after a workout and Fatima found she could relax a bit with her. It was a feeling she had not experienced since her parents were executed by Syrian government soldiers. And that was such a long time ago. She'd almost forgotten what it felt like to feel some contentment, to enjoy her surroundings and not be constantly consumed by hate and rage. Fatima discovered that she could respond to and enjoy feelings of intimacy with Yana.

Fatima still remembered Yana's first overture. It would have been difficult and a great risk for Yana. Islam forbade such feelings. They had worked out together for some time, frequently having lunch together afterward often followed up with great conversation. One time their discussion centered around a new musical artist both women enjoyed. On impulse, Yana reached out and covered Fatima's hand in hers. The touch was electrifying. It surprised Fatima. It felt ... good. It was very ... real. Misreading Fatima's initial reaction, Yana started to withdraw her hand; a frightened look on her face. Fatima caught her hand and gave it a reassuring squeeze. Yana looked up … surprised … and pleased, no longer frightened.

After finishing her work with the free weights, Fatima took a shower at the gym and then walked the four blocks to Yana's apartment letting herself in with the key Yana had given her. Yana worked as a hostess at a posh Washington Mediterranean Cafe that served good food, hookah, and after 11:00 PM … belly dancers.

Fatima knew Yana would be napping at this hour to get ready for that night's shift. Quietly, she slipped into the bedroom and removed her clothing. Yana was sleeping peacefully. Fatima stood there for a few minutes, enjoying watching her sleep. Yana looked so peaceful, without a care in the world. Already Fatima felt some of the rage in her begin to subside. She pulled the cover back and slid in beside her, reaching over to stroke Yana's thigh with her fingers. Yana half awake, rolled over and mumbling something incoherent, snuggled into Fatima's waiting arms. Fatima held her close, enjoying the intimacy. She leaned over and gently kissed Yana's cheek. Yana opened her eyes and look up at Fatima, a happy smile on her face. Fatima leaned over to whisper in her ear.

"I need you, my little dove. I need you badly. There is no one else like you in the world for me."

CHAPTER 27

An hour before sunset two high-speed Mark V special operations boats pulled away from the USS Redmond, an Arleigh Burke-class destroyer. Each towed a rigid-hulled inflatable boat behind it. The Arleigh Burke class of destroyers are some of the most powerful surface warfare ships in the U.S. Navy.

The Mark V, while certainly not in the same class as the USS Redmond, was also a marvel of military design. This fast, special operations boat could carry 16 fully-equipped SEALS out to a range of 500 miles. The Mark V's angular design and low silhouette greatly reduced its radar signature making it very hard to detect. A Sea Hawk helicopter flew along overhead to spot the Hamad and help direct the Visit Board Search and Seize operation from a better vantage point. Two SEAL snipers were on board the chopper. They were there to provide covering fire if needed. Petty Officer Casey was manning the FLIR. It was also his job as a sniper to identify the target using the chopper's forward-looking infrared system and pass the needed information on to the teams in the Mark V's. The

FLIR uses a spherical glass lens mounted on the bottom of the chopper and has a range of over 50 miles. The sniper had a clear view of what was happening on an 18-inch green display, an invaluable tool for such operations. Casey's eyes were currently glued to that display.

Below, in the Mark Vs, the internal communication system crackled to life. "Target vessel spotted."

"Good copy! Standing by," came the response from Lt. Dietrich, the team leader in the lead boat. Petty Officer Casey began feeding him the information needed for a successful VBSS operation.

"Hull length 740 feet. Vessel speed, 18 knots. Twenty-five feet of freeboard." Freeboard is the vertical distance the SEAL team members will have to climb from the water to the hook point along the rail of the vessel. Boarding a ship in this manner is extremely dangerous and must be executed precisely. Any miscalculation can send the boat and its crew to the bottom of the ocean.

"Superstructure's aft and has direct access to the bridge. Nothing stirring on the deck. I'd say you guys can double hook aft."

"Copy that." Double hooking meant two rigid-hulled inflatable boats would approach, one on each side of the freighter. This would allow the sending of two teams on board simultaneously. That was good news.

RHIBs were very fast craft. They had twin diesel engines that delivered 1,000 horsepower, meaning they could race up, keep pace and hug the side of the vessel being boarded as the SEALs climbed titanium hook ladders hung from the rail with quick-release carbon fiber poles.

Lt. Dietrich had his teams in their RHIBs and speeding toward the Hamad. The Sea Hawk was completely blacked out and took up a position hovering off the Hamad's starboard side, about 150 feet above the water. Petty

Officer Casey kept a careful watch over the scene with night vision goggles.

The RHIBs raced in and took up positions along both sides of the ship. It was extremely dangerous work. They had to pin their small craft against the side of the freighter and maintain that position matching the vessels speed, particularly difficult to do in rough seas. Fortunately, it was a calm night.

The ladder man in both RHIBs used the long carbon fiber poles to hook the titanium ladders over the freighter's rails. Working the quick-release lever the poles released the ladders, securing them to the rails. The first men started up the ladders. There was no noise ... no yelling of commands. Each man was a professional. Each one knew his job. The SEALs climbed quickly on board. They had caught the Hamad's crew sleeping and totally unaware. Within ten minutes the captain and crew were confined in a forward storage locker and the SEALs were in control of the ship. No communications had been sent from the Hamad to alert any parties that the ship had been seized. It was a perfect boarding operation. The SEALs quickly began their search of the cargo hold.

The Hamad's hold was filled with 80-pound bags of concrete. Whatever they had hidden, it was sure to be hidden under those bags. It was backbreaking work moving those 80-pound bags one at a time. But SEALs get the job done, so move them they did. Seven hours later the SEALS, covered with concrete dust, struck pay dirt. Buried beneath the many bags of concrete, they discovered a shipping container, And, it wasn't on the shipping manifest.

No real surprise there, Lt. Dietrich thought!

The lock on the container doors was cut and the doors pulled open. Lt. Dietrich, with two other SEALs, entered the container. They found 10 wooden crates about the size of military footlockers securely strapped to wooden pallets. Dietrich gave a nod and Ensign Tillman stepped up to the closest pallet and sliced the straps with two slashes of his razor-sharp combat knife. The two SEALs pried the lid off the crate. Dietrich stepped up to see what it contained.

"Oh shit!" Lt Dietrich exclaimed. He'd never actually seen a real one ... not in real life. He'd only seen diagrams, photos, or mock-ups. But, unless he was badly mistaken, he was looking at a small nuclear device commonly referred to as a suitcase nuke. And, it looked like he had 10 of them right here in front of him.

The USS Redmond and the Coast Cutter Endeavor were both on station circling the Hamad, which was currently sitting dead in the water.

"Kelly," Dietrich ordered. "Get the Commander of the Redmond on the radio asap! We've got some serious-assed shit right here!"

"Yes, Sir!"

It turned out to be one heck of a haul. The primary mission was to ascertain what, if anything, had been loaded on the Hamad in the North Korean port of Nampo, and if dangerous ... seize it. They'd certainly succeeded in that respect.

In addition to the 10 nuclear devices hidden under the bags of concrete, they also captured 32 prisoners, about $250,000 in assorted small U.S. bills, and a large number of weapons including knives, an assortment of handguns, AK-47s, and RPG grenade launchers. There was no sign of any oil drilling equipment, materials, or parts.

Some of the SEALs took advantage of the lull to go over the side and rinse off the concrete dust. Feeling refreshed, they were resting on the deck after the long hours of moving concrete. A few sat on the deck in small groups talking … many were sleeping. Three guarded the Hamad's captain and crew, still confined in the forward storage locker.

Connor's intercom buzzed to life.

"Yes, Laura. What is it?"

"Admiral Spence is on the line for you."

"Thanks, Laura. Put him through." Connors picked up the phone.

"Bob, what up?"

"It seems your intelligence was very good. SEAL Team 3 successfully boarded and seized the Hamad. It was a textbook operation. No messages sent from the Hamad. They grabbed a load of cash and weapons and about 30 prisoners. They also found a locked shipping container buried under 80-pound bags of concrete mix. The container held 10 small nuclear devices. They were not dirty bombs, but small nuclear bombs … probably 2 kiloton yields."

"Suitcase nukes …," Connors stated.

"Right," Admiral Spence replied. "Not real powerful, but 10 of them in 10 different cities … the result would be a real national disaster."

"And small enough to smuggle across the Mexican border."

"Exactly. And if that part of the plot is real, I would assume the rest of it is as well."

Connors had already come to that conclusion. "I asked the FBI director to take a very close look at Brookstone's campaign donations. With Michael Stanley's death and the evidence from the files taken in Afghanistan, they have a good idea of what to look for. If there's something there, they'll find it."

"One more thing," the Admiral continued. "The SAS and Delta platoon SEAL Team 4 will be in place to hit the camp in Somalia early tomorrow morning. Should go down at 3:00 AM local time. No warning went out from the Hamad, so this Atta character shouldn't have any idea we are on to him. Satellite images have identified 17 individuals in the camp ... 10 do look to be participating in training. They will cease to be a threat tomorrow morning. I'll let you know when the mission is completed."

"Thanks, Bob." Connors hung up the phone and sat back in his chair. The leather squeaked a little bit. Connors had always liked that sound. It was comforting somehow.

It was a scary new world, Connors thought to himself. *It was an entirely new ball game.*

Connors had a great deal of experience with the CIA. He'd started almost forty years ago as an analyst. There was a brief period when he had left the CIA and did a stint as a lawyer in private practice. But, he quickly realized he wasn't happy with that and returned to the CIA. It was a job he enjoyed, a job with a serious mission, and he was good at it. Now, he was the Director.

If only there was a way to keep this kind of thing from happening, to make the United States too risky an area for terrorists to operate in. However, in a Democracy, there really was no foolproof way to do that. Connors understood that and truthfully, he wouldn't have had it any other way. Personal freedom comes with risk. If you can't accept that risk, you can always move someplace else. Meanwhile, he would do all in his power to keep the terrorists from being successful.

CHAPTER 28

NSA satellites located the terrorist training camp, designated Camp 27, 135 miles north-west of the Somalian capital of Mogadishu. The training camp was run and staffed by al-Shabaab, an al-Qaeda linked Somali terrorist organization. Several al-Shabaab members had been identified in the satellite photos of the camp. The photos also showed several structures identified as staff buildings, a mess hall, and a barracks. There were 10 individuals currently residing in the barracks building. The trainees couldn't be clearly identified from the photos because they were all wearing ghutrahs, a piece of white cloth worn as protection from the sun and in this case ... probably as a security precaution. They could, however, see that there were 3 of African-American descent, 4 Middle Easterners, and 3 Caucasians. Two of the trainees were female. Just east of the staff buildings the satellite photos identified four parked vehicles, either small trucks or jeeps.

The plan called for the assault on Camp 27 to begin at 03:00 hours Mogadishu time. At that time in the morning, the camp's staff, as well as the terrorists-in-training, would be least prepared, their bodily systems in a low state of readiness.

At 12:00 hours, the Royal Navy's V22 - Osprey lifted off the tarmac at Camp Lemonnier, home of the Combined Joint Task Force-Horn of Africa of the U.S. Africa Command. It was just under two hours to their insertion point five kilometers west of Camp 27 in Somalia. On board were eight SEALs from Delta platoon, Team 4 and a matching number from the Special Air Service anti-hijacking counter-terrorism tcam. Each one of these 16 men was a professional warrior, among the best of the best.

One hour and fifty minutes later, the V-22 Osprey's rotors tilted vertically, and the craft hovered over the desert. The Osprey's rear cargo door lowered, and 16 men quickly and efficiently roped to the desert sand 50 ft. below. In a matter of minutes, the cargo door was closed, the rotors rotated back to a horizontal position, and the Osprey headed back to Djibouti. Upon completion of this joint SEAL/SAS mission, extraction would be handled via a Chinook helicopter from the USS Ronald Reagan. The Chinook with its Apache gunship escort would very shortly be in the air, on route to their location.

It was a clear, cold mid-October night. There was nothing to hold the heat in the desert when the sun went down, especially with no cloud cover. And, tonight the stars were shining brightly in the night sky.

Both teams performed a quick equipment check, the SAS team leader checked his GPS and the 16 operators took off at a ground-covering trot. The mission was right on schedule and the assault team would arrive at the camp a few minutes before 03:00 hours

As the 16 men approached Camp 27, they split into two groups, consisting each of 4 SEALs and 4 SAS operators. Silently, one team worked its way toward the staff area. Al-Shabaab was about to lose some of its members tonight. The second team went straight to the barracks shed where the terrorist wannabees were sleeping.

A sentry near the perimeter of the camp lit a cigarette, a fatal mistake. The flare of the match ruined his night vision. It would take several minutes for his eyes to fully readjust. He stomped his feet, trying to keep the blood flowing in them. His thin shoes were not much protection against the cold night. From behind him, a strong hand clamped over his mouth. There was an instant explosion of agonizing pain as the blade of a Fairbairn-Sykes combat knife thrust up into his kidney. The SAS operative, with a twisting motion, pulled the knife clear of the body. The hand covering the sentry's mouth now guided the dying man to the desert sand. He was dead before he hit the ground. It was a silent kill.

As the first team approached the two staff sheds, they split up again, this time into two four-man groups. Each four-man group approached the door to one of the staff sheds. Without a sound, three men entered each shed while the fourth man stationed himself to cover the door and watch for possible newcomers. The SEALs were armed with the Colt MP4. The SAS operatives carried the Heckler and Koch HK 417, another excellent assault weapon. The quiet night was disturbed only by the coughing sound of silenced assault rifles.

As the first team approached the staff sheds, the second team reached the barracks building. Since the barracks shed had two doors, one at each end, they also split into two groups, one four-man team moving to each door. The same procedure yielded the same results ... coughing sounds from silenced rifles and dead terrorists.

It was over in a matter of minutes. There was no one left alive in the camp. The teams hitting the staff sheds quickly grabbed anything that looked like it might contain useful information for intelligence purposes. The two teams reassembled at the rally point just east of the camp and to maintain schedule, began a fast trot toward their extraction point a few kilometers away. The team arrived just as the Chinook and its Apache gunship escort were coming in.

Director Connors and Admiral Spence left the Oval Office. It had been a good meeting and the President was pleased with the way things turned out.

Both missions had been very successful. The 10 nuclear devices were on board the USS Redmond steaming toward Naval Station Mayport located in Jacksonville, Florida and the Hamad was sailing to Pensacola, Florida, manned by a crew of sailors from the Redmond. It was being escorted by the US Coast Guard Cutter Endeavor.

Terrorist Camp 27 in Somalia was history. Of course, it wouldn't take long for Camp 27 to be up and running again ... but for now, at least, the 10 American jihadists were dead, and the threat of those terrorists, or the nuclear devices, crossing the Mexican border was over.

President Hardeman suggested these two stories be released to the press. It would show that his administration was taking a firm stance in the War on Terror and that the U.S. and Great Britain were united in their efforts. It would let Rahman Atta know that a large part of his brilliant plan had failed.

Neither Connors nor Admiral Spence saw any problem with this. The American people could use some good news after the recent series of small but deadly attacks on U.S. soil.

The subject of the Josephine Warren-Brookstone campaign wasn't brought up by the President. He'd been informed of the evidence earlier and Brookstone, being a member of his party, placed him in a very uncomfortable spot. There was no real need to discuss it now, and Connors saw nothing to be gained by bringing it up. It would have to be dealt with soon enough. He had another meeting later this afternoon with the FBI Director. The President would certainly be kept apprised of the situation and there was no need to embarrass him at this point.

Let the President and the rest of the country enjoy this current moment … and a bit of much-needed good news.

CHAPTER 29

The next morning, after feeding Ajax and getting some coffee at the diner across from the motel, JD and Julie drove the Jeep to Washington, DC to meet JD's parents at a Denny's in downtown Washington. It was a cool morning. The drive was pleasant. A few minutes into the drive, Julie reached over and took JD's right hand in hers.

Arriving in Washington, they found a parking garage close to the Denny's and left Ajax in charge of guarding the Jeep.

Curtis and Mai were very relieved to see that their son was okay. After introductions were made and the waitress brought their orders, the four talked about what needed to happen next. Curtis filled JD and Julie in on his conversation with General Ellerson. Julie wasn't surprised at all that nobody knew about the connection between the terrorists and the Brookstone campaign.

"Stanton would have kept that to himself unless he had no other choice. He would have liked the thought of having a lot of leverage over the new President if she won ... or the means to buy a lot of goodwill by letting her know."

"I think," Curtis put in, "that it was the latter rather than the former. That would explain both his and William Peterson's death and the attempt on your life."

JD nodded. "They were cleaning up loose ends."

"It's like the plot from some Tom Clancy novel," Mai interjected. "It's all so crazy."

"Seems so," Curtis replied. "Unfortunately, we know it to be very real."

"So, what do we do now?" Julie asked.

JD spoke up. "Well, for one thing, we have to find Julie someplace safe to stay. She certainly can't go back to her condo."

Mai didn't hesitate. "She'll come to Knoxville and stay with us."

"I couldn't …," Julie started.

"You not only can, you will. I won't take no for an answer. It makes perfect sense. We can look out for each other."

JD agreed. "I'll have to contact my team and extend my leave. There shouldn't be any problem once the Chief understands the situation, and he'll clear things up with Ft. Bragg. I'm not going anywhere until I know Julie is safe and the people who killed William are caught or dead."

"Okay," Curtis decided. "Looks like we at least have the start of a plan." He looked at JD. "Why don't you and Julie get your Jeep and meet us at our hotel. Your mother and I will check out and we can all head back to Knoxville this afternoon."

Ten hours later, they arrived at the Cordell residence in Knoxville, Tennessee. JD helped with the luggage and then took Ajax for a much-needed walk. Mai volunteered to feed Ajax and JD excused himself and went into the den to place a call to Bagram Airbase in Afghanistan.

Curtis showed Julie to the guest room and told her to make herself at home. The guest room had its own full bath and she knew that very soon she'd be soaking in it.

"Thank you, Mr. Cordell. This looks very comfortable. I really appreciate you letting me stay here. I hope it is not any trouble."

"No trouble at all, Julie. Any friend of JD's is a friend of ours. You are welcome to call me Curtis if you are more comfortable with that. We're all adults here." Julie nodded as Curtis retreated from the room and went back downstairs.

JD, in the den, sat at the desk and began the slightly complicated process of calling his SEAL Team from a civilian phone line in Knoxville, Tennessee. After jumping through a couple of hoops and getting past some incredulous duty officers, he got Chief Whitley on the phone.

"Hey Chief, this is an unsecured line but I need to give you a situation report. I will be careful what I say. But much of it will probably be in the news in the next few days anyway."

"Damn, JD, this sounds serious. What's up?"

JD filled Chief Whitley in on everything from the thumb drive and the terrorist plot right up to taking out the three Syrian assassins at Julie's condo. JD only left out the piece involving Brookstone and her presidential candidacy.

"There's more, Chief … but I can't give it to you over this line."

"Understood," Chief Whitley replied. "Damn it! What a cluster fuck!" Chief Whitley took a second to absorb what he had just heard.

"Okay then. JD, I have you covered on this end. I can certainly get you an emergency extension of your leave. But, let me see if I can call in a few favors and get you a temporary duty assignment in Knoxville. Maybe you and your dog can do 6 months at the Navy recruiting center there. That should make sure you have plenty of time to get things sorted out. Maybe you can even find time to get a few good recruits for us … in between whacking terrorist assassins, of course."

"Damn, that would be great if you could do that, Chief. That should be plenty of time. By the way, this dog, Ajax, is unbelievable. You should have seen him in action at the condo. Ajax is a warrior through and through." JD laughed. "Axel better watch out. Ajax might make him look bad."

"That wouldn't be that hard," Whitley admitted jokingly. "But seriously JD, get this shit handled and then get both yourself and that dog back here in one piece. Maddux is bitching every day about having to do all the team sniper assignments while you're stateside raising a cute little puppy dog. I'm getting sick of listening to his shit."

"Sure thing, Chief," JD replied.

"I'll get your temporary duty assignment orders cut and mailed out to you. It might take a week or so though. I'll have to pull a few strings, but you should have them before your leave is up. Keep me informed as you can, JD."

"Will do, Chief. And, thanks!" JD hung up the phone and went back to the kitchen where Mai, Curtis, and Julie had gathered for a glass of wine. He took a few minutes to tell them what he and Chief Whitley had discussed. Curtis nodded, understanding.

Both Julie and Mai were excited at the thought of having JD around for another 6 months, although most probably not for the same reasons.

Suddenly, Mai looked up at Curtis. "What about Annie? She's still at Clemson. I know she's going to her boyfriend's home for Thanksgiving to meet his parents, but then she will be coming home for Christmas."

Curtis thought about that for a few minutes. "No need to upset her now. I can see no way anyone can connect her to any of this and she is probably safer at Clemson than she would be here right now. This will hopefully all be over before she comes home for Christmas. If not, we will deal with it then."

"If you think that is best, Curtis" Mai replied.

"I think at this point it is. If anything changes, we can go get her or make other plans.

"Okay then. I guess for now that is best."

JD looked up grinning. "Annie has a boyfriend? Who'd of thought?" He looked over at Julie and gave her a wink. Julie laughed. "Is this her first boyfriend?" Julie asked laughing.

"Yep," Curtis replied. "Well, first serious one. We haven't actually met him ... but JD's mother spoke to him once on the phone."

"He's nice," Mai said. "He seems very nice."

'I'm sure he is," Curtis observed. "Annie is smart. She has a good head on her shoulders and I think she would be pretty picky when it comes to boyfriends."

JD laughed. "No doubt about that!"

"Mai, Julie, Come here quick! You've got to see this!"

Curtis was sitting in the den watching CNN. JD was out running with Ajax and wouldn't be back for another half hour or so. They had been back from Washington, DC almost a week now.

"Curtis, what is it?' Mai asked as she and Julie hurried into the den.

"Look at this," Curtis replied pointing toward the television.

A news anchor was reporting on an early morning raid conducted a few days earlier by members of a U.S. Navy SEAL team and elements of the British SAS anti-terrorism unit. The team had conducted a strike against a terrorist training facility in Somalia.

"According to reports, this camp located 125 miles northwest of Mogadishu, was being used to train 10 American citizens who had become radicalized and joined a radical Islamic jihadist movement. The Navy Special Warfare Group reported that the mission was a total success. Seventeen terrorists are dead while members of the participating SEAL and SAS teams suffered no losses or injuries. A good bit of intelligence was also gathered during the raid. This intelligence would be shared between the security agencies of both the U.S. and the U.K."

"Son-of-a-gun," Curtis exclaimed. "How about that!" The reporter went on.

"Spokesmen for the U.S. Navy and the CIA gave a joint press conference early this morning confirming the successful raid on the camp. Neither spokesperson would confirm whether the raid was connected to another recent operation in which the USS Redmond and the US Coast Guard Cutter Endeavor boarded an Iranian registered freighter as it entered the Caribbean Sea. There is no news yet on exactly what the freighter may have been carrying. There is wide speculation that the Iranian freighter may have been carrying drugs or perhaps some sort of explosive devices or weapons. We do know that the U.S. Coast Guard Cutter Endeavor is escorting the impounded freighter to Pensacola, Florida."

The reporter caught his breath ... the news story continued.

"In a statement released by the White House just an hour ago, President Hardeman praised the joint operation conducted in Somalia by both members of the U.S. Navy SEALS and the British SAS anti-terrorism unit, stating that this mission, as well as the recent search and seizure of the illegal cargo on the Iranian freighter bound for Venezuela, are just more evidence of his administration's continuing efforts to fight and win the War on Terror. The President went on to say that these successful operations are a testament to the professionalism and expertise of both the American security services and the U.S. Military, and of course, those of our allies."

Curtis chucked to himself. "Wait until JD hears about this!"

CHAPTER 30

Present at the meeting in a conference room at the Justice Department were FBI Director Charles Flynn, Special Agent Armatto, Special Agent Erdeski, and Attorney General David Rankin. It was a somber atmosphere. No one was happy to be here for the reason at hand.

"I'm not sure we have any choice at this point," David Rankin commented. Spread out in front of each of them was a file containing the information on the thumb drive Curtis Cordell had turned over to General Ellerson. Over the last few days, a lot more evidence had been gathered and added to the files. And, while the investigation was still underway, according to Special Agent Armatto, they already had enough to issue an arrest warrant.

The FBI had started with Brookstone's cell phone number found in the hands of a terrorist. Phone records showed several calls originating in Iran coming to her phone. While they were not always from the same phone, they were from the same place. A mountain village named Masuleh. More damning, however, was a phone call originating from her phone to one of those same numbers in Iran a few days before both Stanton and Peterson turned up dead. It was enough to get transcripts of the calls from the NSA. That was where the really bad news began.

A check into the Brookstone campaign's financial records also showed some interesting patterns. Not too long ago, her campaign was on the verge of being broke. But again, after some calls from Iran ... several sudden surges in donations occurred. The influxes of cash seemed on the surface to be legit, but it was interesting that they often seemed to coincide with calls to or from Iran. Special Agent Armatto also found that many of the credit cards used for the transactions were later reported stolen. There were too many for it to be a coincidence.

Add to this a possible connection to the death of Michael Stanley, a computer hacker wanted for creating Ransomware viruses, and the investigation was heating up. Stanley had been in both Turkey and Iran before being burned alive by Syrian terrorists. Way too many coincidences. The FBI didn't believe in coincidences.

'There is just too much here," Flynn agreed. "And, I don't like that two CIA agents are probably dead because they stumbled onto all this. If Brookstone had anything at all to do with their deaths ... I want her ass in jail."

"I have news along that line, Sir, and it's not good," Erdeski added. "I had a couple of agents pay a discrete visit to Richard Sexton, a senior member of her campaign staff. He's a tough old warhorse but the deaths of Stanton and Peterson shook him up bad. My agents leaned on him just a bit and he caved. It seems Stanton met him to discuss the evidence he had concerning Brookstone's cell number being in that notebook. Stanton was looking for leverage."

Rankin exploded! "He knew about that and kept it from us ... and from Connors? Son-of-a-bitch! Fuck!"

"There's more," Erdeski continued. "Stanton called Sexton sometime later. He talked to Brookstone who was in the room for a meeting. Sexton put the call on speakerphone. Stanton gave her Peterson and Julie Spencer. I understand Julie has not shown up for work in several weeks. Either she is spooked and in hiding, or she's dead. However, from what General Ellerson told us, we believe she is alive and traveling with some Navy SEAL named JD Cordell who got mixed up in this. Cordell was part of the SEAL team in Afghanistan that grabbed the intelligence that started this whole damned thing. He was a friend of William Peterson, which is probably why Peterson trusted him enough to send him a copy of the files on that thumb drive. I understand Cordell took out three Syrians at Spencer's condo. They were obviously sent to kill her. The DC police have them on ice."

"I sent some guys over to pick them up for questioning," Armatto added. "They should be back by now."

Rankin looked over at Flynn.

"Unbelievable!" Flynn nodded.

"The SEAL had help at the apartment. He was stateside to train with a new K9. It seems the dog is with him now." Rankin sighed a long, tired sigh. "Do we know who the Syrians are?"

"We have names," Armatto replied. "I doubt they're real. They've already lawyered up … that Saudi lawyer who always seems to be defending accused terrorists … Assad Al-Joud."

"You can't make shit like this up." Rankin paused. He got up from his chair and walked over to the window. Rankin stood there a few minutes, looking out at the city street below. He turned back to look at the three other men in the room. "You know, despite the magnitude of all this and all the moving pieces, it was really pretty amateurish! They could have made it a lot harder."

"That's often the case," Flynn observed. "The bad guys are often not as smart as they think they are." Erdeski looked up from his notepad.

"I think they may have done this on purpose. Kind of adding insult to injury. You know, the suitcase bombs were the real threat. The campaign interference was just a slap in the face. I can just hear it on the news … American Presidential Candidate Sells Out to Terrorists. Proof positive of the decadence of the West."

"That might be. I think I liked it better thinking they were just stupid though," Rankin commented. He was back at the window, looking at the street below.

"Damn," he muttered. Rankin turned toward the two special agents.

"Armatto, Erdeski, I'll request a warrant. I guess you'd better go pick it up and then, go and arrest Brookstone. We might as well grab Richard Sexton and Carl Sundstrand at the same time. We'll sweat them a little while, maybe get them to roll over on Brookstone." Rankin paused, letting out a long sigh. "I'll go talk to the President. He's not going to be happy about this, but there is no way around it." Nobody in the room envied Rankin that job.

Several blocks away, Fatima Hadhari walked into the small but comfortable law office of Assad Al-Joud. She strode right past the receptionist without bothering to acknowledge her presence. The door to Al-Joud's private office was open. Fatima walked right in.

Al-Joud looked up from his desk. An icy feeling wormed its way into his stomach, but he covered it up the best he could. That woman's reputation preceded her …, especially in radical Islamic circles. Fatima closed the door behind her.

"Hello, Fatima. To what do I owe the pleasure of this visit?"

Fatima did not respond to the greeting. She wasted no time.

"I want the name of the man who stopped my men from killing that Julie Spencer woman. The man with the dog. I want his name. I want to know where he lives, where his family lives and where anyone he might care about lives."

Al-Joud shook his head.

"I cannot be a party to such things. I am a true servant of Allah as you know, but to do what I do for our cause … there are things I cannot be part of … or … or I cannot do my job."

"I do not care about any of that." Fatima's eyes were filled with a look of intensely cold hatred. She slid a knife with a long wicked-looking curved blade out from under her jacket. Al-Joud's eyes widened in fear when he saw the blade. Knowing Fatima, it would be razor sharp.

"You have the connections. You can get me the information I want. You will get it for me … or you will die. I will slit your worthless throat. It's that simple." Al-Joud weighed his options and came up with the only answer he could give under the circumstances.

"Give me a couple of days. I will talk to the people I know. Give me a few days and I'll get you the information you seek." Fatima nodded.

"You have until the end of the week." Fatima turned and strode from Al-Joud's office, slamming the door behind her. The receptionist sat in her seat, eyes fixed on her computer screen, making darn sure she didn't look up from her desk as Fatima stormed by.

Assad Al-Joud wiped the perspiration from his forehead, then pulling an address book out of his top desk drawer, he reached for his phone. Assad Al-Joud knew it was not healthy to disappoint Fatima Hadhari.

CHAPTER 31

It was a beautiful fall day in Masuleh, the temperature a moderate 63 degrees. The morning bus from Tehran had just arrived. A mixture of passengers stepped off to begin their enjoyment of the beautiful mountain village. Most filtered off to the shops in the bazaar. One man made his way through the narrow streets and climbed a set of stairs to the next level of buildings. Masuleh was built as a series of terraces carved into the mountainside. Often the roofs of the lower terrace served as the street or front yards of the next higher terrace. The man came to a stop in front of a building that had, until recently, housed a cafe. The cafe was famous in both Masuleh and Tehran for its assortment of teas, kabob, and a fine assortment of delicate pastries.

The building was boarded up. The man went over and peered in through a window.

"The cafe is closed," another man called from across the street. "It's been closed for some time now I am afraid."

The man turned toward the speaker. "What happened? It was my favorite cafe in all of Masuleh."

"Only Allah knows," the man replied. "I have heard rumors that the owner, Salim Abbas, and his daughter, a beautiful child, returned to Tehran. I do not know if this is so. Salim seemed so happy here in Masuleh. He lived here many years and his business was good. I too miss the cafe, especially his delicious pastries."

The man nodded. "It is very sad. I come every year to Masuleh and have enjoyed visiting this cafe immensely. I shall miss it." The man turned to walk back down the narrow street.

"As Salaam Alaikum," he called to the man he had spoken to.

"As Salaam Alaikum," the local man replied. "Allah Akbar."

The man wandered back down toward the bazaar and turned into a small restaurant on a side street. He nodded to another man sitting at a table and walked over to sit with him. A few minutes later a third joined them, a woman wearing traditional Iranian dress for travel, one piece, with sleeves covering her arms to below the elbows and the dress itself extending down well below the knees.

"The café's boarded up. It looks to have been empty for several weeks. I spoke to one of the locals and he said that nobody knows for certain what happened to Salim Abbas or his daughter. The rumor is they went back to Tehran but some seem to have their doubts about that."

"I've checked around as well. Nobody can tell me what happened to Hadi the gardener either. It seems he just disappeared too. He really wouldn't have been missed by many but Salim, on the other hand, would because his café was very popular with the locals as well as the tourists from Tehran."

The woman joined the conversation. "I've located the house identified by Weiss as belonging to Rahman Atta.

Two men seem to be staying at the residence. From the descriptions Weiss sent us, I've identified Atta. The other one is his subordinate, Hakim. Unless somebody else arrives in the next several hours, we should have just those two at the house tomorrow. Abe is keeping an eye on Atta's residence."

The three sitting at the table, as well as the fourth team member who was watching the house, were all members of Kidon. The Hebrew word "Kidon" translates to "bayonet" or "tip of the spear." Kidon is a highly covert branch of Mossad … and one of the most capable and lethal special ops units on the face of the planet.

Kidon is often spoken of in whispers. Some doubt that this branch of the Mossad even exists. It does.

In 2003, a massive explosion occurred on a North Korean freight train heading for the port of Nampo. According to CIA intelligence reports, ten Iranian nuclear engineers were traveling on that train in a passenger compartment connected to a specially built car containing nuclear fissionable material. All ten of the engineers were killed in the train explosion. Kidon operatives had planted the explosives on the train.

The bodies of the nuclear engineers were later flown back to Iran in lead-encased coffins onboard an Iranian military cargo plane. The explosion site was cordoned off for many days as North Korean soldiers in anti-contamination suits worked to collect the wreckage and decontaminated the area. According to the experts at Mossad headquarters, the North Koreans were also working to recover as much of the weapons-grade plutonium scattered in the explosion as possible.

Just last year, Kidon assassinated a Syrian General who

had been negotiating with the Russian military to purchase next-generation anti-aircraft defense systems. The General was shot while standing on the balcony of his hotel room in Greece. It was a very long shot made from a yacht cruising the waters off the Greek coast. It struck the Syrian General in the chest, very impressive by anyone's standards.

Kidon's missions in Iran also contributed significantly to slowing the growth of the Iranian nuclear programs. This was achieved by simply assassinating nuclear scientists working for the Iranian state.

The four team members of this current Masuleh mission had entered Iran through Azerbaijan. Azerbaijan shares a border with Iran and Kidon teams often worked directly with Mujahidin to counter Iranian efforts in the area. Taking advantage of this relationship, the team slipped quietly across the border into Iran and made their way to Tehran. Once in Tehran, they boarded a tourist bus to Masuleh, blending in with other day-trippers to avoid drawing any attention to themselves. For all appearances, they were just four Iranians traveling to Masuleh to enjoy the Fall mountain air.

The initial recon over, Zoe and Matthew, traveling as a married couple, went immediately to their hotel and began the thorough preparations needed for the team to execute its mission. Zeke went over to where Abe was keeping the Atta house under surveillance. It was time to give him a break, and Abe tended to get very cranky when he missed his meals

Back in their hotel room, Zoe and Matthew donned microfiber cleaning gloves and set about their preparatory tasks. The gloves were a real aid in not leaving any tell-tale fingerprints. The team had smuggled in four 9mm semi-automatic Beretta M9A1 pistols that no longer had serial numbers. These were broken down, cleaned and reassembled. Next, they were fitted with silencers. Each pistol had two magazines holding 15 rounds each. Each pistol component, magazine, and round was wiped down to remove any possible identifying fingerprints. Four light-weight, loose-fitting dark cloaks of the type often worn by traditional Iranian clerics served as disguises for the team members and could be easily disposed of once their task was completed. They also carried forged identity papers. While not perfect, they were good enough for a cursory examination by someone doing an ordinary identity check.

Following through their mental checklists with the utmost care the team made sure there was nothing to connect them to anything that was about to happen in Masuleh. They were experts and it all simply went with the job.

At 3:15 AM there was a quiet knock on the hotel room door. Zoe opened the door and let Zeke into the room. He'd been watching the Atta residence when the final lights went out in two windows of the dwelling. The locations matched sleeping rooms on the house's floor plan. The layout had been provided months earlier, drawn by Zev Weiss based on information provided by Hadi. Architectural drawings for old dwellings found in an Iranian mountain town over one thousand years old simply did not exist.

The three members of Kidon donned the black cloaks and concealed their pistols under them. Zeke also hid the fourth cloak and Beretta under his cloak. Leaving the room, they quietly made their way out of the hotel. Nobody saw them leave.

The three moved stealthily through the dark village

streets. Ten minutes later, Zeke signaled Abe where he'd resumed his surveillance ... a sleeping beggar in a location presenting a great view of the residence in which their targets slept. Abe stirred himself and hobbling like a crippled beggar, moved into the shadows, joining the other members of the team. After Abe donned the cloak Zeke handed him, he took the Beretta.

"All is quiet. The last two lights went out about five hours ago in the rooms identified as the house's sleeping quarters. They should be sound asleep."

"Let's do it!" Matthew whispered. The four moved toward the house. Zoe stayed in the shadows to cover the entryway to the house's courtyard. Matthew, Zeke, and Abe moved quickly into the courtyard. Matthew stopped just inside to cover the courtyard as Zeke and Abraham continued toward a window that overlooked the courtyard. It was the very window Hadi had been listening under when Hakim caught him and slit his throat.

Thank God for ancient dwellings, Abraham thought as he used a pocket knife to pry up the simple window latch. Without a sound, he opened the window.

Zeke and Abraham climbed in through the window. Moving silently across the room, the men made their way into the kitchen. Spotting a collection of cell phones arranged on the counter, Zeke slid three phones into his pockets and Abraham grabbed the other two. It was risky. They could not afford to be caught with these phones during their escape, but it was simply too good an opportunity to pass up.

According to Zev's layout, the bathroom was directly to the left. Night vision would have been helpful, but it was just too much equipment to try and conceal when they slipped across the border. The two doors directly opposite them in the corners of the kitchen were the sleeping rooms.

Zeke took the door to the left, while Abe went to the one on the right. Both men signaled that they were ready. At a nod, they opened the doors and stepped into the sleeping rooms.

Rahman Atta lay there, sound asleep. Zeke wasted no time. He moved quietly up close to the bed. His Beretta coughed three times. Two 9 mm slugs struck Atta in the chest. One struck him in the head. Zeke paused a moment to survey his handiwork and then backed quietly out of the room.

The muffled sound of the Beretta awakened Hakim. He knew the sound of gunfire ... even with a silencer. Hakim sat up in his bed just in time to see a dark silhouette moving quietly toward him. Abe's Beretta coughed four times, each bullet slamming into Hakim's chest. Hakim fell back on his mattress without making a sound. Abraham moved closer and his Beretta coughed once more. A bullet hole appeared in Hakim's forehead. Satisfied, Abe left the room.

Masuleh slept on, totally oblivious to the violent deaths that had just occurred within its ancient streets. Silently, Abe followed Zeke back out through the same window they had used to gain entry. Abraham took time to close the window. Once again, he used his pocket knife ... this time to re-secure the latch. The two men joined Matthew in the courtyard and listened carefully for a moment. Nothing stirred. Seconds later they were back with Zoe in the shadows across the street. It was 4:14 AM. Zeke and Abraham had been in and out of the terrorists' residence in less than seven minutes.

Zoe pulled a heavy-duty plastic bag out from under her cloak. All four guns went into the bag, followed by their cloaks and microfiber gloves. Squeezing all the air out of the bag, it was tied shut and dropped down an old well. The bags fell a good way before Zoe heard a quiet splash. From the information that had been provided, the well was no longer in use … and it was very deep. Who knew what other secrets were hidden in that ancient well.

Less than ten minutes later, Zoe and Matthew were back in their hotel room. Fully clothed, the two stretched out on the sleeping mats grabbing a couple hours of sleep before beginning their long trek back to Azerbaijan. Zeke and Abraham were settled into a room Zeke had rented at a small inn one street level down, also getting some much-needed sleep.

The next morning Matthew wiped down anything in the room that had been touched. Everything was spotless … no trace of their being there would ever be found. Zoe and Matthew enjoyed a breakfast of pastries and coffee in a small cafe near their hotel. The cafe had a great view of the valley stretching out before them.

While they didn't know the fate of Zev Weiss, Rachel Weinstein or the old soldier they knew only as Hadi, it was a safe bet they were dead … and their deaths probably were not easy. The team from Kidon could only hope that their actions during the previous night would help their deceased comrades be at peace in the long sleep.

There were a great many travelers on the bus back to Tehran. It was noisy, the riders happily jabbering amongst themselves about their visit, the silks they had purchased, or the grand sights they had seen. Having enjoyed this nice weekend in the mountains, it was time to return to their lives in the city. They were oblivious to the fact that, hidden among them, four Israeli assassins were just beginning their long journey back across the border and into Azerbaijan.

It was three days before any of the townsfolk in

Masuleh noticed that they'd not seen Rahman Atta or his loyal servant Hakim in a while. The next day, a village police officer stopped by the house with its beautiful gardens to check on them. He knocked at the door but nobody answered. Turning to leave he detected a really bad smell. It was a smell of death. The policeman called back to the office for more officers. Thirty minutes later, they entered the house. It was a shock to all when they discovered the two dead bodies. Obviously, they'd been shot and killed, but nobody could figure out when or why it had happened ... or who had killed them. Nobody remembered hearing any gunshots. Nobody remembered seeing any strangers lurking around town ... just the typical pleasant day-trippers from Tehran. It was quite a mystery. And, one that would probably never be solved.

CHAPTER 32

Josephine sat in the quiet dark of her suite at the Trump International Hotel in Chicago. Her team had selected this location for her Party's election victory celebration. The hotel had also served as her campaign's headquarters for the final days of the campaign. It was in the hotel's Grand Ballroom that Josephine would give either her victory speech or her concession speech. At this moment in time, it looked like it would certainly be the former.

But right now, Josephine simply wanted quiet … to be alone in her thoughts. The campaign had taken its toll. She was damned tired and wanted to be as rested as possible for the big moment only a few hours away. Her team was downstairs, and under the direction of Richard Sexton and Carl Sundstrand, checking final preparations. The staging, the sound system, lighting, balloons, and confetti … it all needed to be perfect. Many members of the press were impatiently milling about, waiting for the final election results. Supporters were talking excitedly about their sure victory and what that would mean.

The only light in her suite was from the large flat-screen

TV mounted on the wall in front of the couch. Josephine tried to relax as she listened to the talking heads on CNN's Presidential Election Night Special. It was difficult!

"CNN can now call the state of Florida for Josephine Warren-Brookstone. Adding twenty-nine more electoral votes to her total, she now has a total of 262 electoral votes."

"That right, Mike. Her opponent, the Senator from New Mexico, Benjamin Steele, is currently sitting at 255 electoral votes. It is a very close race so far, but California is still out there. Winning California would make Josephine Warren-Brookstone the winner."

"You're right, Ted! We certainly can't call it yet, but the odds sure look good that Josephine Warren-Brookstone will be the first woman President of the United States. And on that note, we must take a short commercial break ... but don't go away, we'll be right back with more CNN Election results."

Josephine was ecstatic. She was going to win the election. California, with its 55 electoral college votes would put her over the top with 317 electoral votes. It only took 270 to win and she had California sown up.

She ran through her victory speech in her head. Josephine had already rehearsed it several times this evening. Her speechwriters had outdone themselves coming up with the perfect mix of humility and gratitude, and positive excitement for moving forward into the future.

There was a knock at her hotel room door. Josephine frowned.

Who the hell can that be?

The Secret Service had two agents stationed in the hall outside her door, and they certainly wouldn't let anyone unauthorized get to her door. They knew she didn't want to be disturbed and it was too early for the security detail to escort her to the podium for her speech. Her team had planned this all out carefully. That wouldn't happen until exactly forty-five minutes after the election was called. This was designed to build anticipation and set the stage for her much-anticipated grand entrance.

"Just a minute!" Josephine got up from the couch and crossed the room opening the door. She found the two secret service agents assigned to her security detail outside her door as she expected, but standing next to them were two other men in badly tailored suits. There were also several uniformed Chicago police officers.

"Can I help you?" Josephine inquired.

"Are you Josephine Warren-Brookstone?" one of the suit-clad strangers asked. It was a very professional voice … all business. It was a formality. He knew who she was. Josephine suddenly felt a bit apprehensive.

"I am," Josephine replied. "Is there something I can do for you?"

"I am Special Agent Armatto. This is Special Agent Erdeski," indicating his associate.

"I see," replied Josephine. "And to what do I owe this honor?"

"Ma'am, I am afraid we are here to place you under arrest," Special Agent Armatto replied.

"Arrest me? You're kidding of course? For what? Did I forget to pay a traffic ticket?" Josephine forced a little laugh.

"I am afraid it's a bit more serious than that," Special Agent Erdeski replied.

Josephine turned into the room. "I am calling my campaign manager."

"Ma'am, don't bother. He's being arrested as well." Armatto motioned Josephine back to the door. "We need you to come with us."

"You can't arrest me, I'm winning the election. I'm the President!"

"Not yet, Ma'am. And we're arresting you … on charges of campaign fraud … knowingly receiving illegal campaign contributions. There may be more charges forthcoming. "

"I don't know anything about that. You need to talk to my campaign manager!"

"We will be, Ma'am. You can be certain of that," Armatto replied. "For now, you need to come with us." His voice was suddenly a lot firmer and authoritative.

"You can't do this to me now! I am winning the election! I am going to be the first woman President of the United States!"

"Ma'am, would you rather we'd waited until you were standing at the podium? Please come with us." Special Agent Erdeski moved closer to Josephine. He was holding a pair of handcuffs.

"Really? Is that really necessary?" Josephine asked.

"I'm afraid it is, Ma'am." Erdeski cuffed her wrists together in front of her.

Spotting Josephine's coat lying on the back of a chair, Special Agent Armatto retrieved it and folded it carefully over Josephine's arms, concealing her handcuffed wrists.

"We'll keep this as discreet as possible, Ma'am." Taking her by the arm, he gently but firmly guided her down the hall and toward the elevators.

The two secret service agents stood there in stunned silence. They'd, of course, seen the federal warrants, but were still shocked at what had just transpired. Josephine Warren-Brookstone seemed like such a nice lady!

Bob turned to his partner, "you just never really know with these people, do you?"

319

Steve nodded. "Damnedest thing I've seen in all my years in the Secret Service!"

Bob grimaced. "You know, Steve, I think it's really time for me to retire. Better call this in. Then let's go get a beer!"

"I'm with you on that one!"

The two Special Agents sat in the front seat of the black Lincoln Town Car, chatting quietly about the Chicago Bears and their chances for the upcoming football season. They were only a few minutes from the Chicago FBI field office. Josephine sat in the back seat, alone with her thoughts.

... what the fuck do I do now! Wait! This is not a problem ... just a minor setback. I'll hang the whole thing on Sundstrand. It's my word against his ... they'll listen to me. Not him! ... the American people love me. Wasn't I winning the damn election? I'm the President. Just hang tough, Josephine. You can do this! ... what evidence can they possibly have against me? I haven't done anything! Sundstrand handled the money!

The Lincoln entered the parking garage at 2011 West Roosevelt Road. They circled through several levels before coming to a stop near a set of shiny elevator doors. The two Special Agents got out. Erdeski came around, opened the back door and assisted Josephine as she climbed out of the back seat ... not an easy task with her wrists cuffed together. They walked to the elevator. Once inside, Armatto pressed the button for the tenth floor. Nobody spoke during the elevator ride. The elevator door slid open and Erdeski guided Josephine out and to the right. A little way down the corridor, she was shown into what she assumed was an interrogation room. Seating her in a chair in front of a desk, the two Special Agents left the room, closing the door behind them.

For a few minutes, Josephine found herself alone. Then the door opened and Special Argent Armatto reentered the room, this time followed by another man in a suit. Armatto introduced him as Special Agent-In-Charge, James Fielding. The two men took the seats behind the desk. Fielding opened a rather thick folder. He cleared his throat.

"Ms. Brookstone," Fielding began. "Sorry to have to bring you down here like this, especially on such a big night for you, but we have stumbled on some very troubling information and we're hoping you could clear it up for us."

"If you are referring to any campaign financing issues, you need to talk to Carl Sundstrand. He handled my campaign finances. I'm sure he can answer any questions you may have."

"We have Mr. Sundstrand here. He is a few doors down the hall. When we showed him some of the contents of this file, he began to sing like a bird." Josephine felt a tinge of real fear in the pit of her stomach.

"I am sure I don't know what you're talking about," she replied, trying to sound calm.

Fielding sighed, and pulling a sheet of paper from the file, slid it over toward Josephine so she could see it. She didn't want to look at it.

"This is a summary sheet of most of the information that has come into our hands. It is scary stuff. You should look at it." She still wouldn't look at the document.

Fielding went on, "We have an interesting series of events unfolding here. It seems that a U.S. Navy SEAL team recovered some intelligence in a remote Afghan village when they were trying to capture a known terrorist courier. The intelligence the SEAL team recovered contained some interesting stuff! What we have are detailed plans for a terrorist attack on American soil." Fielding paused, looking directly at Josephine for a moment.

"We have a terrorist mastermind hiding out in the mountains of Iran. Then we have North Korean suitcase nukes on an Iranian freighter bound for Venezuela."

"I have nothing to do with any of that …," Josephine started to interrupt.

Fielding raised his hand to cut her off. "Let me finish." Fielding went on.

"We also have a group of U.S. citizens training to slip across the Mexican border, presumably with said suitcase nukes and detonate them in several key American cities!"

"I still have no idea what all this has to do with me," Josephine replied, fighting to sound calm and indignant.

"Well, Ms. Brookstone, it seems amongst all this other intelligence, we discovered your cell phone number."

Josephine stammered, "What? That's not possible! That must be a mistake!"

"Oh, there's no mistake, Ms. Brookstone!"

"It seems your terrorist friend, Rahman Atta, had quite a system going. That is until Kidon took him and one of his associates out a few days ago."

There was a look of incomprehension on Josephine's face. "Kidon?"

"You haven't heard of Kidon? It's a branch of the Mossad that eliminates serious problems for the Israeli government. They did us a huge favor here." Fielding paused, letting all this sink in.

"You know, Ms. Brookstone, your buddy Atta had quite a cell phone collection. They were all disposable phones. It looks like he had a system and used different phones to call different people, probably an attempt to keep conversations private or separate, sort of a security precaution. Unfortunately for him, or rather for you, now we have them. I am sure the Mossad got any information they wanted from the phones first, but that's okay. We're allies after all."

Suddenly Josephine saw where this was going. She felt sick to her stomach.

How could I have been so stupid?

"Anyway, Atta recorded every call he made to you. I'm sure he planned to blackmail you after you won the election. He had really big plans for you," Fielding stopped.

"Yep! About fifty million dollars' worth, in fact," Armatto added. He had spent most of this conversation gazing intently at a spot on the ceiling. Armatto had supported her and now found it hard to even look at Josephine Warren-Brookstone.

Special Agent-In-Charge Fielding looked over at Special Agent Armatto, who nodded. Armatto shifted in his seat and for the first time, looked squarely at Josephine, who by now had turned quite pale.

"This brings us to the recent murder of two CIA operatives. We know you have spoken on the phone to Associate Director Michael Stanton. We have his cell phone as well. Stanton was brutally butchered in an empty upscale Washington D.C. condo." Armatto paused to let that sink in a bit.

"You may not know his subordinate, William Peterson, who was also murdered ... poisoned it seems! He was found sitting on a park-bench on the Mall near the Lincoln Memorial. Peterson had a wife and two young daughters." Again, Armatto paused. He wanted this woman to absorb every word ... he had two little girls of his own.

"We have some security footage of an attractive Middle Eastern woman entering the condo with Michael Stanton. It seems this same woman also showed up on some security footage near the Mall where Peterson was found. We will identify her eventually." Armatto paused, letting the woman across the table wrap her head around the implications. Armatto dropped the hammer.

"In addition, to the campaign fraud charges mentioned earlier, you will also be charged with conspiracy to commit murder, attempted murder, and possibly, treason against the United States of America."

Josephine began to cry. Both men got up and without looking back, left her alone in the interrogation room.

CHAPTER 33

The dark van rolled quietly up the street, it's engine barely above an idle. Though it was late at night and quite dark, the van's lights were not on. It rolled to a stop near a car parked on the street about thirty yards from the Cordell residence. The van's six passengers were all in black, wearing Adidas running suits and balaclavas on their heads. And, they were armed to the teeth. All six carried semi-automatic pistols of one make or another along with MP-5 submachine guns with heavy cylindrical silencers hanging from their barrels. The woman sitting in the driver's seat had a long wicked-looking knife in a sheath strapped to her right thigh. She watched the house intently.

The five men with Fatima were all Syrians who'd been recruited by Hakim for Atta's organization, every one of them a proven Islamic fanatic. They'd been embedded among the many legitimate refugees and smuggled into the United States as soldiers of the Jihad, the war on the hated West.

The vetting process for refugees was sketchy at best. It was very difficult, if not impossible, to perform thorough background checks in failed states with no functioning government ... or with governments hostile to the United States.

Sitting there in the van, they whispered among themselves in hushed tones and waited for those in the Cordell residence to go to sleep. There was no heat in the van with the engine turned off. They were cold.

Fatima sat quietly, silent but deep in thought. Assad Al-Joud had done well. On the Thursday after her visit, he'd gotten word to her that he had the information she wanted. Most importantly, she'd learned the name of the man she was after, JD Cordell, and that he was currently in Knoxville, Tennessee. He, the woman who had escaped her, and the dog, were all currently staying at the Cordell family home. JD Cordell was working as a recruiter for the U.S. Navy. The man was a Navy SEAL.

Thirty minutes after the last light went out, Fatima turned to her team.

"Let's go ... now," she hissed. The side door of the van slid open and six dark figures slipped into the night and sprinted toward the house where their victims lay sleeping and unaware.

Ajax was suddenly alert. A quiet growl rumbled deep down in his throat. His ears came to attention and he sprang to his feet with a loud growl. Ajax began whining and frantically pawing at the gate on his crate.

Curtis sat bolt upright in bed.

What the hell was that!

He sat still ... silent and listening. Then he heard Ajax's growls and whines. He reached over and quietly slid the Colt .45 semi-automatic pistol from its holster. He'd riveted the holster to the back of his bedside stand. The

Colt was cocked and locked. Seven rounds in the magazine and one in the chamber … an old habit from his time in Vietnam. Curtis shook Mai, gently waking her up.

"What's the matter, baby?" Mai asked sleepily.

"Shhhh! Something is very wrong. Listen to Ajax." Yes … Mai could hear Ajax whining and pawing at his crate.

"What do you think it is?" Mai asked, now wide awake.

"An intruder … maybe more than one," Curtis replied. "Stay here and call the police. I'm going to check it out." Curtis quietly made his way to the closet and slipped into a pair of jeans. He returned to the bedside table and grabbed the second magazine for the Colt, slipping it into his back pocket.

"The phone's dead," Mai whispered.

"Is your cell phone here?" Mai nodded, reaching for the purse on her bedside table.

If they'd cut the phone line, this could be bad! They wouldn't be run-of-the-mill intruders; they'd be professionals, Curtis thought.

"Mai, stay here unless you don't have a choice … that way I'll know where you are in the house. The door is steel. Lock it when I leave. The shotgun is in the closet and there is a box of shells on the shelf."

Curtis hugged the wall as he peered out through the open bedroom door and down the hall. With a reassuring glance at Mai, he slipped through the door and pulling it shut behind him, started making his way down the hall.

Mai locked the door and set herself up with the shotgun and the box of shells. It was a 12-gauge Remington 870 Wingmaster pump shotgun and she was very familiar with it. Sitting on the edge of the bed and opening the box of shells, she slid one into the Remington's loading port. She racked the slide as quietly as she could. There was now one in the chamber. Mai then slid three more shells into the magazine. Ready, Mai pressed 911 on her phone.

Fatima and her team of assassins had synchronized their watches. She and two of her team arrived at the kitchen door on the side of the house. Thirty seconds to go ... and this infidel, who had ruined her employer's plans, along with his entire family would be dead. Fatima felt nothing more than her typical constant rage. These people had foiled her mentor's plans and therefore they needed to die. It was really that simple.

Ten seconds ... Fatima stood and aimed the MP-5 at the door lock. Another team member prepared to kick the door once she'd blasted the lock. *Three, two, one* ... five rounds from the silenced MP-5 slammed into the door lock, smashing it to pieces. A black-garbed figure kicked the door in and the three quickly rushed in, believing surprise to be on their side. The second team hit the front door at precisely the same time.

Curtis was in a position where he could cover the front door. There was no way he could cover both the front and the kitchen at the same time. The house was simply too big for that, but the front door offered quick access to the bedroom area of the house ... where Mai was. Anyone coming in through the kitchen would have more rooms and corners to navigate to reach the master bedroom. Curtis knew the layout of his house where these attackers, hopefully, did not.

He heard the loud crash as the front door was kicked open. The first black-clad figure to enter the foyer caught two .45 hydro-shock rounds in the chest and dropped. The silenced barrel of an MP-5 poked its ugly snout into the doorway and began to spray the room with lead. Curtis cursed, hitting the floor as one of the wild rounds caught him in the left shoulder. He rolled to take a position behind the couch, gun ready … eyes on the front door. If anyone came from the kitchen now, Curtis knew he would be in serious trouble.

He waited. A balaclava-clad head peered quickly around the door jamb, then retreated. Curtis took aim at the point the head had just occupied. The head appeared again. He gently squeezed the trigger, his Colt fired and the bullet struck the center of the balaclava covered forehead. The head disappeared. Suddenly more rounds were being sprayed into the foyer from the doorway.

"At least one more out there," Curtis muttered to himself.

But how many more?

Fatima entered the kitchen followed by the other two members of her team. From the sounds of the gun battle going on in the front of the house, their element of surprise was gone. She motioned for one of her team to go toward the gun battle.

"Take care of that," she ordered. "Make sure whoever that is … is dead!" The black-covered head nodded and headed toward the front of the house. Fatima, followed by the third member of her team, slid through another door and started down a hallway. They'd handle anybody else in the house.

Clearing each room as she went, Fatima passed through a dining room and into a family room. Nothing moved. She next made her way into a large bathroom. Nobody. Moving across the bathroom to another door, she opened it. A hallway! She peered around the door jamb, then cautiously stepped into a hallway.

Bedrooms, she thought. Fatima began to make her way down the hall.

JD and Julie were on their way home from dinner, shopping, and a late movie. They had a great time. Julie was sitting in the passenger seat munching happily on the refilled bucket of popcorn. Another eight weeks and JD, along with Ajax, would be returning to Afghanistan. JD's orders had come through. His six months as a recruiter for the U.S. Naval Recruitment Center in Knoxville were two-thirds over. Soon he'd be returning to his team. Neither was looking forward to that. While JD certainly missed his team and wanted to get back, Julie had made a big impact on him, changing his perspective on some things. They were discussing what options the future might hold when JD noticed the dark van parked across the street very close to his parent's house. It was a small neighborhood. Everyone knew everyone's vehicles.

"That's not a familiar van," JD commented to Julie as he passed it noticing the side door was still open … it appeared to be empty. He'd just swung the Jeep into the driveway when he heard gunshots coming from the house.

"Look!" Julie yelled. She pointed as a black-clad figure fell back out of the doorway of his parent's home and collapsed on the porch.

"Son-of-a-bitch!" JD exclaimed. Despite the lack of noise, it was clear another black-clad was firing a weapon into the house from the doorway.

Silencer, JD thought! *Oh shit … that's not good!*

JD flung open the door of the jeep.

"Julie, drive. Take the jeep. Get down the road and call the police. Get us some help fast." Then JD was out the door and sprinting toward the front porch of the house.

Julie slid into the driver's seat. Jamming the transmission into reverse., she backed out of the driveway and down the street, moving away from the van so she could keep it in sight. Slamming on the brakes, Julie brought the jeep skidding to a stop and slammed it into park. She reached for her cell phone.

CHAPTER 34

Fatima slowly worked her way down the hall, checking each room as she went. Her remaining team member worked with her, keeping his eye on the way they had come. Fatima checked JD's room and saw the dog in his crate, pawing frantically at the door trying to get out.

The dog can wait, Fatima thought. It is caged. We'll kill the animal later. First, this infidel and his family.

It dawned on Fatima that the son and his girlfriend might not be here. Surely, he, a U.S. Navy SEAL wouldn't be hiding in his room; he'd be confronting his attackers.

There was one door left. Fatima tried the handle. It was locked. Fatima motioned to her partner to come up and kick open the door. He kicked the door near the doorknob. It was a powerful kick but the steel door held. Fatima motioned him back and aimed her MP-5 at the doorknob. She pulled the trigger. A spray of bullets hit the doorknob, disintegrating the locking mechanism. Without waiting for her partner, she kicked in the door and stepped into the room. Her partner moved to follow her in.

Ajax hurled his body against the crate door again. His front paws were bleeding from frantically pawing at the gate to get out. Back in K9 warrior mode, Ajax hurled himself furiously at the crate door again and again. Suddenly, it flew open. Ajax rolled to his feet and was through the bedroom door.

The assassin was at the door to the master bedroom, ready to follow Fatima in when sixty-five pounds of canine fury hit him from the side. He felt the dog's powerful jaws as they closed on his left arm, yanking him off his feet. He rolled over, frantically kicking at the dog, his foot contacting the dog's ribs. Ajax never made a sound. He rolled, sprang to his feet and immediately launched himself at his enemy. The dog seemed to sense this was life or death ... he was defending his pack.

The assassin, rising to his feet, brought his MP-5 around and squeezed the trigger. A bullet grazed Ajax's left side just before he again slammed into the man, this time hitting him squarely in the chest, knocking him over. Amal felt the dog's powerful jaws as they again closed, this time on his right forearm. He screamed in agony as he felt the dog's teeth rip into his skin, chomp forward, and shatter the two bones of his right arm. Ajax, doing what he was trained to do, used his weight to drag the killer to the floor.

As Fatima stepped into the bedroom she saw Mai standing there, leveling a shotgun at her from the partial cover of Curtis' dresser. Fatima dove for the floor as the shotgun fired. The buckshot missed her by mere inches. She rolled to her feet and brought the MP-5 around as Mai worked the action of the Remington 870, chambering another round. Mai fired again. This time most of the shot struck the MP-5 near the bolt. A few of the pellets struck Fatima in the left bicep.

Fatima screamed in rage as she dropped the now useless submachine. Drawing the knife from the sheath strapped to her right thigh, she threw herself at Mai. There was a look of animal fury on her normally beautiful face. Mai moved back as she attempted to work the shotgun's action again, but she wasn't fast enough. The shotgun flew from her grip as Fatima slammed into her. Mai lost her footing, falling back onto the bed. She rolled across the bed and came up on the other side, turning to meet Fatima as the enraged woman came across the bed, knife held low in a blade-up grip. Mai circled back warily. She was at least twice this woman's age, but she was still her father's daughter ... and this woman would not know that. She'd be overconfident facing an older woman. That gave Mai an advantage.

Fatima cursed. "Infidel bitch! I'm going to gut you like the filthy swine you are. I am going to kill all of your filthy family."

"You'll have to get past me first," Mai stated calmly, controlling her breathing, working to calm herself. Mai circled back slowly as Fatima advanced on her ... knife at the ready. No more energy was wasted on words.

Fatima advanced confidently. Suddenly she sprang forward and slashed across at Mai's midsection. Mai leaped back, the blade missing her abdomen by scant inches. Fatima moved in again, reversing the slash and again the blade barely missed. Changing tactics, Fatima lunged forward once more, this time thrusting the blade straight at Mai's stomach. This was exactly what Mai was waiting for. Pivoting on the ball of her right foot, Mai twisted her body to the right, pulling her abdomen back and out of the way as her left hand deflected Fatima's thrust, guiding the knife down and slightly past her. Mai's right hand came up and both hands trapped Fatima's wrist in a strong grip, bending it back against itself. Again, Mai pivoted sharply on her right foot pulling her left foot back fast. Fatima found herself flipped over backward.

"Ugghhhh!" Fatima landed hard on her back, the air rushing from her lungs with a loud noise. She lost control of the knife ... it was now in Mai's hands. Her sudden loss of breath slowed Fatima. She tried to roll over to regain her feet. Seizing the opportunity, Mai moved fast, stabbing down hard with the knife. Fatima let out a bellow of rage and pain as the blade passed through the back of her hand and buried itself deep in the hardwood flooring. Mai sprang back and turned, diving for the shotgun. She came up off the floor, racking the slide as she turned again to face Fatima, who was now struggling to pull the blade from the floor to free her hand.

"You move ... and I'll blow you in half!" Mai was standing there with the Remington leveled ... pointing straight at Fatima.

"Infidel woman ... you haven't got the guts!" Fatima gave a last hard jerk on the knife handle and it came free. She turned to spring at Mai.

The explosion from the shotgun was deafening. Fatima was flung back as the buckshot slammed into her chest, the knife falling to the floor. Fatima did not move again.

JD reached the steps of the front porch just as the terrorist stopped firing through the doorway and was preparing to rush into the room. Concentrating on the task at hand, he'd not seen JD coming. He dove at the Syrian assassin and tackled him like a professional football player. They both hit the floor in the entryway. JD rolled quickly to his feet. The assassin made it to his knees and struggled to bring his weapon around toward JD. Before he could complete the movement, JD slammed his right knee into the terrorist's jaw with as much force as he could muster. It was a lot. There was a sickening crunch as the entire left side of the terrorist's face caved in under the force of the knee strike. The assassin dropped to the floor and lay still.

JD retrieved the assassin's MP-5 from the floor and glanced around the living room. He'd counted two more dead terrorists near the front entry. They'd both been shot coming through the door. A fourth figure burst from the hall, screaming in Arabic, his MP-5 spraying bullets wildly around the room.

"Allahu Akbar!"

JD dropped to one knee and dropped the assassin with a short, controlled burst from the MP-5 he'd picked up.

It was suddenly quite still. JD called out in a loud whisper.

"Dad, are you okay?"

"I'm okay," Curtis replied from behind the couch. "I got hit in the shoulder, but I'll live. I got two of the bastards. Check on your Mom. I heard the shotgun go off in the bedroom."

JD crossed the living room, glanced down the hall, and saw that Ajax had a fifth terrorist by his shattered arm. He was growling as if he was daring the terrorist to try something … anything.

"Afblijven … zit!" JD commanded. Ajax released his bite on the terrorist's arm and backed away. Still growling, Ajax sat, keeping his attention glued on the injured assassin. JD retrieved the terrorist's weapons and unloading them, tossed them into the guest bedroom.

"Mom … Mom … are you okay?" JD heard a movement from the bedroom.

"JD? Oh my God! I'm alright. I'm not hurt." Leaving Ajax to guard the wounded terrorist, JD hurried into the bedroom where he found his mother sitting on the bed still holding the shotgun. A dead woman lay on the floor near a wicked-looking knife with a long curved blade. There was also a damaged MP-5 lying on the floor near the door.

"Mom," JD said quietly. "Let's get you and Dad out of here. Dad's okay but he's been shot in the shoulder. He needs your help." Mai looked up.

"Curtis!" Mai got quickly to her feet. JD led her down the hall giving the wounded terrorist a wide berth. Mai didn't even glance at him. Ajax was still scope-locked on the terrorist and if the terrorist even twitched, Ajax gave out a low menacing growl.

Mai took one look at Curtis and went to the kitchen to get a dishtowel.

"Let's go out on the porch," Curtis suggested. "There are chairs and it will be better to not be in here when the police arrive." They could hear the sirens in the distance. Together, JD and his mother helped Curtis to his feet. Once on the porch, Mai used the dishtowel to apply direct pressure to the bullet hole in Curtis' shoulder.

"Damn!" Curtis exclaimed. "That hurts!"

"Be quiet, you big baby." Mai chided gently. "This is nothing compared to the injuries I treated for you in Vietnam."

"I was much younger then, Mai."

JD listened to this exchange. It sounded like they were both just fine.

Seeing JD, Curtis, and Mai out on the front porch, Julie pulled the Jeep into the driveway and got out. The police sirens were getting louder now.

"Dad, don't you have some duct tape in the kitchen?" JD asked.

Curtis nodded. "Second drawer down, to the left of the refrigerator."

"Good. I am going to secure that wounded terrorist and then put Ajax in the Jeep before the cops get here. I don't want them to shoot my dog … even accidentally."

"That's for sure," Curtis replied. "Ajax probably saved our lives. He warned us … and stopped that guy in the hall from getting to your mother." Curtis went on, "If they shoot that dog, your Mom will be very mad. I may have to shoot them."

JD took off for the kitchen and the duct tape. A few seconds later he returned followed by Ajax who happily jumped up into the back of the Jeep. Once Ajax was secured, JD returned to the porch.

"Ajax ripped his feet up a little getting out of that crate. I need to get him to the vet as soon as I get a chance."

The sirens were very close now and a few seconds later, several police cruisers pulled into the driveway. JD stepped out to meet them, both hands empty and held high in the air.

CHAPTER 35

The holidays had come and gone. Annie did come home for Christmas. Curtis, Mai, Julie, JD, and Ajax all met her new boyfriend, Robert ... who, it turned out, was a very nice young man studying to be an orthopedic surgeon. They learned over Christmas dinner that Robert wanted to go into sports medicine.

When Annie learned of the events of the last few months, she took it all in stride. She was quite taken with Ajax who seemed more than happy to have another member of his pack.

"A typical day in the Cordell family," was her only real comment. Nothing seemed to phase her. And after all, everyone was okay. Robert, on the other hand, did not know quite what to think.

JD was leaving for Afghanistan in three days. Mai and Julie had gone shopping at the mall, so JD and his father took Ajax and went for a hike at Frozen Head State Park. While it was cool, they had a great time hiking the Panther

Gap Trail. Ajax had a wonderful time, covering at least four times the mileage the two men did. They were now back at JD's Jeep enjoying some hot coffee JD had packed in a thermos bottle for the trip. Ajax had a bottle of water ... poured into his water bowl, of course.

"What have you and Julie decided to do, JD, if you don't mind my asking?"

"I don't mind. We've decided not to decide anything until my team rotates back to the U.S. It should be about six more months or so, I figure."

"Are you going to reenlist?" Curtis asked. "You have about a year or so left if I remember right."

"Before I met Julie, I certainly would have ... no hesitation. Now I am not so sure. I've got my twenty in. I could retire now. But I feel like I can't abandon Ajax, especially after all he and our family have been through. He's got five more years before he would be done." JD paused taking a sip of his coffee. "I wonder if she would mind being married to a SEAL for one more enlistment period?"

It was nice just sitting there enjoying the warmth of the hot coffee. Curtis spoke again.

"Hard to believe what's been happening in the world lately. A thoroughly corrupt presidential candidate, terrorists ... suitcase nukes? What a nest of vipers!"

"Yep!" JD replied. "I guess it's probably always been that way. We just hear about it more now. But, we should be alright as long as we're always prepared to stomp on any of these evil serpents that raise their head."

"I guess so," his Curtis agreed.

"Come on, Ajax. Let's load up and head home." JD stood and opened the gate on the back of the Jeep. Ajax leaped up, ready to go. "Maybe I can talk Mom into making fried rice once more before we head to Bagram."

About the Author

Darren C Gilbert was born in 1960 in Ilion, NY but grew up in the Berkshire Mountains of Massachusetts. An avid reader, he particularly enjoys military history, epic sagas, spy novels, and historical fiction. In addition to serving in the U.S. Army from 1979 to 1983, Darren has over 33 years of martial arts training including managing his own martial arts school for 12 years. He has earned both undergraduate and graduates degrees from the University of Tennessee and Western Governors University respectively. He is also a graduate of Executive Security International's Advanced Executive Protection Program and is a Certified Protection Specialist. He currently lives in Cary, NC with his German Shepherd, Sophie.

62098466R00194